MINUTES
TO
DIE

Center Point
Large Print

Also by Susan Sleeman and available from
Center Point Large Print:

Fatal Mistake
Kill Shot
Seconds to Live

**This Large Print Book carries the
Seal of Approval of N.A.V.H.**

HOMELAND HEROES BOOK TWO

MINUTES TO DIE

SUSAN SLEEMAN

CENTER POINT LARGE PRINT
THORNDIKE, MAINE

This Center Point Large Print edition
is published in the year 2021 by arrangement with
Bethany House, a division of Baker Publishing Group.

Copyright © 2020 by Susan Sleeman.

The text of this Large Print edition is unabridged.
In other aspects, this book may vary
from the original edition.
Printed in the United States of America
on permanent paper.
Set in 16-point Times New Roman type.

ISBN: 978-1-64358-769-1

The Library of Congress has cataloged this record
under Library of Congress Control Number: 2020946526

MINUTES
TO
DIE

For my family

Your support and the many sacrifices you make enable me to write the books of my heart and share God's message. He has blessed me beyond measure.

CHAPTER 1

Exposed. Kiley felt exposed.

Standing there. In the dark.

Waiting. Waiting.

The moon hunkered behind heavy clouds. The streetlights dim. The quiet Washington, D.C., suburban shopping area shrouded by foggy mist.

A whisper of wind broke through the trees, carrying the damp, earthy smell from nearby planter beds packed with vivid yellow-and-rusty mums. The rustle of branches created the only sound and movement. A normal fall night.

And yet . . . Kiley couldn't relax. Maybe her FBI agent instincts were warning her to be careful. Maybe. Or maybe it was more.

She looked at her watch, the green number glowing in the eerie fog. 11:20 p.m.

What was taking her confidential informant so long? Firuzeh had promised to arrive by eleven. Had something happened to her?

She'd called Kiley at eight to warn of an imminent terrorist threat. A threat so grand, Firuzeh said it would make the tragedy of 9/11 pale in comparison. Millions of lives could be impacted. Kiley had heard exaggerations like this in the past, but Firuzeh's intel had always been credible.

Millions.

Kiley shuddered and hoped Firuzeh was wrong this time. Not that she ever had been. Not since Kiley first met Firuzeh when she called the FBI a year ago with a tip related to one of Kiley's investigations.

The hum of an automobile droned in the distance, grabbing Kiley's attention.

Finally.

She stepped deeper into the shadows, took a long breath, and held it. She focused her night-vision binoculars across the narrow street where she and Firuzeh often met. Headlights drifted through the fog, two solid beams forming as the small white Toyota drew closer. Kiley zoomed in on the license plate.

Yes. Firuzeh's car. At last.

Kiley released her breath, the puff of air evaporating in the mist, but continued to glass the area with her binoculars, her attention sharp.

The car pulled to the curb and stilled.

Kiley's phone vibrated against her leg. Seeing Firuzeh's name on the screen, Kiley answered. "I see your car."

"Where are you?" An edge of worry cut through Firuzeh's tone.

"Across the street by the coffee shop."

"I can't see you."

"It's foggy, but I'm here."

"I'll be over in a second." Firuzeh's car door

opened. She stepped out and glided across the street like a waif, the ends of her brightly colored headscarf fluttering behind her.

Kiley took a long look through the shadows cloaking the storefronts. Made one more check of the road, wet with September rain, and glanced down the street at parked cars.

Nothing out of the norm for a Saturday night in the quiet suburb.

She stepped out to greet the young woman who'd always impressed Kiley with her self-sacrifice for the greater good.

Kiley respected Firuzeh's sacrifices and wouldn't waste any of her time with small talk. "Tell me what you know."

"I cannot." Firuzeh's big brown eyes widened, and she glanced around as she bit her full lower lip. "Not until you promise to bring my entire family into witness protection."

Kiley's mouth fell open at the unexpected demand. "That's not how WITSEC works. I need the information first, and then we can assess the need for security measures."

"No. No." Firuzeh shifted her stance, and her wide-legged pants in a bright paisley print floated with the movement. "If anyone finds out I talked to you, they will kill us. I cannot keep silent. Not with a threat this big. Millions of lives are in danger, Agent Dawson. Millions! But I need to protect my family first."

Kiley searched Firuzeh's earnest face, the muscles tight, her eyes wide.

She really believed she was in danger, and Kiley had to help. Question was, how was she going to get WITSEC approval without details? She had no standing with the U.S. Marshals. She *was* a member of the elite Rapid Emergency Deployment team, or RED team, made up of interagency law-enforcement officers, and they had a deputy on their team. Plus one of their team member's fiancées was also a deputy. Perhaps together they could make this happen.

She smiled at Firuzeh to ease her worry. "Give me a second to make a call."

Firuzeh clamped her hands together. "Please. Hurry. I am worried about my family. So very, very worried."

Her panic cut through the quiet night, and Kiley knew right then and there that this threat was real. No question. Firuzeh and her family *did* need to be protected, and it was a matter of urgency.

Kiley dialed teammate and Deputy U.S. Marshal Mack Jordan.

"Mack, good," she said after he answered. "I need a favor, and I need it now."

"Hey, slow down." His rumbling Texas drawl stretched out over the line. "Catch a breath."

"No time to breathe." Kiley relayed the Abed family's situation.

"Millions? Isn't she exaggerating?" His skepticism was deserved. He didn't know Firuzeh like Kiley did.

"For anyone else I might say yes, but not for Firuzeh. She's not a player. If she says she has intel this big, she does."

"Okay. Let me see what I can do." His instant trust in her judgment was a hallmark of their team's support. One for all and all for one, she liked to joke.

"Thanks, Mack," she said, watching Firuzeh searching the darkness as if she believed someone was coming for her now. "Every minute counts."

"Trust me. I get it."

"Maybe I should've called Eisenhower." She hated to sound like she doubted Mack when she didn't, but as the ICE special agent in charge of the Cyber Crimes Center, their team supervisor had more clout.

"Do it, and we can work this from different angles." Mack's lack of offense and steadfast cooperation was typical of his kind and compassionate personality lurking under a He-Man façade.

"I'll get back to you as soon as I can." He disconnected the call.

She turned to Firuzeh. "My associate's a U.S. Marshal. He's working on your request, and I'll call my supervisor too."

"Thank you." She adjusted her purple tunic edged in gold trim. "I am so very appreciative."

"If this is approved, I'll need contact information for everyone in your family."

"I don't know the numbers, and I left my phone in the car. I'll get it while you make your call." She quickly turned toward the street.

Kiley watched her disappear into the haze and offered a short prayer for Firuzeh and her family's safety as she tapped Eisenhower's number on her contact list.

"Barry Eisenhower." His confident voice rumbled deeply through the phone.

"It's Dawson," she said.

A gunshot split the quiet, ripping through the night like a car backfiring in the distance. Firuzeh's body went limp. Dropped to the ground. Sprawled in an awkward pose.

"No!" Kiley shoved her phone into her FBI windbreaker and drew her weapon.

She searched the darkness, her heart thundering in her chest as she made a thorough sweep to assess the threat.

Firuzeh stirred. Moaned in pain.

No. No. No. Not this. Kiley had to help Firuzeh even if the shooter had his weapon trained on them.

Please, please, please. No more shots and let Firuzeh be okay.

Kiley charged across the street. One foot in front of the other, her pulse racing. Waiting for the bullet to come. To pierce her back. Her side. Anywhere.

She reached Firuzeh. Dropped to her knees. Saw Firuzeh's chest rise and fall. Still alive.

Thank you.

A bullet bit into the road by Firuzeh's head, the report an echo in the eerie quiet. Sharp shards flew, piercing Kiley's face. Maybe the shooter wasn't a good shot. Or he was warning Kiley. She didn't know which. Didn't matter. She had to move Firuzeh to a protected area.

Kiley holstered her gun, took a good hold under Firuzeh's arms, and tugged backward. Sticky, warm blood congealed on Kiley's hands. Fear blazed a path down her back, so raw she could almost smell it. She swallowed it down. "Hold on, Firuzeh. Hold on. I'll get you to a safe place and call for help."

Firuzeh slipped in Kiley's hands, and she shifted to get a better hold. Another bullet cracked through the night, razoring past Kiley's head. If she hadn't slipped, that bullet . . .

No, don't think about that.

Kiley gritted her teeth and moved backward. Faster. Faster. She bumped around the front of the car. Another slug slammed into the metal behind her. She nearly yelped but held it together and gently lowered Firuzeh to the ground.

"Agent Dawson?" Eisenhower's voice came from the phone in her pocket. He was still on the line.

Oh, thank you!

15

She fumbled in her pocket until her slick hand circled the phone. "It's Firuzeh. Someone shot her. Is shooting at me! I need backup."

Kiley took a breath. Searched her brain to cut through the panic and think of their address. Shouted it into the phone. "I have to help Firuzeh!"

"Stay put, and don't try to be a hero."

Hero, right. Kiley just needed to stay alive. To tend to Firuzeh and keep her alive as well.

She ended the call. And it hit her. She was on her own here. Alone. All alone.

Panic raced in. Took hold. Her hands trembled.

Stop. Get control. Firuzeh is depending on you.

She shone the light from her phone on Firuzeh's body, the beam wobbling under Kiley's trembling hand. Firuzeh was still breathing. Barely. Blood pumped from her chest. Spurting.

Kiley dropped her phone. Shrugged out of her jacket. Balled up the fabric and pressed it against the wound. Blood soaked through the cloth and coated Kiley's hands.

"Stay with me, Firuzeh," Kiley pleaded, her heart in her throat. "For the love of God, stay with me."

The mere thought of a terrorist attack so big it made 9/11 seem like a warm-up sent a chill over ICE Agent Evan Bowers' body. In the ditch overlooking the Port of Tacoma, he stared

16

through his binoculars at the dock and couldn't think of a more important mission than stopping this impending threat.

A cold wind swept across the docks while crickets chirped in the background. Thankfully, insects mingling with the rush of water lapping the port wall were the only sounds. No cranes were moving. No trucks hauling. No workers rushing around. Perfectly still as he'd hoped for at eight o'clock on a Saturday night when most of the workers were off for the weekend and only a minimal crew remained on-site.

He scanned the distance, where tall orange cranes rose like giant skeletons above the murky water steaming from the nighttime cool-down. Stacks of metal shipping containers lined the docks, waiting to be moved, and Evan locked his binoculars on the green one in question.

He'd worked similar covert operations in his job with ICE, and for years as an Explosive Ordnance Disposal technician in the Navy. When an EOD tech, he operated with Special Forces like SEALs and Rangers and also with the Secret Service and State Department to protect the president, vice-president, and other state and foreign officials. He also supported Homeland Security as well as U.S. Customs, the FBI, and state and local police bomb squads.

But that was all in the past. Now he hunted terrorists. The most dangerous threat of all.

"Looks clear to me." FBI Agent Ryan Cartwright poked his head up from where he crouched in the ditch beside Evan. "We should get moving."

Evan's gut warned him to take another sweep before breaching the port's perimeter. "Not yet."

"What's the point of sitting here when our contact is waiting?" Cartwright was a cowboy—rushing in instead of evaluating and planning. The kind of guy who could get himself and Evan killed.

Evan wouldn't risk a trigger-happy security guard or a startled terrorist training a gun on them, and he sure wasn't about to explain that his caution stemmed from an incident a few years back when an FBI agent lost his life. Since that day, Evan knew it took only minutes to die and had erred even more on the side of caution, and no better time to be extra careful than when facing brutal terrorists.

He scanned the dock again, questioning the plan. "I honestly don't like this approach."

Cartwright scoffed. "What's not to like? We have a warrant. We're just slipping through the back door to keep from alerting port staff with questionable ethics. No way we'll let them stand in our way and risk having the container moved before we reach it."

"I get that." Evan took a long pull of the fifty-degree air tinged with the smell of diesel. "But

I like to complete my due diligence. Tonight that means one more sweep for potential threats before we go."

"Well, I'm done. You coming or what?"

Evan chose the *or what*. Cartwright started to move, and Evan grabbed the guy's ankle to pull him back down.

Evan glowered at Cartwright. "We go when I say we go and not until then."

Cartwright didn't respond, simply lifted his binoculars and pointed them at the container.

Evan did the same thing but kept his hearing tuned to Cartwright in case he moved again. Evan watched the guard drive his utility vehicle slowly past them. He was five minutes ahead of schedule, and he checked the area with a more thorough focus than he had on the past round. If Evan had let Cartwright move, they would've run right into this guard, resulting in an altercation Evan surely didn't need tonight.

He kept his eyes pinned on the containers and waited five full minutes before shifting his focus back to Cartwright. "Okay, we go."

Cartwright lowered his binoculars and lifted his radio to his mouth. "Making entry. Rendezvous at container."

"I'm waiting," the port's night supervisor answered.

Cartwright dropped his binoculars and got to his feet. This cowboy didn't know the meaning of restraint and control and could get himself killed. Evan wouldn't mind if the guy learned a lesson, but Evan didn't want him to die, and if Evan was going in, he was leading the way. He eased in front of Cartwright and slowed the guy's approach.

Evan signaled for Cartwright to follow, and the agent fell in line behind Evan as if he were lead on the Joint Terrorism Task Force where they both currently served. JTTF leadership fell to ICE Special Agent Harley Watson, though Evan was in charge of this op.

He climbed the bank, inched toward the chain-link fence, and resisted shaking his head at the minimal security. A simple fence and occasional guard patrol were the only things standing between them and stacks and stacks of containers. Way too easy of a breach in Evan's opinion.

He strapped his rifle over his back to climb the ladder and scale the fence. His tactical boots hit the ground, sounding like an explosion in the quiet.

Cartwright scrambled over the fence, and they lowered the ladder to the ground. Rifle outstretched, Evan signaled to move toward the long metal containers in rusty blues, greens, and oranges. He slipped between a row stacked four high and let out a breath for making it this far unseen. He crept down the dark row, the security lighting doing little to show the way. Unfortunately the light was too bright for NVGs, yet their path remained dark and uncertain.

At an open lane, he paused and listened. A motorized vehicle sounded nearby. The next guard detail. He held up his hand, warning Cartwright to hold.

Headlights swept over the area. Evan backed into the shadows and held his breath. The vehicle passed. He waited two minutes and lifted his hand to signal their forward progress. He rushed across the lane and moved quickly along another bank of containers. Then another—and another, his back now slick with perspiration under his body armor.

He spotted a tall, stocky man standing near the next row, wearing a port security uniform and white hard hat. He held a walkie-talkie and clipboard.

Evan glanced at Cartwright. "Radio our contact. Let's see if this guy picks up."

Cartwright grabbed his device. "In view. Coast clear?"

The man lifted his radio. "Yes, but hurry before someone starts asking questions."

"We're right across the lane," Cartwright said. "On the move."

The dock supervisor started to turn, and Evan set off again, reaching the man before he could make a complete turn.

"ICE Agent Evan Bowers." Evan displayed his credentials.

The supervisor shined a flashlight on the ID and nodded. "Tony Lopez. I'll need the warrant you promised me."

Evan produced the paperwork from his pocket.

Lopez snatched it as if grasping for a lifeline, shone his light on the papers, and flipped through the many pages. He gave a single nod and fixed the warrant to his clipboard. He set it on the concrete and picked up a pair of bolt cutters. "This container's odd. Has a small side door. It has a less sturdy lock. Easier to cut. I'll start with that one."

He flicked on his headlamp and stepped around the side of the container. He hefted the bolt cutters in solid arms and made quick work of snapping the lock and opening the door. Looking proud of himself, he stood back.

Evan brushed past him to the entrance and swept the inside of the container with his flashlight. His mouth fell open. "What in the world?"

Cartwright joined Evan and let out a low whistle. "Never expected to find this. Not in a million years."

"Yeah, me neither." Evan ran his gaze over the space in front of him, his heart sinking. "But it looks like the terrorist threat is real. Very real and more sophisticated than we could've ever imagined."

CHAPTER 2

"C'mon." Mack took hold of Kiley's arm and lifted her out of the fog swirling over the pavement. "There's nothing you can do for Firuzeh here."

"No. You're right. I already failed her." Tears pricked Kiley's eyes, and she swallowed them down. She wanted to lean into Mack for a hug. He'd give her one. He was this teddy bear of a man underneath his muscular, fierce protector exterior and a very good friend. But she would never break down in front of him or the rest of her team. Never.

For starters, she was a female in law enforcement with an information technology concentration. Both male fields, and to top it off, at only five-foot-seven, many of the men in her field towered over her. And growing up a geek, she was pretty introverted. She didn't need being a crybaby added to the list.

She pulled back her shoulders and marched toward Sean's car, where the other agent on their team waited with the responding detective. At six-foot-three, Sean was a head taller than Detective Lancaster and a few inches taller than Mack.

Sean ran a hand through his rich chocolate-colored hair, cut short on the sides and longer on top, leaving a bit of a curl. He caught her gaze with his dark brown, nearly black piercing eyes and transmitted his sympathy. She responded with a quick nod.

"I'm assuming Agent Dawson is free to go," Sean said to Lancaster, who had the intense look of a lawman.

Lancaster lifted his sagging shoulders in his rumpled gray suit coat worn over a white shirt, the knot of his tie hanging loose on his chest. "You can go if you promise to stop by in the morning to sign an official statement."

"I don't really have anything to add to what I told you. I didn't see the shooter or shooters, and the shots came from the south, taking Firuzeh out instantly."

"You may remember something else by tomorrow." Lancaster handed her a business card.

Mack took it. Normally she'd protest his stepping in on her behalf, but not when her hands were covered in dried blood. She gave him a nod of thanks, and he waved it off to open the passenger door of Sean's SUV.

She slid onto the leather seat and noticed the warm scent of vanilla that seemed at odds with the night, but Sean kept his SUV spotless, an air freshener always present. As she lifted her legs with bloody knees into the vehicle, she stared down at Mack's worn cowboy boots. Something about a familiar sight eased her angst a bit. He slammed the door, quickly erasing any relief she'd gained.

Sean got behind the wheel and handed over a pack of wet wipes. She gave him a wobbly smile as she ripped the package open to attack her hands. She couldn't possibly do anything with her clothing, but at least she could have semi-clean hands.

Mack climbed in back, and she glanced over her shoulder at him. He was more rugged-looking than Sean, with red hair, warm grayish-green eyes, and a ready smile, where Sean was more reserved.

"Thanks for coming for me," she said, balling up a wipe stained red and pulling out another one.

"Of course," Sean said. "What do you need from us?"

Yes, what? She hadn't thought ahead at all. Not even to getting in this SUV and driving away, leaving Firuzeh lying on the cold ground. "Give me a sec, okay?"

"Sure." Sean got the vehicle started and heading toward their office.

She scrubbed at her hands, using ten wipes before feeling the least bit clean. Sean held out a trash bag for her.

"Thanks," she said again.

"Hey, no need to keep thanking us." He gave

her a tight smile. "We're here for you. Just accept it."

"Okay," she said, and would try. Until joining this team, she really never had friends or family whose love didn't come without strings attached. Not since her dad died when she was nine, and her mother couldn't cope with the loss. Worried she might lose Kiley too, her mother tightly controlled Kiley's life and didn't care how she felt about anything. It was all about her mother preventing the loss of her only child. One of the reasons Kiley went into law enforcement. To push the boundaries. Memories she didn't need to dredge up ever but especially not now.

She lowered her window and let the brisk air rush over her face. Firuzeh had sacrificed her life for her country, and the very least Kiley could do to honor her was to pull herself together and lead the charge to find the killer.

She'd never taken lead on an investigation. She was always glad to let Sean or Mack do it and work in the background where she felt more comfortable. This one was different. She would fight for lead. And she would make sure Firuzeh's family members were all brought into protection for the short term. The long term too, if it was warranted.

She took long gulps of the chilly air for the first time, catching the scent of sugary sweetness from a nearby bakery. Over and over, she breathed. One breath after the other, yet when Sean pulled into their secured parking lot, her nerves remained jangled. She lifted her shoulders for confidence, the very last thing she would normally do when faced with stress. She was more of a retreat-and-regroup kind of person.

Tough. That couldn't—wouldn't—happen here.

"I'm going to ask Eisenhower for lead on this investigation." She pinned her focus on Sean, nearly daring him to argue with her, maybe itching for a fight to forget about losing Firuzeh. "And I need you guys to back me on it."

"Sure," Sean said easily. "If you want lead, I'll support you."

"I do." She clamped her lips into a hard line and swiveled to face Mack, the anger building inside and itching for release.

He gave a firm nod. "We have your back, kiddo."

Okay, fine. No fight here. That was really what she wanted, right? The three of them working together to hunt down Firuzeh's killer? She'd have to find another outlet for her anger and frustration, or just internalize it as she'd done for years.

She turned back to Sean, thoughts of how to proceed now pinging through her brain. "I need to grab a quick shower and change. While I do, will you locate the address for Firuzeh's parents? They own a mailbox store in Tysons. I figure they live nearby. And call Lancaster to tell him I'll take care of notifying the Abeds about Firuzeh. They need to hear the difficult news from someone who knew her."

"Sure thing," Sean said.

She tried not to picture the upcoming conversation and move ahead. No point in looking ahead to something that would be nearly as difficult as seeing the life vanish from Firuzeh's eyes.

She caught Mack's focus again. "Can you keep looking into WITSEC for the family? Besides Firuzeh's parents, she had two sisters, a brother, and sister-in-law. We'll bring them into protection tonight for the short term, then decide on a long-term plan once we know what we're up against."

Mack gave a crisp and confident nod. "No problem. I almost had it arranged anyway."

"Thanks," she said, then bit her tongue, as they'd told her to stop thanking them. She was so grateful for her teammates that it was hard to remember not to express it. "There's something I didn't tell Detective Lancaster. Before Firuzeh died, she got out a few words. Port, coma, and Box 342."

"She probably meant a mailbox at her family's business, but the other words?" Sean frowned. "Odd."

"I know, right? I'll ask her family about the box number, but I have no idea what she meant by *coma* and *port*. Still, it's a place to start the investigation. Be thinking about it, and I'll get Cam looking for any intel referencing these terms." If the information existed on the internet, their team's analyst would find it.

She reached for the door handle and glanced between her teammates. "Any questions before we go?"

"No, but I like this new bossy Kiley." Mack grinned, his wide jaw covered in red whiskers lifting.

She managed to eke out a smile, his intent she was sure. They exited the SUV, the air tinged with the fresh scent of rain that was falling now at a hard rate, and strode together into their building. The fifth floor was dedicated to their team and support staff, and the minute they entered the bullpen area filled with desks, the few workers present went quiet. The silence, more than anything, made Kiley want to sit down and cry.

Before a tear could form, Barry Eisenhower marched out of his office, and his pointed look ended all thoughts of crying. In his fifties, he was fit and lean, and she'd never seen him dressed in anything except a tailored suit that didn't seem to wrinkle, not even during his very long workdays.

He towered over her, and she looked up at him. His gaze softened for a fraction of a second, but then his hard-set expression quickly returned. "Sorry about the loss of your CI, Agent Dawson."

"Thank you, sir." She swallowed and plunged ahead before she lost her courage, which was already trying to make a run for the hills. "I'd like to take charge of her murder investigation."

He ran a hand over black hair buzzed close to his scalp. "We don't do homicides. The locals will handle the investigation."

Kiley didn't like his response and pulled her shoulders back. "This isn't a simple homicide. Finding her killer could lead to the biggest terrorist threat our nation has faced in years."

"Inside. Now." He tipped his head toward his corner office. "All three of you."

He spun and charged for his office at his usual supersonic speed. Feeling like she'd somehow let him down and was headed for a firing squad, she marched after him.

No matter. He could fire away. She would find Firuzeh's killer with or without his permission. And she knew her teammates would support her in her quest.

He dropped into a chair at a round table and motioned for them to join him. She sat across from him so she could read every nuance of his expressions. Mack straddled the chair to her right and rested his arms on the back. Sean sat on her other side, his posture rigid. Not surprising. He was pretty much always on guard at work.

Eisenhower locked gazes with her. "Tell me what you know about this threat."

She relayed her conversations with Firuzeh. "She was a straight shooter, sir, and wouldn't be blowing smoke. I may not know the details yet, but the threat is credible. You can bank on it."

He didn't speak. Didn't move.

She felt like wilting under his study. Instead, she hardened her resolve and sat up straighter. "If you don't want to take over the murder investigation, let us at least look for additional intel to confirm her claim. If we find something, we can assume jurisdiction."

He placed his perfectly manicured hands on the table. "I'm not inclined to mess with the locals at any point, but I do support you wanting to run this intel to ground."

"To take lead in running the intel to ground," she amended and lifted her chin.

He tipped his head and watched her for a long moment before swinging his focus to Sean. "You agree with this?"

"I do."

Eisenhower looked at Mack. "You too?"

"Absolutely."

Eisenhower stood. "Then congratulations, Agent Dawson. You're lead on your first investigation."

She thought if this day ever came she would feel like celebrating, but there would be no celebrating. Not with Firuzeh dead and a major threat to the country in the offing. Only sadness and determination. "Thank you, sir."

31

"Just know"—he hardened his tone—"if this gets too big or ugly for you to handle, I'll revisit my decision."

"I won't let you down, sir."

His penetrating gaze met hers and held. "See that you don't."

Shock coursed through Evan's body as he stared at the container turned into a mini-home. He caught a whiff of cinnamon and another spice he couldn't name, totally at odds with the fact that terrorists had crossed the ocean in this vessel.

The front area of the container served as a sitting area and held a sofa, television, several video gaming systems, and stacks of games. Next was a small kitchen, complete with running water and appliances. The back wall held two doors. Evan would investigate what was behind them when he figured out what to do first.

"It's like one of those tiny houses you see on TV," Perez said, drawing Evan from his reverie.

He faced Perez and eased the guy out the door before he got a better look at the place. Evan had already let his surprise keep him from action, and Perez had seen more than Evan should have allowed. "You don't speak of this to anyone. You got that?"

Perez gave a halfhearted nod.

Evan got in his face. "Seriously. If I find out word got out on this, you'll be looking at prison time."

"Okay. Okay." Perez held up his hands. "I get it. I won't tell anyone."

He noticed Perez's wedding band. "Not even a word to your wife. Or parents. Or best friend."

He nodded again, this time adding a nervous twitch to it.

Evan hated scaring this man, but he had to guarantee his silence. "I'll need the bill of lading for the container and any other details you have on the shipment."

Perez ripped a sheet from his clipboard and handed the paper to Evan.

He took a quick look at the document to confirm the container number on the page matched the one sitting in front of him. "Thank you. You're free to go."

"I . . . um . . . I . . ." Perez swallowed hard. "I can't leave you alone here. You don't have the right credentials."

Evan eyed Perez.

He stood strong for only a moment before his expression yielded. "Okay, fine. You're ICE, and you'd be approved if you applied for clearance. I still need to call the head of security to tell him I let you in."

"Good. Do that. Tell him I want to talk to him."

Perez nodded and slowly backed away as if waiting for Evan to object. Evan gestured for Perez to keep moving, and he bolted toward his small pickup truck.

Evan went back to Cartwright, who remained near the container door, phone to his ear as he arranged for an FBI Evidence Recovery Team to process the scene. Evan thought Cartwright was jumping the gun in assuming his agency's team should take lead on forensics.

"I put in a request for ERT." Cartwright shoved his phone into his pocket.

"You call Watson?"

Cartwright shook his head. "Local FBI office."

Evan didn't respond. No need. The JTTF supervisor would decide which agency's forensic team handled processing the container.

"You thinking what I'm thinking?" Cartwright asked.

"If you mean terrorists crossed the ocean in this thing? Then yeah. We're on the same page."

Smuggling in terrorists via shipping containers had been happening for years. This container was different. The elaborate interior said whoever entered the U.S. in this box had to be higher up in the terrorist food chain, as the place was totally tricked out.

"They had to spend weeks in this box." Cartwright stared in awe. "Crazy."

Evan ran his flashlight over the exterior, looking for anything unusual. "There has to be some sort of generator or maybe solar panels to run the electronics we saw inside."

Cartwright shook his head. "Panels would draw attention in the move."

Despite the agent's comment, Evan's intuition said he was right and they would find a source of power. Too bad he couldn't see additional details, but the streetlight above barely broke through the fog now thick and heavy rolling in from Commencement Bay. "We need to light this place up."

"ERT will bring lights."

"We need booties and gloves to take a look around the inside." Evan got out his keys and tossed them to a surprised Cartwright. "Grab some from my vehicle."

He looked like he wanted to complain but then spun and stormed off.

Evan took a walk around the exterior of the container, feeling the walls for additional cutouts. He found several that he suspected were windows the stowaways opened for fresh air while at sea. Other than the potential windows, he found nothing unusual.

Cartwright returned with the gloves and booties and shoved them along with the keys into Evan's hand.

"Thanks," Evan said.

Cartwright scowled. "I'm not your lackey, you know."

Evan didn't bother responding. Cartwright was one of those agents who did the bare minimum to get by, and Evan had bitten back his response with the guy many times over the years. Tonight included.

Evan slipped into booties and gloves and entered the container. He shined his light over the box he estimated at eight feet wide by thirty feet long. He started for one of the two lofts suspended high in the space and climbed the ladder. On the floor he spotted a twin bed, the bedding a tangled mess, and a prayer rug lying next to it. He went to the other loft. Discovered similar items. He checked for clothing or personal belongings. Found nothing.

He glanced at Cartwright, who was standing at the door, apparently not interested enough to come inside. "Looks like two people traveled in here. They left a prayer rug behind. No clothing."

"Male or female, do you think?"

Evan shrugged and came down the ladder. "Muslim faith wouldn't allow an unmarried man and woman to travel unsupervised, so likely male. Unless we're dealing with a married couple."

"So not likely a woman," Cartwright said

For once, Evan agreed with Cartwright. Not that females didn't take up terrorist causes. They did and were becoming more common in terrorist organizations. Still, law enforcement knew nothing more about them other than they were less likely than men to be involved in planning or carrying out terrorist attacks. They were more apt to act behind the scenes in supporting roles. And if the gender roles held true here, Evan was looking for two men.

"There's got to be a bathroom. Maybe with products to help us determine sex of the occupants." Evan stepped through the kitchen to one of the back doors. He found a tiny bathroom with a composting toilet, the faint odor of bleach permeating the air. He opened the medicine cabinet where he spotted two toothbrushes and toothpaste. Nothing more. He looked in a tiny shower. Saw only a bar of soap.

"Nothing in here to suggest male or female." He backed out and opened the other door to a large closet running nearly the width of the back wall. "Generator's in here, along with a water tank and other controls."

"So this threat is for real, and we have two terrorist stowaways." Cartwright blew out a breath. "I'm gonna step outside and run this up the FBI flagpole."

"We should start by informing Watson," Evan said, knowing full well where Cartwright's loyalties lay—with the FBI—and he would try to move this investigation out of the JTTF and under the FBI's jurisdiction.

"Nah. Something this big? It's every man's agency for themselves right now." Cartwright disappeared into the night.

Evan was appalled by the man's lack of loyalty to the team he'd worked on for two years. Evan probably shouldn't be surprised. This could be a career-making case where many agents would lose sight of what *team* meant. Evan had the career he wanted, and he was glad to share this investigation, but he did want to take lead. Run the investigation. Capture these men.

He stepped outside into soupy fog, inhaled the moist air laden with a fishy odor, and dialed Watson. He hated late-night phone calls, so Evan prepared himself for a testy response.

"This better be important, Bowers." Watson didn't disappoint.

"It is, sir." Evan gave a quick recap of the night's events.

"I want the container locked down tight. No one goes in there until I give them clearance." His gruff tone left no doubt of his command. "No one. Hear me?"

"Yes, sir. I can manage security for now, but Cartwright has other ideas and is contacting the FBI's Seattle office. I'll need you to get with the bureau on this thing."

"Then get off the phone and let me get to it."

Evan glanced at Cartwright, who was pacing and waving his free hand as he talked. No way Evan would let that guy have this investigation. "Before you go, I want to make sure JTTF keeps control of this investigation."

"I'll do what I can, but you know how these things go."

Yeah, Evan did. Politics all the way, and the reason why he was bringing it up. "I don't mind working with other agencies on this, but I don't like having done all the legwork to lose out completely."

"I'll keep your request in mind. Now secure the container." Watson disconnected.

Evan approached Cartwright and waited for him to get off the phone. "You can call off your forensic team. We're locking this place down until further notice."

He scowled. "Already called off."

"Not happy with your call, I take it."

"The ASAC told me to call Watson." Cartwright shook his head. "Can you believe that? The investigation of a lifetime, and he's too shortsighted to take the ball and run with it."

"Sounds to me like he's politically savvy." Evan let the comment hang in the air, hoping Cartwright would catch on and emulate the assistant special agent in charge of the Seattle field office and show some smarts.

"Yeah, well, so is Watson," Cartwright said. "He's gotta be on the horn to his supervisor already, and it's going to shoot up the ranks all the way to D.C."

D.C., right. It might as well be the moon as far as Evan was concerned. Only way he would retain control of this investigation was if he had a connection in the capital with someone who had major clout.

An adorable dark-haired woman's face came to mind. Kiley. Kiley Dawson. He knew her—had once known her pretty well. Even had a thing for her. Before she became a member of the elite RED team.

With her high-profile job, she likely had the clout he needed to keep control of the investigation, but would she use her influence for him?

Doubtful. Totally unlikely, actually.

With their history, she'd as soon laugh in his face as help him out. There was no point in calling her. No point at all.

CHAPTER 3

Kiley rubbed the foggy steam from the locker room mirror and looked at her face in the remaining haze. She'd showered and put on clean clothes she kept at the office for her many all-nighters. Black tactical pants, an FBI logo collared shirt, and her worn tactical boots. Her daily work ensemble. Comfortable and efficient. And when she went to see Firuzeh's parents she would look the part of a law-enforcement officer. Strong. Capable. When she felt anything but at the moment.

"You can do this. Her parents deserve your best." She studied her hands again to make sure she'd cleaned off every pinpoint of blood, yet she could still smell the metallic odor and wondered if the scent of Firuzeh dying would ever leave her.

She couldn't linger on those thoughts. Not if she wanted to do her job—find the killer. Something more important to her than breathing right now. She went to the door and marched straight to Mack's cubicle, praying he'd have some information about protection that she could share with the Abed family.

The nutty scent of fresh coffee brewing permeated the air. Something she could use right about now. She would grab a cup on the way out the door. Maybe the warm liquid would erase the cold emptiness she felt inside.

Mack leaned back in his chair, phone to his ear, one booted foot on a desk cluttered with files and stacks of paper. He claimed to know where every item was located. She had her doubts about that.

"Get back to me ASAP." He dropped his boot and looked at Kiley. "Taylor will meet you at the Abeds' home. We'll get them settled in temporary quarters, then arrange movement to a permanent city if needed."

Kiley nodded at the mention of Sean's fiancée, Taylor Mills, who served as a WITSEC deputy. "*If* the Abeds go for it."

"You think they might not?"

She shrugged. "They could have deep family ties in the area and won't want to move."

"Or leave their business behind."

"Could you come with me to explain the process to them in case they have questions? I'm not sure your legendary Texas charm will work on this family, but if anyone can convince them that going into protection is the right move, it will be you."

"I'll do my best, ma'am." He mimicked tipping an imaginary cowboy hat. "We'll at least get them to accept temporary quarters while they consider any future plans." He stood and shrugged into his leather jacket. All he needed was the hat to look exactly like the cowboy he was deep down.

She tried to embrace a cheerier attitude, but sadness enveloped her as she grabbed her backpack and a clean windbreaker from her cubicle. They stopped in the break area for to-go cups of coffee, Kiley adding a liberal dose of cream to hers, while Mack liked his black and "Texas strong," as he called it. They took the long hallway to the parking garage. Kiley tried to concentrate on the warm cup in her hand, the fresh and tantalizing smell of the coffee, but each step pounded in the reality of their upcoming mission.

A family's life was about to change in a way she knew only too well from past experience. The thought chilled her. She tugged her jacket closed with her free hand but lifted her face to the rush of air sweeping through the parking garage to clear away any residual thoughts of crying. Though telling the Abeds about Firuzeh was going to be hard, Kiley would hold herself together for the sake of the family.

She saw Mack's old truck parked by Sean's SUV and remembered her car was still at the crime scene. "Can we pick up my car on the way back? I also want to see what Detective Lancaster found."

Mack unlocked the passenger door for her. "You sure you want to talk to Lancaster?"

She slid onto the seat and took comfort in the cab that always smelled like savory barbecue. "Why not?"

He arched an eyebrow. "First, Firuzeh was your CI, and you're still in shock. And second, Eisenhower made it clear he didn't want you interfering with the locals."

"Then he won't like it. And Firuzeh being my CI is precisely the reason I need to know Lancaster is doing a thorough job." She pulled the door closed to end the conversation.

Mack took his place behind the wheel and steered his truck out of the parking structure. He kept glancing at Kiley.

"Enough already," she said. "You'd do the same thing in my position and you know it."

"Yeah, but I like to live on the edge. You're a by-the-book person." He pointed the vehicle in the direction of the Beltway.

"Well, not anymore. Firuzeh deserves my best effort to find her killer." She took a long pull of the creamy yet sharp coffee, nearly burning her tongue.

He nodded, but his narrowed gaze said he wasn't convinced she should pursue the murder investigation. "How did Firuzeh come across her intel?"

"I didn't get the chance to ask her. In the past, she'd overheard things at her parents' mailbox business. The box number she mentioned could very well be the key."

"Tell me about the business," Mack encouraged.

"It's a basic mailbox rental and package

shipping store. Her parents are semiretired. She ran the business with her older brother."

"It would be risky for terrorists to communicate using written mail."

"True, but when she's behind the boxes distributing the mail, they might not know she's there and feel free to talk."

"But this attack is hyped as something big. *Huge.* Seems too careless to be talking about it in public." He merged into the Beltway traffic, which was light at this time of night. "Have you given any more thought to the other words she said?"

"In the shower. Unfortunately, I didn't come up with anything. Maybe she was trying to tell me there's someone in a coma who knows more."

"Sounds possible." He reached for his coffee cup but paused before sipping. "But how would a coma relate to 'port'?"

"Yeah, that's the weird part." Kiley stared at the cup in her hand and tried to focus her thoughts. "What kind of ports are there? And did Firuzeh mean port as a noun or verb? Like a place where ships take harbor or to port information like in a software upgrade?"

"Or even a wine. Or did she mean airport, and you only heard port?" He shook his head. "What kind of background did she have that might have informed the word?"

"Her family emigrated from Iran when the last

shah was overthrown in the late seventies. Her father was just a baby. Her grandfather bought the business when they moved here, and it's been in the family ever since. In addition to working there, she was going to school part time for legal studies."

"I don't know how any of that informs the word *port,* but she could've gotten her intel at the university."

"I'll text Cam to run background on her university connections." Kiley set her cup in the holder, sent the message to Cam, and traded a few more texts with their team analyst where he expressed his sympathies.

Cam was the only civilian on the team, but his work was on par with everyone else's, and he'd made it very clear that he wanted to become an agent. A problem for him because the bureau didn't want to lose an incredibly talented analyst.

Mack turned off at Tysons. The Abeds' house was only minutes away.

Kiley's throat felt dry, and she reached for her coffee but changed her mind as unease swam in her stomach like a sea of acid. She was out of her depth here and prayed she was ready to help this soon-to-be grieving family through the loss of their precious daughter.

To protect the scene's integrity, Evan had waited and waited some more, testing his patience as he sat with Cartwright for three hours in an FBI incident response vehicle that reeked of stale microwave meals. But finally—finally—they had action. A top-notch FBI Evidence Recovery Team from Quantico pulled into the area Evan had cordoned off with crime scene tape. He'd fought to keep the forensics under ICE's HSI Forensic Laboratory, as they were familiar with ports. He might have won the battle if there hadn't been an FBI Quantico team in Seattle finishing up another investigation.

Two males jumped down from their mobile lab and two females got out of a black SUV. They went straight to the truck's side door and opened it.

"Go time," Cartwright said and, without a backward glance, bolted down the steps.

Evan followed. Not being with the FBI put him at a disadvantage here. No matter. He planned to do his best to direct this team's evidence recovery efforts and joined them at their truck. Cartwright had introduced himself but hadn't yet started dictating priorities.

"ICE Special Agent Evan Bowers." Evan held out his credentials and looked at each member of the team, hoping the leader would step forward.

A short, wide male without a strand of hair on his head stuck out a pudgy hand. "Gerald Philips. I'll be heading up our team."

Evan shook hands. "As you can see, we've

cordoned off the scene. Agent Cartwright and I had a quick look around inside. Wore gloves and booties. No one else has been in the container."

Philips nodded. "We need full access to the container. Means the ones on top will have to be moved."

Cartwright snapped his jacket, wrestling to gain control against the harsh port wind. "I'll arrange to have them moved."

Evan held up a hand. "That will require a crane, destroying the scene. Moving the top ones will have to wait until after the exterior is processed."

Cartwright frowned but didn't argue.

"We'll start outside, work our way in, and I'll let you know when to bring in that crane," Philips said. "Any priorities inside?"

"Fingerprints," Evan said before Cartwright could speak. "The container should be filled with them, unless the suspects wore gloves the entire trip, which is unlikely. I'd like the prints processed first in hopes of confirming ID and number of occupants."

"You got it." Philips gave a tight smile. "Anything else?"

"DNA," Cartwright said.

DNA was also a priority. Evan got that, as it was another way to ID the terrorists. But running DNA samples would take days when fingerprints were much faster.

"Prints first," Evan said, taking charge. "And

then do your thing. Process the place top to bottom. Let me know if you have any questions."

Philips turned to the others. "You heard him. Let's get suited up and get the scene photos and sketches going so we can start printing the exterior of this monster of a thing."

Evan's phone rang, and seeing Watson's name, he answered and stepped out of hearing range.

"Got the details back on the container," Watson said without fanfare. "Originated in Mundra, India. Arrived in Tacoma four days ago."

Evan made a mental note of the information so he could enter it in his phone's notes app when he ended the call. "Odd that the container is still here after four days. I'll talk to the port supervisor to see if there are orders to move or store it. If it's scheduled to remain on-site, then our occupants might be planning a return trip in the same container."

"True, *if* we're not dealing with a suicide mission."

"I gotta figure such nice accommodations means these guys aren't flunkies who plan to wear a suicide vest."

"Good point. The container was shipped via Golden Lion Shipping. They're a reputable line."

Interesting name. "I'll research the company and the owner as soon as I can."

"Get back to me on that and any forensic leads the minute they come in." The call went dead.

Evan entered the information into his app and shoved his phone in his pocket as he climbed the steps of the command truck. He didn't like being dependent on another agency for a command vehicle, but he had to admit the FBI had all the bells and whistles in here. A bank of monitors and cameras took up one wall, surveillance equipment and a command desk on the other. Plus televisions with computers, all with internet access, and secured phone lines were at their fingertips.

Evan sat at the main desk and called the port office. He'd been dealing with Jim Gadsden, the head of security, ever since Perez had reported the incident and Gadsden begrudgingly came into the port.

"Help you." His cranky tone left no question about what he thought about having to report in on a weekend.

"I need to know if this container is supposed to be moved or stored here," Evan said.

"We don't store anything on-site."

"Then when is the move scheduled?"

"Let me check."

While he looked it up, Evan opened an internet window on the computer and entered *Golden Lion Shipping* in the search engine. Their colorful website with a border of gold lions loaded on the screen. He clicked on the About section. Ormazd Malouf owned the company that his father founded eighty years ago in Iraq. He'd originally called the company Malouf Shipping, changing the name to Golden Lion in the early sixties. A shipping company tied to Iraq raised a ton of red flags. Evan would most certainly be talking to Malouf.

"Here it is," Gadsden said. "It's scheduled to leave Terminal 18 tomorrow. Going to Golden Lion's storage facility."

"Is it usual for a container to sit here for a few days like this?"

"It's not unheard of, but we try to move 'em out as fast as we can. Don't have the space to keep 'em on-site."

"And how are these orders generated?"

"Electronically from the shipping company."

"You ever have any issues with Golden Lion?"

He didn't answer for a moment. "We have issues with every shipping company. If you're asking about something illegal, nah. Nothing like that."

"I need the contact information for the owner. Not Golden Lion's office number but Malouf's personal cell, if you have it."

"Let's see what we have. Hmm . . . yeah, here's a cell number, but I'm not sure it's his." He rattled off the number.

Evan jotted down the contact information and read it back to Gadsden.

"Yep. That's it."

"I need you to email those shipping orders to me. In fact, email everything you have on this container."

"I . . . well . . . honestly, I probably shouldn't have told you what I did. I'll have to talk to the boss man about that and get back to you."

"Then call him. Immediately."

"But it's Sunday. He's not gonna like it."

"Tough," Evan said. "While you're at it, get permission to release your security footage for the entire month, and every worker's name and hours worked for the same period."

He groaned. "Aw, man, you don't know what you're asking for here."

Evan did know, and he didn't expect Gadsden's supervisor to cooperate without a warrant, so the minute he ended the call, he would request one.

"Say, what's this all about anyway?" Gadsden asked. "What did you find in the container?"

"I'm not at liberty to discuss that, but you can be assured there is no immediate danger to anyone here." Evan disconnected, hoping—no, praying—he was right.

Because truth was he couldn't promise anything. Not when they had no idea where these terrorists had gone and where they planned to unleash their horrific attack.

CHAPTER 4

"We have expected a day like today," Mr. Abed said as he stroked his bearded chin and shifted on the sofa in their well-appointed living room.

Kiley took a deep breath of the air filled with the cloying smell of incense and tried not to stare at him for such a statement after learning his daughter had been brutally gunned down.

He ran his hands over his flowing white pants paired with a beige high-necked shirt and a blue paisley overshirt. "We feel great sorrow, but we are proud of our Firuzeh."

Kiley tried to process his comments but couldn't make sense of them. "I'm sorry, but exactly why did you expect this?"

"When Firuzeh was born, we wanted her to be strong." Mrs. Abed smiled and patted her shoulder-length black hair liberally woven with threads of gray. She, like Firuzeh, didn't cover her head in the privacy of their home.

"We wanted Firuzeh to be a person who could fight anything and survive," Mr. Abed took over. "We chose to name her Firuzeh, which means 'woman of triumph.' We soon realized the name was appropriate." He smiled fondly, even as he gripped his knees. "From a child on, she stood up for injustice. In our world that can often mean death. So we prepared ourselves for something like this. And here we are." His chin trembled, but he took a deep breath and let it out slowly.

Kiley still couldn't believe this stoic acceptance of their daughter's death, but maybe they were putting on a strong face for her and Mack and would fall apart when they were alone. "Can you think of anyone who might want to hurt Firuzeh?"

"No. No." Mrs. Abed clutched her chest. "She was well loved."

"I agree." Firuzeh's brother, Raheem, looked at her, his full black beard making his long face seem even longer. "Our customers really took to her."

"She told me she had information regarding a terrorist plot," Kiley said, hating how Firuzeh's parents cringed at the news. "Do you have any idea where she might have heard about that?"

Her parents shook their heads while Raheem clutched his wife's hand and bit his lip. With her free hand, she straightened her tailored green blouse and cast him a questioning look. They knew something they were afraid to mention.

Kiley needed to know what they were hiding. "Is there something you want to share, Raheem?"

His dark eyes somber, he nodded. "Firuzeh was very involved in politics on campus. She even went to group meetings at other universities with friends."

"She attended Northern Virginia Community College, right?" Kiley asked.

"She was recently accepted at Georgetown full time for next spring," Raheem said.

"Getting accepted to such a prestigious college was a major accomplishment." Kiley felt even sadder for the young life cut short.

"She worked hard to save money so she could attend." Pride filled Raheem's expression.

"Do you think her intel could have come from the business?" Mack asked.

Raheem rubbed his hands over the legs of his worn blue jeans. "It's possible, I suppose, but I think the schools are more likely."

"She mentioned box number 342. I think it could be located at your business, and we need to find out who rents it," Kiley said gently to try to make this seem optional when in fact she expected them to turn over their customers' details.

"I can look it up for you when I go back to work." Raheem sat up higher. "And I am glad to listen for any information that might help find my sister's killer."

"About that." Kiley looked directly at Mr. Abed, who would likely be the decision-maker here. "We believe your lives could be in danger, and we want to move you to a secure location for your safety while we investigate."

Mr. Abed pinched the bridge of his long nose

and lifted his shoulders. "We will not run and hide. Not from these scoundrels."

Mack slid forward on the sofa. "No disrespect, sir, but think of your family. They could wipe all of you out in one attack."

Mrs. Abed clutched her husband's arm. "We cannot put the children at risk. We must do as they say."

Mr. Abed drew in a long breath and seemed to deflate as he exhaled, looking like a smaller version of himself. "We will do as you ask. For now."

Mack nodded. "Then we ask that you pack your bags. Take nothing that could identify you. No driver's licenses, birth certificates, credit cards. Nothing. Deputy Taylor Mills will arrive soon to take you to a safe location and will provide everything you might need."

Raheem shook his head slowly. "What about our business? The income supports our entire family."

"Do you have anyone else who could run it?" Mack asked.

Raheem glanced at his father, who nodded, and then Raheem looked at Mack again. "We have an employee I could train to keep things going for the short term."

"Then we'll arrange for the two of you to meet when you look up that mailbox owner for me," Kiley said. "I also hate to tell you this, but the local police will want to search Firuzeh's room.

We'd like to take a quick look before they do."

Mrs. Abed's eyes widened. "But her privacy—"

"Has already been violated," Mack said. "Kiley cared very much for your daughter, and she's the best person to make the initial sweep."

Raheem stood. "Come, everyone. Pack. I will show them to Firuzeh's room."

Mr. Abed helped his wife to her feet and led her into the hallway. Raheem motioned for them to follow him through a kitchen filled with the pungent scent of curry that seemed to be infused into the walls.

He looked back at Kiley. "My wife and I shared the in-law suite with Firuzeh."

His wife passed them, her jasmine perfume lingering as she quickly climbed the stairs. He started up slowly, as if lifting his sneaker-clad feet took too much effort.

In the large room at the top landing he pointed at blue-and-red-striped curtains running the width of the space. "We have the bedroom, and we curtained off a section for Firuzeh in the main area."

"May I ask why she didn't have her own room?" Mack asked.

"She would have to share with our younger sisters, and Firuzeh felt too grown up for that." He shook his head. "She was too grown up for sharing since she was a teenager. Such a serious girl, she was, and so passionate."

"Is there anything you might have overheard

out here? Like a phone call maybe?" Mack asked before Kiley could ask the same question.

"No," Raheem answered. "I have told you everything I know. There is nothing more. Please, look at her things. I am going to wake my sisters and get them packing, then help my wife."

He plodded away, his shoulders slumped. Kiley's heart broke for him and his family, and she headed for the curtain. She loved her job and wouldn't want to do anything else, but some days she hated it, and today was one of those days.

She stepped behind the curtain and caught a whiff of Firuzeh's flowery perfume, bringing fresh tears to Kiley's eyes. She forced herself to focus on Firuzeh's meager furnishings. A neatly made twin bed with a purple-and-gold bedspread. A nightstand with burnished bronze lamp. A tiny scarred desk, along with a small dresser and a clothes rack.

Mack headed straight for the desk. "She didn't have much."

"Sounds like she didn't need much." Kiley joined him and slid Firuzeh's laptop to the corner. "I'll take an image of her hard drive while we're here. Be sure to look for any hidden flash drives."

He gave her a wry smile. "I *do* know how to search a place, you know."

"Yeah, sorry. I just know this will be our only chance to access Firuzeh's space before Lancaster takes over, and I don't want to miss a thing."

"Then let's get to it."

She grabbed her backpack and pulled out an external drive and her laptop to connect to Firuzeh's computer. Due to the limited memory on Firuzeh's machine, the drive would finish quickly. Kiley left the image running and moved to the nightstand. The top drawer held assorted pens and a notepad.

Kiley switched on the lamp and angled the paper under the bulb's warm glow. "There are indentations on this pad. I'll take it for forensics to process. Hopefully they can figure out what she'd last written."

Mack looked up. "Lancaster won't like that."

"I know, but a local lab might not have the tools needed to process it. Our lab will." Kiley grabbed an evidence bag from her backpack and dropped the notepad inside.

They continued through Firuzeh's belongings, working in silence for nearly an hour, searching under the mattress, through her bedding, and all the while Kiley searched for sense in this tragedy. Questioning where God was in all of it. Wondering if she'd chosen the right words in breaking the news to the Abeds.

Right words. Hah! Like there was anything right about this situation or any words to make it better. There *were* words to make it worse. She knew that firsthand. She'd heard them when her father had died.

She'd grown up in Buffalo, New York, and her dad worked in the steel mill until it went out of business in the early eighties. He struggled to find gainful employment for years, doing odd jobs and losing them as he developed a drinking problem. When she was born years later, he had regular work, but he still drank heavily. The night he died, he'd slammed into a family of five, killing himself and the entire family.

When the officer came to tell her mother, Kiley was in the hallway listening. She would never forget each harsh word the officer had uttered about her dad. A drunk. Monster. Killer. The pointed barbs cut through her with razor-sharp anguish both then and now. He was much more than that, but the horrible accident was now his legacy.

Frustrated from sinking into the pain of old memories at her age, she dropped to the floor and looked under the bed. She couldn't continue to let the past impact her life and decisions. She had to get beyond it. Let it go once and for all. She just didn't know how to do it without confronting her mother and hashing out the past. Not something she was ready to do. Especially when she didn't think her mother would take her seriously. She never had before.

Kiley banished her thoughts and pulled out two soft-sided suitcases. She jerked hard on the zippers but found both suitcases empty and shoved them in the dark recesses more forcefully than needed to ease out her frustration. She drew Mack's study, but she didn't care. It had felt good and alleviated a bit of her anguish.

She inserted Firuzeh's backpack in an oversized evidence bag and set it by the curtain without looking inside. Kiley wanted to give the pack a thorough look when she had plenty of time to review each item. "Lancaster has likely recovered Firuzeh's phone. I'll have to get her records from her telecom."

Mack frowned. "With no standing in this investigation, getting a warrant for her phone will be problematic."

She didn't want to admit he was right, but he was. No judge would approve a warrant for an investigation not under their jurisdiction. She would have to find another way to get the call logs. At the moment, Kiley didn't know how she would accomplish it. At least she couldn't think of a legal way to obtain the records. She could hack the telecom. She wouldn't, though. As Mack said, she operated by the book, and it would take extreme circumstances for her to hack a legitimate business.

Kiley looked at Mack where he squatted by the bottom dresser drawer. "Firuzeh said millions of lives were at stake. I haven't really had time to give that much thought, but what could threaten a million or more lives?"

His hand stilled over the drawer. "Off the top of my head? A weaponized toxin. Chemical plants. Liquid natural gas. Could be any of them and more."

Frustrated, Kiley planted her hands on her hips and looked around the space. "There has to be some clue here."

Mack looked over his shoulder. "If so, I'm not seeing it."

"She said it was to be carried out within a week." Kiley's computer dinged, telling her the image had completed.

Mack stood. "Anniversary of 9/11?"

"I was thinking the same thing. It's hard to believe this sweet college student stumbled on a sinister plot and might have lost her life because of it."

Mack frowned. "We need to finish up here. Get back to the office. Make an action plan."

"You're right. We're done here. Let's go." Kiley packed the external drive and her computer and shouldered her backpack to leave. On the way out, she grabbed Firuzeh's backpack and found Raheem near the stairs, a large black suitcase that matched the pair under Firuzeh's bed in his hand.

Kiley looked around the room at overstuffed furniture with a contemporary flair. "Is there anything out here belonging to Firuzeh?"

He shook his head. "She felt like she was

infringing on us so she was very tidy and never left anything behind."

"What did she like to do for fun?" Kiley asked, as she wanted to see more than this very serious side of Firuzeh.

"She was really into dancing. Especially traditional Persian dances like the Bandari. Our parents do not approve of dancing, so this they do not know."

"Where would she go to dance?"

"This *I* did not want to know, so if my father found out I would not have to lie to him."

Kiley could understand his position. She tapped Firuzeh's backpack. "I would like to take several items with me. I also made a copy of her computer hard drive."

He gave a firm nod.

"Thank you for your cooperation, Raheem."

"It is for my sister that I do it." He met Kiley's gaze and held it. "Please promise me you will find Firuzeh's killer."

Kiley found herself nodding and gritted her teeth. What on earth had she been thinking to make such a promise?

One of the first rules of law enforcement was never to promise anything to grieving families. Now she had to find a way not to make a liar of herself.

CHAPTER 5

Kiley watched Taylor's car holding the bereaved Abed family wind up the parking ramp at the U.S. Marshals' office, and she turned to face Mack, who sat in the driver's seat of his truck. "I don't like leaving the Abeds before they're settled in a safe house."

"You know they're in the best hands with Taylor." Mack wasn't exaggerating because Taylor was engaged to Sean. She was a top-performing and well-respected WITSEC deputy, and an overall wonderful woman.

"I already appreciate having her here in D.C. as a friend," Kiley said, "but tonight I appreciate her a little bit more."

"Yeah, I get that. Having people you can count on to do what they say they're going to do is a rarity these days." Was he thinking of his wife, Addison Leigh? They'd been separated for over a year but had never divorced.

Kiley looked at him. "You thinking of anyone in particular?"

He shrugged, a faraway look in his eyes that said *end of subject.*

She wanted to probe, yet she'd hate it if he ignored her desire for privacy, so she clamped her mouth closed and sat back for the drive to Firuzeh's crime scene.

Still, Kiley felt insanely proud of herself for even noticing his desire not to talk. Figuring people out was a nuance she was just starting to get good at. Thanks to her mother's overprotective nature, outside of school hours Kiley had spent her teen years pretty much locked in her room with her computer. She didn't have friends other than online friends, and there were no nuances in their written messages. Plus video was rare back then, and even the little bit she'd participated in wasn't really interacting with a person up close and personal. So she'd had to learn the skills as an adult. Skills she would need when she faced Detective Lancaster, who was emerging from the shadows near Firuzeh's car.

Mack parked by the yellow crime-scene tape. Kiley got out and caught Lancaster's eye. His hair was plastered against his forehead. He brushed it back with an angry swipe as he marched across the street. Kiley planted her feet and prepared herself for a testy encounter.

"Agent Dawson," Lancaster began, "think of something I might need to know?"

"I came to pick up my car." She poked a thumb over her shoulder at her vehicle. "Thought I'd stop by to ask if you'd found anything of interest."

He eyed her, probably hoping she'd squirm

under his study and leave, but she stood fast. "We recovered five slugs," he finally said.

Kiley let herself replay the shooting, counting the rifle reports, wincing with each one. "I heard five shots. Means the bullet that killed Firuzeh must have been a through-and-through."

"Seems like it. The ME will confirm."

"You get a make on those rounds?" Mack asked.

Lancaster shifted his focus to Mack. "I didn't catch your name when you were here before."

"Deputy U.S. Marshal Mack Jordan. One of Agent Dawson's RED team associates."

"Ah yes, the hotshot team." Lancaster spit the words out as if they tasted like sour milk. "They're rifle rounds, but I'm not into weapons so can't tell you more than that."

"So the shooter used a long gun," Kiley said. "Jells with why I didn't hear anyone or a car speed off."

Lancaster nodded. "Trajectory puts him on the roof of the nearby mall. We recovered a casing lodged in a crack. Otherwise the shooter policed his brass."

The mall was half a mile away or more. *Sniper.* She didn't say it aloud because she didn't want to get into a discussion neither of them knew enough to hold. Better to stick to facts she *did* know about. "Firuzeh never stood a chance."

"No."

Kiley thought back to the shooting again. "Takes time to find a way to the roof of a mall and set up a shot. He wouldn't have had time to follow Firuzeh here, then get to the mall. Means he had to know where she planned to be."

"You've met here before, right?" Mack asked.

Kiley nodded.

"So, he could've put a tracker on her car and phone, giving him the time he needed."

"I already had techs check her car for one," Lancaster said. "It was clean, but I'll have them check her phone."

Kiley stepped closer and tried to convey a sense of urgency in her body language. "I don't mean to be difficult here or prideful, but I'm one of the best electronics techs you can find. And I'm fast. Why not let me handle the phone for you? I could extract the data and get it back to you by morning. That's before you'll even get a tech to look at it."

Lancaster widened his stance. With his defensive posturing she prepared herself for a big fat no.

"I'll give you the phone," he said, "but on one condition. You tell me what you took from her house."

"What makes you think I—"

He flapped up his hand. "Save it. We both know you couldn't miss the opportunity to conduct a search while doing the death notification call."

She always planned to share with him, so this was no hardship. "I imaged her hard drive. Also took a notepad with indentations. Plus her backpack."

He ran a hand down his blue striped tie, leaving it rumpled. "And you're in possession of these items?"

She nodded. "It's not like I'm withholding evidence. I planned to give the notepad to our forensics lab and the rest of it to you after I reviewed it tonight."

"Right." He scoffed, then quickly cleared his expression. "Phone's yours so long as it comes back to me by ten a.m. along with everything else, other than the notepad."

She started to nod but then decided to push her luck. "Why not let me take the slugs and casing too? Get the FBI's Firearms/Toolmarks Unit to examine them for you? I can have FTU start right away and rush it for you."

He nodded. "We'll do that too, but I better not find out you're playing me."

"No," Kiley said earnestly. "I just want to help you find Firuzeh's killer."

"I'll get the items for you." One last lingering look and he marched away.

Mack faced her. "That was easy."

"Surprisingly so," Kiley said, her focus still on Lancaster as he talked with a white-suited tech. "Maybe he knows our lab techs have far more experience than most locals and wants the best."

"Or he's too tired to argue with you."

"Could be," she said as Lancaster disappeared into the fog near Firuzeh's car.

Less than three hours ago Kiley was on the ground in those shadows fighting to keep Firuzeh alive. Trying to stop the bleeding, her hands saturated with the sticky liquid. She held them out and stared at her fingers, the soft mist dampening her skin. They still felt as if they were coated in blood. How long would it take to recover from the first ever homicide committed in her presence? Or did one ever recover from such a thing?

"It'll get better," Mack said softly. "But it'll never go away completely."

She lowered her hands and looked up at him. "My thoughts are that obvious?"

"I've been through it so I recognize the signs. You might want to consider counseling."

"Have you ever gone?"

"I hear it helps."

She was about to ask why he chose not to answer her question when Lancaster returned with the evidence bags and a chain-of-custody form requiring her signature.

He held the bags just out of reach and met her gaze. "Ten sharp, with everything minus the notepad, slugs, and casing, Agent Dawson. Don't make me come looking for you."

"You won't have to." She grabbed the bags and turned to leave. For some reason she couldn't make her feet move. Trying to figure out her reluctance, she looked around and focused on the investigation instead of her emotions. "I don't see any CCTV cameras here. Are there any in the area of the shooter's hide?"

Lancaster sighed. "We haven't gotten that far."

She was disappointed no one had looked into possible videos yet. She would get on locating them right after she started extracting the phone data. She faced him. "Have you considered this murder might not have to do with my meeting with Firuzeh?"

"Of course."

"So you'll be requesting Firuzeh's banking and credit card information. And checking her social media."

"I *do* know how to run an investigation, Agent Dawson." Lancaster curled his fingers into fists. "And I'd get a lot further if you'd stop second-guessing my every move and let me get to work. Remember," he added before she could get out an apology. "Evidence back to me by ten." He strode away.

"You trust him to do a good job?" Mack asked as he walked her to her car.

"Seems capable, doesn't he?"

Mack nodded. "But you'll still gather the information regardless?"

"Yeah."

"That's my girl." Mack grinned. "You can leave the backpacks in my truck, and I'll bring them in when we get to the office."

She started to thank him, then remembered their earlier conversation and slid into her car. A takeout bag of Mexican food she'd scarfed down on the way to meet Firuzeh left the air saturated with a spicy aroma that turned her stomach.

She ignored it and shoved the key into the ignition. Mack stood watching until she got her car going before giving her a tight smile and getting in his truck. He could come across as gruff and pushy—a holdover from his days as an elite Army Night Stalker—when he wasn't laying on the Southern charm and was often misunderstood, but he was a great guy. Three years older than Kiley, she thought of him as a big brother.

On the road, she slowed for him to catch up and merged onto the Beltway headed into D.C. A text-to-speech message from Sean came over her car's speaker.

"You on your way back yet?"

"Few minutes out," she replied and waited for him to explain why he questioned her location, but miles flew by without another text. He wouldn't check on her unless he had something important to tell her. She pressed on the gas pedal and glanced back to be sure Mack kept pace all the way to their reserved parking spaces.

He met her at the door with the evidence bags and Kiley's backpack.

She swiped her keycard down the wall-mounted reader. "Sean text you?"

He nodded and held the door open for her. "Something must be up."

Eager to find out what was going on, she raced down the hall and found Sean and Cam waiting by their office entrance.

Mack was right. Something *was* up. Something big. All team members were go-getters and didn't wait around for anything. Not even Cam, who was often laid-back. Tonight, his eyes were narrowed, and he shoved a hand into his blond hair already in a messy style. Intensity radiated from his toned body just as it did from Sean.

"We gotta move," Sean said. "We're on a plane to Tacoma leaving now."

She blinked a few times to let his comment register. "Tacoma? As in Washington State?"

"Yes." Sean moved closer and lowered his voice. "We have a report of two known terrorists entering the country. A JTTF out of Tacoma intercepted a shipping container tricked out as living quarters. Arrived four days ago out of India. Eisenhower arranged for us to catch a military hop out of Andrews."

Kiley couldn't leave. Not even for the Joint Terrorism Task Force's discovery. Not now. "But Firuzeh . . . I need to . . ."

"I think we'll find there's a connection to her," Sean said.

"Think about it." Cam tapped his temple. "Port. Coma."

"Oh my gosh. Yes." Her mouth fell open. "Of course. Port of Tacoma. That's what Firuzeh was trying to tell me."

"Likely," Sean said.

But what did this mean for the investigation? "Did Eisenhower say he still wants me in charge?"

"Yes," Sean said.

This was big. Huge. Freaking huge. Her confidence completely evaporated.

"I've already loaded our gear into my vehicle," Sean continued. "Go pack your personal things so we can get moving."

Mack spun, and her backpack hanging over his shoulder shifted.

"Wait," she said. "I've got evidence from the homicide. I need to review it, and Lancaster wants it back by ten a.m."

"No time for that. Our hop is the last plane of the day, and they're holding it for us. We'll be putting down at Joint Base Lewis-McChord near Tacoma. Either leave it behind or maybe we can get the evidence returned on another flight."

She shook her head. "I need equipment to review Firuzeh's phone. I can't do that on the plane, and there's no way I'm leaving it behind.

It'll just have to be late, and I won't worry about it."

"What about the evidence we need to get to Quantico?" Mack asked.

"We'll leave it here." She retrieved the items, along with the chain-of-custody form, and held them out for Sean. "While I pack, can you arrange to get this to the lab with my name listed as the contact person?"

Sean nodded and took the items. "Harrison is here. The rookie's always looking for a way to help. She'll camp out on the lab doorstep until they open and get this submitted with top priority."

Kiley took Firuzeh's backpack from Mack and shoved it at Cam. "Hold on to this for me."

Kiley jogged to her cubicle, making a mental note to text a heads-up to Eisenhower about the evidence in case Lancaster wanted to call foul. She took a quick look at her desk to decide what to take. The team traveled with a mix of equipment—electronic, forensic, and law-enforcement supplies—always packed and ready to go at a moment's notice, so she didn't need to add much. She stowed frequently used electronics and cords in her pack that already held extra clothes. If she forgot something in the rush, she could buy it in Tacoma. She heard Mack doing the same thing in the cubicle next to her.

"Ready?" he called out.

She shouldered her pack and met him in the aisle. Sean had returned to the doorway with Cam, and the four of them raced for Sean's department-issued SUV. With his need to control things they usually let him drive, and tonight was no exception. She rode shotgun while Mack and Cam took the back seat.

After Sean got them on the road, which was slick with rain, she swiveled to face him. "You mentioned a JTTF. Is this an FBI group?"

He shook his head. "Mixed agencies, but I don't know the makeup."

She wished they knew more so that she had an idea of what she would be facing. "Either way they won't like our interference."

Sean shrugged. "Locals never do, but it's in the country's best interests to have the most capable people on this investigation."

"And that's us." Mack chuckled.

"We *are* the best," Cam said matter-of-factly. "We really are."

Rolling her eyes, she looked over her shoulder. "And modest."

"Hey, facts are facts." Cam grinned.

She frowned. "I expect everyone to lose this attitude before we get to Tacoma."

"See, Cam," Mack said. "I told you she's stepping up."

"Totally," Cam said. "It's kind of hot."

She eyed him. "You did *not* just say that."

"Sometimes I lose my filter." His little boy smile beneath his blond good looks made it hard to be irritated with him.

"Sometimes?" Mack asked.

She shook her head but totally understood their joking. They all did it to combat the tension of daily potential life-ending situations. Common behavior for law-enforcement officers. Even more so for an elite team like theirs. Even when losing someone like Firuzeh. Especially then, or the on-the-job stress would render them incapable of doing their jobs day in and day out.

And as lead on this high-profile investigation, Kiley would be subjected to more stress than usual. She had to be proactive and formulate an investigative plan.

She sat back and thought ahead to their arrival at the port. First action item would be wrestling the investigation away from the agent in charge of the JTTF investigation. With this being her first time as lead, she could only hope he was a friendly sort who wanted to cooperate—who wanted to put the investigation first and not try to claim jurisdiction. Do the right thing no matter what.

Right. And pigs flew.

"They can't," Evan snapped, and regretted it when Watson didn't comment. "Sorry. I spent weeks cultivating this lead, and right when it gets interesting the RED team swoops in and takes over."

"I've requested we be included in the investigation, but the ball's in their court."

Evan's heart fell. Kiley would never let him work this investigation.

"You better practice playing nice, because they'll be on scene anytime now," Watson said.

"Here? Now? How?" Evan looked out the command truck's window. "Takes hours just to get through the airport and security in D.C."

"Military transport."

Of course. The wonder team would have such connections.

"Be professional," Watson continued, "and don't make a scene."

The call went dead, and a little bit of Evan went dead inside too. He wasn't an emotional guy, not usually, but mess with his job and he could get good and mad. And losing this investigation? That just plain stunk. Still, it didn't mean he had to let it go. He could work things on his own time even if Watson would have a fit if he found out.

And Evan wouldn't let his irritation stop him. He wouldn't sit inside the command vehicle and sulk. Not when he still had time to get forensic details from Philips before Kiley and her team arrived to kick him to the curb.

He stormed out the door and down the steps. The sun was climbing over the port, fingers of yellow and orange creeping over the water's surface. He would stop to enjoy God's beauty, but he had little time to waste.

Cartwright leaned against the truck and glanced up from his phone. "Someone take away your toys?"

"So you haven't heard then?"

Cartwright lifted an eyebrow. "Heard what?"

"DHS's RED team out of D.C. is taking over the investigation."

"I thought they predominantly worked internet crimes."

"They do. I tracked this lead on the dark web. Maybe they did too." Evan didn't bother to explain the dark web, as Cartwright knew all about the deep and murky layer of the internet where criminals conducted illegal sales transactions.

Cartwright yawned. "Then there's nothing we can do. I won't ruin my career by going up against them. I'll call in and get my marching orders."

"You do that." Appalled at the agent's easy acquiescence, Evan couldn't comprehend not desperately wanting to put these murderers away and protect innocent lives. That was what got Evan out of bed each and every morning since the day six years ago when Agent Olin Foster lost his life on an op. Evan was in charge of planning the ill-fated op, and Kiley was on the team too.

Evan clamped a hand on the back of his neck. He would soon see her again and relive Olin's death. His day was spinning out of control and he didn't like it one bit, but he wouldn't let it stop him from hearing about any discovered evidence.

At the container, he put on booties and gloves and stepped over the threshold. This time he noticed savory ginger lingering in the air, and the place was lit by several Klieg lights. He spied Philips in the back loft where he was lifting evidence with a tweezer.

Evan climbed the ladder. "Got time for a quick review of your findings?"

"Sure, why not?" Philips bagged the item as he sat up, his head brushing the top of the container. "This is quite the operation. Self-contained water system with a large enough tank to provide fresh water for four weeks for two people. Composting toilet with container in back for disposal. Solar generator, and I expect when the containers on top of us are removed, we'll find the panels."

The comment drew Evan in like a puzzle might do, but it didn't make sense. "The panels would be seen and questioned by dockworkers."

"They've cut windows in the sides, lining up the cuts with a painted logo to camouflage them." He tapped the ceiling. "This isn't the container's exterior. When we're able to see the top, I expect we'll find sliding doors that open to reveal the panels."

Evan shook his head. "They thought of every-thing."

"Looks like it. Except they didn't count on you finding the container."

"As sophisticated as they seem to be, it's a good thing I did."

Philips nodded. "We've lifted a crazy number of latents. I did a quick comparison. We've got five distinct prints."

"You think five people came over in here?"

He shook his head. "The rest of the evidence suggests only two. I suspect the other prints were left by people preparing the container."

Evan got out his phone to add the information to his notes program. "You'll get those processed as soon as possible?"

"We have an agent standing by to fly the prints and DNA samples to our lab in Quantico today. You should also know I found explosive residue and bomb-making supplies."

Evan had been afraid they'd find evidence of explosives. Not only did his EOD experience tell him such a thing was likely, but so did his years as an ICE agent. Most people thought ICE was all about deporting illegal aliens. They did that, sure, through the Enforcement and Removal Operations, but they also focused on transnational crimes by investigating the illegal movement of people and goods and funds into, within, and out of the United States, which included terrorism.

And that meant Evan needed to know what the tech located. "Specifically what did you find?"

"The most concerning thing so far is fragments of white phosphorus. I located a jar of it in a large storage bin under the couch."

"That's not good." Evan knew the compound was highly unstable and very dangerous. "I'm a former Navy EOD tech and saw it used to make IEDs in Afghanistan. Rained down fire on soldiers, and they couldn't put it out."

"Yeah, it's bad stuff. Eats through clothing, skin, metal. You name it. Smothering it with dry sand or submerging in water will extinguish it, but it'll ignite again the second air touches it. Fragments in a bomb can cause unthinkably horrible burns."

"What else did you find?" Evan asked, as if the white phosphorus wasn't bad enough.

"Electronics mostly."

"I need to see them."

"Already cataloged and in the truck. You're welcome to take a look."

"I'll check it out and come back for the rest of your update."

"Suit yourself."

Evan dropped his booties at the door and headed outside. Cartwright was still leaning against the command truck, his phone in hand. Evan had no idea what the guy was doing. Likely playing games.

In the back of the vehicle about the size of a package delivery truck, a white-suited tech was cataloging and storing the evidence.

Evan smiled at her. "I'd like to take a look at the recovered electronics."

"Here you go." She slid a container across the floor, the grating sound rising into the quiet morning and joining the chatter of birds.

He took pictures of the basic electronics the terrorists would use to create a timed device. One of the bags held a switching device. He studied it, his gut knotting. Cellphones were often used to detonate a device, but this switch enabled the bomber to send a signal over Wi-Fi to detonate the explosives.

Evan photographed the switch and went back to the container, but his gut wouldn't let go of his growing unease over the impending attack. The level of sophistication and organization here was very disturbing.

A swab in hand, Philips looked up from the same spot. "You get a look at the electronics?"

Evan nodded and left it at that. There was no point in worrying this tech. "What else do you have?"

"I found two handguns. Makarovs. And several boxes of 9.27mm caliber ammo."

"Russian," Evan stated, as he was familiar with the semi-automatic pistol still widely used by Russian police, military, and security forces.

They were also often found in the hands of militants in Iraq and Syria. "Odd that they left them behind."

"Serial numbers were filed off."

"We can't trace them."

"Didn't say that." Philips grinned, revealing a gold tooth. "Our firearms people can probably recover at least part of the number. I don't think the guns will be found in any U.S. database, but Interpol might have them. We'll be working this scene for some time, so the weapons can go out with our agent to Quantico too."

"Great work, Philips," Evan said enthusiastically. "I'm glad they called you in to lead this team."

He arched an eyebrow. "You weren't at first."

"Honestly, no, but you've proven your abilities." Evan backed down the ladder and wondered if the RED team would be the same way—that he'd dread their taking over at first, yet in the end he would be glad of their presence.

CHAPTER 6

The massive Air Force transfer jet touched down with a solid thump, and Kiley exited past airmen who'd already gotten to work removing and stacking the RED team's equipment containers while their lieutenant handed her the keys to a black SUV. She should probably be impressed with the service they were receiving, but this red-carpet treatment wasn't unusual. The team's logistics coordinator was excellent at her job, and even at a moment's notice in the middle of the night, they received special treatment.

She put her backpack in the SUV and looked at her teammates. "Would you guys get the gear loaded while I make a few calls?"

They didn't question her request but headed toward the airmen stacking the crates.

She got out her phone and called Agent Harrison in D.C. "I wanted to be sure you've got Firearms working the slugs and casing and that you took the notepad over to forensics."

"Turned them over the minute the lab opened," she replied with her usual enthusiasm. "We're in luck on the ballistics. I was able to convince Adam Garvin to run the tests." Though Adam was tops in his field, as the department manager now, he rarely ran tests.

"How'd you manage that?" Kiley asked.

"I told him we're hunting terrorists and we needed it immediately. He didn't have a free tech so he agreed to handle it."

The rookie's persuasive skills impressed Kiley. "Did Adam say when to expect results?"

"Late today or first thing tomorrow. I gave him your phone number, and he'll call you directly."

"I owe you," Kiley said sincerely. "A month's lattes on me."

"Not necessary. Just glad to be of help."

"You were. And thanks." As Kiley disconnected the call and phoned Taylor, she vowed to find tasks for Harrison to do in the future that weren't all bottom-of-the-barrel jobs rookie agents were frequently saddled with.

"How are the Abeds holding up?" Kiley asked after Taylor answered.

"As well as can be expected, but the shock has worn off and grief is taking a toll." Taylor sighed. "I wish I could do more for them, but it's just going to take time."

Kiley remembered the ever-changing stages of grief from losing her father. Nothing comforted her. Not even prayer.

"I was just getting ready to take Raheem to their store so he can train their worker," Taylor continued, "and he said something about looking up the name and contact details for one of their mailboxes for you."

Kiley tried to let go of her worry over the Abeds and refocus her thoughts. "We think it could be related to our shooter or the terrorist threat."

A long silence filled the phone.

"I know you can't tell me what you're working on," Taylor said, "but I assume you all got safely to your destination."

Kiley smiled over Taylor's not-so-subtle way of asking about Sean. "Yes, and Sean is fine."

Kiley's phone rang, and seeing Lancaster's name, she quickly said good-bye to Taylor and answered.

"Just a friendly reminder that evidence is due here soon," he stated plainly.

Exactly what she was afraid he'd say. "Unfortunately, it's going to be late. I'm sorry, I—"

"I'm coming over to your office to pick it up," he snapped.

"About that." She inhaled a long breath of air laden with the caustic smell of jet fuel before having to explain. "I'm in Tacoma, Washington, and it's with me."

"What? Just what are you trying to pull here?" A sharp edge of anger tinged his tone.

She couldn't let his irritation bother her, as she couldn't do a thing about the problem right now. "I'm not trying to pull anything. We received a strong lead last night and had to immediately hop a plane. The notepad's in our forensic lab, and the slugs and casing are with our firearms examiners.

I'll evaluate the phone as soon as I can and overnight it to you plus keep you updated on the forensics results."

"This lead," he said, sounding a little less mad, "care to share?"

She forced herself to sound positive and cheerful. "I can't yet, but if it pans out and you're cleared to be read in, I'll call."

"I'd appreciate that."

"Any progress on your end?" she asked, making sure she didn't sound like she was grilling him.

"It's early stages yet. I did receive Firuzeh's banking and credit card information. Nothing out of the ordinary. No large deposits or withdrawals in her checking account. But I'll be tracking down a few recent charges on her credit card. I'll let you know if they give me anything to go on."

Thinking the call went better than could be expected, Kiley thanked him for his cooperation and battled the bitter wind whipping across the tarmac to open the car door. She grabbed her FBI windbreaker from her backpack and slid onto the passenger seat.

Sean closed the hatch, and she took comfort from their equipment piled high in the back as it made her feel more prepared. He jumped behind the wheel. Cam and Mack took the back seat. In minutes, Sean had them out of the base and on the road for the quick twenty-minute trip to the port.

He glanced at her. "When we reach the scene, do you want me to get on the phone to our local office and arrange for a command center?"

"Perfect." She smiled. "That'll free me up to start assessing the port findings right off the bat."

"What's your plan in handling the JTTF agents when we get there?" Mack asked. "You thinking about including them in the investigation?"

She swiveled to face him. "Since we don't know anything about them, I thought I'd play it by ear."

He frowned. "Odds are good they won't be happy with our interference."

"Yeah," she said. "It's hard if fellow agents get their backs up when we all have the same goal in mind."

"Having a reputation as the best usually opens doors, but it can also get in the way," Sean said, and she knew he spoke from experience in leading investigations.

"Doesn't help when some of us get cocky." She eyed Cam.

He held up his hands. "Message received. I'll tone it down."

"At least until we establish our rapport with this team and decide on how we'll handle their involvement."

Sean took a longer look at her. "I'm glad you're keeping your options open and not ruling out their help, but don't let these guys play you."

She crossed her arms. "Sounds like you don't

have a lot of confidence in my leadership ability."

"It's not that at all. I've always thought you'd be a strong leader if you ever wanted to take control. The thing is, though, you're emotionally invested here, and following emotions rarely results in sound decisions."

"Don't worry, I got it," she said quickly. But did she really? Was she wrong in asking for lead on this investigation that now seemed as if it would be far bigger and wider reaching than she'd first imagined? Maybe far beyond her abilities and control?

She had the knowledge and technical skills. The team had worked many terrorism investigations, as the internet and dark web were often used to recruit and communicate with terrorists. So they all stayed up-to-date on the current terrorism scene and knew the major players and their preferred methods of operating. But as lead, she would have to be careful to keep her emotions dialed in. Not let them dictate her actions. Not let the vision of Firuzeh falling to the ground sway her judgment.

She closed her eyes and meditated on a saying she'd had to embrace to find the courage to move out from under her mother's control and become a productive adult.

No one has power over you unless you give it to them. You are in control of your life and your choices. Decide your own future.

Sure, God was ultimately in control, but if her day-to-day actions fell within His will, they were hers to command. And right now, she needed to stay focused. Not worry. Act on what she could impact and do her very best to lead. Think ahead more. Plan.

She opened her eyes. "After we get up to speed on the container, we need to brainstorm the most logical target."

"Not sure how we can narrow it down," Cam said. "Unless they found something in the container to help."

"I'm hoping they did, because so far we have nothing to go on." She met Cam's gaze. "Firuzeh was involved in several political groups. Get started on writing an algorithm to search for connections between other group members. Look for anything radical."

"On it." He took out his laptop, and she was thankful for his sense of urgency.

For the remainder of the drive, she reviewed the to-do list she'd made on the plane and added a few additional items, so when Sean pulled up to Terminal 18 on the quiet dock, she was prepared to take charge.

She leaned forward to view the many lanes leading up to security booths ahead with cameras pointing at the arriving vehicles. "First thing we need to do is request video footage for this terminal if the JTTF agent in charge hasn't done so already."

"I can do that," Mack said.

She nodded but turned her attention to Sean as he displayed his credentials for the guard, who leaned out of the booth at the security checkpoint. He studied the ID and checked his computer monitor that looked like it hadn't been updated in years. Hopefully that wasn't indicative of the rest of the port's security measures.

"Hang tight and my supervisor—name's Tony Lopez—will take you back," the guard said and closed the window on his booth.

Lopez arrived in a small white pickup to escort them onto the property. With it being a weekend, only a few workers were present. Two large ships bobbed at the port wall, and colored steel shipping containers filled several lots. She could easily imagine the organized chaos that would exist when truckers arrived on Monday morning to pick up containers.

Sean parked near a stack of four containers roped off by yellow crime scene tape fluttering in the breeze. Kiley got out, and if she thought the wind was strong at the base, it buffeted her here, and she had to plant her feet wide to take in the scene without losing her balance. A large FBI command truck and forensic truck were parked next to several personal vehicles, and a young man in an FBI windbreaker and khaki pants stood sentry. He held a clipboard, obviously serving as the officer of record. When he caught sight of them, his expression perked up.

"Let's go find out who's in charge here." She snapped her jacket closed and crossed over to the man to display her credentials. She heard her teammates' footsteps right behind her. "I need to speak to the agent in charge."

He poked a thumb over his shoulder at a man in tactical attire staring at his phone by the command truck. "Agent Cartwright's been working the scene."

She noted he didn't say Cartwright was in charge. Still, she could gain access through this agent and later sort out the hierarchy.

"Agent Cartwright," she called out instead of sending this guy to get him.

Cartwright frowned before a broad smile crossed his face, and he eagerly strode toward them. He was tall, slender, confident looking, and had a thick head of ebony hair that ruffled in the wind.

"You must be the RED team. Was just reading about you." He held up his phone. "Agent Ryan Cartwright. Seattle office."

Kiley introduced herself and shook hands with him. "So you located this container?"

"Sure did." His shoulders rose even higher. "Got a warrant. Arranged for security to meet me at the gate and bring me back here."

"You do all of this alone?" she asked.

Cartwright shook his head. "Me and an ICE agent. He's inside the container with forensics. Knowing this was big, I called in a super team out of our Quantico lab."

This agent must think she was an idiot. There was no way he would have the authority to call people in from Quantico, and even if he did, he surely would be interested enough to be inside with the techs. He was obviously exaggerating, but what else was he embellishing?

She shared a look with Mack, and he gave a nearly imperceptible nod of understanding. Seemed like a good time to move on and talk to the ICE agent. "I'd like to see the container now."

"Sure, sure. Sign in and it's all yours."

"What? You give up just like that?"

"We all know how this will go down, so why fight it, right?" He gave her a snarky grin.

His reaction made her mad, but then she remembered Sean's warning and swallowed down her irritation. She signed the log and smiled at the agent of record. "I'd like a copy of the log. I'm assuming you have a copier in the command truck."

"We do."

"I'll stop back for it after getting a look at the container." She ducked under the tape and waited for the others to sign in and join her, allowing them to start across the lot as a complete team. To be honest, she was counting on the shock-and-awe value of the group to help her keep her guard up and not give in to any of the JTTF members.

A man stepped out of the container's side door. The ICE agent. At least she thought his tactical attire and wide shoulders said law enforcement and not forensics.

His steps halted, and he stood staring, his face deep in shadows. She couldn't make out his features, yet she felt like she knew him. It was something in his stance. Eager to get a better look at his face, she picked up speed. He stepped out from the shadows and locked gazes with her.

"No. No. Can't be." Her legs went weak, and she stumbled to a stop.

"Hey," Mack said, grabbing her elbow. "What is it?"

"Him." She pointed at Agent Evan Bowers in the flesh. "It's Evan Bowers. He killed Olin."

She didn't care if she said it loud enough for him to hear. She had nothing to hide.

He kept coming, a frown on his rugged face.

She took a deep breath and looked him in the eye. He had the same brown hair with sun-kissed blond streaks as when she'd known him years ago. The same chiseled jaw. Same piercing blue eyes, muscular build, and confident stride. And he still had the long scar on the side of his face, which he'd sustained when he tackled her to the ground to protect her after Olin had been shot.

She swallowed hard and tried to figure out what

to say. What to do. How to act. He shouldn't be here. He worked out of the Seattle office, not Tacoma.

"Kiley," he said, his voice low and husky—just like she remembered.

Despite her anger at him, his tone settled over her like a warm blanket. "You're the other agent who found the container."

He stopped in front of her, planting his feet on the pavement. "Not other. *The* agent."

Yeah, just as she'd thought. Cartwright exaggerated his role.

"And now you're here to take over," Evan said and shifted to offer his hand to Mack. "ICE Agent Evan Bowers."

Mack shook hands with Evan. "Deputy U.S. Marshal, Mack Jordan."

Sean reached out next, and then Cam, both introducing themselves. Somehow she felt their greeting was a betrayal when deep down she knew they were simply extending professional courtesy.

Evan faced her again. "I know I'm the last person on earth you would want to see, but if you'll hear me out for a minute, I think I can help you."

She didn't want to listen. She wanted to run screaming. Or maybe punch him.

Remember, you're lead here and you need to be impartial.

She curled her fingers, letting the nails bite into her palms. "Go ahead."

He took a wide-legged stance so common for him, making him seem larger and in charge. "You're not familiar with the area or with the terrorist network on the West Coast. I've been working it for years and know the ins and outs. I know bombs inside and out too. And I'm the only one who located this container. No one else can tell you about that. You need me."

She planted her hands on her waist and widened her stance to try to match his. "I don't need—"

"A minute, Kiley," Mack said.

She jerked her gaze from Evan to see Mack's sharp focus pinned on her. He stepped out of earshot, and she had no choice but to join him. "What?"

He peered down at her. "Remember our conversation. Think before telling him to shove off. He has a point. If it was any other agent with his credentials standing there, what would you say?"

"He isn't any other agent!" she got out between gritted teeth. "He's Evan Bowers. Killer of Olin."

Mack looked like he wanted to sigh. "You're being unreasonable. We reviewed the investigation of Olin's death, remember? And I don't think he was any more at fault than anyone else on the team."

He'd never told her that. "Are you saying Olin and I had a part in his death?"

"No. I'm saying things happen on an op. Things we can't plan or predict. Some things that are almost too big to come back from. Don't let this be yours." He eyed her. "Lives depend on you thinking with your head, not your heart."

He was right. She didn't want to admit it, but she had to. "Fine. He works with us. Are you happy?"

He shook his head. "Not until I see you change your attitude."

"You're a pain, you know that? I don't want to change my attitude about him." She knew she was sounding like a spoiled child pitching a tantrum, but this was about the worst thing she could be faced with at the moment. At any moment really.

"And I don't want terrorists to kill people, but they do," Mack said, somehow his slow Southern accent making the words sound even more horrific.

His comment brought everything back to the matter at hand—truly the worst thing she could be facing. She could overcome working with Evan. She might hate every minute of it, but to stop murderous terrorists, she could suck it up and accept his help.

She took a long breath and let it out. Took another, fisted her hands, spun and marched back to him.

"You're right, Agent Bowers," she said with

the most professionalism she could muster. "Our team does need your help, and we'll be happy to have you work the investigation with us."

His mouth dropped open, and his gaze clung to her like an unwanted cobweb.

"You can start by showing us the container." She waited for him to turn before letting out a seething breath.

She would do the right thing here. She had to. But as she trailed him into the container, she had to wonder why doing the right thing was rarely, if ever, easy.

CHAPTER 7

Evan stopped just inside the container door and watched Kiley as she scanned the interior. She had no idea how beautiful she was. None. Even now. She looked tough and commanding in her tactical pants and FBI windbreaker, but he knew underneath the law-enforcement façade that she'd once been shy, sweet, and socially awkward, all bundled up in an amazing package.

She backed into him, and he reached out to steady her. She bolted away from his touch, but his heart thundered over her nearness and the sweet pear-and-vanilla scent of her perfume. How pathetic was that? She couldn't stand the sight of him, and yet he was still attracted to her.

She took a few extra steps away from him, her face a mask of indifference. "Tell me what we have so far."

He resisted blowing out a breath and explained the container's setup, making sure he didn't get locked in those enticing green eyes. Not even when she cocked her head at the mention of solar panels, her eyes narrowed in a cute inquisitive look he'd always found endearing.

He'd had a thing for her from the moment he'd first met her and had been thrilled to work an assignment together in Atlanta. They once had great chemistry, even if she'd never admitted it. Especially not after the tragic op where things had gone south. She blamed him for Olin's death and could barely look at him, but that didn't mean Evan could turn off his feelings just like that.

She shifted her attention to her teammates, and he noticed the pencil holding her thick hair in a sloppy knot. She'd always said the hairstyle served two purposes. To hold her hair up, as she thought the look made her appear older, and to have something to write with at all times. He found it adorable that she continued the practice.

"You'd have to be motivated to risk weeks at sea in this thing," she said. "Any number of things could've gone wrong."

Mack planted his hand on his sidearm. "That kind of motivation speaks to the level of the threat."

"As do the players themselves," Evan said. "We aren't dealing with some suicide bomber taking out a train station or church. Men warranting such luxury accommodations are higher up the network, and they're here to carry out the impending big attack."

"Agreed," Kiley said, but her eyes still simmered. "Who's in charge of forensics?"

Evan introduced Philips and stood back to listen to Kiley's questions. She raised the same ones Evan had asked, and Philips, who'd moved to the other loft, patiently answered them.

"I want the usernames for any games on

the video consoles ASAP." She handed him a business card. "Overnight the consoles to the lab and put me as point of contact. I'm lead on this investigation, so everything goes through me."

"Actually, I have an agent taking evidence to Quantico in a few minutes." Philips rubbed his eyes. "If you want, she can take the consoles as well, but I'm not sure it's that urgent since there's no evidence terrorists actually communicate via video games, right? Just stuff that movies are made of."

Evan watched Kiley carefully to see how she reacted to being questioned by a forensic tech.

"There's also no evidence that they don't," she said matter-of-factly as if the question didn't bother her in the least.

Cam snorted. Obviously he didn't think this was a viable lead to pursue.

She didn't even bat an eyelash at her team-mate's response. "I also want scene photos emailed to me within the hour."

Philips opened his mouth like he planned to complain but then nodded.

Evan kept watching the woman who'd become far more confident over the years. She seemed to have grown into quite a force to be reckoned with. And foolishly he wondered if she was thinking about how he'd changed. She probably wasn't thinking about him at all, other than as a pesky bug she wanted to swat away.

She spun and exited the container, the others following. Evan trailed after them and felt like he was five again, wanting to play with his older brother and the big kids when they didn't want him anywhere near them.

Kiley stopped six feet out and stood staring at the container. "We need to figure out how Firuzeh learned of this container."

"Firuzeh?" Evan asked.

"She was my CI," Kiley said, quickly masking a dark shadow that had crept into her eyes. "She'd learned of a terrorist plot she said would impact millions of people and would occur in five days. We were meeting so she could tell me about it, except she was gunned down before she could provide any details. She managed to mutter the words *port, coma,* and *Box 342.*"

"I'm sorry for your loss," Evan said sincerely.

She eyed him suspiciously, like she didn't believe he could honestly be sorry, but her gaze quickly cleared. "At this point we have to assume she meant the Port of Tacoma and the two investigations are related."

She obviously wanted to keep this all business, so Evan would comply. "What about the mailbox?"

"Her family owns a packaging and mailbox store, and I suspect that could be where she got her intel. One of our agents is following up to see who rented that box number at their place."

"Sounds like a solid lead," he said, hoping

it would pan out. "And what have you learned about her shooting?"

"Nothing much. We'd barely notified her family of her death when our focus expanded to the container, and we don't have the homicide investigation dialed in."

"It'll be interesting to see how your CI learned of this plot from the other side of the country."

Kiley eyed him for a long time. "How did you hear about it?"

"Social media."

She narrowed her gaze. "Social media?"

He didn't like her skeptical study, but he was confident in his work and could hold up under it no matter how long she chose to grill him. "Chatter on the dark web said something big was going down soon. No details. Just cryptic comments, but they seemed credible to me, and I wanted to follow up. I have this friend at MIT who was working on a social-media study. He claimed he could predict terrorists by posts on social media before they even mentioned anything threatening."

She pressed her lips into a fine line. "I read about that study referencing extremist groups using social networks. They use it to harass users, recruit new members, and incite violence. The problem is rapidly growing, and they said Twitter shut down 360,000 ISIS accounts."

Mack let out a low whistle. "Seems like too big of a problem to get your head around."

"It is," Evan said, "and it can be overwhelming. But if you take it one terrorist at a time—focus solely on the one investigation until you resolve it—then you can keep going."

"So, your MIT friend helped with that?" Sean asked.

Evan nodded. "They used statistics to develop a method to predict new extremist users. They can tell if an account belongs to a prior user and predict where an account suspended by the social-media company will pop up under a new name. They were even able to identify seventy percent of additional extremist Twitter profiles."

Mack gave a firm nod. "That's impressive."

Kiley didn't look nearly as impressed. "And they used this method to help you?"

"They did," Evan said. "We worked together to take the information down to the local level, and my friend gave me a list of profiles to review. Of course, the conversations were cryptic, but I pieced them all together, worked and reworked them until I figured out they were communicating about the port and this container in particular."

"No surprise they used the container," Kiley said. "Smuggling terrorists in them isn't anything new. Been going on for years."

Evan was impressed by her knowledge. "What *is* surprising here is that they claim their goal is bigger than 9/11."

Kiley stared at the container and tapped her chin—her thinking mode. "And even after seeing these social-media posts, you have no idea who these men are or their target?"

"No. They didn't use their real names, and the accounts disappeared in a day."

She turned to Cam. "I want you to find these accounts and monitor the dark web too."

Cam gave a crisp nod and handed a business card to Evan. "I'll need the list you got from your MIT buddy, plus a list of the dark websites visited ASAP."

Evan palmed the card. "I'll email them both to you."

Agent Cartwright bounded down the command center steps and started their way. Evan wished the guy would go back to Seattle, but maybe Kiley was already second-guessing adding Evan to the team and wanted someone in her agency who knew the local scene to stick around.

Kiley gestured at Cartwright. "Is he someone we need to keep involved?"

Evan wouldn't bad mouth anyone and would stick to an honest evaluation. "He's a solid agent but is more of a follower. So if that's what you want . . ." He shrugged.

Cartwright stepped up to her, an admiring look in his eyes. "Hear you're heading up the investigation, Agent Dawson."

She nodded. "Thanks so much for your help so

far. You can go back to Seattle. We'll take it from here."

He glanced at Evan. "But he—"

"Has been working a very interesting social-media angle, and we want to keep pursuing it," she said.

"Well, I . . ."

"Again, thank you, Agent Cartwright." She held out her hand and kept her gaze pinned on him. "If I have any questions after I read your report on last night's op, I'll be in touch." She released his hand and turned away.

"Catch you later, man," Cartwright said.

Evan watched the guy storm off. It wasn't lost on Evan that he could just as easily be sent packing at any time and had to be sure he kept making serious contributions to the investigation to make sure that didn't happen.

Kiley turned to Evan. "Did you get security footage for the dock yet?"

He shook his head. "The port's head of security—a Jim Gadsden—insisted on a warrant. I've requested one for the video files and for details on the shipping company. Should have it soon."

She clenched her hands. "Maybe then we can determine when these terrorists crept out of their hidey-hole and hopefully get a look at their faces to identify them and then put out an alert."

• • •

Kiley stood outside the command truck where the team and Evan were waiting for her to finish her call to Eisenhower, but she wouldn't rush things with their supervisor. She would need a small army to work this high profile of an investigation, and he was the key to gathering the necessary people and keeping the big wheel rolling.

"So the threat is real." Eisenhower sucked in a sharp breath. "RED team will continue to take the lead, but you'll need a cadre of analysts and agents working behind the scenes on this one. And forensics techs at your disposal twenty-four seven. I'll get on the horn to HSI to secure additional manpower for the investigation, and we'll form a task force back here to coordinate interagency workers."

"Thank you," Kiley said, glad to know Homeland Security would be backing them up with much-needed resources.

"As of now, I'll clear my plate and run things from this end while you manage the upfront team. I'll need twice daily written and verbal reports from you. In turn, I'll provide you with the same thing. And if things move quickly, be prepared for even more frequent updates."

"Understood."

"Call me at the end of the day today, and we'll go from there."

"Will do." She hung up and felt like she was

being thrown into a fiery furnace. Yet she'd asked for this responsibility, so she would buckle down and rise to the challenge, starting with setting the immediate priorities.

She climbed into the truck, where Cam sat in a chair up front, his face buried in his laptop, likely working on his algorithm. Sean was on the phone to the local FBI office, arranging a war room. Mack was looking at his phone. And Evan was leaning against the console, watching her.

She should look away, but he had this confident way of standing that was totally relaxed yet fully alert at the same time and always captivated her. She found the dichotomy fascinating, as she'd never seen anything like it. Take Sean and Mack, for example. They were either hyper-alert or relaxed. Never had she seen them mix both in a single stance, while Evan brought them both together, and she could hardly look away.

Maybe it came from his former career as an EOD tech, embedding often with SEALs and Rangers. He had to train in many areas to become certified in EOD. Explosive ordnance disposal skills, of course, but also water diving and skydiving. And then to support Special Forces he had to train in parachuting plus weapons and small units tactics. So he was well-rounded in his skills. And so rock-steady she'd never seen him startle or lose focus. Which was why it was such a shock when Olin lost his life on an op under Evan's leadership.

Stop it. Just stop thinking about him. This job will be tough enough without wasting time on something so futile.

She cleared her throat to gain everyone's attention. "Eisenhower's calling HSI to gain additional manpower in D.C. so we'll have analysts and forensics at our disposal. And he'll coordinate the team there." She faced Evan. "Barry Eisenhower is the ICE special agent in charge of the Cyber Crimes Center and our supervisor."

"C3, right?" Evan asked.

"That's right," she said, impressed that he knew this detail about their team affiliation. "Before we get going for the day, is there anything else we need to know that I haven't asked about?"

He took a shaky breath and blew it out. "The bomb-making supplies Philips found trouble me, but the white phosphorus is more concerning. Are you familiar with it?"

"It's used in incendiary devices often to create smoke, right?" she asked.

Evan nodded and shoved his hands into his pockets. "It combusts the moment air touches the substance and eats through anything and everything. It's so unstable that it has to be kept underwater to prevent it from bursting into flames."

"Sounds incredibly dangerous," Sean said as he joined them.

Evan gave a clipped nod. "In addition to causing severe burns, inhaling the smoke can be deadly."

Even worse than Kiley thought. "Is it available in the U.S.?"

"Not legally, but you can make it out of red phosphorus. In fact, it's a by-product of using red phosphorus to make meth."

"So it's around then," Mack said.

"Yes," Evan said. "Combine it with explosives and you have a fiery rain that will inflict great harm."

Kiley couldn't even begin to imagine the devastation. "You said there were things that troubled you. What else?"

"The bomb-making supplies included a Wi-Fi switch."

"Wi-Fi?" Mack asked. "As in use *it* to detonate the device instead of a cellphone?"

"As backup to the cellphone," Evan said.

"Terrorists are slowly learning that law enforcement blocks cell signals at big events," Kiley said. "So they've had to get more creative. They're using Wi-Fi trigger mechanisms as backup."

Cam looked up. "But Wi-Fi doesn't travel far. Anyone who's had to deal with network dead spots in their own house knows that."

"That's changing." Kiley looked at Cam. "I've read that in previous attacks using Jemaah

Ansharut Daulah militant network, and with careful construction of routers and amplifiers, militants extended the range as far as a kilometer."

"More than half a mile?" Cam shook his head. "Wow."

"And JAD is tied to ISIS, so . . ." Kiley didn't finish her statement. She didn't need to. Everyone understood. They weren't looking for run-of-the-mill uneducated terrorists here. They were looking for a cut-above bomber with strong electronics skills.

"The Makarovs and ammo left in the container seemed odd too," Mack said.

"You're questioning why they left them behind?" Sean asked.

Mack nodded. "I was thinking they might be planning to come back and leave this country the same way they entered. In case they lost the weapons I assume they're carrying, they wanted to be sure they had protection waiting for them."

Kiley shifted her focus to Evan. "Do you think they're going back home in the same container?"

"Possibly," Evan replied. "Golden Lion Shipping is handling this container, and they're scheduled to move it to their place tomorrow. I immediately requested a warrant. After it came in, I planned to stop by the company to see what I could learn about the plan. I've already called the owner and persuaded him to meet me today."

She was glad for his proactive move, but there

was no way she would let him visit Golden Lion Shipping without her. However, the entire team didn't need to go along. She faced Sean. "No point in all of us waiting around for the warrant. You go ahead and get our office accommodations finalized."

Sean nodded.

"Cam." She looked at him. "Go with Sean. Finish your algorithm and get started on the social-media information from Evan and start searching the dark web for any intel."

Cam closed his laptop and stood. "You got it, boss."

She wrinkled her nose at his boss comment, and he grinned. Clearly he wanted to mess with her, but she let it go.

"I should go with them too," Mack said. "Check in on the murder investigation and see if Lancaster uncovered any leads. Then get a murder board set up."

She'd planned to keep him here as a buffer between her and Evan. Mack likely figured out her plan, and he was leaving so she would have to face her demons with Evan before the investigation got going. She wanted to insist Mack stay, but she couldn't find fault in his logic. A murder board with their leads, scene photos, et cetera would be of great value, so she nodded. "I'll need a car to head over to Golden Lion."

Evan frowned. "I can drive you."

She might not want to work with him, but he was a real go-getter and independent thinker. That was what she needed on her team, and she would do her best not to stifle his efforts. Besides, he knew the city and it would be faster for him to chauffeur her.

"Okay, thanks." She turned back to her team. "Keep me posted on any developments. Otherwise I'll see you back at the office."

She watched the trio of men whom she'd become close to these past six years exit the command center and felt Evan's gaze on her. His presence seemed to grow, to take over the space, and she didn't know what to say to him.

His phone dinged, and thankfully he turned his attention to the screen. "Warrant's in for the dock video. We can serve it to Gadsden on the way to Golden Lion."

He tapped his screen, and the printer in the corner started whirring. Without speaking, he grabbed the pages and headed for the door.

She stepped out after him to find a large crane hovering over the container. The crane's motor churned and groaned as it swiveled away with the last container that had been situated on top of their suspects' home. Philips was climbing up a ladder leaning against the wall.

Evan cupped his hands around his mouth. "Philips! Any solar panels?"

The forensic tech looked over his shoulder and

nodded. "Under doors cut into the container just like we suspected."

Evan nodded his understanding and looked at Kiley. "To power the place."

She shook her head. "They really thought of everything."

"And that should tell us the skill level of the men we're up against." Frowning, Evan spun to lead the way to a black Chevy Tahoe and opened the passenger door for her. He didn't wait for her to get in but rushed around front and slid behind the wheel.

She'd barely gotten her seat belt clicked in place when he peeled out, spitting loose gravel behind the tires.

"There a fire I don't know about?" she asked, taking a look around his immaculately clean vehicle. She was organized at work. Her car and personal life not so much, and she'd always appreciated his neatness.

He glanced at her. "No fire. Just five days and two or more terrorists wandering free in our country hell-bent on hurting millions of people."

She appreciated his sense of urgency, but his comment tightened her stomach into a ball of worry. He could've also pointed out that she was in charge of ensuring the country's safety, a thought that made her stomach contract more.

He parked in front of the port's security office, and they headed for the door together. He jerked it open and stepped back to allow her access. She'd forgotten what a true gentleman he was. Or maybe after Olin died, she'd purposefully wiped that bit out as it didn't fit with the blame she was heaping on Evan's head.

She looked around the small reception area with a tall desk, worn chairs, and a nautical-themed décor that looked as tired as the chairs.

"Mr. Gadsden," she called out and resisted tapping her foot as she waited.

A man with curly black hair, a large nose, and wide jaw stepped into the room. His blue security uniform was worn and needed a good pressing. "And you are?"

"Special Agent Kiley Dawson with the FBI." She extended her hand.

He paused a moment before grasping her hand in a punishing grip. She had no idea if this was an intentional thing, showing his irritation at being called in on a weekend, or if he just had a firm grip. Either way, she worked hard to keep from yelping in pain.

Evan introduced himself and held out the warrant. "We'll take the security video now."

Gadsden glared at Evan. " 'Bout time you got here. I been cooling my jets for hours when I coulda been home watching the game."

"It's not always easy to find a judge on the weekend," Evan said, holding back obvious frustration over this man's lack of cooperation.

Gadsden scratched a heavy five o'clock shadow but didn't take the warrant from Evan. "You do realize how many gates we have at this place, right? Gonna be a huge file."

Kiley pulled a flash drive from her pocket and plastered a smile on her face. "If you'll show me to your computer, I can help you compress the files, and they'll fit very nicely on my drive."

Gadsden glanced at Evan for permission.

"I'm lead on this investigation, Mr. Gadsden," she said. "So please. Let's not waste any more time."

He didn't move and sought Evan's confirmation. He nodded, and she wished he hadn't thought it necessary to do so.

Gadsden spun and took them to the back of the building, the wood floor groaning underfoot. He opened a door to a chilly room holding large servers and a desk with multiple monitors, each displaying a live feed of a particular gate.

He leaned over the desk, typed in his login, and brought up the video files. "How far back you want?"

Evan laid the warrant on the desk. "A month."

He flashed an irate look at Evan. "But the container's only been here a few days."

Kiley agreed thirty days was overkill and would take her team way too many hours to review all of the footage, but she also agreed with Evan's request. "It's better for us to take what we anticipate needing so we don't have to bother you again later."

Gadsden looked at her as if he had no idea what to do. She didn't have time to waste. She dropped into the chair by the monitor displaying the files they needed and plugged in her flash drive. She waited for Gadsden to argue. He didn't speak, so she started compressing the video files and transferring them to her drive.

He moved closer to the desk. "You're not taking the original files, are you?"

She shook her head. "The zip program is creating new ones."

"What's in that container anyway?" Gadsden asked.

"We're not at liberty to say," Evan answered.

Gadsden frowned. "Must be something big if it's got so many Feds out here."

Evan didn't respond to the comment and neither did Kiley as she looked up at Gadsden. "Has anyone else been around asking questions about the container?"

"Nah. At least no one asked *me* about it."

"I'd like you to contact all of your staff to see if anyone has talked about it or if they've seen anything odd."

He pinched the bridge of his nose and sighed. "If anyone saw anything odd, I'd already know about it."

"Not if your guards were paid to keep quiet," Kiley said.

He crossed his beefy arms over the start of a paunch. "My guys are all on the up and up."

"Please don't insult my intelligence, Mr. Gadsden." She held his stony gaze. "We all know you have workers who are looking the other way for certain shipments. For all I know, you might be one of them."

He sputtered, his mouth opening and closing like a fish out of water. "Well I'm not."

"I noticed you didn't say others weren't."

He tightened his arms and didn't reply.

Evan tapped the warrant again. "Now would be the time to gather the list of dockworkers and the hours they worked for the last month. Be sure to include management and dock staff."

Gadsden scowled. "Gonna take some time to pull all of that together."

Kiley had enough of this guy's stonewalling and overall testy attitude. "An operation this big must use a computer-aided scheduling and payroll system. Either you can print out the reports for us now or you can log me into your system and I'll do it."

He lifted his chin. "I don't have access to those programs."

Kiley fixed a penetrating stare on him. "Then I suggest you get on the phone to the person who does and get them down here. Because we aren't leaving without the reports, and that means you're not heading home."

CHAPTER 8

Unreasonably glad to have Kiley with him, Evan glanced across his Tahoe's console at her. The same sadness he'd caught a few times since she'd arrived was darkening her usually bright and energetic eyes. He didn't know if her sadness was fueled by her CI's death or because seeing him reminded her of losing Olin. Or maybe it was none of the above. He knew nothing about this woman anymore. Case in point, the way she'd handled Gadsden.

He glanced at her. "You've changed. You're much more confident. You handled Gadsden like a pro."

She frowned. "Actually, I messed up."

Not at all what he expected her to say. "How's that?"

"I got mad when he thought you were in charge." She sighed. "I'm tired of having to prove a woman can be in charge in law enforcement. You'd think by now those old stereotypes would be gone, but they're alive and well."

"Yeah," he said, as he witnessed gender discrimination often enough on the job. Not only from the public but also from other law-enforcement officers.

"I shouldn't have let it get to me. If I hadn't, maybe I would've handled him better."

He didn't like seeing her second-guess herself this way. "His cooperation was forced when I talked to him on the phone, and you probably would've ended up in the same place with him."

"Maybe."

He studied her, trying to determine if there was more behind her comments than she was letting on, but she faced the window.

The miles rolled on, the tires spinning over the asphalt and tension seeming to grow with each turn of the wheel. He knew asking to discuss Olin was a risky move. After all, she could kick him to the curb, but he also knew it would be better for the investigation if they got things out in the open.

"We should talk about Olin," he said matter-of-factly.

She shot him a testy look. "No. We really shouldn't."

He wouldn't back down yet. "It's best to air out our differences."

"And I think we should let it lie." She slumped down in the seat. "Bringing it all up will only make it seem worse."

He looked at her then, long and hard, seeing her sullen expression and crossed arms. "You never did like conflict."

Her eyebrows lifted. "Where you, on the other hand, liked to stir things up."

"Yeah." Once upon a time he'd liked questioning things just to question. Now he had to have a good reason to do so. He considered pointing out that he'd changed, but hopefully she'd see the difference soon enough.

"You like working on a task force?" she asked, her change of subject so obvious it was painful.

Fine. He wouldn't try to get her to talk about Olin now. He couldn't make her do anything, and that included staying out of his thoughts when he should be focused on finding deadly terrorists. "I like being at the forefront of stopping terrorism. If working on an interagency team is the best way to accomplish my goal, then so be it."

She swiveled to face him and honestly looked interested. "Don't politics get in the way?"

He kept his eyes on the road but felt the intensity of her stare. "More often than I would like. What about your team? You're multi-agency."

"Sean and Mack had some issues, but they worked all that out. Now things are great and we're all friends."

He'd often wanted the same thing for his task force.

"Of course, on this investigation we'll only be the point team, and there'll be hundreds of people working behind the scenes with Eisenhower in D.C."

He was so impressed with how far she'd come since he'd last seen her and wanted to know more about how she accomplished it. "How did you end up on the RED team?"

"I was still an agent in Atlanta working the cyber squad," she said, then paused.

He waited for her to add *after Olin died,* as the three of them had worked on the multi-agency investigation in Atlanta back then.

"And Barry Eisenhower came to the office to interview Agent Spelling for the RED team. A kidnapping occurred while he was there, and he inserted himself into the investigation. I hacked the teen's car information system to get the girl's last GPS location, and she was found. Eisenhower said he was impressed. Not that hacking the car was a big deal, but that I thought to do it when Spelling didn't."

"So he offered you the job instead."

She snorted. "Not quite that easy. He checked out my credentials, and we had several intimidating interviews first. And not until after he'd hired Sean and Addison. She's Mack's wife, but they're separated."

"Did Eisenhower hire Mack at the same time?"

"That came later, when he showed up at the office to complain about how Sean handled an incident." She smiled as if the memory was a good one. "Eisenhower had Sean's back in the situation, yet he liked how Mack wasn't intimidated into backing down. And Eisenhower thought Mack's fugitive apprehension experience would benefit our team."

"This Addison, is she still on the team but isn't here with you?"

Kiley shook her head. "She left us when she split up with Mack."

"I'm not surprised that Eisenhower was impressed with your background," Evan said. "Even as a rookie agent you thought outside the box and brought several high-profile investigations to a close. It's no wonder he wanted you on his team."

She glanced at him.

"Hey, I'm not trying to butter you up here. You've always been a natural agent, and Eisenhower simply recognized that."

She still looked skeptical at his comment, but then her phone rang, taking her attention. "Hey, Taylor," she said and listened. "Is the registration form handwritten or computer-generated?" She tapped a finger on her chin. "Okay, then can you scan and email it to me?" After giving a sharp nod, she said, "Thanks. I'll let you know if I need anything else and give the Abeds my best."

She rested her phone on her leg. "That was Taylor Mills, the WITSEC deputy who arranged a safe house for the Abeds. FYI, she's also Sean's fiancée. She has the registration information for that mailbox in question. It's registered to a Badriddin Hilali in D.C."

"Never heard of him."

"Me neither." Kiley's phone dinged. "That'll

be the guy's registration form. Let me get Eisenhower to assign a top D.C. agent to pay this guy a visit."

She looked at her phone and started typing, so Evan concentrated on the drive. When the shipping company came into view, he focused on a large golden lion statue sitting in front of a guard shack by the road.

Kiley stowed her phone and leaned forward. "I wonder what the lion's significance is."

Evan shared the brief history he'd read online. "I plan to ask about the name change."

At the small booth, he held out his ID. "Agents Bower and Dawson to see Ormazd Malouf."

The uniformed guard had a blond buzz cut, sharp nose, and square jaw that made Evan think former military.

"Hang tight," the guard said and darted back into the booth to grab the phone while keeping an eye on them like he thought they might make a run for it and break through the gate. He listened intently and came to attention as if whoever he was speaking with was watching him.

Evan looked for a camera inside the booth but didn't see one. Malouf would be a seriously paranoid owner if he watched the guard shack.

"Yes, sir." The guard hung up, looking a little less sure of himself. "Straight ahead to the main building. Someone will meet you at the door and take you to see Mr. Malouf." The gate groaned upward, and he stood watching as Evan drove through.

Kiley glanced out her window. "Tight security."

"Makes sense that a shipping company would have top-notch security, but this is feeling more extensive than needed."

She continued to take in their surroundings. "We both should keep our eyes open on the way in. Never know what we might see."

"Agreed." Evan parked in a visitor spot outside the four-story building with a curved front.

They got out and crossed a grassy median separating the parking lot from the building. The property was protected from bay winds, and the temperature hovered around sixty in the bright sunshine. They passed a large water feature lined with iridescent turquoise tiles and holding an even bigger lion spraying water from its mouth into a koi-filled pond, the water glistening in the sun.

"Pretty lavish for a shipping company," Evan said.

Kiley held her hand over her eyes and surveyed the area. "We need to find out if Malouf's a savvy businessman who can afford all of this or if his money comes from something illegal."

Evan nodded and followed her up the steps to a large veranda running the width of the building. Gold-and-black umbrellas protruded from wrought-iron tables surrounded by chairs with matching cushions.

A powerfully built armed guard wearing black pants and a white shirt with a gold lion embroidered on his chest pushed open the door. If Evan thought the other guard was serious, this one gave the word a new meaning. "Follow me." He marched across a two-story lobby to a pair of elevators.

A golden lion statue sat on the floor between them. One set of doors etched with the company logo split open. They entered the mahogany-walled car, and after selecting the fourth floor, the guard planted his feet in a wide stance, his focus pinned on the numbers above the door.

Evan looked for the guy's nametag but found none. "Do you work for the company or are you contract?"

"Company," he replied, his gaze remaining on the numbers.

"How long have you been employed here?" Kiley asked.

"Ten years."

"Good place to work, I take it."

Kiley received a sharp nod in response but that was all.

"Do you know how long the company has been based in the U.S.?" Evan asked.

"No." Clearly he was a man of few words.

On the fourth floor, he walked to glass double doors at the far side of a small lobby and swiped a card down a wall-mounted reader. The door popped open, and a tall regal-looking man dressed in a black pinstripe suit, white shirt, gold tie, and gleaming patent-leather shoes strode confidently toward them. His skin was brown, his hair the blackest obsidian. He was fit and stood around Evan's six-foot-two height. He held out his hand, his nails manicured, and gave Evan a tight smile. "You must be Agent Bowers. I'm Ormazd Malouf."

Evan shook hands, not surprised to find the man's skin soft instead of callused like his dockworkers. "Thank you for meeting us on such short notice."

A bushy eyebrow rose. "I'm afraid you made it sound like I didn't have a choice."

Evan waited for Malouf to introduce himself to Kiley. He gave her a crisp but indifferent nod.

His obvious dismissal made Evan mad. "This is Special Agent Kiley Dawson with the FBI. She's the lead agent on this investigation and will be directing our interview."

Kiley had to look up at Malouf, but his height didn't seem to bother her as she shoved out her hand and confidently met his gaze, giving him no choice other than to shake her hand or appear rude.

He pumped her hand only once and then spun. "Follow me."

She looked at Evan and rolled her eyes. He nodded his agreement. The man had been painfully condescending, perhaps a holdover from his culture. In today's business world, surely he ran into professional women and didn't alienate them this way too. Or maybe he did or even refused to deal with women.

He stepped into an office facing the curved portion of the building. One wall was filled with glass-and-chrome bookshelves holding ancient artifacts, sculptures, old and likely rare books. Another wall held gilded-framed photos of Malouf with men in flowing robes, celebrities, and politicians. For a Tacoma-based shipper, this man seemed well connected.

"Sit," he commanded as he pointed at a glass-topped conference table with the company logo etched into the center.

Kiley nodded at the logo as she sat in one of the white leather chairs. "What's the significance of the lion?"

A flash of annoyance tightened Malouf's expression before he cleared it. "My father founded our company in Iraq under Nuri as-Said's rule. My father was a huge supporter of the ruler's largely pro-Western policy. When he was assassinated, and his supreme government overthrown, my father moved to the United States and changed the company name, using the lion from the Iraqi coat of arms as a symbol of his support." Malouf sat and folded his hands on the table. He focused on Evan. "Now, what can I help you with?"

Evan nodded at Kiley and waited for her to begin the questioning.

"We're interested in learning more about a specific container your company shipped. It originated in India and has been sitting in the Port of Tacoma for four days." She took a paper from her jacket pocket and slid it across the table to him. "This is the shipping manifest."

He didn't even glance at the page. "I'm afraid I can't be bothered with the details of a single container. I *can* refer you to a clerk tomorrow who I will authorize to share additional details."

Evan saw Kiley's shoulders rise a hair. Just enough to tell him she was getting mad. After their conversation in the car about her getting upset with Gadsden, he knew she would work hard to control her emotions.

"You'll have to bother yourself with the details of this particular container," she said, her voice so calm it felt lethal. "It's not optional."

He sniffed in a breath and cast her a disdainful look. "Really, I have no idea on how to even look the shipment up in our system."

"Then I suggest you get someone in here who can show you." Kiley didn't move a muscle. She didn't have to. Her pointed tone did all the heavy lifting for her. "Unless of course you'd like to take a trip to our local office where we can delve into your reasons for not cooperating."

"One moment." His whole body was tight with

anger, but his tone was saccharine. He rose and strode from the room.

Kiley let out a pent-up breath. "Do you think his problem is with me or he's got something to hide?"

"Hard to tell."

"Then let's find out. You go ahead and handle the questioning when he returns."

"Are you sure?" he asked. If their roles were reversed, he wouldn't want to back down.

"It's for the good of the investigation, so yeah, I'm sure."

Impressed at her willingness to sacrifice her pride, he nodded.

Phone to his ear, Malouf returned and went to the open laptop on his desk. He put on gold wire-rimmed glasses, propped the phone between his ear and shoulder, and started typing. He talked condescendingly to a Henry on the other end of the line in much the same way he'd spoken to Kiley. Maybe he was just an equal opportunity jerk.

"I've got it." He said good-bye without thanking Henry.

Malouf must pay his guards well, as there seemed to be no other logical reason why the guard who'd escorted them had worked for this man for so long.

Malouf laid his phone on the desk and brought the computer to the table. "What is it you want to know?"

"The container arrived a few days ago and sat at the port since then. It's scheduled to be moved here for storage tomorrow. Is it normal for a container to sit at the dock like that?"

"Normal? No, but not unheard of."

"Is it scheduled to remain here, or what is the disposition?"

Malouf stared at his screen and frowned. "It was to remain here until the thirteenth, then be shipped back to the originating port."

Two days after the anniversary of 9/11, lending credence to Evan's theory about the terrorists planning a return trip. Evan might get this, but Malouf seemed to be in the dark.

"You look like you think this is odd," Evan said.

"It is most unusual. It would not have been unloaded at the dock or here, so why send it out only to return?"

Evan knew the reason but obviously wouldn't share it. "How did the shipment originate, and who placed the order?"

Malouf glanced at his computer again. "It was an online order placed by a Haval Barzani."

Evan was surprised he gave up the shipper's name. "So, if I wanted to ship something with your company, I could create an order online like this Barzani guy did?"

Malouf raised his gaze to Evan. "You would need to have an approved account to do so. I

131

doubt you would have the financial backing to be approved."

Though the guy knew Evan was speaking hypothetically, he had to get a jab in. "Barzani has this approval."

"Correct."

"Has he shipped with you in the past?"

"Let me check." He typed on his computer. "Yes, he has been a customer for some time."

"Exactly how long?" Evan asked.

"Since 1992."

"Does Barzani work for a company, or is he an independent shipper?"

Malouf squinted at the screen. "He's a licensed ship broker with a container-chartering focus. His company is independently owned."

"What's a ship broker exactly?" Evan asked.

"They're specialist intermediaries or negotiators, if you will," Malouf replied. "They consult between shipowners and charterers who use ships to transport cargo. They also work with vessel buyers and sellers."

"I'd like a printout of all of Barzani's prior shipments with your company, along with his contact information."

Malouf crossed his arms. "That's not something I'm willing to provide."

Evan sat forward. "We can have a warrant within the hour to compel you to provide the information. Why not hand it over and save us both the hassle of coming back on a Sunday?"

Malouf lifted his chin and pointed it at Evan like a sharp sword. "You'll have to get a warrant. I did not get to where I am in the business world by divulging client information."

Evan expected this response, but he had to try.

"Is there a reason you're being so difficult, Mr. Malouf?" Kiley asked.

Evan was shocked at her straightforward confrontation of the man, so unlike the old Kiley he'd known, yet he sat back to watch the guy respond.

He sniffed. "Difficult? No. I prefer to think I'm being discreet on behalf of my customers. This business is based on relationships, and I cannot afford to alienate anyone and keep the company my father founded afloat in this competitive world." His eyes blazing with passion, he crossed his arms. "I won't *ever* do anything to risk the business. My father meant way too much for me to do that. So, without your compelling me to legally comply, I will decline."

Evan took the man's point to heart. Even so, they would still get the warrant and insist Malouf cooperate. For now, Evan would move on. "In the meantime, tell me more about the container. Do you track it in each port of call? And were there any special shipping instructions?"

"We do track ports." Malouf looked at his screen. "The container didn't have special orders at initiation but was changed to top tier right before loading."

"Top tier?" Evan asked.

"Containers are stowed on a vessel by bay and tier," Malouf explained in a taxed tone. "To determine loading order, a computer takes into account the vessel's route, ports of call, schedule, other cargo, and expected cargo. Planners also classify the loading data according to the kind of cargo, the size and shape of the containers, and their destinations. So, for example, refrigerated cargo needing to be plugged in goes on the bottom tier. Same is true of unusually heavy cargo or potentially leaky cargo. Dangerous cargo is stored away from other cargo. Beyond these criteria, the containers are stored in order of discharge. In this case, the company Barzani brokered for paid extra to ensure this container was placed on the top of the stack."

"What was the cargo of the container listed as?"

Malouf looked at his laptop. "Computers."

"Something that wouldn't seem odd coming from India," Kiley said. "And probably not odd for being a top-tier container either."

"Correct," Malouf said.

"Is asking for top tier a normal request?" Kiley asked.

"Normal, no," Malouf said. "But not uncommon and would draw very little attention other than the flag to place it in the correct tier."

"Are these containers inspected?" Kiley asked.

"Less than five percent of all containers coming into the United States are inspected. To put this into perspective for you, ninety-five percent of the world's cargo is moved by ships. Each year, more than eleven million containers arrive at U.S. seaports. So it would be impossible to inspect them all."

"And even if they were," Evan said, "people can be bought and containers overlooked."

Malouf sharpened his gaze. "I would like to say that's not true in my company, but yes, of course there will always be people out to make some extra cash on the side."

Evan nodded his appreciation for the man's honesty. "How are these orders conveyed?"

"Our planners transmit them electronically to container terminals that discharge containers and reload them if needed to complete the process."

"Is it possible these plans aren't followed?"

"With stowage plans transmitted electronically, modern pirates working with organized crime syndicates have intercepted them in the past. Not only to have them changed but also to tell these pirates where the most coveted cargo is stowed. So when they board a vessel, the container they seek is accessible and they know exactly where to look."

"Were there any incidents with the ship carrying this container?"

"I would have to research that and get back to you."

Evan nodded. "I also want a list of all containers on this ship."

He sniffed. "You realize our ship carries around five thousand containers."

Evan knew the ship would hold a large quantity, but nothing like this.

A smirk slid across Malouf's face. "Of course, I will require a warrant for that information as well."

Evan stood. "We'll be in touch as soon as the warrant is available."

"I'm not sure I'll be available."

"No problem," Kiley said calmly. "We can serve the warrant to your guards if we have to."

She marched toward the door, and Evan followed. The guard was waiting right outside to escort them out of the building and watch them as they headed to the parking lot.

Kiley glanced over her shoulder at Evan. "I don't trust Malouf. What about you?"

"No. He was more than forthcoming about basic shipping information but tight-lipped on internal processes." Evan clicked his key fob to unlock the Tahoe's doors. "I don't know if the historical connection to Nuri as-Said means anything, but I'll get an analyst started on reviewing it."

Kiley flashed her gaze to him. "You think there'll be a terrorist connection?"

He opened her door. "Don't you?"

"I do," she said. "I really do."

CHAPTER 9

Nathaniel Stadler, supervisory special agent in charge, a tall gangly man wearing an olive-green suit, met Kiley and Evan at the door of the satellite office called a resident agency by the FBI. The small office was located in a high-rise in downtown Tacoma and had a hint of mustiness about it.

Kiley noticed how the pair of agents working on a Sunday tracked her movements as she followed Stadler through the bullpen filled with old desks and well-used chairs. She knew they had questions about their team, and thankfully she'd showered and changed clothes last night, because terrorists didn't care about giving her or anyone else on the team time for personal hygiene and looking their best.

Stadler stopped near a conference room—the RED team's home for the foreseeable future—and pointed at the door. Mack or Sean would have already told Stadler the room was off-limits. By remaining outside, he was respecting the privacy of their investigation.

"IT has the computers and logins set up so you can access our network," Stadler said, scratching a cleanly shaved jaw. "Agent Nichols has the information. You need anything, just ask. Bowers knows where my office is located."

"Thank you," Kiley said.

He nodded and strode away.

Kiley watched him leave. "I'm impressed he isn't trying to insert himself into the investigation. Small offices like this one aren't likely to see this kind of action, and many supervisors would push to get involved."

"He wants to move up fast and has the political smarts to make that happen. Which means leaving this alone."

"You know how bad I am at politics." Kiley mocked a shudder.

"Yeah, you'd rather tell things as they are. Probably a good thing you're on a hotshot team so your straight-shooting doesn't get you in trouble."

"True. Though I do admire people who can play the game. Sean's good at it, which is why he often takes lead on our investigations."

"So how did you get lead on this one then?"

"We vote as a team, but ultimately it's Eisenhower's decision. Because of losing Firuzeh, I asked for lead and the others supported me."

Evan nodded, and a moment of understanding passed between them. Acutely aware of him, she quickly brushed past him into the room with drab beige walls before she said or did something stupid. She greeted the others seated at the long table as Evan sat down behind one of the provided laptops. She looked down the table at the tote holding Firuzeh's items and wanted to get to work on processing them, but as team leader she needed to set priorities. And at the moment, the shipping container took precedence over Firuzeh's murder.

Kiley set down her backpack and quickly brought the team up to speed on their interviews with Gadsden and Malouf. "I'll get warrant requests going, and then we'll do a status update and brainstorm possible targets. DHS will be clamoring for a threat assessment soon. I want to be ready to advise them on our country's threat level."

Threat assessment. Threat level. She couldn't even believe those words were coming from her mouth. Her, Kiley Dawson, an average person from Buffalo, New York, growing up in a working-class neighborhood, having a say in the country's threat level. *Unbelievable.* As was the sheer magnitude of this investigation and the grim reality that if she made one mistake—one slipup—millions of people could be in danger.

She reached for a laptop, and her stomach grumbled. She hadn't eaten much of anything for twenty-four hours. *Tough.* Getting warrants issued was her priority. Hunger could wait.

Mack put his hand over hers, stopping her from opening the computer. "We had lunch brought in. Sandwiches are in the break room refrigerator.

You and Evan go eat. I'll get the warrants started."

She couldn't waste time. "You don't know the details."

"I know enough to fill in the forms while you scarf down a sandwich. Then you can come back and finish them up."

"But I—"

"We have to find a receptive judge first," Sean said. "I'll do that."

She frowned at her teammates.

"We're better off fueling up for the long haul," Evan said.

She thought to keep arguing but knew when she was outnumbered and looked at Evan. "Lead the way."

He charged for the door. *Right.* He was hungry. A good leader would've thought to grab some food while they were out. Now it was pushing five o'clock and they hadn't even had lunch. And yet he didn't complain or ask. With their history, he likely thought she'd say no, or maybe he didn't think he should even ask.

If so, things had to change between them. He was on the team now, so she needed him to be an effective member, and she had to let him know she would welcome his input and suggestions. She still held him responsible for Olin's death— that would never change. Even if she appreciated his willingness to have her back in the meeting with Malouf and make the situation easier for her.

He opened the refrigerator and pulled out a tray of sandwiches. "Turkey, roast beef, or ham."

"Turkey." She took the sandwich and sat to open the package. The thick wheat bread piled high with turkey, lettuce, tomato, and avocado made her mouth water, and she was suddenly ravenous.

He went to a soda machine and came back with a Dr Pepper and Coke. He set the Dr Pepper in front of her. She paused, sandwich in hand, to stare at the can. He'd not only thought to get her a drink but also remembered her drink of choice. Why did he have to keep reminding her that he was a great guy?

He popped the top on his soda, the fizz sizzling into the air. "I figured some extra sugar and caffeine might help after pulling an all-nighter."

She smiled her thanks, and as he dug into his meal, she finished chewing her bite and pondered what to say to him.

"I didn't want you on the team," she said, instantly regretting the start to her conversation.

He shot her a surprised look and swallowed.

She held up her hand. "But you are. And I want you to know I'll do my best to be civil, and I want you to feel free to say or do what you might normally say or do on an investigation."

"Okay." He took a long swig of the Coke.

"I mean it. I remember how smart and intuitive you are. This investigation is bigger than all of us, and I'm glad for your input."

He gave a firm nod and took a large bite of the crusty roll with mounds of thick roast beef. Thankfully he didn't seem inclined to string the conversation out, and she focused on her own food.

He set down his sandwich. "It would help if I knew more about Firuzeh."

Her bite turned to sawdust in her mouth, and she had to wash it down with a gulp of the sugary Dr Pepper. "I've told you all I know about her death."

"You haven't shared what's making you look so sad when you think no one's looking." He arched an eyebrow, making the scar on the side of his face stretch out. "Unless there's something else, I have to assume your sadness is from losing her."

Kiley turned her can around on the table, looking at the wet ring trailing behind. "Firuzeh was really special. The kind of woman who lit up a room. She was always cheerful and thought of others before herself."

"And you feel responsible for her death."

Kiley nodded.

"I understand that. Trust me."

She knew he meant Olin, but she wouldn't go there, so she sipped her soda and stared at the table.

"Tell me exactly what happened," he said, his tone gentle and not at all demanding.

Kiley wanted to ignore his request, but she'd just told him she valued his input, and she didn't want to shut him down right off the bat. She gave him background information on Firuzeh and her family's business and replayed the night, looking down at the table and reciting details of the shooting as if it happened to someone else so she didn't get teary-eyed.

"You did nothing wrong," he said with conviction.

She looked up to find compassion and understanding in his eyes. "Technically, no, but . . ."

"But you lost a woman who was more than a CI to you, and you feel like you should've been able to protect her."

Kiley nodded. "I should never have formed a personal attachment. Maybe I'd become too relaxed around her—let my guard down—and would've been more objective if I didn't have that attachment."

"How could you have predicted a shooter waiting a half mile away?" he asked. "You couldn't, and continuing to second-guess yourself won't help find her killer."

He had a point. "Our supervisor doesn't even want me to be looking into it."

He grabbed his sandwich with red onion slices dangling from the sides. "Why not, when her death seems to be connected to this investigation?"

"We rarely handle homicides, and he's pretty adamant about letting D.C. homicide handle the investigation. They're more than capable of doing a good job, and my focus needs to be on whoever arrived in the container."

He stared at his sandwich for a moment before setting it back down. "You might've changed over the years, but it seems like your greatest fear is still losing people you care about. I know you. You're planning to work both investigations."

She'd forgotten she'd told him about losing her dad and living with her mother's paranoia, drilling the fear of getting hurt into her so frequently Kiley had once lived with the constant terror of losing others. This had even informed her career choice. Computers were controllable. She told them what to do, and they did it. Sure, there were always kinks to work out, but *that* she could control.

When the network she administered was hacked, she didn't like the loss of control and had signed up to become an agent. She didn't want others to feel the same anxiety and didn't want the hackers to get away with the hack. So she'd spent the last six years as an agent ferreting out every kind of criminal and making them pay. All the while trying to move beyond the anxiety her mother's warnings brought.

Would they go away for good if she ever got up enough courage to confront her mother? To hash out their differences? Did she even want to do that?

He bent closer until she let go of her wayward thoughts and looked at him.

"Which means you plan to work the murder when you should be sleeping," he added.

"So?"

"I can help you."

"You need to sleep."

"So do you, but you won't do it. If I help, maybe you'll at least get a couple of hours a night."

She searched his face for any hidden motives. Found nothing in his expression other than concern and caring.

"To find Firuzeh's killer, I will accept your help. Thank you. We'll have to work out of our hotel. Maybe you should arrange to stay at the same place as the team."

"Sounds good to me."

"Give me your phone number, and I'll text you the details."

He shared his number, and she quickly sent him a text. For some reason she felt like this action was cementing something between them. What, she didn't know, but a bit of her anger over Olin evaporated, and she didn't like the hole it left behind. She'd been holding on to her anger for years, and it had become a part of her—a driving force.

If I let it go, God, then what?

She balled up her sandwich wrapper and heaved it at the trash can. Evan watched her every move as she grabbed the Dr Pepper and marched to the door. She didn't wait to see if he followed, but she heard his firm footsteps behind her.

"I'll get started on reviewing the CCTV footage from the port," he said as they stepped back into the conference room. "Unless you want me to do something else."

"Do the videos. Thanks." She handed the flash drive across the table to him and dropped into the chair next to Mack.

He gestured at the computer left for her use. "I emailed the form to you, and it's ready for your input."

"Judge Moreland is on standby." Sean slid a piece of paper down to her. "His email."

Evan looked up. "Good choice. Moreland's flexible and easy to please."

"We have Stadler to thank for the recommendation," Sean said.

Kiley made a mental note to thank the SSA next time she saw him. She logged into her email and opened the form to fill in the details, making sure she clearly stated the probable cause for her requests. She entered the judge's email address, wrote him a quick message, included a thank-you for his assistance on a Sunday, and sent the email.

Finally feeling a sense of accomplishment, she sat back and took a look around the room. On one wall, Mack had created a murder board as he said he would. It held Firuzeh's picture, the crime-scene photos, and a to-do list. As much as Kiley wanted to step over to take a better look and begin working the investigation, she grabbed a marker and went to the whiteboard filling the wall at the head of the table.

She faced the group. "I'd like to spend a few minutes brainstorming, starting with how this threat is different from what we've recently seen."

Evan looked up from his computer and grabbed his phone. "I'm not sure what you're getting at, unless you mean this has to be a hard target when recent attacks have been diverted to soft targets. Particularly large gatherings of people."

"Exactly what I meant." Kiley was reluctantly impressed with his ability not only to understand her but also his knowledge of the current terrorist landscape. "In the past, terrorists have directed their attacks at security forces, government buildings, and other official buildings. With these targets being increasingly hardened and protected, they're more difficult to attack."

A beam of late afternoon sunlight filtering through the dirty window caught Mack's face, and he got up to close the blinds. "Then are we dealing with someone new to terrorism, or is this cell getting bolder?"

Evan looked around the group, then up at her, as if he was still hesitant to speak. She gave him a quick nod.

His gaze cleared. "Normally in an investigation, I'd suggest we come up with a profile for our suspects, but I doubt we'll be able to do so here until we know who they are."

Cam closed his laptop. "But aren't there certain characteristics we can expect from terrorists?"

Evan shook his head, looking fully confident now in participating. "Each new terrorist incident shows us we're no closer to figuring out what leads people to turn to political violence. Their motives differ based on the individual."

"They have nothing in common?" Sean asked.

"There's one thing. Behavioral analysts have learned that terrorists always have a grievance, and it's often based on actual pain or injustice."

Cam narrowed his eyes. "So if we determine our suspects' grievance, it could help find the target."

"I doubt we'll learn the grievance until the suspects are in custody." Evan frowned.

"Instead of focusing on a profile, I say we review the watch list. See if we can come up with who might be helping our stowaways, because I'm sure they'll need help to pull off such a big event." Kiley noted the item on the board.

"Agreed," Evan said. "But we can't stop at the watch list. We also need to consider new recruits." He paused and looked at the others. "And don't be fooled into thinking the stereotype of a Muslim, Arab, immigrant male is the most vulnerable to extremism and are the only people to consider. This isn't characteristic of many of today's recruits."

"So, what is?" Sean asked, a hint of respect in his tone.

"They're likely to be born in the United States. Primarily male, but increasingly female. Caucasian or African American. Younger and less educated. And converted to Islam as part of their radicalization process."

"What about immigrants?" Kiley asked.

"We have to look at them, of course," Evan said. "But currently there's a risk that second-generation immigrants are more vulnerable to recruiters. They don't want their parents' culture *or* Western culture. Both are increasingly sources of self-hatred, and they're embracing terrorism."

"What you're saying, then, is that we need to keep an open mind. Look beyond Arab Americans, but also look *at* them," Kiley clarified.

Evan nodded. "Like I said, there's no known profile."

"I'll get analysts reviewing the watch list, but

until we know more, let's go at this from the angle of potential targets." She tapped the board. "Toss out ideas and I'll write them down."

Mack straddled his chair. "Impacting a million people brings a nuclear bomb to mind first. I don't know of any known terrorist group with nuclear capability, though."

"Agreed," she said and noted it on the board. "Our nuclear facilities are virtually impenetrable. Regardless, we should still evaluate the potential risk. I'll discuss this threat with Eisenhower to see if he thinks we should pursue it or if it's too much of a long shot to spend our time on."

"The white phosphorus in the container says we need to consider chemical plants," Mack said.

Evan nodded vigorously. "White phosphorus or not, terrorists are already on record as saying there's no need to make a weapon. They exist in mass quantities in chemical plants and are already located near major population centers. Terrorists simply have to find a way to set them off. The same is true of fertilizer plants and liquid natural gas."

She noted chemical, fertilizer, and natural gas facilities on the board and looked at Mack. "Can you make a list of these facilities? With the container arriving days ago, our suspects could be anywhere in the country by now, so make it country-wide. Follow up with a risk assessment to home in on the most vulnerable sites."

"Will do." He leaned back and draped an arm over the chair next to him.

She marked the number one by the word *chemical*. "Any additional indication it could be chemical?"

The others shook their heads.

"Okay, what else?"

"We could also be looking at dams," Evan suggested.

"Yes. Of course. Blow up a large one and the downstream flooding would be catastrophic. Or they could launch a cyber attack to open spillways. In any event, it would cut off water supplies and electricity too." She noted dams. "Do we have anything else to suggest this is a possibility?"

No one spoke.

"Sean, I want you to bring up all dams in the U.S. that if destroyed would threaten millions of people. Prioritize them by greatest risks and distribute the list to everyone here."

"You got it."

She noticed Evan tapping on his phone, and she couldn't believe after their talk in the break room that he wasn't taking this discussion seriously. "Are we boring you, Agent Bowers?"

He looked up. "What?"

She gave him a pointed look. "Your phone."

"Oh, that." He smiled. "Just taking notes. I like to keep everything with me."

She felt churlish for calling him out when he was simply doing a thorough job. She should apologize, but for some reason the words stuck in her throat.

"Though this would be considered a soft target," Mack said, and she was thankful for his bailing her out, "what about some sort of weaponized toxin released across the country in major transportation hubs?"

Evan stopped typing. "Sounds possible *if* an organized network exists, but there weren't any masks or other indicators of such a plan found in the container. Still, I can compile a list of known terrorists who've shown a preference for biological weapons."

"Great idea," Kiley said. "But reviewing CCTV files for the dock is top priority."

He nodded, and she was glad he didn't argue.

"I'm almost done with the algorithm, and I can do it," Cam offered.

"Have at it," Evan said, not sounding the least bit troubled at being upstaged.

He'd always liked being part of a team. He'd once told her the thing he enjoyed most about being in the Navy was the absolute trust and belief in the guys around him. When he knew the planning had been done and the others had gone through the same training, it wasn't hard to do a dive. Or even jump out of a plane, because no one would ever send one of their brothers or sisters into harm's way without adequate planning and training and making sure the equipment was ready.

Which was why it was so very hard to accept the fact that he'd bailed on planning the op that resulted in Olin's death just to go out on a bender with a few agents the night before.

"Kiley?" Sean asked.

She snapped back to the present, noted the item on the board, and jotted Cam's name next to it. "We need to find someone to get a printer and shredder set up in here."

"I know some of the staff and can arrange it," Evan offered.

She gave a nod of appreciation.

He smiled, lopsided and as devastatingly cute as she remembered. She especially appreciated his help with the grunt work. She hated to find anything she liked about him, but she did like the fact that he didn't think any task was below him. And maybe his smile.

Shut that down right now.

"I'll get a list of tasks and assignments going." She marched to her computer and caught Mack watching her. She gave him a look that said *so what?* He shrugged. Still, she knew he'd noticed her moment of infatuation with Evan.

She sat, curled her fingers into fists under the table, and made sure not to look at Evan, even though she wanted to check his expression. She couldn't be attracted to *that man*. Just couldn't. Sure, she'd been interested in him way back when, but she'd had those feelings before Olin died.

And now what? What did she feel for him on a personal level?

She'd have to be dead not to see he was still a very good-looking man, but other than that she felt only disgust for him, right?

CHAPTER 10

Evan stepped into his room with a queen bed covered in a white comforter in the posh downtown hotel. The fan hummed from under the window, blowing the scent of lavender from a bundle of dried flowers on the pillows. Contemporary nightstands held orange lamps, and aqua side chairs sat in front of the window. He didn't much care what the place looked like. It was somewhere to shower and sleep if he could convince Kiley to knock off early tonight.

He dropped his bag and got the shower going, cranking the temp as hot as he could stand it, the steam curling up and fogging the room. Every time he stepped in a shower, he talked to God. He'd done it since he was a kid. His dad had the same habit, and Evan learned it and so many other things from the most amazing dad a guy could hope for. The washing away of surface grime always left Evan knowing if he confessed his failings and sins that God washed those away too, and he emerged completely clean and refreshed. Hopeful.

It didn't always work. Especially not right after Olin died. Evan had taken tons of showers following the ill-fated op, and his fingers were often wrinkled. He still wasn't free from his guilt in the matter, but he could at least bear up under the weight and be productive.

He turned his face to the biting spray and prayed. For the team and for the wisdom and the ability to do his job to the best of his abilities. For the country. For Kiley and the tension between them. That she might see his heart and realize he truly felt bad about Olin. And that Kiley could mend things with her mother, because after their conversation in the break room it was clear that the fear of losing others still controlled her.

Evan had been raised with two wonderful parents in a loving relationship. He knew what he could have with a woman if he only let himself believe he deserved it. But Kiley? She'd never witnessed a loving relationship between husband and wife—with a child. She'd known only turmoil and anguish.

Let her get over that, Father. She deserves to move on.

He quickly finished up and dressed in a pair of tactical pants and plain black T-shirt. In the bedroom, he dropped into one of the blue chairs to review notes he'd taken on his phone and added points he'd forgotten to record.

He'd once tried to stop noting everything, yet time and time again since he'd started the practice, he'd find something in his notes he'd forgotten, and it helped with his investigations. Not to mention helped him sleep at night, as he could rest assured he'd done everything he possibly could in his job for the day. He recorded a few items he wanted to follow up on, grabbed his laptop, and headed to the team's suite.

He knocked on the door and waited for Kiley to answer, wondering how she might look at him this time. At times today, he caught hints of the old respect and interest in her eyes, and he'd take whatever positive vibes he could get. *Pitiful.* He'd become pitiful. Like a puppy waiting for a pat on the head.

She answered the door and gave him a quick once-over, the intensity of her gaze kicking up his pulse. He caught himself staring and also caught a whiff of a fresh tropical scent that matched the shampoo he'd used. Her hair was wet, and damp tendrils hung down her back. She'd put on gray yoga pants and a white T-shirt, displaying her very curvy shape.

She suddenly stepped back. "Perfect timing. We're ordering dinner."

He strode past her to find a large living area with four doors leading to the bedrooms. The space held a small kitchen with full-sized appliances in sparkling stainless steel. The guys were lounging in chairs, watching a sports-channel update.

Mack tossed a room-service menu to Evan. "Cam's placing the order. Tell him what you want."

Evan nodded and took a seat in a club chair. He didn't waste much time on the menu since he knew what he wanted. "I'll have a burger and fries."

The others looked at him.

"Yeah, I'm *that* guy," he said, not at all embarrassed. "The one who has a fancy menu in front of him and gets a burger and fries."

"It's pretty much what we're all having." Cam grinned and grabbed the room phone to place the order.

"Mack stocked the fridge with drinks," Kiley said. "Go ahead and help yourself. When Cam's done ordering we'll get started."

He wanted a Coke, but honestly he was more content with watching her. He liked seeing her in casual mode. She seemed more approachable and like the Kiley he knew before Olin died.

She passed the sofa, rearranged the multicolored pillows, and chopped them in the middle to leave a V. He'd forgotten that she liked to decorate, and when she was stressed she moved things around. Made him wonder what her home was like these days. Had her tastes changed in décor too, or was she still into traditional things?

She eyed the pillows one last time, shifted one of them, and then went to a whiteboard propped up on an easel. She wrote the word *Leads,* and next to it she jotted down *Assigned.*

She turned and caught him watching her.

He should probably look away, yet he wasn't embarrassed for her to know he found her captivating, and the guys were busy with the TV show and wouldn't notice.

She set down the marker, swept her hair up in back, and shoved a pencil in, a mask of calm remaining on her face as if his study didn't impact her. "Since Cam's finished ordering, we should get started."

Sean turned off the TV, and Mack dropped his cowboy boots to the floor from the table. He looked out of place in this highly modern environment, but if he was uncomfortable, he didn't show it.

Sean's phone dinged. He looked at the screen and frowned before shoving it back in his pocket.

"Bad news?" Kiley asked.

"Not good," he said. "The latest Montgomery lead didn't pan out."

"Montgomery lead?" Evan asked.

"We've got an ongoing investigation we're still working," Mack said.

"Not really ongoing," Cam said.

"Okay, fine." Mack scowled at Cam. "A cold case we're working in our own time."

"You know," Cam said, looking at Evan, "one of those you don't solve and can't let go."

Evan nodded. "Sounds like a rough one."

Sean nodded. "Three girls went missing in Montgomery, Alabama. We failed to bring them home. As Cam said, we keep working new leads, but they quickly dry up."

The same sadness he'd seen inching into Kiley's eyes all day darkened them again. "We have a ton of resources at our disposal. *A ton.* So how could three girls just vanish and we can't find them?"

Evan totally got her angst. "I've had several cases where women went missing and we never found them. Mine were all cartel-related, though. Unfortunately not an unusual occurrence."

"At least knowing who did it gives some closure," Sean said.

Did it? "I suppose, but I also know how brutal these cartels are and the fate the young women probably met."

Kiley frowned, and he wanted to press out the wrinkles forming on her forehead and tell her everything in life would be okay. It wouldn't make a difference if he did. As a law-enforcement officer, she would know he was spouting a platitude they told themselves to get through tough days. Sure, she believed in God and knew He was ultimately in control. So did Evan, but when faced with senseless killing after killing, holding on to that belief was a struggle at times.

She shook her head. "I don't know how you deal with the cartels, but I'm thankful you're willing to do so."

Her respect for his work warmed him clear

through. "I could take a look at your Montgomery case files if you have them with you. Not that I think I'm a better investigator than any of you, but fresh eyes and all that."

Kiley shook her head hard. The pencil flew from her hair, and glossy waves tumbled down to her shoulders. "No need—"

"Great," Sean interrupted. "Kiley's scanned everything and can give you a flash drive with all the information on it."

She slowly picked up the pencil, and Evan had to keep his gaze pointed straight ahead not to look at how the yoga pants fit her curves. She gathered her hair in a tight twist and jabbed in the pencil like she might be envisioning slamming it into Evan's chest for interfering in yet another area of her life.

She ran her gaze over her team. "Everyone in agreement on this?"

"Can't hurt," Mack said.

"Might help," Cam added.

"Okay fine." She turned to Evan. "I'll give you the file before you go, but don't let it distract you from the case at hand."

He didn't acknowledge her warning, as he had to believe she'd based it on their past, and their personal connection wasn't anyone else's business.

"There are a few things I want to follow up on before we eat and get back to work." She jotted down *Dark Web* on the whiteboard under Leads.

Cam sat forward and rested his elbows on his knees. "I checked in with D.C. and there's been some chatter suggesting something's coming. Nothing specific, but hints that it will happen on the anniversary of 9/11."

Kiley sucked in a breath. "Just like we suspected, and now we have a ticking clock to battle."

Evan did the math—a little more than four days to find and stop these terrorists.

"They're working twenty-four seven to try to track the logins to real people," Cam added. "But you know how the dark web works."

Kiley nodded. "Pretty much guarantees anonymity."

"They'll keep watching and will alert me of anything concrete," Cam said.

Kiley wrote down *Follow Up on Forensics,* then turned back to the team.

Mack took a long pull on a can of Red Bull. "I can call the lab tomorrow and light a fire under them, but you know forensic testing often can't be rushed."

"No, but it can be prioritized." She noted his name next to the item and wrote *Review Scene Photos.* "I looked them over, but nothing stood out at me. Anyone else see anything unusual in them?"

"It's hard to know what's normal at a dock

scene," Sean said and looked at Evan. "But you've had quite a bit of experience with ports, right?"

Evan nodded. "Other than the container cutouts, nothing out of the ordinary as far as I could see. I'll give them another look, though." He added it to his list in his phone.

She wrote his name by the item and scribbled *Barzani Worker Lists* in the Leads column. "Since the warrant forced Malouf to turn over the information we needed on Barzani, I'll meet with him in the morning. It would help if someone could review the printout of his shipments and the manifest tonight, so I know if there are any red flags to raise when I talk to him."

Mack tightened his fingers on the can. "You're planning on working Firuzeh's murder investigation tonight?"

She nodded. "But if no one can review these files, I will, and Firuzeh's evidence will have to wait."

"I can do it," Mack offered. "Did you let Eisenhower know you still have the evidence?"

"Not that I *still* have it, but I gave him a heads-up at the beginning."

"You reported in today, right?"

"Yes, and the subject just didn't come up," she replied.

Mack shook his head but didn't say anything, even though he looked like he wanted to. Evan was starting to get to know these guys, and he could almost imagine what Mack might say. Something to the effect that the evidence didn't come up because she didn't bring it up when she should have.

Evan didn't chime in. He'd committed to help her look into the murder, and he was on her side. And while he was at it, he would do his best to help make sure she didn't get into trouble with her supervisor.

She tapped the board with the marker. "Anything I've forgotten?"

"Not unless you want to talk about Firuzeh's murder," Mack said. "I assume you got a look at the murder board in the office."

She nodded. "I took pictures of it and will review the details tonight after I process the evidence from her place."

"You want help on that?" Sean asked.

"I've got it covered."

Mack eyed her but didn't speak, and neither did she.

She clapped her hands. "Okay, that's it for now. Keep me updated on your other assignments."

Everyone took out an electronic device of choice and got to work. Evan opened his laptop and queued up another video from Terminal 18. Analysts were reviewing video from other terminals too and would cover an entire month just to be sure they didn't miss anything. He'd started this afternoon with the most current recording and reviewed the footage all the way back to Friday morning. He ran them at a faster than normal speed and paused when something caught his eye so he could get through them all without it taking days to complete.

A knock sounded on the door. Cam leapt to his feet and rushed across the room. The waiter rolled in a squeaky cart filled with metal dome warmers. Cam signed the receipt while Kiley lifted the domes and released the tantalizing smell of grilled burgers and onions.

Cam saw the waiter out, and they sat down to eat. Evan expected conversation during the meal. Not so. Everyone brought their device to the table and continued working. He grabbed a Coke and set his open laptop by his plate. He started the video running and chomped into his juicy burger. The flavors exploded in his mouth as the video time-stamped at eleven p.m. the prior Thursday started running.

Boring footage played of empty lanes leading out of the North Harbor area, which covered three terminals, including Terminal 18 where the container still sat. He leaned in for a seasoned fry when movement on the far side of the screen caught his attention. He slowed down the video and zoomed in on the hazy scene.

He dropped the fry and shot his hand up. "Got them!"

Kiley looked up. "What?"

"Two men. On foot at the Terminal 18 gate. Hightailing it off the property. Has to be our guys."

Kiley dropped her chicken sandwich and rushed to stand behind him. He tapped the area on the screen she should focus on and forced himself to ignore her close proximity.

"Zoom in more," she commanded.

He did. The image was grainy, and with the camera facing the entrance, it caught the men but only from behind. They wore American clothing—jeans, hoodies, sneakers—and had bulging backpacks hanging from their shoulders.

"Could be anyone," she said.

"You're right, it could be." Evan didn't understand her lack of excitement. "But at this terminal in the middle of the night? Leaving the place on foot? I'd put money on it being our guys."

"C'mon. C'mon. C'mon. Turn around or glance back." She clutched the back of Evan's chair and shook it as if he could somehow make the men turn.

The guy on the right suddenly spun as if he heard something. A bright light obscured his entire head.

"What in the world?" Evan squinted at the screen.

Kiley slammed a fist on the table. "He must have LEDs on his hood."

Evan swiveled to look at her. "Explain please."

She swatted at a stray strand of hair. "Infrared security cameras like the one that recorded this video have an auto iris that adjusts for the average light level of the scene it's capturing. Shining a bright light like an LED will confuse the camera. In fact, it'll partially blind it and record only the bright light."

Mack shook his head. "He's a cut above the usual terrorist if he was smart enough to plan ahead like this."

"Look at their body language," Kiley said. "They're calm, their shoulders relaxed. They don't expect to be caught."

"Because they thoroughly planned their escape," Evan said. "Maybe ran a dress rehearsal back home. And had local men watching the port—scoping out security and knowing the patrol schedule."

Sean scowled. "They're not newbies, that's for sure."

Evan focused on the pair on the screen as they kept moving straight ahead and out of camera range. He grabbed the arms of his chair and held tight, anger pulsing through his fingertips. They'd finally seen their terrorists but couldn't ID them other than by their build and clothing, which they would surely have changed by this point. Essentially the team had nothing to go on. Nothing.

"This occurred almost three days ago." Kiley charged back to her computer. "They could be anywhere in the country, and we need to find them. Starting with where they went from here. Someone turn on the TV, and I'll display an area map."

Cam turned on the large flat-screen TV, and she tossed a cord in his direction. Burger in one hand, he took a bite and then plugged the cord into the back while she connected the other end to her computer. A map of the area displayed on the screen.

Still by the TV, Cam swallowed and tapped the glass. "Looks like the most direct route into town is the Murray Morgan Bridge over the waterway."

"I've worked the port neighborhoods many times, and it's covered by CCTV cameras," Evan said. "We should be able to get footage from them. But not if these guys went north on the Hylebos Bridge. No cameras there."

Cam looked at him. "They'd take that bridge if they were heading to Seattle to hop a flight, right?"

"I doubt they'd risk flying even *if* they have fake papers," Sean said, fry in hand. "Buses or trains are more likely. But honestly I doubt they'd risk public transport at all. Still, I can get an analyst on retrieving all flight manifests from SeaTac for the following morning."

"That'll be a long list," Evan said. "And without names, how will you weed through it?"

Sean shrugged. "If it's at all possible, we have to look at it. I don't think it will yield much, which is why I'll pass it off to someone else."

Evan wasn't used to having unlimited resources at his disposal, and something like this would be put on a list to do if time ever became available. It rarely did.

Kiley squinted at her computer screen. "The bridge is about a four- or five-mile walk from the port. They could've done it on foot. Someone could've picked them up too. Or they called a cab or rideshare."

"I doubt there would be many rideshare drivers in this area," Evan said, "especially in the middle of the night. A cab would be more likely. But would someone who was smart enough to find a way to baffle cameras get in a cab where they could be identified?"

"Seems like another long shot, but I'll check it out," Cam offered. "And I'll get police incident reports for the area. Maybe a cop remembers seeing them."

"I'll put out feelers with my local CIs to see if anyone's heard anything." Evan grabbed his phone so he could send texts to contacts he'd used in the past. If anyone knew where these men went, he hoped it would be someone who frequented the same circles.

"Thank you," Kiley said. "Because we need to figure out who on earth these men are, and what kind of terror they plan to unleash. And we need to do it quickly."

CHAPTER 11

Kiley and the team continued back through the videos to the day the container arrived, in case these guys had crept out of and back into their container before Thursday, but they didn't even poke their heads out the door. So she kept running the video over and over, replaying it to look for leads as the atmosphere in the room went from tense to atmospherically tense.

Now more than ever, she felt the pressure of her responsibilities. Hearing chatter about the date and seeing the men with backpacks that could contain explosive devices made the impending threat more real. Everyone was right. These guys weren't newbies. They were experienced. Their organization valued them. Valued their skills. And the country was in for a world of hurt if the team didn't find them soon.

More determined than ever, her teammates settled into the television seating area to get started on their assignments. Evan remained at the table, sending texts. She could no longer stand the pungent smell of their forgotten dinners and moved the dishes to the cart. She pushed it into the hallway, ignoring an irritating wheel and weighed how this new development impacted her game plan for the rest of the night.

Now would be a perfect time to call Eisenhower for an update. She dug out her phone and stepped to the other end of the room to phone him. Despite the late hour in D.C., he answered on the first ring. She brought him up to date on their progress, or lack of it, and raised the question about investigating a nuclear connection.

"Seems like a long shot to me, but not one we can rule out just yet," he said. "Leave it with me, and I'll get the team here working that angle."

"Any word on Badriddin Hilali?"

"Nothing," he said. "The registration information was bogus. The address is a vacant lot. And interestingly enough, the name is that of a Persian poet. Not sure if this guy's trying to say something by that, but I have a team researching it and trying to track down the box holder."

"Of course it didn't pan out," Kiley said. "Would be too easy."

"Indeed." He took a long breath. "Still, I was able to obtain a warrant for the box, and we're intercepting all incoming mail. Plus the staff knows to watch for this guy and call if anyone shows up to check the mailbox."

"That's all we can do then."

"It is," he said resolutely. "Harrison will gather any mail, and she knows to keep you updated."

After promising to update him again in the morning, Kiley thanked him, ended the call, and passed on the information Eisenhower had shared.

Evan set down his phone. "I've put feelers out to my guys. Hopefully one of them knows something. What can I do next?"

She frowned. "I'm not sure. I need to regroup."

He watched her, and she didn't like his study because she couldn't fathom what he was trying to figure out.

"No need to change our plans, right?" he asked. "Not when there isn't any action you can take on these guys at the moment."

"He's right," Sean said from the sofa. "The video doesn't have anything actionable in it."

Kiley didn't want to let the lead go. She wanted to keep replaying the video to find something she could move on. But what was the point when the file revealed nothing? She had to quit wasting her time wishing for a lead and find one before it was too late.

"You're both right. I'll stick with my plan." She grabbed a roll of white paper, masking tape, and a pair of latex gloves for Evan. "Clear the table and cover it with the paper."

He followed directions as she placed her laptop on a nearby credenza to connect Firuzeh's phone. As with computers, law enforcement didn't directly access phones when at all possible. Just turning one on or waking it up could alter the evidence and call into question other files at a legal trial.

Her computer screen moved through prompts

for imaging startup but skipped the field where Kiley would add Firuzeh's password. "This is odd. Firuzeh didn't have a password on her phone."

Cam mocked a shudder. "I can't even imagine going no password, but a lot of people don't want the hassle."

"Yeah, but with Firuzeh's CI role, I would have thought she'd be extra careful," Kiley said, a slurry of guilt starting to build in the pit of her stomach. "Maybe I should've told her to take better care."

The others looked at her, their expressions mixed with sympathy and something else she couldn't quite read.

Did she fail Firuzeh? Should Kiley have warned her CI to be more careful? Kiley had never worked with a CI before Firuzeh. Maybe she should've asked Sean or Mack for advice on how to handle the role, but until Firuzeh died, Kiley never believed her CI was in any danger. And now she was dead.

Kiley grabbed her can and chugged, trying to wash away the pain. At some point she would need to find time to be alone and cry. To release all of this guilt and anguish so she could start the process of moving on. But not now. Not when there was so much to do. She would have to simply fight the urges and fill each moment with work.

Searching the image of Firuzeh's laptop was the next logical step, but Kiley wanted to be extra careful in preserving evidence for trial. No way she'd let a technicality allow Firuzeh's killer to escape punishment. Making an image of the image would give her an unaltered copy for trial should she need it.

She started the copy running, then joined Evan at the table and took Firuzeh's backpack from the large evidence bag. She removed textbooks and notebooks and slid the textbooks to Evan across the papered table. "Start with these. Look for anything with a terrorism connection."

He didn't question her but grabbed a basic algebra book and cracked it open, his attention focused and sharp, and Kiley was suddenly very thankful to have him here. Not a feeling she ever expected to experience again in relationship to Evan.

She grabbed a calculator and opened the battery compartment. Finding only batteries, she set it aside and dumped out a few pencils and pens. A ruler. Eraser. She twisted the pens open. Nothing unusual. She located a makeup bag holding mascara, blush, lipstick, and a powder compact. A quick roll up of the lipstick tube revealed the pale pink lipstick Firuzeh favored, and a twist of the mascara tube, a black wand.

Kiley dropped them back into the bag and reached for the compact. The case rattled. She quickly snapped it open to lift the puff. A shiny gold key rested in the empty powder area, and her heart rate ratcheted up. She displayed the key for Evan. "Found it hidden in her makeup."

He turned the key around in his gloved fingers. "Looks like it could be for a locker or padlock."

"The fact that she concealed the key makes it a promising lead." Mack swiveled to look at them. "Maybe the place where she dances has lockers. It would be a perfect place to hide something."

Kiley nodded. "Hopefully we'll find dance studio information on her computer or phone."

Mack looked across the room. "You're making a copy of the computer image you took at her place?"

Kiley lifted her chin. "I won't risk the D.C. forensics staff blowing the image they take. I want to be sure we have an unaltered copy for when we find Firuzeh's killer, and he goes to trial."

Mack raised his eyebrows. "A bit excessive, don't you think?"

"I get it. Totally." Evan gave her a tight smile, but unease lingered beneath the surface. "You can never be too careful."

Clearly Olin's death or another incident had impacted Evan in ways she hadn't yet seen, as this man—this careful, take things slow, take copious notes in case guy—wasn't anything like the spontaneous agent she'd once known.

Thankfully Mack let it go and went back to work on reviewing the ship manifest. Kiley heard the pages whisper in the book Evan was looking through while she emptied the rest of the backpack to feel every inch of the fabric for hidden items. The well-worn canvas revealed nothing else, so she stowed the evidence and grabbed a notebook to begin wading through page after page of class notes. As time ticked down, she kept her ears tuned for the ding of her computer, and the moment it sounded, she charged across the room.

"In a hurry much?" Cam laughed.

"Phone's done at last." She eagerly opened the files and navigated to Firuzeh's recent texts, finding messages to her family members and a friend named Alicia. Kiley browsed the files looking for email, but Firuzeh didn't have an email app on her phone. She did have a Twitter account, and Kiley reviewed it to discover several D.C. political groups Firuzeh followed.

Kiley jotted the group names down on a legal pad for further follow-up and moved on to recent pictures. Several candid shots of her smiling family made Kiley's heart ache even more for their loss, yet she forced herself to search the images for any leads. The final photo was of her dance class, though the picture didn't hold identifying information on the studio.

The hard drive image completed too, and

she quickly dug into the data, starting where she always started—with deleted files. People erroneously believed they could trash a file and empty the trash making the information disappear—hiding secrets or things they didn't want others to see. But the only way to completely eliminate information on a hard drive was to overwrite the files with new data. Few people knew to take this extra precaution, allowing forensic techs to recover many of the deleted files.

She set the program to restore the emails, and as the computer churned, she read through Firuzeh's Inbox. Most of the messages related to her schooling. Her teachers praised her papers, and she received top grades. Except for one professor.

"I found a dispute here between Firuzeh and her professor," Kiley said. "He didn't like her dissident take on the subject of immigration and downgraded her paper. There are several heated emails between them, and Firuzeh ended things with threatening to go above his head."

Sean looked over his shoulder. "But is that enough of a reason for murder?"

"Threatened people can often feel cornered and do rash and unthinkable things," Evan said.

"I agree, and we should at least talk to this guy." Kiley added Yancy Flagel, the testy professor's name, to her notepad.

She finished reviewing the Inbox and moved to the restored emails. The first message referenced a dance class at a studio called Dance Jewel.

Kiley quickly looked the place up on the internet. "Dance place in Firuzeh's email is called Dance Jewel. They offer classes in authentic ancient Persian dance. The owner's name is Alicia, and Firuzeh texted someone by that name."

Evan looked at his watch. "Too bad it's almost three or you could call her. Would be good to know if Firuzeh has a locker there."

"Exactly." Kiley continued down the recovered email list, and her eyes locked on a message referencing a group called The Righteous—a known terrorist group and one of the organizations Firuzeh followed on Twitter.

Stunned at the connection, Kiley sat back to think. She'd heard of The Righteous in passing, but the RED team never encountered them in their work. She read the email in which Firuzeh vehemently disagreed with Nasim Waleed, leader of The Righteous, and his plan to protest an incident between the police and an immigrant from Iraq. Waleed threatened retaliation if she interfered with his plans.

She noted his name next to the group on her legal pad and swiveled to look at Cam. "I have a D.C. political organization I need you to watch for in your search. Firuzeh opposed a protest they had planned on Saturday and traded heated emails with the group's leader. It's unclear if she's a member of the group, but they're called The Righteous."

"The Righteous." Evan's head popped up. "I've been tracking them for years. They're not just D.C.-based. They're international and have strong ties to ISIS. Nasim Waleed is their leader."

"Yeah, he's the guy she was emailing with," Kiley said.

Evan frowned. "Then she was in bad company. Waleed's suspected of masterminding several suicide bombings around the world, and two assassinations here in the U.S. He's also a former Iraqi sniper. If Firuzeh opposed him, he could very well be the one behind her murder."

Memories of the shooting flashed back in vivid color, and Kiley's stomach knotted.

Mack turned to look at her. "A sniper is a good possibility given the way Firuzeh was taken down."

"We also think the shooter was monitoring her communications or he wouldn't have known where she'd be last night," Kiley added, as she hadn't shared this information with Evan. "Her car was clean, but I haven't been able to check her phone for a tracker until now."

Evan's eyes narrowed. "You should know. Waleed's in information technology. A network administrator in his day job, and a recruiter of other IT professionals in his role with The Righteous. He could easily use Wi-Fi to detonate a bomb."

That knot in Kiley's stomach cinched tighter. "If this goes beyond Firuzeh's death, and he's involved in the terrorist plot, we could be looking at some sort of computer-generated attack."

"Like what?" Evan asked.

Thoughts pinged around in Kiley's brain, and she struggled to organize them. "Computers control so many things these days, like critical infrastructure control systems to energy pipelines, hydroelectric projects, drinking water systems. Even nuclear power plants."

"Dams and chemical plants are computer-controlled too," Cam added.

Kiley jumped to her feet and thought about actions they should take regarding this discovery. "Cam, keep on top of this with the analysts monitoring the dark web and let me know of anything that might corroborate an upcoming cyber attack."

Cam gave a sharp nod.

"I'll get Eisenhower to check with Counter-terrorism to see if they've heard any chatter on a computer-driven plot," she said, sitting back down. "And I'll check for a tracker on Firuzeh's phone."

Kiley located a hidden app that not only was tracking Firuzeh's GPS but also texts and phone calls. She thought about a faceless monster following Firuzeh and felt like she might throw up. "Tracker was installed on Friday at 1:15 p.m."

Evan met her gaze. "So where was Firuzeh then, and who was she with at that time?"

Kiley navigated to the date on Firuzeh's calendar, and her stomach dropped. "She met with Waleed for lunch that day. Without a password, if she left her phone unattended, he could've installed the tracker."

"Sounds like we really need to talk to the guy." Evan's tone spoke of a burning desire to face Waleed. "And before you say I can't go with you when you talk to him, I know this guy better than anyone here, and I *will* be in on the interview."

Kiley had never seen him this adamant, yet she couldn't let his desires play into her decisions. They would have to travel back to D.C. together for the interview, and she didn't want to spend hours in a plane with him.

"Evan has a point," Sean said. "He can bring you up to speed on the trip, and you'll be better prepared for the interview."

"You can go to the dance school too," Mack added, "and check for lockers."

She *did* want to visit the studio, and she also wanted to talk to Professor Flagel, though with a long-range rifle shot it was unlikely her professor killed Firuzeh. Still, he could've hired someone to take the shot, and Kiley could leave no stone unturned. But she certainly didn't need Evan's

181

help with the interview or to check the lockers.

"I . . ." She fumbled for a reason to leave him behind but couldn't come up with one. "First, I can't rush off to D.C. with so much going on here, and second . . ." Her phone rang before she could continue, and she almost shouted hallelujah for the interruption. Until she saw the name on her screen. "It's Eisenhower."

"Never good when he calls." Mack's dire tone raised her angst. "Especially not in the middle of the night."

Evan didn't like seeing the pressure mount on Kiley's face or the way she was holding her body so rigidly as she stepped across the room and lifted the phone to her ear. He glanced at her teammates, who were sharing a concerned look.

"Sir," she said, her hand moving a lamp on a table by the window a few inches to the right, telling Evan her stress had reached decorating level. She suddenly stumbled and grabbed on to the credenza, her fingers turning white.

No one moved to go to her aid. Evan started to get up. Mack fired a warning look, telling Evan to stay put. He wanted to ignore Mack, but the guy knew Kiley better than Evan did these days, so he remained seated.

"Where?" Her shoulders pulled back into a firm line. Something bad had nearly taken her down, and she was struggling to climb out of it.

Evan still wanted to go to her. Instead, he slung an arm around the back of a nearby chair to keep from acting on his impulse. He wasn't with a group of friends hanging out. They were law-enforcement professionals, and she needed to be treated as such. Even more so since she was leading the investigation.

"I'll decide and let you know." She gave a firm nod. "We'll be there."

She lowered her phone to the credenza and planted both hands on the edge, her head bowed.

Was she crying or praying? Evan didn't know, but he desperately wanted to figure it out. The first required help. The second distance.

She took a long breath. Let it out and took in another, then released it too. She removed her hands from the credenza and slowly pivoted. Her face was pale, her eyes dark with anguish.

"There was a bombing in Pittsburgh," she said, her voice sounding disembodied, as if she'd distanced herself from the situation to maintain her sanity. "A train. Not passenger. Freight. Suspected target was a chlorine gas tanker. Thankfully the device exploded early and didn't rupture the tanker. At least three people were killed, and countless others injured. Two male suspects described as Arabian or Middle Eastern descent were seen in the area before the bomb detonated."

Evan shot to his feet. "Are you thinking it's our guys?"

She responded with a wooden nod. "If so, this bombing was a warm-up to the main event. Even if the tanker *had* ruptured, it wouldn't have subjected anywhere near a million people to danger."

"The chlorine gas would've killed or harmed a large number, though," Mack said.

"True. Eisenhower mentioned that a single railcar holds ninety tons of the chemical, so it's not hard to imagine the damage an exploded tanker would've caused."

Cam closed his laptop and planted his feet on the floor. "We should've considered chemical transport and not just plants producing them."

Evan wasn't as certain. "Shipping would have to involve a large network of coordinated events to target a million people."

Sean eyed Evan. "Then maybe we've got it wrong. Maybe the threat isn't a single attack but an accumulation of attacks or many simultaneous ones."

Kiley frowned, her face continuing to look washed out. "Eisenhower has requested the national threat level be raised."

Mack shook his head. "Don't much like that. People on the watch list might go to ground, making our job that much harder."

"Which is why we need to work faster," Kiley said, sounding stronger now. "Eisenhower has booked the last two seats on the first flight to

Pittsburgh in the morning. I'll be going and need to decide who to bring with me."

"Evan," Mack said quickly. "Take Evan. He knows the players better than we do, and he's an explosives expert."

"I agree," Sean said.

"As a bonus," Mack said, "when you're done in Pittsburgh you can hop a quick flight to D.C. to check out the dance studio and interview Waleed."

"I've got the interview in the morning with Barzani," she said, as if thinking how the interview would impact her decision.

Sean stood. "Mack and I can do that. He's been reviewing the information anyway, so he's up to speed on the guy."

"I'll even make one of my famous omelets for you before you leave." Mack smiled. "So no more excuses. We can handle things here while you're gone."

"Fine." She shifted her focus to Evan. "We need to leave for the airport in an hour. Be ready."

He nodded, but her reluctance to travel with him cut him to the core. Tension was bound to linger on the hour drive to the airport plus the five-hour flight at her side. Yet Evan would do his best to put that aside so he didn't make things more difficult for either of them.

"Eisenhower's forwarding scene photos, along with a preliminary report from Pittsburgh," she said. "We can review those on the plane."

"I've got a written background report on Waleed I did for another investigation," he said. "I'll print that for you to review too."

She ran a hand through her hair. "You ever worked a bomb investigation before?"

"Car bomb," he replied as the horrific images played in his brain. "Four fatalities."

"Then you have some idea what to expect here. Other than the train engineer, the injured and dead are innocent people in a car by the tracks. One's a three-year-old boy." She shuddered.

The desire to comfort her again burned in Evan, but now definitely wasn't the time to try to take her into his arms and hold her while she worked through the pain. Now was the time to act as her co-worker and help her investigate this horrific bombing.

"I'm gonna go pack a bag." She walked out of the room, her head down, shoulders drooping.

Evan let out a long breath.

Mack walked over to him. "Keep an eye on her. Make sure she eats and gets plenty to drink. She has a tendency to get dehydrated at the drop of a hat. And make sure she gets at least a few hours of sleep."

"Sounds like you should be the one going with her."

Mack shook his head. "I meant what I said. You have experience with explosives and a deeper understanding of terrorism and the players involved. And—" he paused and met Evan's gaze—"I think you're just the person she needs right now."

Evan was about to ask what Mack meant by that, but the guy strode across the room and knocked on Kiley's door, then disappeared inside.

Evan would like to be a fly on the wall in her room, but he had to grab his bag from his own room. Knowing Kiley, if he was even one second late, she'd leave him in the dust.

CHAPTER 12

Evan took Kiley's overnight bag from her shoulder. She thought to argue with him, but he meant nothing by it. No power play. No assertion of strength. Just common consideration to lift it into the airplane's overhead bin. He'd always had impeccable manners, and this was simply Evan being Evan. Embracing the manners he'd learned in his wonderful family growing up.

She got that. Totally. So why as she dropped into the window seat did it feel like she was surrendering something to him?

Oblivious to her turmoil, he settled into the aisle seat next to her. "You always fly first class?"

She stowed her backpack on the floor. "Only when we have to be somewhere quick and they're the only seats available. Or there aren't any military hops."

He stretched out his long legs. "It'll be no hardship, that's for sure."

She nodded, thinking the same thing. Bigger seats allowed her to sit farther away from him than the cramped coach seats. She'd just survived an hour in his Tahoe, and now this. She would give Mack an earful when she got back from the trip. He was clearly trying to throw them together. He'd wanted her to deal with

Olin's death for years. She got it. Truly she did. But Mack's wishes, or even what Evan wanted, didn't mean she desired the same thing. She'd much rather leave the whole thing buried in the back of her brain where she'd forced the trauma so she could go on. Now the angst was creeping out, nearly paralyzing her when she needed every bit of her focus to find these terrorists.

"How often do you catch military hops?" Evan got a stack of folders out of his computer case and shoved it under the seat.

"Pretty regularly actually," she said, glad he'd found something safe to talk about. "In fact, Eisenhower has the Tacoma base on standby in case we need something faster than commercial flights right now. They'll scramble a flight if needed."

He shook his head. "Each time I think I realize the power of your team's influence, something else surprises me."

"Well, don't think we have the military at our beck and call all the time. This is one of those ultrahigh priority investigations."

The flight attendant brought coffee, and Kiley took a sip, savoring the full body of the above-average airplane brew.

Cam's ringtone sounded from her phone. Glad for the distraction, she grabbed it. "Is this something Evan needs to hear?"

"I didn't have a chance to update you on my

progress before you split," Cam said. "Must've been wiped. So anyway . . . yeah, either let him listen in or you'll have to update him yourself."

"Hang on." She got out her wireless earbuds with talk feature and handed one to Evan. "It's Cam, and I don't want anyone overhearing us."

He nodded and leaned close, plugging the bud into his ear. She should have thought about how sharing earbuds would bring Evan closer, but she couldn't very well jerk the bud from his ear now.

"Go ahead, Cam," she said as she focused on passengers slogging down the aisle instead of Evan's nearness.

"With the chlorine gas now in the picture, I'm expanding the list for potential bombers to include terrorists who've experimented with biological weapons. Hope to have something for you by the time you get back."

She was always thankful for the way Cam went above and beyond what many analysts brought to the job. "Thanks for adding to the search."

"Yeah, sure, and I'll email you the list of organizations Firuzeh belonged to. It's a short list, and nothing looks out of the ordinary for a student except The Righteous." Cam took a long breath. "I also made a list of those who unloaded the container and moved it. And a list of security guards who worked Terminal 18 since the container landed. Sean and Mack will interview Barzani this morning, and after that Sean will interview as many of the workers on my list as he can."

"Great," Kiley said.

"Did my guy from MIT call you back?" Evan asked.

"Nah, man," Cam replied. "Maybe you should give him a ring and light a fire under him."

"Will do," Evan said.

"Okay, that's it," Cam said. "Now go destroy that Waleed guy." Laughing, he ended the call.

Evan pulled out the earbud. "Cam might like to joke, but he's really good at his job, isn't he?"

She wrapped up the cord. "One of the best analysts I've ever worked with."

Evan rested his head against his seat and looked at her. He was so close she could see the details of the scar trailing from his eye to his jaw, and she wanted to run her finger over the raised white skin.

She scooted back instead and asked the first thing she could think of regarding the investigation. "Do you still have dock video to review? If so, maybe we should send the remaining files off to analysts."

He arched an eyebrow, the scar rising.

She sat on her hand. "I'm not questioning your work. I want you to focus on the bombing and our upcoming interviews."

"I don't have any left." His expression relaxed. "Let me send a text to my guy at MIT before we take off."

She watched his thumbs fly over the small keys on his phone. He'd been so helpful and proactive from the moment he'd joined their team. Sure, they'd had their share of tension, though she was the cause of it, not him. But then he was the guilty party here. He was the reason Olin died.

She let the moment play in her brain for the first time in years. She recalled the approach to the suspect's door. Her on the left. Olin in the middle. Evan on the right. The door jerking back. The suspect opening fire with an automatic rifle. The booming rifle reports cracking the quiet morning air. Bullets flying. Evan reacting too late to drag Olin out of the gunfire but hurling himself at her and knocking her to the porch. Then swiveling to take out the shooter with his handgun, slicing his cheek open on a metal boot scraper as he landed hard.

And her, what had she done to help before Evan tackled her? Nothing but gape and reach for her gun. Was she excusing her failure to quickly respond to the fact that Evan was in charge? To the fact that as a woman she might not have been able to move a big guy like Olin to safety?

Could Mack be right? Was she blaming Evan for something that wasn't his fault at all?

No. No. A thousand times no. He was responsible for the plan. For crafting an effective suspect apprehension op, and that didn't happen. All because of some drinks with the guys.

She eased out a long breath and shoved the memory back into the recesses of her brain.

"You're worried about the investigation," Evan said.

She looked up to see his concerned gaze pinned on her and chose not to share her thoughts, but instead simply looked at him.

"I get it," he said. "I've worked terrorism full time, and there are things I haven't begun to experience. Just when you think you've figured these guys out, they get more and more sophisticated."

She decided to go with his assumption about her mood, as it gave them something concrete to talk about. "Especially in computer programming and electronic communications."

"I know no one has proved terrorists communicate via video games, but it would be great if these guys *did* use the gaming systems," Evan said. "And it would be nice if video-console makers could find a way to monitor the chats. Maybe then we'd finally know if terrorists *are* using them."

She'd once thought the same thing, but it was an impossibly big problem and a naïve thought. "All the violent games make it hard to distinguish between game talk and actual conversations. And with roughly thirty million PlayStation Fours alone out there, you can imagine the size of the problem."

He frowned. "I guess it makes sense that

console makers can't even begin to deal with chat monitoring."

She nodded. "I'm most interested in party chat held outside the games. It involves a much smaller set of users and could be monitored more easily, but it would still be a big number."

"Even so, isn't it all encrypted?"

"Yes, but it's data in surface-level environments, and access could be made through back doors." Their discussion had gotten too off point for any meaningful dialogue, and she needed to bring it back into focus. "At this point, we're better off with our analysts monitoring the social-media accounts your MIT friend located."

He shook his head in disbelief. "What's it like to have people at your disposal all the time?"

"Honestly," she said, "I haven't thought about it in years. It just is and has been this way since the team was formed. We don't have unlimited resources, but we do have deep pockets. Very deep ones." She smiled at him.

He gave her one of his lopsided smiles in return. Her heart cartwheeled, and she fought hard to keep her cool and not do something stupid like trace his scar. Thankfully the flight attendant made her way down the aisle to refill their cups. Kiley gripped hers like a lifeline to wakefulness.

Evan opened a folder on his tray. "I printed out your Montgomery Three case file to read if I have time on the flight."

Kiley still didn't know if they should have let him into their inner circle on this investigation, but as she opened her mouth to say something, her phone rang. The name Zoey Ryden appeared in caller ID, and Kiley quickly answered the call from the top FBI electronics tech. "Zoey. Good to hear from you."

"I've been working the PlayStation game consoles for your investigation," she said, direct and to the point as usual, "and I have the login names and passwords."

Talk about a timely call. "Can you email them to me?"

"You got it. FYI, these guys played The Witcher Three for hours and hours. Like nonstop for days on end."

Not a surprise. Most role-playing games had heroes, but not The Witcher. The main character, Geralt, was a Witcher—someone who was both feared and needed by everyone from the aristocrats to the villagers. Being detested by most people gave him complete freedom to treat them however he wanted. Something she could see terrorists totally embracing.

Kiley thanked Zoey and sent a text to Eisenhower requesting the 24/7 resources needed to monitor the logins. He replied with an affirmative, and she texted Mack to locate agents to handle the monitoring.

"A lead?" Evan asked.

"Maybe," she replied. Hoping for once this information actually produced something actionable, she shared it with him.

The flight attendant interrupted with her official announcements and closed the front door. After she came down the aisle and collected their cups, Kiley got out Evan's report. "I want to read your info on Waleed, and then we'll look at scene photos together, okay?"

He nodded and flipped open the Montgomery Three folder.

As she read, she was acutely aware of his presence next to her, yet it wasn't awkward or uncomfortable. A sense of comradery and the sharing of a singular goal made it feel more like the days before Olin's death when they'd spent hours working that investigation together. Some of the happiest hours of her life.

Kiley sat back to think about what she'd read in the report on Waleed and sip the rich, dark brew the flight attendant delivered the moment they hit cruising altitude.

Evan rested his cup on the tray where the Montgomery Three report lay open, revealing notes he'd jotted in the margins. "There's no description of the abductor in your case files."

"Right," she replied. "No one saw him."

"And that has me thinking." He looked at her, his gaze tentative as if he didn't want to rock the boat.

"Go on," she encouraged.

"You briefly entertained the idea of the abductor being female, but when the profiler got involved, you dropped that possibility."

Her shoulders went up, but she forced them to relax and took a sip of the coffee before answering so she didn't sound defensive. "It's not like we didn't interview the women in these girls' lives. We thoroughly vetted them. But yeah, the profiler *did* make it clear that a male likely abducted the girls."

Evan continued to drink his coffee, and that uneasy hint of treading lightly with her remained in his expression.

While she appreciated his consideration, she wanted to find the girls more than anything. "Spit it out. I can handle it."

He placed his palms flat on the tray table, then looked back at her. "I only bring this up because I recently worked an investigation near the border where women were going missing. It's not unusual for illegals to disappear, and especially not in or near Mexico. Turned out in this investigation that a woman—one of their own—was leading them out of the country and turning them over to a cartel to traffic them."

Kiley didn't want to believe a woman would do this, but Kiley didn't doubt he was telling the truth. "Why would a woman do such a horrible thing to another woman?"

His fingers curled into fists. "The cartel threatened her children, and you know mothers will do anything to keep their own children safe. Even hurt other children. Or friends. Even family."

"So, you think we should give more thought to a female abductor?"

He shrugged. "You know the investigation better than I do, but if it was my investigation, I would run it down more. It would be hard for a man or woman to take three girls at a time without one of them freaking out and screaming or trying to run away. So maybe these girls went willingly with this person, and they would be more apt to go with a woman."

"Yeah, maybe. But I really feel like we exhausted that avenue." She stared into her coffee, swirling it in the cup, the sloshing liquid an image much like her brain of late. "The only person to see anything that night recently remembered the van they drove off in had a red circle with green letters on it. We investigated and didn't turn up any businesses with such a logo. Maybe if we factor in a woman as the business owner or former owner with these details, we might find something."

"Sounds worth the effort."

"Yeah. Thank you for the fresh look. Maybe it'll pan out." She smiled.

"I have another thought." He sounded even more tentative, not at all his normal mode.

Maybe she'd been coming across as defensive, and he thought she didn't want him butting in. "Please. Tell me."

"It's about the van." He tapped one of the notes he'd made. "Cartels deal with suspicious vehicles by burning them or hiding them in tunnels and caves. I don't know anything about Montgomery's topography, but maybe a cave or tunnel is a possibility too."

Kiley pondered his suggestion. "We did a statewide search for the van, but we didn't specifically look at the abductor dumping a vehicle up north where the state is hillier. So yeah, we should look into it. We're running this investigation on the sly, so I can't task an analyst to find a most likely location for me. If Cam wasn't already swamped, he could do it."

"I can read a map," Evan said.

"That would be great," she said with enthusiasm. "If you want to, that is."

"Glad to do it for you." He smiled, a soft, intimate number lifting the corners of his mouth—a smile she hadn't seen in years.

The smile called to her, and she was powerless to look away. The ache in her chest since Firuzeh's death simply let go, leaving a flutter of butterflies in her heart. Kiley suddenly felt like she'd agreed to much more than a search for caves or tunnels. So much more, and mistake or not, she didn't mind. Not in the least.

CHAPTER 13

Evan followed Kiley toward the smoldering carnage. Caustic smoke rose into the air permeated with the stench of diesel and charred metal. They'd both donned Tyvek suits, booties, gloves, and respirators, not only to prevent scene contamination but also to protect them from chemicals and noxious gases.

Kiley shuddered, and her footsteps faltered. Evan stopped next to her and thought about taking her hand. Not that he would act on it. He wouldn't do something so personal in front of her peers. Instead, he moved closer to her and hoped she understood that he was here if she needed him.

He'd never seen anything like the sight before him. A locomotive remained on the track, the front completely blown away and the insides hanging out as if someone had cracked it open like a raw egg. A hole the size of a railcar revealed daylight on the other side of the torched metal. The remaining cars lay on their sides, jackknifed off the tracks.

Hazmat workers and firefighters attended to the large tanker farther down the tracks where it balanced precariously on a slope. They'd secured the heavy car with thick ropes and wood cribbing.

And amongst all of that, FBI agents and forensic techs combed through the scorched wreckage, as did paramedics.

Evan took a deep breath and let it out through the respirator. The scene in front of him was nearly unfathomable. Gruesome. Unspeakable. What would an attack that was intended to harm millions look like if they didn't stop the terrorists from carrying out their planned horror? He had to fight not to shudder at the thought and turned his attention to Kiley instead.

She ran a trembling hand over her hair, her eyes wide. Evan hoped never to see a sight like this again, and he wished at the moment that Kiley didn't have to take it all in. He wanted to protect her from things nightmares were made of. He couldn't, of course. Not if she was going to do her job. Which he knew she wanted to do more than anything. Certainly more than she wanted his support and comfort.

"This is worse than I expected," she said, her voice muffled behind the respirator.

Evan nodded and swallowed hard.

Her phone rang, and she reached inside the suit to grab it. "It's Gerald Philips."

"Agent Dawson," she answered and held the phone close to Evan. "I have Agent Bowers with me, and you're on speaker."

"I've got the DNA results from the container's interior," Philips said. "Based on the disbursement of the samples recovered, I still think we're looking at two men, though we were able to definitively locate five DNA profiles. No match in CODIS for any of them."

Not finding names linked to the DNA in the FBI's DNA database was a huge setback but not a surprise to Evan. Not with the terrorists living in another country.

Kiley narrowed her eyes. "So we struck out."

"Yes and no," Philips said. "We may not be able to give you an identity from these profiles, but we can give you an approximate age for the two most likely suspects. One is thirty-three, the other twenty-eight."

"And that's it," Evan snapped as he looked at the disaster in front of him that these two men may have perpetrated.

"No," Philips said calmly, despite Evan's outburst. "My supervisor said I should pull out all stops for this investigation, and I have a friend with access to technology that could give you an electronic sketch of your suspects. So with your permission, I'll send DNA samples to her to get the sketches generated."

"We've never used this technology," Kiley said.

Evan moved closer to the phone. "I've never even heard of it."

"The process is called phenotyping," Philips explained. "Basically, DNA can now be used to provide physical characteristics that are compiled in a composite sketch. There have been great results in locating suspects this way."

"If it works that well, why isn't your lab using it?" Evan asked.

"There are still too many variables to make it an exact science, and it can't be used in court. Plus it's costly."

"How costly?" Kiley asked.

"Depends on the DNA sample," Philips replied. "But it could range from fifteen hundred dollars up to seven thousand."

"Whoa." Evan gaped at Kiley.

She didn't react at all, but when it came to budgets her team had deep pockets—even more so on this investigation.

"I can't approve five profiles," she said. "But go ahead with the two most likely ones."

"There's something else you should know." Philips's tone deepened. "We confirmed the substance in the jar is indeed white phosphorus."

Kiley sighed, her mask muffling the sound. "Anything else?"

"No. That's it for now."

"Thanks for the update. Get me those sketches the moment you have them." She ended the call and fired a quick look around the scene. "You think they used white phosphorus here?"

Evan shook his head. "It would still be burning, and we'd see evidence of it all around us. To be safe, though, we should inform the agent in charge so he can warn forensics to be on the lookout for it."

"We'll do that first." She took off, winding through workers toward a large FBI truck parked near the inner perimeter.

Inside, four people sat at consoles, headsets and mics perched on their heads. A well-built agent wearing navy tactical pants and matching polo shirt embroidered with the FBI logo stood behind them, his fingers plunged into ebony black hair. He turned to look at Kiley and Evan, and the weight of the tragedy lingered in his brilliant blue eyes as his hand fell to his side.

Kiley lifted her respirator and offered her hand. "Special Agent Kiley Dawson, and this is ICE Agent Evan Bowers."

"Special Agent Pierce Quinn." He shook her hand and nodded at Evan.

Evan returned his nod with one of his own, lowered his respirator, and got out his phone to take notes.

Quinn focused his penetrating stare on Kiley. "The director tells me you might have insight into our bombers."

"It's possible, but it's likely you can tell us more." Kiley tipped her head at the window. "What happened here?"

Quinn grimaced. "As you can see, the engine was destroyed, but we believe the target was the chlorine gas tanker, and the bomb detonated prematurely."

"How's that?" Evan asked, as he couldn't see how they could possibly know the bomb's timing.

"We compared fragments to a video recorded at the time of detonation."

Kiley's eyes widened. "Someone got the explosion on video?"

Quinn nodded. "A kid was working on a school project and was filming the train from a safe location on the hill above. We've already recovered enough of the timer to tell it went off a minute before the scheduled detonation. Engineers did the math and tell me if it had detonated at the programmed time, it would have been the precise moment the chemical tanker reached the bomb."

"Did the kid capture the suspects on video?" Kiley sounded so desperate for information her tone put an ache in Evan's gut.

Quinn shook his head. "Kid arrived after the bomb had been set. The image he caught of the device prior to detonation should help our team in reconstruction efforts, though. Maybe allowing us to connect it to known bomb makers."

"Any potential suspects yet?" Kiley asked.

"Yes and no. Two men of obvious Arabian or Middle Eastern heritage were seen earlier today walking along the road by the tracks. Both men are around five-foot-ten, medium build, and sporting thick beards. Witnesses to the explosion didn't see them at the scene." Quinn looked at

Kiley. "I know the descriptions are vague, but are these the men you're seeking?"

"Right build, but . . ." She paused as if she was considering what information to share.

"What else do you know about these men?" Evan jumped in to give her time to decide.

"Unfortunately nothing yet, but we're checking for CCTV in the area."

If these men were the same ones with the special LED lights in the port video, Evan doubted they'd be dumb enough to be caught on camera.

"Our suspects could be targeting chemical plants or shipments like this one," Kiley said, "and I have reason to believe our investigations are linked."

Quinn worked the muscle in his jaw. "The reason the country's threat level was raised."

Kiley didn't acknowledge his statement, and neither would Evan. This wasn't a two-way street here. As a RED team investigator, Kiley held the upper hand and didn't have to tell Quinn anything, whereas his job was on the line if he didn't cooperate.

"Anything else we need to know?" she asked.

He stared over her shoulder as if the weight of the investigation was already taking its toll on him. "We're sending the recovered bomb fragments to TEDAC in Alabama."

"Terrorist Explosive Device Analytical Center,"

Kiley said, explaining the acronym that Evan was already familiar with as he trained at the Hazardous Devices School located in the same facility.

Quinn nodded and looked at Evan. "BAU is located there, and they're our best bet in recovering prints from the device."

Evan might be an ICE agent, yet he knew involving the FBI's Biometrics Analysis Unit Latent Print Squad would be critical to their success. "Did anyone report seeing white smoke or sustain burns from falling shards?"

Quinn shook his head. "Sounds like you're looking for something specific."

"White phosphorus."

Quinn narrowed his eyes. "I'm not familiar with that."

"We consider it highly unlikely that you'll find the phosphorus here," Kiley explained. "Still, you'll want to warn the forensic and recovery staff to be on the lookout for it."

"If it was deployed," Evan said, "it could be stable in water or buried under rubble. It'll ignite again when it hits air."

Quinn grimaced. "As if this wasn't bad enough."

Kiley took out a business card and handed it to Quinn. "I need you to keep me up-to-date on developments as they break. Call any time of day. And I'd like the teen's video within the hour."

Quinn gave a frustrated nod. Evan understood how he was feeling. Evan had felt the same way when Kiley and her team came waltzing into his investigation. At least Quinn didn't have to fear that she would take over here.

"Mind if we have a look around the site?" she asked, her question a mere formality that Quinn couldn't say no to.

"Don't get in anyone's way." He widened his stance. "You might be royalty, but I still have two bombers to bring in."

"Thank you for your time." Kiley offered her hand.

Quinn gave a quick shake and looked at her like he thought she carried the plague. Evan scowled at him, but Kiley didn't react at all as she stepped out the door.

Evan caught up to her. "How do you deal with it?"

"What?"

"Being a pariah with investigators like that."

"Nothing much to be done about it. Just try not to make it worse, let it roll off your back, and move on." She slipped her respirator over her mouth.

Evan still didn't like how Quinn treated her. Frustrated, he put his respirator in place, and they walked toward the road where the young family had been caught by the blast. The small SUV was torn in two and incinerated. A car seat lay burned on the roadway, a scarred teddy bear nearby, both saturated with water used to extinguish the blaze.

Anger rose in Evan's gut, and he curled his fingers into tight fists. Kiley cleared her throat, her hands trembling as she took out her phone to snap pictures. Evan wanted to draw her into his arms and shield her eyes. The heck with the whole professional thing. But then he imagined the look she would give him. Maybe disdain or even rage that he'd held her at a crime scene.

She was doing her best to hide how the horrors of this scene were impacting her. She obviously didn't want him or the others to see her emotions, but he cared too much for her to stand back when he could let her know he was here and that he felt the same anguish. He gently touched her arm.

She looked up at him and lifted her shoulders into a resolute line. "We need to make these guys pay."

"We will," he said, but he didn't know any such thing. At least not yet.

She spun and marched down the tracks toward the mangled engine. Sweltering heat rose up as if they were slogging through desert sand, not the Pennsylvania countryside, keeping workers at a distance. Evan began snapping pictures but halted when he caught sight of a body burned beyond recognition in the twisted metal. His stomach heaved, and he closed his eyes and took a long cleansing breath before he lost his cookies. He only hoped Kiley didn't see the body that Evan suspected was the train engineer. Evan offered a prayer for the man's family and for the family of the victims in the SUV.

He opened his eyes, the horror seeming even darker now. The heat and caustic burnt smell didn't stop Kiley. She picked her way through the debris, then lost her footing. Evan grabbed her elbow to steady her. He doubted she appreciated his help in full view of the others who were staring at them.

"Thanks." She looked over her shoulder at him. Her eyes above the mask were clear and earnest.

Okay then. He was wrong about her again. Maybe face-planting in front of the others was a less desirable outcome.

Together they made their way down the tracks until a hazmat worker stopped them. Kiley flashed him a belligerent look but didn't speak as she snapped pictures of the tanker. The massive size of the railcar had Evan's mouth falling open, and he couldn't begin to imagine what they would be looking at here if it had blown.

Thank you for not letting this be worse.

Kiley spun to look at him. "Anything else you want to check out?"

He wanted to leave. To get Kiley out of here too, yet they weren't quite done. "The device could be the key to tying this back to Waleed or the guys from the container, so I'd like to get a look at the recovered fragments."

She gave a sharp nod. "We'll need to get with forensics for that. Just know the techs will be irritated with us, and so will Quinn."

He hated to put her through more stress. "I think it's worth it."

"Then I'll follow your lead."

"Letting me make them mad, are you?" He grinned and hoped she could see the humor in his eyes, as the respirator hid his smile.

She shook her head, the horror of the bombing washing from her eyes for the briefest of moments.

"I'll remember this." He joked, but he was serious too. He would remember this moment like he remembered everything about her. And like he would remember the horrific scene. How could he forget? The carnage and smell were permanently etched in his mind and senses.

On the way to the evidence truck, Kiley's phone rang. She dug it out. "It's the firearms examiner working Firuzeh's murder investigation." She eased away from the workers and held the phone out, allowing Evan to listen in on the conversation.

"Please tell me you have something for me, Adam," she said. "You're on speaker, and ICE Agent Evan Bowers is with me. He's part of the team. Feel free to be candid."

"I have something, but not likely as much as you're hoping for," Adam replied. "We're looking at a 7.62x54mmR."

Evan let out a long whistle. "Russian. Sniper."

"Correct," Adam said. "This caliber was initially developed by the Russians for their Dragunov sniper rifle. It's been around for over a hundred years and is commonly used by terrorist organizations."

She nodded as she stared at the phone. "Makes sense with Russia's past connection to these groups."

"Exactly," Adam said. "We don't often see it in the U.S., as the .30-06 will outperform the 7.62x54mmR if same-length barrels are used. But .30-06 Springfield firearms are generally sold with much shorter barrels than 7.62x54mmR firearms."

Kiley honestly looked confused, and Evan didn't blame her. He was a gun enthusiast, and he barely kept up with Adam's statement. "Either way we're probably looking for a shooter with sniper experience."

"That's right," Adam said.

Kiley lifted the phone closer to her mouth. "What about prints or DNA on the casing? He might have left trace evidence when loading the magazine."

"We ran it through trace before we started," Adam said. "They got a partial print but not enough to search the database. They swabbed for DNA. I put a rush on it. Should have the results for you in a day or so."

Evan wished they could push the lab, but there was no way to rush the DNA process.

"DNA tech is Veronica Jennings." He shared her phone number.

Evan tapped the name and number into his phone's contacts.

"We got excellent rifling marks on one of the slugs. It'll give us a good comparison when you find the weapon."

"Anything else I need to know?" Kiley asked.

"Other than be careful if you run into this guy?" Adam said, his tone deepening. "No. I'll email the reports to you."

"Thanks for making this top priority." She disconnected and shoved her phone into her pocket.

"Firuzeh traveled in some tough circles if she brought this kind of heat from someone," Evan said. "Most ISIS snipers—if in fact we're dealing with one here—aren't going to be caught. Waleed included."

Kiley lifted her chin. "Most snipers don't have the RED team after them. This one does, and he *will* be caught. I can assure you of that."

He loved her confidence and enjoyed seeing the fire back in her step as she marched over to the evidence truck. She displayed her ID for the woman in charge of cataloging and storing what would be trucks filled with evidence bags by the time the investigation concluded.

Kiley looked up at the white-suited woman. "I need to see all recovered bomb fragments."

She narrowed her eyes above her respirator. "I don't have the authority to show them to anyone."

Kiley planted her feet. "Agent Quinn can confirm my clearance, but why don't you save us both the hassle of disturbing him?"

She eyed Kiley for a long moment before spinning into the truck and sliding a bin to the edge in front of Kiley. She took out the plastic evidence bags and laid them out on the floor while the tech watched Kiley as if she thought Kiley planned to steal something. Evan didn't blame the tech. She was responsible for every item in this truck, and she was doing a good job of guarding everything.

Kiley carefully looked at each item and took pictures, then passed them on to Evan. He knew she possessed a basic understanding of explosives and would likely know what she was looking at, but as the bomb expert in the group, it was up to him to evaluate the items and look for a signature of sorts. So he took his time on each bag.

On the last one, she gave him a pointed look. He studied the Wi-Fi switch that matched the one found in the container. Excitement for the connection to their suspects mixed with worry in his gut, and he locked eyes with her. She held up an index finger. Okay, she might not be a bomb expert, but she clearly understood what she was looking at and was warning him to wait until they were out of the tech's earshot to discuss the switch.

She took several detailed pictures of the mechanism and put everything back into the bin.

"Thanks for your help," she said to the tech as Evan stepped away and waited for Kiley to catch up.

"Wi-Fi," he whispered, worried someone would hear.

"Same switch as the container. I'm not sure using it in this scenario makes sense, though. There's no likelihood the police were jamming radio frequencies here." She moved closer, her focus intense. "What if this was simply a dry run, a test to see how well the network performed?"

He looked over the horrific scene and didn't want to believe she could be right.

"The bomber would need to have at least a passing knowledge of technology to deploy this switch," she added.

"Waleed or his people?" Evan asked.

She nodded, her eyes narrowing. "If we weren't already planning to question him, we would be now."

CHAPTER 14

After two nights with only catnaps, the rumble of the plane's engines should have lulled Evan to sleep. Flying time to D.C. was only an hour. Basically up and down again, yet it was enough time to catch a quick nap. But he was too amped to sleep, the pressure of the timeline building in his gut.

Kiley, on the other hand, was breathing softly and regularly, her eyes tightly closed. They'd boarded the plane, this time in coach with a window and middle seat. After she dropped into the window seat, the ballistics report from Adam Garvin arrived in her Inbox, and she forwarded it to Lancaster. Then she returned a text from Mack, who'd followed up on the Makarovs and the boxes of ammo. Nothing helpful found. No prints. No more information after additional analysis of the residue. Another lead failing to pan out. Evan expected her to be upset. Instead, she'd closed her eyes and drifted off to sleep.

She shifted in her seat, and her head dropped to his shoulder. Her soft hair brushed against his face, and he caught the lingering smell of burning rubble from the crime scene, underneath it a hint of tart apples. He imagined her waking up. Finding him close. Smiling softly and bringing his head down for a kiss.

Yeah, right. Reality was more like she'd come awake and scream in fright.

She moved again, curling her arm around his and snuggling close. He couldn't resist resting his head on hers and closing his eyes. But his mind remained on the bomb and trying to figure out the terrorists' next target. If indeed this train was detonated by the container guys and their plot did include a bomb. At this point in the investigation, they couldn't even confirm that detail.

"Sir." Someone tugged on his arm.

He opened his eyes to see the flight attendant leaning over his seat. "Seat back up for landing, please. Your wife too."

"Sure thing," he said and was glad Kiley was still asleep so she didn't hear the wife comment.

He gently extracted his arm and eased her head onto her seat. He raised her seat back, and she didn't stir. Mack's warning came to mind. Make sure she eats, drinks, and sleeps. They'd had breakfast on the first flight but no lunch or dinner. Despite the burning desire to get to Waleed and find out if he was part of the plot, Evan would insist they stop for something to eat on the way to the interview and grab several bottles of water. Maybe even Gatorade. Neither of them was any good to the investigation unless they took care of themselves, including grabbing short naps whenever possible, like Kiley had managed to do.

The plane touched down at Dulles at seven o'clock in the evening D.C. time, and Kiley woke with a start.

"We're here," he said.

She rubbed her eyes and looked out the window. "Man, I was out of it."

You don't know the half of it.

She shifted her focus to him. "Did you get any sleep?"

"No," he replied, finding it hard not to move a wayward strand of hair clinging to her cheek. He shifted his focus out the window, pinning it there until the plane came to a stop at the gate. He wasted no time grabbing their bags from the overhead bin. She shimmied into her backpack and bolted from the plane, taking him on a race through the airport. She'd never been one to rush into anything. She'd always been controlled and cautious. Apparently another thing that had changed about her.

He reached out for her arm, slowing her and tipping his head at a sandwich shop. "Let's grab something to eat and some water for the road."

"Good idea." She jetted into line and ordered a roast beef and Swiss on a ciabatta.

He got a turkey on wheat loaded with sprouts, cucumbers, hot peppers, lettuce, and tomato, his mouth watering just thinking about food after only a tiny bag of pretzels on the plane.

She glanced up at him. "You think you can fit something that big in your mouth?"

"I'll do my best."

"I like my sandwiches without all the rabbit food on it."

"I remember."

She didn't look pleased by his comment. He got it. She didn't want to be reminded of their past, but they really needed to talk about Olin. Evan would try to find time on this trip without the team around to bring up the subject again.

He moved down the counter to grab four bottles of water and to pay. Surprisingly she let him, and let him carry the bag of food and drinks as well. At the curbside pickup area, a woman with a blond ponytail and wearing a gray pantsuit, a gun at her hip, leaned against a black Escalade. She had *agent* written all over her.

Kiley opened the back hatch and introduced him to Special Agent Gabby Harrison.

"Nice to meet you," Harrison said and held out the keys to Kiley. "Vehicle's all yours."

"What about you?" Kiley set her backpack on the floor. "How will you get back?"

The woman gestured at a small blue Toyota behind them. "My boyfriend will take me to the office."

"Tell him thanks for me, and thanks to you for delivering the wheels," Kiley said.

"Gives us a chance to spend some time together, and you know I'm always glad to help."

Kiley opened her backpack. "I have evidence I

need delivered as soon as possible to Detective Lancaster at Metro. Can you handle that for me?"

"Sure thing."

Kiley got Firuzeh's possessions from her tote and had Harrison sign the log before handing them over to her. "Thanks again."

"No worries." Harrison took the evidence and headed for the little sedan.

Kiley darted to the Escalade, quickly sliding behind the wheel. She continued to act like there was a fire somewhere. Evan supposed she could be running so she wouldn't have time to think about the bomb—about seeing the car seat and teddy bear. He knew he'd like to forget it. Or she was energized again and wanted to move forward in the investigation. He preferred the second thought as he carried their meal to the front and climbed in.

She plugged her phone into the vehicle's information system, the screen displaying her texts. She tapped through them. "There's one from the D.C. analysts. They tracked Waleed down. He's holding a meeting at his headquarters in an hour."

"How far away is it?" Evan set the bag on his lap and put a bottle of water in the cup holder.

"Fifteen minutes. Means we have time to drop in on the professor and still get to the meeting before it breaks up." She fastened her seat belt.

"After hearing about the Dragunov, you still

220

want to talk to the professor?" He opened a water bottle and handed it to her.

"I don't think Flagel killed her. Especially not with a Dragunov. But he could've hired someone." She lifted the water to her mouth and guzzled half the bottle in one drink.

"Still, it's not likely." Evan buckled his seat belt.

"Yeah, but if we only ran down likely leads, we wouldn't be doing our job, would we? And we have the time, so . . ." She looked in the mirrors and merged the SUV seamlessly into the heavy airport traffic.

"What about the dance school?"

"Don't worry. No way I'd miss out on stopping there. They don't close until ten."

"Sounds like you're really counting on finding something in the locker." He took a swig of water and put the bottle in the holder.

"Counting on it, no. Hoping. Honestly, Firuzeh could've simply hidden the key because she didn't want her parents to find out she was dancing."

"We'll know soon enough." He felt the zing of excitement in knowing a lead could pan out, and he got out her sandwich. "You good to eat and drive?"

"No time to take a break." She held out her hand, and he laid the sandwich on her palm. "One of the reasons for no rabbit food. Makes eating and driving much less messy."

She opened the package, took a bite, and glanced at him as she chewed. "I forgot to mention. Your report on Waleed was extremely thorough. He's something else."

He pulled back the sandwich wrap. "He is indeed. And slippery. I honestly don't know if he was personally involved in the bombings, but he *was* the shooter on the two assassinations. We just never found enough physical evidence to prove it."

She chewed and tapped her thumb on the wheel. "One thing I found odd. It's unusual to turn from the Iraqi army to ISIS."

Evan nodded and washed his savory bite down with water. "He blames the U.S. for the drone strike that killed his father, and joining ISIS is a way to get back at us."

"But why, when there's zero proof it was one of our drones?" She clicked on the blinker, moved into the left lane, and kicked up her speed.

"Only he knows his motives, but I suspect his brother Ibrahim had a hand in it. He's a known ISIS operative. He likely persuaded Nasim of our guilt to get a top sniper to immigrate to America and join his cell. Or he just needs to accuse someone. I mean, if I lost my dad that way, I'd be looking for someone to blame."

A flash of pain crossed her face.

"I'm sorry," he said. "That was insensitive. You're thinking of what happened with your dad."

"Not your fault." She set her sandwich on the

paper in her lap and waved a hand. "My father made a mistake and other people died. I saw their family's grief in news reports often enough to know the toll it took on them. So I guess if Waleed feels this way, I can understand it. Not that he's embracing a life of crime as a result, but feeling a need to blame others."

Evan wasn't quite so sympathetic. "You'd think he would be even more unwilling to hurt others."

"Hurting people do irrational things," she said, and he had to wonder if she was thinking about Olin. "Another thing I don't get is how Nasim was even allowed into our country with a brother in ISIS. Makes no sense."

Evan had once thought the same thing. "Seems hard to believe now, but at the time his brother wasn't on our radar as a potential ISIS operator. In hindsight we can see they both took the long-game approach. Nasim married an American citizen to speed up his path to citizenship. And he's managed to escape any convictions, so he remains in the country. Same is true of Ibrahim."

She gripped the wheel with both hands. "If Nasim's responsible for Firuzeh's death, I *will* find a way to prove it."

"I often thought we might be able to get to him via his brother."

She glanced at him. "What is it with brothers in terrorism? I know it's pretty common."

Evan nodded. "Sometimes they join up in

tandem, or like these guys, one brother radicalizes the other."

She swallowed. "Do the Waleeds have sisters?"

Evan swiveled to face her. "You're thinking of the characteristics of the 9/11 attackers."

"Yeah. They all had younger sisters who the terrorists acted to protect."

"But the 9/11 attackers also had violent alcoholic fathers. Not true of the Waleeds. However, their mother is deeply religious, and they had poor social achievement like the 9/11 attackers. Though you wouldn't know it by looking at Nasim today. He's very charismatic."

"Like you said before, they don't all join up for the same reason." Her comment carried a heavy weight of the reality they were facing. Not knowing enough about terrorists' motivations was common because they often died in their attacks, allowing no explanation.

She picked up her sandwich, and he attacked his while she whizzed through the busy D.C. metro traffic and headed toward Professor Flagel's address.

As they strode up the severely cracked sidewalk to the professor's brick bungalow, Evan took in the ivy smothering the house and the crumbling mortar between the bricks.

Kiley knocked on the black door in desperate need of a fresh coat of paint. A tall man with snow-white hair and mustache opened the door.

"Professor Flagel?" she asked.

"Yes." He narrowed his eyes behind thick wire-rimmed glasses.

"Special Agent Kiley Dawson, FBI." She held out her ID. "And this is Agent Evan Bowers with ICE."

"ICE?" Bushy brows rose above his glasses.

Odd. The professor only seemed to think ICE was unusual but didn't seem to consider an FBI agent on his doorstep unusual as well.

"We have some questions to ask you about one of your students. Could we come in?" Kiley sounded cheerful, though Evan knew she was upset with the professor for the way he'd treated Firuzeh.

"Yes, of course." He stepped back. "Come in."

They entered a small living room with traditional furniture, including a blue camelback sofa and matching armchair. Heavy mauve drapes hung over the large front window, leaving the room dark and oppressive. A hint of garlic lingered in the air, and he heard dishes clanking in the next room.

"Sit, please," Flagel said as he closed the door. "Can I get you something to drink?"

"Thank you, but no." Kiley perched on the edge of the sofa, and Evan sat next to her.

Flagel took a seat in a rigid-looking high-back chair. "Now, who is it you wish to talk about?"

"Firuzeh Abed," Kiley said.

The professor stiffened. "What about her?"

"It seems the two of you had a disagreement about a paper she'd written." Kiley rested her hands on her lap, and Evan saw her flex them as if relieving tension. "She believed her opinion on the topic shouldn't be taken into consideration for her grade. Only the quality of her work and research and the paper itself."

"And?"

"And she threatened to go above your head." A hint of irritation entered Kiley's voice. "That must've made you mad."

"Darn right it did!" Flagel planted his hands on the knees of his black dress slacks. "She had no reason to question my grading. No reason at all."

"Was she right?" Evan asked.

Flagel jerked back and eyed Evan. "I beg your pardon?"

"Was she right about you downgrading the paper because you didn't like her opinion on the topic?" Evan clarified.

Flagel rolled his eyes. "No, of course not. Her paper was filled with flaws. It was pedantic and amateurishly written."

"That's odd, isn't it?" Kiley asked. "When all her other professors praised her skills in crafting fine research papers."

He shrugged, but a trace of worry entered his eyes.

"Did Firuzeh report you to your superiors?" Kiley asked.

He shook his head. "She's a most difficult student, so I suspect she plans to."

"Plans to?" Kiley eyed him.

"There's still plenty of time in the semester for her to lodge a complaint."

Kiley looked at Evan, and he nodded his understanding. Either this guy still thought Firuzeh was alive or he was a very good actor.

"Firuzeh won't be reporting you," Kiley said.

Flagel blew out a breath and sagged in the chair. "Thank goodness."

"Because she was murdered on Saturday night," Kiley added.

"Murdered?" Flagel's eyes widened. "Oh my. How horrible."

Kiley kept watching him.

He squirmed in his chair. "Wait. You're here because you think *I* killed her? That's absurd. It was *just* a grade."

"She had firm standing to dispute it," Kiley said, "and your obvious prejudice could have cost you your job."

"I'm an open-minded man and would have come through any inquiry with flying colors." His wavering tone didn't bear out his statement.

"Where were you on Saturday night around eleven?" Evan asked.

"Here. With my wife." He cupped his hands around his mouth. "Willa! Come here!"

He tapped his foot until a petite woman with a

dark cap of short hair and wrinkles upon wrinkles entered the room. He reached out for her hand and nearly dragged her to his side. "Tell them where I was on Saturday night at eleven."

"Here. Reading. With me. Like we always do on Saturday nights." She glanced between Kiley and Evan. "Why?"

Flagel lifted his head higher, that haughty expression returning. "They're with the FBI and ICE, and they think I might have killed one of my students."

Her mouth fell open, and she shook her head. "You're way off here. Yancy can't even kill a spider, much less a person."

Kiley stared at the professor. "Since you claim not to be involved in Firuzeh's death, I'm sure you won't mind giving our team access to your email, phone, and financial information."

Flagel let go of his wife's hand and crossed his arms tightly over a sagging chest. "I don't understand why."

"Because"—Kiley locked gazes with the man, and he fidgeted—"you may not be able to commit murder, but that doesn't mean you didn't hire a killer to end Firuzeh's life."

CHAPTER 15

"You're not really liking Flagel for this, are you?" Evan asked after Kiley got the Escalade headed toward Waleed's headquarters.

She shook her head. "I might've had multiple motives for visiting him."

Evan looked at her. "How's that?"

"Firuzeh died before she could hold this guy accountable for his prejudice. So it's possible I wanted to make him squirm for being so mean to her as much as I was doing my job and following up on a lead."

He'd suspected as much. "You always did have a thing for standing up for the underdog."

"Yeah." She suddenly whipped the vehicle into a clothing store parking lot and opened her door. "Hold on. I'll be right back."

She ran for the front door and disappeared inside. Why on earth was she risking not getting to Waleed on time? With the threat hanging over their heads, he knew everything she did was motivated by the investigation, so it had to be important. He took the time to text his MIT friend again. This time he got an immediate promise to call Cam. Evan updated Cam just as Kiley came out of the store carrying a red-and-purple paisley scarf.

In the car, she ripped off the tags dangling from the material. "Thought I should cover my head when we meet with Waleed."

Evan stowed his phone. "Do you really think that guy cares if you respect his religious beliefs?"

"No, but he claims his messages are religious in nature, and there might be others there who *do* care. No point in inciting people if we don't have to." She wrapped the scarf around her head, adjusted it around her neck, and pointed the SUV out of the parking lot.

The vehicle hummed through the heavy traffic, and he watched out the window, leaning forward when The Righteous's red logo appeared on a whitewashed two-story box of a building with a red front door. The headquarters was located in a typical older retail neighborhood with various mom-and-pop stores in worn buildings.

Kiley backed into the first free parallel space down the street. She cut the engine and glanced at him. "I'll take lead on this interview, but since you know Waleed better, feel free to add any questions you have."

He nodded, thankful she was letting him play a vital role in their fieldwork when she hadn't wanted him to accompany her on this trip. He was impressed with her ability to put her personal feelings behind her and do her job.

She got out, and he kept his head on a swivel

as he followed her, looking each man in the eye as they passed to see if he recognized any ISIS operatives. At the door to a large meeting room, Evan spotted a sign-in sheet, and Kiley quickly took a picture of the names. They stopped in the back of the room by a literature table filled with IT recruiting materials.

"That's him at the podium, right?" Kiley whispered.

"Yeah." Evan shoved his hands in his pockets and took in Waleed's every detail.

Dressed in a pricey black suit with white shirt open at the neck, he had a broad nose, big eyes, and a thick head of gleaming black hair in a fashionably messy style. His beard was equally dark and close-cropped. He looked like he'd stepped off the cover of *GQ*, not like the stereotypical terrorist most people pictured.

The mere sight of the killer standing tall and haughty as he sweet-talked the audience of mostly young people—teens to early twenties, male and female—increased Evan's urge to pummel the guy. Waleed had the audacity to appear in public, to flaunt his group even when he was fully aware that law enforcement knew the place was a front for ISIS activities.

Though Kiley seemed less agitated than Evan, she still had a sour look on her face. She picked up each of the pamphlets and fliers on the table and glanced at them. A man with a full beard and lifeless gray eyes was seated behind the table and eyed her suspiciously. She simply nodded and pocketed the brochures. Of course, none of Waleed's literature would have any ties to terrorism, but Evan suspected there were hidden messages in the propaganda, which Waleed explained to individual audience members once they'd reached recruiting stage.

He wrapped up his speech to a standing ovation, and a female minion wearing traditional garb met him with a cup of pink punch from a refreshment table piled high with sweet confections. Waleed moved into the crowd to speak to his audience more personally. Evan snapped covert pictures and planned to run facial recognition to try to match the attendees to the names on the list.

When Waleed said good-bye to the final trio of people, he turned his attention to Kiley. He mocked surprise and ran a hand over his jaw. Evan knew the guy had seen them the minute they walked in and had been waiting for everyone to leave. Wouldn't do his image any good to engage in a public altercation with law enforcement.

He crossed over to them, his head at a cocky angle. He was nearly the same height as Evan and had a muscular build. His eyes were as black as his hair and likely his personality.

"Let me guess," he said, his English perfect with no hint of an accent. "Homeland Security."

"FBI." Kiley displayed her ID and introduced

herself, but Evan didn't bother to identify himself.

"I was hoping you might answer a few questions for me, Mr. Waleed." Kiley's tone was overly polite, and her consideration of this killer grated on Evan's nerves.

"Of course, Agent Dawson." He jerked his head at the man still sitting at the literature table, a single flick of his head telling the guy to leave.

Evan didn't know where the man was going and feared he planned to bring back reinforcements, so Evan moved to a location where he could keep his eye out for any threat to Kiley. No way he'd let anyone hurt her.

She must have perceived a threat too as her gaze sharpened and she rested her hand on her sidearm. "How well did you know Firuzeh Abed?"

Waleed tapped his chin. "That name doesn't sound familiar to me."

Kiley narrowed her gaze. "Let's not waste time claiming you don't know her when in an email you threatened to retaliate if she interfered with your recent demonstration."

He gritted his teeth for a second before a broad smile revealed perfectly aligned and pearly-white teeth. "Yes, of course. I remember now. She didn't share our visions, and I forbid her from joining our group."

"Just kept her out of the group? Nothing more?"

"That's correct. I assume if you read the email, you know there was nothing more."

"Not in emails, no, but you met with her the day before your demonstration."

He arched a brow. "Did I?"

"You're on her calendar."

Unease flickered in his eyes, but he quickly controlled it. "Perhaps she fantasized about us meeting. I don't recall such a thing."

"The coffee shop has video," Evan claimed, yet he had no idea if it did or not.

"I'm pretty sure you're bluffing." Waleed smirked. "I think I've been to the coffee shop she frequents, and I don't recall seeing any cameras."

"Right, you would never meet anywhere your dirty work could be confirmed," Evan ground out between his teeth. "With your IT background you know what to look for."

Waleed's smirk widened, and Evan instantly regretted losing his cool and playing into the lowlife's hands.

Kiley stepped closer to Waleed. "If you weren't at the coffee shop, where were you at lunchtime on Friday?"

"Right here, preparing for the protest. There are many people who would have seen me and can vouch for my whereabouts."

"Do you have an office here?" Evan asked.

Waleed tipped his head at the back wall where a door stood open.

"Mind if we glance inside?" Evan asked.

"I do mind." A deadly intensity darkened Waleed's expression.

Evan wasn't at all put off by the man's threatening behavior. "And where were you Saturday at eleven p.m.?"

"I'm not sure why that time's important, but several of us were cleaning up from the demonstration."

"And let me guess." Evan let sarcasm fill his tone. "The same people can vouch for you then."

"Why, yes, that's right." He blinked innocently.

"I'd like a list of those people and their phone numbers," Kiley said.

"Of course. I'll get it to you."

"Now," Evan growled.

"Now, now." Waleed held up his hands. "No need to get testy. I'll be happy to write them down. I left my phone in my office. Wait here."

He took a leisurely stroll toward the back of the room.

Evan had no plans to stay there. "Let's get a look at his office."

He gestured for Kiley to go ahead, as he wanted to make sure she was safe. On the way through the room, he snapped pictures of bulletin boards to later analyze for any leads. He also grabbed the drink cup Waleed had set down and pocketed it to have it run for DNA for comparison purposes.

By the time they got through the office door,

Waleed was seated behind his tidy desk, phone in hand. The room held a unique scent Evan couldn't place. Maybe it was musky cologne or mild incense. Computers hummed from a wall-to-wall credenza behind him, and a laptop sat in front of Waleed on his polished desk. He lifted his head and fired a heated look at Evan. Evan didn't care. He'd seen what he needed to see—an exterior door.

Evan marched across the space and jerked it open to reveal an alley. Waleed could easily use this exit to leave while others thought he was in the office. Not that it was even necessary to hide his subterfuge when the members of his group would readily lie for him. But maybe, just maybe knowing about the door would help them catch one of his people in a lie.

Evan closed the door and watched as Waleed planted his hands on the desk and slowly got to his feet. He held out a list of names and phone numbers.

Evan snatched up the paper and quickly reviewed the list. He should start for the door, but he couldn't seem to get his feet going. He didn't want to leave without getting more out of this jerk.

Kiley slapped her business card on the desk and held Waleed's gaze. "Don't stray too far without notifying me, Mr. Waleed. We'll be in touch."

She spun and exited, and Evan had no choice but to follow. He glared at Waleed on the way out. Kiley waited on the sidewalk out front, appearing calm and in control.

Evan looked at her. "How could you keep calling that creep Mr.?"

She untied the scarf and draped it around her neck. "Because it irritated him when he couldn't get a rise out of me."

"Unlike me, you mean. I played right into his sick desires."

"Yeah, you did, but I don't blame you. You've been wanting this guy brought in for a long time. Me, not so long, making it easier for me to keep my cool."

Evan appreciated her understanding, and her acceptance of his failure gave him a reason to calm down. Simply put, he'd do it for her. He took a few breaths and glanced up and down the street to figure out their next move.

"Looks like the convenience store across the street has a camera facing this way." He assumed Kiley would be with him in wanting to get ahold of the video and held out a hand. "After you."

At the store with windows filled with handmade signs touting everything from fresh vegetables to goat cheese, he confirmed the single camera mounted under the eaves was indeed pointed at Waleed's headquarters.

"Perfect," he said and pulled the door open for Kiley.

He might have just eaten, but the sweet smell

of fresh-baked bread wafting out of the small store sent his mouth watering. He glanced around at tables filled with fresh produce and a variety of breads. More traditional refrigerated items in coolers circled the space. Thankfully there were no customers, so they could speak freely with the burly and bald cashier. Silver hoop earrings dangled from both ears, reminding Evan of Mr. Clean, and the sleeves of his black T-shirt were rolled around tattooed biceps.

Kiley flashed her ID at him, not at all taken aback by the enormous and daunting-looking guy. "Manager in?"

He planted his meaty hands on the counter. "No manager. Just the owner, and he's gone for the night."

Evan stepped forward. "Does your outside camera catch any action across the street?"

"Yeah. We've had some vandalism problems with those foreigners, so the owner made sure it did." His disgusted tone rumbled through the space like a violent thunderstorm. "There's been other issues with them too."

"What kind of issues?" Kiley asked.

"Fights. Harassment." He crossed his arms, the muscles bulging. "Called the police a bunch of times."

Evan tapped a reminder into his phone to request those reports. "Do you know how long your manager keeps the video files?"

"No, but it's a long time. He says there's no way he'll miss catching them in the act."

Kiley smiled up at the man. "Mind calling him for us?"

He arched a brow. "They in trouble?"

"Something like that."

"Then, yeah, I'll call. You bet I'll call." He grabbed a handset from a charger and hit a button. A dialing sound emitted as he lifted the phone to his ear.

Evan stepped away and motioned for Kiley to join him. "While you wait for the manager, I'll take a look in the alley behind Waleed's office."

"What are you hoping to find?"

He shrugged. "I just know I have to look. I don't want to leave town without something actionable on Waleed."

Evan grabbed his phone in the dance studio lobby as Kiley checked out the locker room. He hadn't located anything in the alley, but he wasn't giving up on finding an actionable item before leaving town. Not yet anyway. He sent off the pictures from The Righteous meeting to Homeland Security's Counterterrorism Unit for review and identification.

He stowed his phone and tried not to look out of place as he waited. But he totally felt uncomfortable here. The music pulsing in the background reminded him of his awkward high school years. He'd never been a good dancer, so he'd avoided any situations that included dancing. Even when he wanted to ask a girl to a dance, he'd chickened out. He knew dance was good exercise, but he'd take jogging and weight training any day over this, thank you very much.

Kiley returned carrying a stack of vibrantly colored books, a wide smile on her face. "Firuzeh's journals. Looks like we hit pay dirt."

"At least one of our interviews will produce some results tonight," he said, thinking about Waleed.

She shifted the journals in her arms. "I'll need to get these in evidence bags, then I want to talk to Alicia."

"Let me help."

"Bags are in my pack." She offered her back to him.

He took a moment to appreciate her slender neck below her hair that was twisted up with the usual pencil. He fought hard not to lean forward and plant a kiss on the soft curve. He'd always wondered what it would be like to kiss her, a question that still plagued him.

She looked over her shoulder at him. "Is there a problem?"

Yeah, a big one. I still have feelings for you, and you won't give me the time of day.

He shook his head and located a large bag. The plastic crinkled in his hand as he opened it and stepped around her. She slipped the journals inside and shrugged out of her pack to settle the bag inside.

"Anything else in the locker?" he asked.

"Dance clothes and deodorant." She slung the straps of her backpack over her shoulder and looked at her watch. "C'mon, already. We have so much to do, and they pick tonight to run long."

The music stopped as if on cue.

"Finally." Kiley pushed through couples exiting the studio, their faces glistening with perspiration.

A woman wearing a flowing skirt and fitted top was putting away equipment in a nearby storage cabinet, her delicate hand braced on the door. Her hair was piled in curls on top of her head, and her nametag read *Alicia Inglesby*.

She smiled, taking emphasis away from her long chin. "Can I help you?"

Kiley flashed her ID and introduced them, her tone hurried and to the point. "We're interested in finding out when Firuzeh Abed took classes here."

"Firuzeh?" Alicia's pleasant smile morphed into concern. "Is she okay?"

Kiley frowned. "I'm sorry to say she's been murdered."

Alicia gasped and clamped her hand over her mouth. She stared at Kiley before lowering her hand. "Murdered?"

Kiley nodded. "And we're investigating."

"You're not here because . . . you don't think someone in her classes killed her, do you? Because if they did . . . well, I'm the owner here . . . and I—" she dropped onto a nearby chair— "my gosh, this is horrible."

Kiley stepped closer to Alicia. "We don't think this has anything to do with the studio. We're just gathering background on Firuzeh's schedule."

Alicia nodded. "Okay, well . . . she actually taught a class here Wednesday and Friday nights. Old Persian dances."

Taught? Evan shared a surprised look with Kiley, then shifted his focus back to the instructor. "How long has she been teaching here?"

"Hmm . . . three months. Maybe a bit longer."

"When was the last time you saw her?" Kiley asked, that urgency to find a lead pulsing through her tone.

"On Friday night at seven for her class."

"And did everything seem okay with her?" Evan asked.

"Yes. She was cheerful as usual. The only thing she ever worried about was her parents discovering she was dancing. They didn't approve."

Evan hoped they never had to find out. What would be the point of their being disappointed now? "Did she ever bring a friend or boyfriend here?"

"No. She was very professional in her approach to teaching and took it seriously." Alicia bent down to unbuckle shiny black shoes.

"I need a list of students enrolled in her classes," Kiley said.

"Sure, but, well . . ." She slipped off her shoe and looked up. "You won't contact them, will you? I mean, I'm barely making ends meet here, and I couldn't afford a scandal."

"We'll have to talk to them, but we'll make sure they know Firuzeh's death had nothing to do with your school."

"Thank you." Alicia attacked the other buckle, jerking it hard. "Seriously, thank you. If you follow me, I'll print out a roster."

She pushed off the shoe, leaving the pair lying on the floor, and ran from the room, her bare feet thumping on the wood flooring, the pitch deepening when she hit the hallway tile. Her office was filled with racks stuffed to overflowing with a rainbow of costumes, and stacks of papers covered her desk. She sat behind her computer, and Kiley tapped her foot as if she wanted to move the woman faster.

The printer soon whirred to life, and Alicia handed the page to Kiley. Evan got a quick look at fifteen names, all female. Hopefully Firuzeh confided something in one of the women, and they would shed more light on her last days.

"Can you think of anyone who might want to

harm Firuzeh?" Kiley asked as she folded the list and shoved it in her back pocket.

"No . . . definitely not. She's been coming here for years, taking classes before she started teaching. She never fell out with anyone. Or even had an argument. She was just a genuinely nice, happy person." Tears glistened in Alicia's eyes. "I'm going to miss her."

Kiley looked like she might be tearing up as she handed over her business card. "Call me if you think of anything."

They left Alicia behind and stepped into the cool night. Kiley stood staring ahead. The bright city lights against the dark sky, reflecting off the Potomac, made a striking landscape. He could easily imagine being on a date with her in the moonlit night, but he doubted she was even seeing the sparkle. He knew she was thinking about finding that breaking lead.

"What's next?" he asked.

She jumped.

"Sorry, didn't mean to startle you."

"I want to review Firuzeh's journals." She dug out the keys to the Escalade. "They'll need to be processed for prints and DNA first. Let me call someone to meet us at the office so we don't waste any time." She hurried to the vehicle and climbed behind the wheel.

Evan slid in and held up Waleed's cup. "Can they run DNA on this too?"

"Yes. And good thinking on taking it, by the way." She made a call and held an enthusiastic conversation with a forensic tech before starting the SUV. "Once they finish processing the journals, you can copy them while I run an ALPR search on Waleed's vehicles."

Evan knew all about Automated License Plate Readers—cameras mounted on police cars and sometimes fixed locations to record license plates as vehicles passed. Once recorded, ALPR footage was run against a database known as a hot list containing information on potentially stolen cars or ones linked to criminal offenses or terrorist acts. Hopefully they could use the database to track Waleed's movements the night of Firuzeh's murder.

"Does D.C. have many plate readers?" he asked.

She maneuvered the vehicle out of the parking space. "A pretty good network. On police cars, like many cities, and on fixed poles too. I read once that the local cameras record up to eighteen hundred plates per minute, catching cars driving up to a hundred miles per hour."

He let out a low whistle. "Impressive number."

"Impressive, yes, but in our case only helpful if it captured one of Waleed's vehicles near the mall."

Her phone rang, and she accepted the call. "Agent Dawson."

"Quinn here." The agent's deep voice thundered through the car's speaker.

"Agent Bowers is with me, and you're on speaker," Kiley told him.

"Our suspects were caught on video outside a gas station. Facial recognition ID'd them as Bilal and Gadi Amari. I'll email the video to you."

Kiley shot Evan a questioning look and whispered, "Know them?"

Evan shook his head.

"I'm not familiar with these men," she said.

"They're from Virginia Beach. Were radicalized by ISIS about a year ago when one of their uncles was killed in Iraq. He was taken out by U.S.-trained forces, though our military had no actual role in the death. Still, they blame us and want to make us pay."

"A powerful motive for retaliating," Kiley said. "Do you have their prints or DNA?"

"No. They moved to Iraq six months ago and weren't on our radar until recently. They've been spouting terrorist propaganda as the foreign arm of a radical faction called The Righteous."

Evan shot Kiley a surprised look. "Nasim Waleed's group."

"That's right," Quinn said. "I take it you're familiar with him."

"We just talked to him," Evan said.

Quinn went quiet for a long moment. "Not about the bombing or these suspects, I hope."

"No," Kiley said, giving Evan a pointed look that told him to keep their conversation with Waleed to himself. "But sounds like we need to go back to see him again."

"Look," Quinn snapped, "you're cleared to be read in on this incident, and I've been told to give you everything you need. Came down from the director himself. So you have pull. I get that, and I can't stop you from questioning Waleed concerning the bombing. But one word of this to him, and you could be sabotaging my investigation, and two bombers could walk free."

Kiley glanced at Evan, a question in her eyes. He wanted to honor Quinn's request, but more than that, he wanted to nail Waleed to the wall. "You have any proof Waleed was involved in the bombing?"

"Not yet," Quinn replied.

Evan looked at Kiley and shook his head.

"We'll discuss it," Kiley said, apparently not caring for Evan's response, "and give you a heads-up if we plan to talk to Waleed again."

"See that you do."

The call ended, and the screen went black.

Kiley glanced back at Evan. "You don't think we should talk to Waleed?"

He firmed his shoulders for an argument. "Not yet. Not when there's no evidence of his connection to these men. Like Quinn said, talking to Waleed now might spook him. Let your super team find the evidence we need and *then* we go back and nail him."

He waited for the argument, but instead she simply nodded and told CarPlay to text the team. "Find everything you can on Bilal and Gadi Amari. Homegrown terrorists affiliated with ISIS and members of The Righteous. Suspected of Pittsburgh bombing. And maybe . . . just maybe our pair of terrorists."

CHAPTER 16

Kiley strode down the hall of her office building, heading toward her cubicle. They'd dropped off the journals and Waleed's drink cup with a forensic tech, and he promised to call the minute he finished printing and lifting DNA from the journals so Evan could copy them and begin reviewing them.

She sank into her ergonomic desk chair that she often thought resembled a spider. She'd been gone less than two days, but it felt much longer. Could be because she was awake for most of the time. Or it could be because of the pressure of the investigation and the threat of an unbelievably large number of people dying. It made each minute seem more precious than gold, and as she spent them, the weight grew heavier and heavier.

Evan stood at her cubicle entrance, staring at her. "You okay?"

"Fine." She sidestepped his concern as it would do no good to talk about her feelings. Hoping he would sit down and quit looking at her, she pointed at the side chair.

He remained standing and let his gaze rove over the area. "So this is where the hotshot RED team works."

"You don't sound overly impressed."

"Well?" He shrugged.

"Not real fancy, is it?" With the red carpet treatment they received, he probably thought they occupied a very plush office, when in fact the space was extremely ordinary. "You'd be impressed if you saw all our toys, though."

He grinned, his wide smile cutting right to her heart. She clasped the spider arms of her chair to keep from doing something dumb like taking his hand and holding it.

Feeling too closed in with him, she shot to her feet. "I'm gonna grab a cup of coffee. Want one?"

"That would be great," he said while giving her a knowing look.

Fine, he figured out she was still attracted to him. So what?

She marched to the break room and brewed two cups of coffee, added cream to his, and returned to hand him the mug, making sure not to touch his fingers or look into those bottomless walnut brown eyes.

He took a seat in the chair by her desk and propped his leg on his knee. She could feel him watching her over the coffee mug as she settled into her chair. Maybe he was thinking about the fact that she remembered he liked cream in his coffee. She ignored him, booted up her desktop computer, and sipped the rich coffee as the hard drive churned to come alive. Her phone rang, and seeing Mack's name, she put him on speaker.

"Evan's with me," she said by way of answer.

"Then you'll both get to hear my report on today's interview with Barzani."

Eager to hear what he had to say, she sat forward. "How'd it go?"

"Slippery fella," Mack said. "But we finally got him to admit the client who booked the container was American."

"American?" Evan asked. "Seriously?"

"That's what he said, and it was when Sean tripped him up on a question that it came out, so we think it's legit."

Kiley liked knowing this information, but it wasn't enough to take action. "I hope you either got his records or a warrant for them."

"Warrant." Mack sounded offended that she even asked. "Sean and I already served it, and we're reviewing the files now."

Evan leaned closer, his attention rapt. "And?"

"Here's the thing. Barzani's business is set up with electronic records only, and his top clients are listed in his files by code numbers, not names. He knows who each code belongs to but claims he doesn't have them written down anywhere, and he won't produce the client information."

"Tell me you got him to give it to you," Kiley snapped, regretting letting the pressure get to her the minute the words came out so harshly.

"Gonna take a judge to compel him to reveal it."

"Sorry I bit your head off," she said. "I know you're doing your best."

"Yeah we are," Mack stated, and she could easily envision him fixing a tight stare on her. "And Eisenhower's working on getting the judge to rule on it. Problem is, Barzani's got a slick lawyer, and it'll likely take time."

"Time is one thing we don't have," Kiley said, making sure not to sound panicked in front of Mack and Evan even if that was how she felt.

"Exactly," Mack said.

"Waleed's American," Evan said. "You think this might tie back to him?"

"It's a good possibility," Mack replied. "But right now that's only speculation."

Kiley wanted to slam her fist on the desk. She needed something to go their way. Desperately needed something—anything. The clock was ticking down and they'd made little to no progress. "What about the ship manifest? Did that tell us anything?"

"A couple of things actually, but the only relevant item is that the container took on fresh cargo at a Cape Town port."

Evan clutched the edge of the desk, his fingers turning white with the pressure. "What cargo?"

"It's not something that was officially recorded, but we obtained all port footage, and this video caught a grainy picture of two guys loading two crates. We've thoroughly reviewed all the documentation and video. Found nothing else, but Eisenhower's got our foreign contacts looking for the dockworkers."

"There weren't any crates in the container," Evan stated.

"Maybe they off-loaded them at another port," Kiley said.

"Possibly." Mack paused for a long moment. "We have no footage showing that or, like I said, anything else."

Kiley sighed. "Have you located any information on the Amari brothers?"

"Nothing actionable as yet. Cam's working on it, so if anything exists he'll find it. They weren't even on the watch list." Disgust deepened Mack's tone.

Evan shook his head. "If these are our guys, they've been on their own for days and could be anywhere doing anything."

"One thing's for sure," Kiley said. "If they're meeting up with Waleed, Agent Quinn will have people waiting."

"Let's hope so," Mack said. "By the way, Cam wanted me to tell you he finished checking with cab and rideshare companies for the port area. No one picked up our suspects, so they either had a private ride or hoofed it."

Kiley had to admit to being disappointed again. She'd hoped this would turn into a strong lead. "Thanks, Mack. Keep me updated. Any time of day."

"Yeah, sure. And hey, we're gonna find these guys."

"I know," she said, and she believed it. She really did. She just wasn't sure they'd find them in time.

Her stomach now burned with acid, and she shoved the coffee mug aside before she added to the problem. Evan sat back, his eyes narrowed as he stared at his mug. She didn't have time to waste brooding, so she opened DMV records and searched for vehicles registered to Waleed. A Toyota Land Cruiser came up first, the very vehicle Evan had photographed in the alley. Next up was a Honda Accord, then a BMW M6 convertible.

"Waleed has three vehicles." She swiveled the monitor to face Evan.

He squinted at the screen. "Some pricey ones there."

She nodded. "I'll get the ALPR search going."

Her team had long ago gotten access to the local ALPR database and other D.C. police data, so she opened the program and entered all three of Waleed's plate numbers. She watched the search run, her brain spinning almost as fast as the circular icon on her screen. They investigated so many leads in a very short period of time, and yet they didn't have anything actionable.

Please let this be one that is.

Her computer dinged, returning a long list of

records. She sorted by date and ran her finger down the screen. "Nothing for the night of Firuzeh's murder."

"Maybe he scouted out the location in advance," Evan said. "Can you sort by address?"

She nodded and made the change. She scrolled down the page. "Nothing near the mall at all going back a month."

"What about trying his brother's vehicles?"

"Good idea." She started at the beginning and ran the report for Ibrahim. "Nothing for that night."

"I guess we shouldn't be surprised," Evan said. "Nasim is smart enough to rent or borrow a vehicle."

She nodded. "So I'll do a location search and have local agents check out every car near the mall that night."

Evan's eyebrows rose, but he didn't say anything. He didn't have to. She knew the report would be long, and it was unlikely even with the additional staff working the investigation that they had enough manpower to check out a large number of vehicles before 9/11 rolled around. But that didn't mean she wouldn't try. She generated the report and emailed it to Eisenhower, who, to her surprise, wasn't still in the office.

"Kiley, good." Agent Harrison's cheerful voice came from behind. "I was just going to text you."

Kiley faced the younger woman, whose pantsuit was rumpled. "What's up?"

She held out a plastic evidence bag containing a legal-sized envelope. "Someone mailed this letter at the Abeds' mailbox place with Box 342 as the return address. We ran it for prints and DNA. No match on the prints. DNA is processing. Text is nonsensical. I'm wondering if it's code."

Interesting. Kiley put on latex gloves from a drawer and held out her hand.

Harrison handed over the envelope holding bold scrawling penmanship addressed to B. Amari at a post-office box in central D.C.

The Pittsburgh bomber?

She showed the envelope to Evan. He perked up. She gave him a warning look to keep silent, as Harrison didn't have clearance to be read in on the bombing.

Kiley's heart was racing over the potential lead. Still, she forced a casual tone into her voice to keep from raising Harrison's interest. "Any progress in finding the account holder for that box?"

The rookie shook her head. "We exhausted all possibilities. Figure he used the poet's name so it couldn't lead anywhere."

Kiley took a photo of the envelope and carefully withdrew the letter. Seemingly thrown-together sentences filled paragraph after paragraph.

She laid the page on her desk to take a picture, then looked up at Harrison. "Could be written by someone with dementia, or as you suggested, it could contain code." She slid the letter back in the envelope and handed it back. "Let's get this to CRRU for examination. Make sure they have a sense of urgency about it."

"CRRU?" Evan asked.

"Cryptanalysis and Racketeering Records Unit," Harrison answered before Kiley could.

"Keep monitoring the mailbox, and let me know the second DNA comes in." Kiley started to look away but remembered her plans to give Harrison more responsibility and turned back. "I also need someone to check out the Capitol Café for security cameras. It's in Tysons. Can you do that?"

"Glad to."

"If they *do* have cameras, we'll want footage from Friday around noon until about three."

Harrison glanced at her watch. "They're probably closed, but I'll be on their doorstep the minute they open in the morning."

Kiley shared the information they'd learned on Firuzeh's dance class. "I also need you to start interviewing the women in Firuzeh's class. See if she confided anything. A boyfriend. Or had an argument with anyone. Had a falling-out. Things like that. I'll email a copy of the names before I go."

Harrison nodded. "Are you staying in D.C. now or heading back to Tacoma?"

"Catching the first flight west around six."

"Have a good trip, and I'll let you know what I find on the café and the interviews." Harrison departed, a buoyancy in her steps.

Evan rubbed tired eyes. "Is she always that eager?"

"Rookie excitement," Kiley said, trying to absorb some of the energy for the tasks ahead.

Evan leaned back in his chair. "What did you think about the 'B. Amari' on the envelope?"

"Could be our guy. Let's take a look at that video from Quinn." She located the email and started the convenience-store footage running, pausing on a clear shot of both men.

Evan leaned closer. "These guys are definitely the right build, but honestly, so are millions of other men."

Kiley agreed but desperately wanted a lead. She memorized the men's faces and grabbed a few still shots to send to her phone for future reference. "I'll have Eisenhower assign an agent to track down the D.C. box this letter was addressed to."

"Why not have Harrison do it?"

"I respect her work so far, but it's too important of a task for a rookie." Kiley fired off a text to her boss and looked at Evan again. "With Amari's name on the envelope, I'm hoping the letter really is code and CRRU can crack it quickly."

"Yeah, hopefully."

She texted the photos of the envelope and letter to Cam, asking him to be watchful for the information in his searches. Her phone rang in her hand. "It's Sean."

"I just got a call from Vivian Vaughn," Sean said without a hello or greeting.

"Hold on." Kiley stood to look over her cubicle walls to make sure no one was within hearing distance. The team never discussed the Montgomery Three investigation in the office, and she wouldn't risk anyone overhearing her conversation with Sean about the mother whose house the Montgomery teens disappeared from. "What did she want?"

"I updated her on the latest lead falling apart, and she's spinning out of control. You have a way with her, and I thought you might be able to talk her down."

Kiley pictured Vivian slumped at her worn kitchen table, her usual mug of coffee sitting in front of her, along with a cigarette burning in an ashtray, her face contorted with pain and guilt. Endless days of wondering. Worrying. Crying.

Kiley's heart broke for the distraught mother, yet she wanted to give Vivian time to cool down or she would just blow Kiley off as she'd done with Sean. "I'll give her a call in the morning."

"Not from the office," Sean warned.

Kiley didn't take offense at his warning. Being reminded not to compromise their covert investigation would never be the wrong thing in her mind. "Of course not."

"Let me know if there's more I can do."

"You mean other than find her daughter?" Kiley sighed.

"Yeah, other than that."

Evan watched the electric blue front door of the police station until it swung open and Kiley exited, her steps seeming a bit lighter as she rushed from the brick building and across the rain-slick street. She climbed behind the Escalade's steering wheel, bringing in a wave of humid air with her and tossing her backpack onto the back seat. Fatigue clung to her, and he felt her tiredness across the seat.

The investigation couldn't stop, but they needed to get some sleep. Just a few hours. While they grabbed that much-needed rest, they could take comfort in the fact that many people would still be working the investigation. He just had to convince Kiley of that.

He buckled his seat belt and decided to ease into the topic. "Journals successfully delivered?"

"Lancaster was still working." She cranked and gunned the engine, the roar splitting the quiet night. "And he was actually pretty civil when I expected him to still be mad about my not turning the other evidence in on time."

Evan faced her. "Did he have any updates on the murder investigation?"

She pulled out of the parallel space and onto

the deserted street. "He finished tracking down the questions on Firuzeh's credit card and found nothing unusual. And he reviewed her social media. Nothing there either. Oh, and he got the CCTV files for the mall."

"Let me guess. Nothing." Evan hated sounding so negative, but since seeing the train blown to bits, he felt the horror that awaited them if they failed and wondered if they would ever catch a break.

"Exactly." She stopped at a red light with high-rise buildings dotting the landscape, the lights reflecting off the damp city streets. "But that's not surprising if we really *are* looking for a trained sniper."

Evan was glad his negative mood didn't bring her down, as that was the last thing he wanted to do.

"So where to now?" he asked, easing into his subject.

She looked at her watch. "Our flight's in less than four hours, and I'm beat. Figured we'd head over to my place to grab some sleep."

And here he thought he would have to convince her of the need. "I don't want to impose. Maybe you should drop me at a hotel."

She looked over her shoulder and changed lanes. "With the price of D.C. hotels, that would be a big waste of resources for a few hours when I have a perfectly comfy couch I'm willing to share. Besides, we'll just waste time looking for one. Time we could be sleeping."

"Okay," he replied and didn't mind at all that he was about to see her apartment.

Something he probably shouldn't be glad about, but he'd totally enjoyed spending time with her. Professional or personal, he liked being with her. But that would be short-lived. Come 9/11 or before, she would walk out of his life. He might not have any hope of a future with her, but he really did want to secure her forgiveness before they parted ways again.

Question was, what was it going take for her to forgive him? He knew forgiveness wasn't even possible until he explained what had happened with Olin. "Now would be a good time to talk about Olin."

She fired a sharp look at him, her eyes narrowed.

He didn't let her reaction deter him. "We have time to kill. Talking would be easy."

"Yeah, *if* I wanted to talk." Her fingers tightened on the wheel.

He hated making her tense, yet he needed to let her know how he felt. "Please hear me out. Talk if you want. Or don't. Either way, I need to say my piece."

Her focus remained on the road ahead, her fingers opening and closing tightly. "I'm listening."

He opened his mouth to start, then suddenly thought better of having this discussion in a moving vehicle. He didn't want to be looking at her profile when he bared his soul. He wanted to be facing her, reading her expressions. He obviously hadn't chosen the time or place wisely.

Didn't matter. He'd started the discussion and now needed to finish it.

"Well?" she prompted.

"You said I didn't do my due diligence on the op," he stated plainly and with no emotion, although the anguish of Olin's loss was churning in his gut. "That I was too hungover."

"Yeah. So?"

"I wasn't hungover. The others went out the night before. Not me. I was up all night doing the due diligence you claimed I blew off."

She glanced at him, her gaze digging deep—measuring, weighing. He felt the immensity of her search, but he wouldn't stop now.

"I thought I was prepared for the op, Kiley. Fully prepared. Had everything planned down to the second." He took a long breath before going on. "But Sapin had a weapons charge as a juvie, and I didn't consider his juvie records. He didn't have any reference to weapons as an adult, so I thought it was all in the past. But it wasn't, and I should've factored the prior charge into my plan. If I had . . ."

He couldn't say the words as that old familiar

guilt gnawed at his gut, and he wanted to end this conversation, but he would get it out in the open no matter what she thought of him going forward. "Couple that with lack of experience when the shooting started, and I didn't react as quickly as I could have. I've played the shooting over and over in my mind. Hundreds, maybe thousands of times. I could've reacted faster. Just a second would've made the difference, and I could've yanked Olin out of the way *before* he took the hit."

She shot him another fiery look. "So, you finally admit you're responsible. You knew Sapin had a past with guns, and you played down the risk. Made Sapin out to be nonviolent, and he opens up with an AK-57 before we get a word out."

He took her criticism but didn't buckle under it. "I relied too much on our current-day threat assessments. Dry runs. Kevlar. Our own assault rifles. We were ready. Just not for him to jerk open the door and start firing."

"Wait, are you saying you don't feel any responsibility for what happened?" Barely controlled anger filled her tone.

"I didn't say that—would never say that." He curled his hands into fists on his legs and stared out the window. "I take full responsibility, and not a day goes by when I don't think about what happened to Olin and blame myself for it." His voice broke, so he stopped speaking. He hated that talking about the op could still make him nearly lose control when he only wanted to project a strong façade.

She didn't respond when he desperately wanted her to say something. He glanced at her and found her honestly appraising him. She turned away, her lips clamped tightly closed.

"Okay," he said, ready to end the discussion as he'd said his piece, and she didn't seem inclined to discuss it any further. Now everything was up to her. "I wanted you to know I didn't shirk my responsibility, but I made a mistake, a big one, and I take full responsibility for my actions. I won't bring it up again or try to defend myself. Please know I'm sorry. Very sorry."

She nodded. Once. Quick, like she still didn't completely believe him but figured if she responded affirmatively, the discussion would end. And it did.

He sat back, gazing out the window, watching the city lights speed by. They didn't speak again until they stepped into her apartment. And even then, he took in the space before saying anything, as he figured the décor would tell him a lot about the woman he hadn't seen in years.

A blue velvet sofa with more pillows than he could imagine in lively patterns caught his attention first. A glossy yellow coat of paint covered the coffee and side tables, and blue glass lamps with white shades sat on top. She'd mounted framed landscape photos on pale-yellow walls, and the adjoining kitchen island held a laptop along with various chargers, the cords tangled like a bowl of spaghetti.

He noticed a Leatherman on the coffee table. His imagination fired and not in a good way. Was the multipurpose tool hers or had a guy left it there? He hadn't even thought to ask her if she was dating. She was an amazing woman. Beautiful. Smart. Kind. Good sense of humor. A real catch. Why wouldn't she be dating?

He looked around more carefully this time, searching for any indication of a guy regularly hanging out here. What he thought he might find he didn't know, but he saw nothing.

She dropped her backpack on the floor and straightened a throw at the end of the sofa. "Want something to drink?"

More than anything he wanted to wash off this day and pray. Maybe forget how she reacted to the conversation in the SUV. "Actually I have a favor to ask."

She arched a brow as she stepped to the refrigerator and grabbed a bottle of water. He looked at the contents, seeing only yogurt and bottled water.

She took a long drink of the water. "What do you need?"

"Can I take a shower? I feel like I need to clean the bomb scene off me."

Her mouth dropped open for a moment. "Oh . . . yeah, sure. I . . . I guess."

His request was too much for their professional relationship. "If it's a problem, I understand, but we have a full day tomorrow and—"

"Of course. Let me get some towels and soap for the guest bathroom." She rushed away, and he hated that he'd put her on the spot for the second time in less than an hour. If she hadn't scurried out of the room, he would have taken back his request.

Antsy, he wandered the wide-open space, still wondering if she had a significant other. The simple thought of her in a relationship put a sharp pain in his heart.

She returned carrying a stack of lemon-yellow towels and wearing a tight smile on her face. "Sorry if I sounded a little freaked-out there. Your request just seems personal, and I'm really trying to keep things all business with you."

His regret intensified. "I blew that for you, didn't I? First on the ride over here, and now asking to shower."

She looked at him and held his gaze. "I'm glad you shared your side of things with Olin."

Her reply shocked him, and he stood there like a fool, staring at her until his mind cleared.

"Does it change anything for you?" he asked and hated that he felt the need to do so when he'd promised not to bring it up again.

She nibbled on her lip, and her eyes locked on his again. And there it was. What he'd hoped to see. Longed to see. Interest for him burning in her expression. He was suddenly very aware of being in her apartment with her. In her personal space. Close enough to touch her. Alone.

She broke eye contact and drew in a deep breath. "I really need to think about it."

Her breathing was ragged, and his heart began racing. He could hardly think straight.

She shoved the towels into his hands. "Bathroom's first door on the right."

He didn't want to leave the room. He wanted to kiss her. Nothing more. Just kiss her. He wouldn't, not when she was reluctant even to think about anything personal with him. He grabbed his duffel. "Thank you for letting me use your shower."

She nodded. "I'll get some bedding for the couch while you do."

"Thanks," he said, and the atmosphere grew even more awkward.

"We need to leave for the airport at four. See you then." She nearly bolted from the room.

He stood frozen in place. Watching. He'd hoped explaining about the day Olin died would clear things up between them. It had the opposite effect. Made things more uncomfortable, and he honestly doubted it would ever be easy between them again.

CHAPTER 17

Ready to leave for the airport, Kiley stopped at the end of her apartment hallway and looked into her living room. She loved the bright colors, but with the stress of the investigation weighing heavy on her, she longed for something more soothing. And seeing Evan sitting on her sofa, the bedding neatly folded, didn't help with finding that relaxed feeling.

He was concentrating on his phone and didn't notice her standing there. She should turn away. Should, but she didn't. Instead, she took in his freshly shaven face, his solid jaw, and a body built by hours spent in the gym.

The sizzling look that had passed between them last night came rushing back. Though he'd made it perfectly clear he was interested in more than her forgiveness, she didn't get it. How could a good-looking guy like Evan with such an amazing personality be interested in her, a socially awkward computer nerd?

She had no answer, and yet the same warm pull she'd felt last night was drawing her toward him this morning. She was clearly attracted to him. Maybe more than attracted. And now, if she stopped to think about their conversation about Olin, she might be able to remove that obstacle.

Not that it mattered. She still wouldn't follow these sincere and, if she was being honest, wonderful feelings. Years of her mother's constant warnings about not putting herself in a place to lose a loved one wouldn't disappear because of a warm feeling. Here she was over thirty years old and was still letting her mother control her life, even when her mother wasn't part of Kiley's world anymore.

But the fear was very real. Visceral even. Especially fear for Evan, who worked a very dangerous job. And if by some miracle she could get past all of these complications—maybe head to Arizona to confront her mom—Kiley didn't really possess the necessary social skills to keep a relationship going.

Professional. That was what she needed to be with Evan. And only needed to be. She let out all her feelings on an exhaled breath and stepped into the room. "Ready to go?"

Evan ran his gaze over her from head to toe, and she flushed. She'd put on her usual tactical pants and T-shirt, then added a button-down shirt to cover her holster. Nothing special, and definitely something few women would wear to impress a guy.

"Morning," he said, his voice husky and low as his eyes connected with hers in a heartfelt, intimate way. His look washed over her like a warming balm.

Oh, man, she had to let this go. She had an investigation to run. Millions of people counting on her. Lives at stake. A threat to annihilate. She took another cleansing breath and focused her thoughts to make sure she sounded businesslike. "Good morning."

He stood, looking tough in his green tactical pants and tan tactical polo stretched taut across his chest. She caught a whiff of his minty scent and had to force herself to ignore the tantalizing smell.

He smiled. "Thanks again for letting me crash here last night."

She nodded, and when she was about to ask if he got any sleep, she clamped her mouth closed and grabbed her keys on the way out the door.

"Any updates from your team?" he asked in the elevator.

"The results came back on Firuzeh's notepad. She'd written Waleed's name but nothing else."

"You think he's involved in the plot?"

She shrugged. "She might have noted his name because she planned to meet with him."

"Yeah, could be as simple as that."

"Also, our analysts finished reviewing the other port videos. No additional sightings of the men."

He shook his head. "I was hoping we'd get a look at their faces. Maybe see what they hauled out in their backpacks."

"Yeah, me too."

He parked a shoulder against the wall and crossed his ankles. "I heard back from HSI's Counterterrorism Unit on the pictures I took at The Righteous meeting. None of the people were on the watch list or under surveillance."

She had to fight to keep her mind on his words and not his mouth, the mouth he might have used to kiss her with if she hadn't run off like a scared little girl last night. "Not surprising as it was a recruitment meeting."

"Exactly, but at least we have the list of names in case we need to cross-reference it."

"Speaking of lists, our analysts finished their review of the watch list and provided a culled list of terrorists who've been active on the West Coast. Eisenhower's team forwarded it to the field offices and asked them to get eyes on these suspects and report any unusual activity."

"Let's hope they find something actionable."

They rode the rest of the way down in silence, tension clinging, and climbed into the Escalade. She didn't know what else to talk about, so she kept her mouth closed as she navigated the early-morning traffic.

A few miles down the road she caught sight of a large SUV on their tail. She kept her focus on the vehicle as it made all the same turns she did. "I think someone might be following us."

Evan shifted, casting a subversive look over his shoulder. "Make a few left turns to be sure."

She slowed and took the first turn. The SUV fell back but followed. Another turn and another, same results.

Evan gritted his teeth. "We've got a tail all right, but who?"

"Someone on Waleed's team maybe?" She glanced in the mirror and noted the plate number.

"Pull up ahead and I'll check them out." Evan lifted his sidearm and rested his free hand on the door handle.

She stopped at the light and gave him a pointed look. "Be careful."

He nodded and jumped out, gun raised, to charge toward the other vehicle. Heart racing from the sudden adrenaline, she leaned out her window and snapped pictures of the driver.

He gunned the engine, the gruff growl a warning.

Evan kept marching forward, weapon still raised.

Fear for his life choked Kiley. She grabbed her sidearm and jumped out to back him up.

The SUV lurched into gear, the powerful engine roaring. He raced past her, the wind from his vehicle blowing her back. He careened through a red light and swerved wildly, narrowly missing a passing car that squealed to a stop.

Kiley ran for the Escalade to tear after him but left her shaking hand resting on the gearshift. They couldn't miss their flight. Besides, they had the plate number and pictures. She would track the SUV later.

She quickly texted the photos to Cam with a request for him to locate CCTV footage for the area in hopes of running facial recognition on the driver. He replied right away, confirming he would look into the vehicle registration.

Evan slipped back into the Escalade, his chest rising and falling, his eyes alive from what she could only assume was adrenaline, similar to the rush coursing through her body.

She shifted into drive, not surprised to see her fingers trembling. "I sent Cam pictures of the vehicle to follow up on."

Evan nodded. "I wonder if they were tailing us last night too."

"Could be. I was honestly too tired to notice. Or if it *is* one of Waleed's goons, he assigned him in the night."

"Not sure who else it could be," Evan said as he sat back, a contemplative look on his face.

"If so, it means we made Waleed nervous. A good thing. Means it's more likely he could make a mistake. Once we confirm the owner of the vehicle, I'll contact Quinn so he knows Waleed might be spooked."

At the airport, she parked in the long-term lot and quickly opened the hatch to get her belongings. A harsh wind blew through the concrete space, and she shivered in the cool morning temperatures.

"Let me text Harrison our location so she can pick up the vehicle." She didn't need to share her every action but still felt jittery from being tailed, and it just came out.

"Seriously, I could use some minion agents working for me." Evan chuckled as he grabbed their bags.

She sent the text and got an immediate reply. "She'll pick up the car."

"She works as much as you do," Evan said.

Kiley couldn't tell if his tone held judgment or not. She was probably looking for hidden meanings when they didn't exist. She grabbed her backpack and took off toward the terminal, not saying another word all the way to the gate, concentrating on slowing her breathing to release the residual adrenaline.

They were assigned seats nowhere near each other, and Kiley saw Evan take out copies of Firuzeh's journals. The minute she could use her phone, she plugged in earbuds to tune out the excited kid in the seat next to her and calm her frayed nerves. She'd been tailed before, but never when the stakes in an investigation were this high. She half wondered if she'd done the right thing by leaving town. Maybe she should've gone after the driver and made him talk.

An image popped into her head of grilling him under some hot light in a dark warehouse and made her snort, drawing the attention of the man across the aisle. She shrugged and opened Firuzeh's first journal. Willing her mind to focus, Kiley read the first few pages. The entries were personal. Very personal. Firuzeh had written about struggling to be a woman in her very traditional family. To honor her parents' beliefs yet live her own life. She often commented about wanting to move out from under their roof, but she couldn't do so until completing her degree.

Kiley's emotions were mixed. Invading Firuzeh's privacy brought discomfort, yet Kiley's heart broke for Firuzeh too. She'd been living for something that would never happen now. Her life cut short when she was on the brink of realizing her potential. Kiley could tell from Firuzeh's writings that she would have left the world better off for having been in it. She'd already made a difference by warning Kiley about the threat.

Could Kiley take a lesson from this? Think about what she was living for and if she was on the right path?

Am I, Father?

Lost in thought, she startled when Evan stopped next to her and bent close. He jabbed a finger at the journal copy. "Did you see she wrote about her meeting with Waleed?"

She nodded. "She really hated him."

The woman next to her looked at them, curiosity with a hint of unease in her expression.

Evan smiled and straightened. "Catch you later."

Kiley didn't like that the woman's interest had chased Evan off. She didn't want to admit it, but she was getting used to being with him and sharing whatever came to mind. Despite their recent tension, it would've been nice to review the journals together and discuss Firuzeh's writings. But other than dancing, it was appearing as if Firuzeh lived as simple of a life as her family claimed.

Kiley kept busy for the rest of the flight reading the remaining journals and assessing Firuzeh's phone logs. She turned up nothing. They were soon in Evan's Tahoe heading out of SeaTac and toward Tacoma under gray skies and dark clouds threatening heavy rain.

Her phone chimed. "Text from Cam. Vehicle tailing us was a rental. He's working on getting the CCTV footage for the area and a warrant for the records."

"With little probable cause, the warrant's a long shot at best."

"We could still get facial recognition on the driver." Her phone signaled a new email message. "The analyst looking into the significance of the lion sent her report. Malouf was telling the truth. The Golden Lion represents the Lion of Babylon in the Iraqi Coat of Arms until 1959 when Nuri as-Said was overthrown. She also says Malouf's father has ties to the Muslim Brotherhood."

Evan shot her a look. "They're not a terrorist group, though, right?"

"Not most factions," she said and looked at the details again before she misquoted the facts. "But he belonged to the Iraqi branch—the Iraqi Islamic Party—formed in 1960. It was banned a year later, and they were forced to go underground. Then after Saddam Hussein's government fell, the Islamic Party reemerged as a big advocate of the Sunni community. They've been sharply critical of the U.S.-led occupation of Iraq, and the imams encourage anti-infidel jihad."

"And Malouf's father was part of that?" Evan worked the muscles in his jaw.

"Intelligence reports show him as a financial supporter, funneling money to charities with ties to the group. Malouf has continued the support."

"Then we need to get a warrant for his financial information."

"I'll email this information to Eisenhower. He can run it up the chain of command, so we don't step on any ongoing counterterrorism efforts."

Evan shook his head. "This investigation is getting bigger and bigger."

She had to work hard not to punch her fist into the dashboard. "And yet we're not getting any closer to finding our terrorists or their target."

"We do have the bombing suspects' names now, and hopefully your team will have located intel on them. If not . . ." His voice fell off.

She thought to ask him to finish his comment, but then what was the point?

They had less than three days to stop the attack, and Kiley knew the consequences of failing to do so. She knew it all too well. Especially after seeing the devastation left by the Pittsburgh bomb.

It was what nightmares were made of.

Kiley almost sighed in relief when she walked into the Tacoma FBI conference room and saw her teammates looking up at her. She had a huge puzzle to solve in very little time, and the three talented men sitting at the table were the key to stopping the horrific threat. And she couldn't forget Evan. He'd become a valuable member of the team as well, and she'd started to count on him in more ways than she liked to think about.

"Welcome back," Sean called out. "You look awful."

"Hey, thanks." She wrinkled her nose. "Just what a girl needs to hear."

"You're not a girl," Mack joked. "You're one of the guys, and you know it."

Surprise flashed on Evan's face, and she almost hugged him for noticing she wasn't indeed one of the guys, but she had zero time to dwell on how she looked or for joking around. She needed to update her team and get a status report.

She quickly filled them in on their trip and noted the Amari brothers' names on the whiteboard.

"You're going to freak when you see this." Cam tapped a few keys on his laptop and turned the screen to face her.

She saw Firuzeh's name at the top of a Facebook profile with a picture of a group of young people standing outside Firuzeh's college. A smiling guy had his arm slung around Firuzeh's shoulders. Kiley leaned closer to get a better look at his face.

Her mouth fell open, and she shot Cam a look.

"What is it?" Evan asked.

"Firuzeh's looking awfully chummy in a picture with Bilal Amari," Cam said.

Evan charged over to them and bent over the screen. "When was this taken?"

"A little over a year ago," Cam said.

"Before he was radicalized." Kiley stood back, trying to wrap her head around this new development. "It would make sense that they were friends from before he'd joined ISIS, but did the friendship continue after he turned?"

"Nothing to suggest it did or didn't," Cam added.

"It can't be a coincidence that she mentioned a box number connected to a letter with his name on it." Evan leaned back. "She could've gotten her information from him."

"Why would he tell her?" Mack sounded skeptical. "He's clearly still involved in terroristic acts."

Cam pulled his laptop back in front of him. "Maybe he has family who could die if the upcoming plot is carried out. He's conflicted. He wants it to happen, but wants to stop it too."

"It would make more sense to warn his family, wouldn't it?" Evan took a seat. "So they could get out of the hazard area."

Kiley met Cam's gaze. "Find out if his family still lives in Virginia Beach and see if there's been any movement. I'll follow up with Quinn to see if Waleed is hunkered down or if he's on the move with his family and brother."

Cam nodded but pointed his chin at her.

She recognized that look. He was questioning her. "What?"

"I don't think the Amaris are our container suspects," he said, then held up a hand before she could comment. "Sure, they no longer live here, but they weren't on the watch list. As U.S. citizens they wouldn't draw any attention returning to the country and wouldn't need to be smuggled in."

"They could've done so to be cautious," Mack suggested.

"Maybe Cam is right," Kiley said. "The Amaris are new to the terrorist world. Would you trust a big event to rookies?"

Evan shifted to look her in the eyes. "If they had the skills I needed, I'd consider it. Think about Harrison. Sometimes rookies are overly zealous and use the enthusiasm to accomplish more. And they're further down the food chain so, if needed, they're easily expendable."

Sean leaned forward. "From Pittsburgh we know they like bombs, but it looks like they screwed up on the target, so they might not be proficient yet. Still in training, so to speak."

Kiley turned to Cam. "Do either of these guys show up on the list you're compiling on terrorist preferences?"

Cam clicked a few keys on his laptop and shook his head.

"Did you turn up anything else useful on them?" she asked.

"Gathered all kinds of personal info, but they're really too new on the terrorist scene to have a record."

"Did Firuzeh know both of the Amaris?" Kiley asked.

"I found nothing to indicate she knew Ibrahim."

Kiley's questions were racing wildly through her head, and she didn't know which one to ask first. She took a breath to organize her thoughts. The image of their tail to the airport pinged to the surface. "What about an association with Waleed? Can we connect the container to him?"

"Barzani did say an American consigned the shipment," Mack said.

They were missing something here, yet Kiley couldn't pinpoint it. "Do you have any more of a feel for Barzani's affiliation with a terrorist organization?"

Mack shook his head. "I got the feeling he's apolitical and would broker a shipment for anyone if he could make a buck on it."

"And then we have Malouf whose only terrorist affiliation we can find is with the Muslim Brotherhood," Cam said. "But does he use his shipping company to help other organizations?"

Kiley wrote *Malouf, Barzani, Waleed,* and *Amari* on the whiteboard and underlined each name with a harsh slash of her marker. "We need to find the connections between these players or with Firuzeh. Sean, can you head that up?"

He nodded.

"Okay, good." She gave him a smile of thanks. "I've been thinking Firuzeh is the key here, and this picture makes me lean more in that direction. You can get the list of groups she belongs to from Cam."

"Sending it now," Cam said, his fingers flying over the keyboard.

"After that, Cam, see if you can locate a list of group members and cross-reference them to the women in Firuzeh's dance classes." She pulled out her notes from the plane and slid the pad across to him. "I've made a list of dates and times of all group meetings from her journals. I thought you could also do some digging on that, see if the dates coincide with any terrorist actions."

He set the pad by his computer. "Sure thing."

She turned back to the board and tapped the prior action item regarding chemical plants when her phone chimed a text. She glanced at it. "It's Harrison. Capitol Café doesn't have video footage, but the bank across the street does. Firuzeh and Nasim Waleed are seen arriving and departing about the same time."

Evan shot up in his seat, his eyes lighting up. "So they *did* meet."

"Not that we'll go back to interrogate Waleed again, but this gives us proof of their meeting in case we or Quinn need it." She tapped the word *chemical* on the whiteboard. "Where do we stand on your research, Mack?"

"I've finished the target list and cross-referenced the plants by size of city and the potential exposure numbers. But I have to say, unless we're dealing with a chemical that might blow downwind or pollute a stream, these guys would be hard-pressed to expose millions of people without a large network of operatives."

"Anything stand out as a particular risk?" Evan asked.

"A few places. I've highlighted them in my report. After the bombing I started working on tracking hazardous chemical shipments, but it's nearly impossible to get an accurate real-time report."

"If our suspects are planning several events instead of a large one, they might be counting on that," Evan said. "Could I get a copy of the list for my records too?"

"I'll email it now." Mack turned to his computer.

"I finished with my list of dams," Sean said. "I'll email it to everyone."

She kept her focus on Sean. "Did the dock-worker and security guard interviews turn anything up?"

He shook his head. "Unfortunately, none of them noted anything suspicious. Also, I got word on the flight manifests from SeaTac. Nothing stands out there either. I've asked them to take another look for the Amaris and let you know if their names appear on the list or their images on any video footage. I'll let you know if I hear anything on that."

"And the video-game chat is being monitored." Mack shook his head. "There can't be an analyst left in D.C. we're not using."

"Eisenhower must be looking at a massive budget overrun, but money isn't important here," she said. "You can't put a price on keeping millions of people safe."

Her comment brought the conversation to a halt as they all looked at each other for a long moment, the severity of their enormous task feeling as if it sucked all air from the room.

Evan broke eye contact and shifted his focus to Cam. "Did my guy at MIT get back to you?"

Cam nodded. "He's pulling together a list of potential accounts we should be monitoring. Said he'd get back to me today."

A knock sounded on the door, and ASAC Stadler poked his head in. "Lunch is in the break room."

Kiley looked at her watch, feeling off-kilter due to the three-hour time change from D.C. "Okay. Good work, everyone. Grab some lunch, then hit the assignments hard. We'll hold another meeting later today."

As her teammates filed out, she texted Quinn asking for a written report on the Amaris, to see if the Waleeds were on the move, and to tell him about their tail to the airport. She expected Evan to leave with the guys. Instead he opened his laptop.

"You should eat too," she said. "No telling when you'll get another chance."

"There's something I want to follow up on first."

She watched him for a moment. He really was a different man than she remembered. Back in the day, he was an easygoing life-of-the-party kind of guy, the first one to suggest social gatherings. Which was why she'd accused him of being hungover and not doing his due diligence in the op where Olin died.

But this guy sitting here, his face buried in his laptop? He was more somber. Not at all the person who jumped at going to lunch with the others and taking the time to get to know them better. She had to admit she was gaining respect for his dedication to the job. It was almost like he was driven by some unknown force to find these terrorists in much the same way she felt driven by Firuzeh's death.

Maybe his intense focus was because of Kiley—he didn't feel comfortable with her around—and she should try to put him at ease more often.

No. She wasn't here to bring back his playful smile that had tripped her heart any number of times since she'd known him. She was here to find terrorists. Only that. And to do it before the days raced by to 9/11.

Evan knew Kiley was watching him, wondering what he was doing, but he wouldn't share unless he succeeded on his hunch. He'd tried to get information on the container suspects' movements from his CIs but to no avail. However, he hadn't tried the local police. While Cam had struck out with them, Evan had contacts at the department, so maybe he could get somewhere.

He grabbed his phone and called a Tacoma Police lieutenant he'd worked with on past investigations.

"Lieutenant Neighbors," he answered.

"Evan Bowers."

"Hey, Bowers." He actually sounded glad to hear from Evan. "You working whatever's going down at the port?"

"I am."

"And let me guess. You need my help?"

Evan ignored the suspicion in the man's tone. "We have two suspects who left the port on foot around eleven p.m. last Thursday. We know they didn't catch a cab or rideshare, but we're not sure if they hoofed it or were picked up by associates. Can you check your calls to see if your officers encountered them?"

"Hold on." The sound of his fingers clicking over a keyboard came over the phone.

Evan resisted tapping his foot as he waited, but he felt this burning need to move. To take some physical action. To force a lead that they could act on. Despite time racing past, they only had a ton of questions and no answers.

"Hey, yeah," Neighbors finally said. "I might have something here. Officer Pilcher talked to two guys on East 11th Street around that time. They were on foot."

Evan jumped up and charged toward the local map on the wall. He ran his finger over the roads until he located 11th Street, a logical direction for their suspects to travel. "Tell me more."

"Not much to tell. Two males wearing jeans, hoodies, and Mariners caps were stopped, but they seemed legit, so Pilcher let them move on."

The description fit the container suspects, though it could also fit an unlimited number of men. "I'll need to see Pilcher's body-cam footage and interview him."

"Not my sector, so I don't have the clearance to show the video to you or even to bring Pilcher in for an interview."

Evan slammed his fist into the wall, making Kiley jump. He took a breath and let it out. "I need you to get me access to Pilcher and his body-cam, or I'll have to go the warrant route."

"You call me for help and then threaten a warrant?" Neighbors' voice rose. "Unbelievable."

Evan felt bad for pushing the guy, but he wouldn't back down. "This is a matter of national security, and I'll threaten even more to get the information I need if I have to."

"Okay, take it easy before you blow a gasket. I get it. I'll go see my captain."

Evan let out a silent breath. "Thanks. I owe you."

"Yeah, you do, and you know I'll collect."

Evan disconnected and turned to find Kiley watching him.

"You got something?" she asked.

"Maybe." Evan shared about his call.

"These could be our suspects." Kiley came to her feet. "We need to question this officer right away and get a look at that body-cam footage."

"My contact is already working on getting that."

"Make this meeting happen, and I'll let you come with me to interview the officer." A slow smile spread across her face.

Evan nodded, and if he didn't hear back from Neighbors within the hour, Evan would follow up. He would also do just about anything to make Kiley's dazzling smile land on him again. But more important, he desperately wanted to catch these terrorists.

CHAPTER 18

The contemporary building housing the Tacoma Police Central Substation was smaller than Kiley expected, but all that mattered was that Evan secured an appointment with the sector-one commander. She could give them access to Officer Pilcher, and Kiley was overjoyed at finally acting on a lead and hopefully moving the investigation forward.

Lieutenant Gail Singer met them at the door to her neat office painted a cheerful yellow. Her blond hair was cut short, and the department's navy-blue uniform fit her tall and slender body perfectly. She gestured at the chairs by her desk as she circled around behind it.

Evan took a spot leaning against the wall and grabbed his phone for those copious notes he liked to take.

Kiley wished she could look so relaxed, but the pressure to succeed still pressed down on her, and she was too amped to sit. She planted her hands on the chair back instead. "I'd like to get right to our reason for being here."

"Pilcher." Singer flattened her palms on the desktop. "I've got him on standby in the conference room."

Kiley was glad to see the lieutenant had the

same sense of urgency about this interview. "I'd like to see the body-cam footage before meeting with him."

Singer dropped into her chair and started typing on her keyboard. She squinted at the monitor, her forehead furrowed. "That's odd."

Kiley didn't like that look. "What's wrong?"

Singer raised her head, her expression puzzled. "The footage isn't here."

"Not there." Kiley charged around the desk and scanned the screen.

"The video for the call before he encountered the men you're interested in is right here." Singer tapped the screen, then ran her finger down to the next file. "And this is the call after. So you can see he uploaded his footage, but the one you want must have been deleted. I don't know how that could happen."

"Several possibilities," Kiley said, and she didn't like any of them. "Body-cams have vulnerabilities that allow a hacker to access footage directly from the camera. They can download it or make changes and re-upload it, and we wouldn't know about their changes. They could also delete footage. Or your server could have been hacked and the file deleted that way."

Singer frowned. "You'd have to have some strong hacking skills to do any of that, right?"

Kiley nodded but didn't explain that if their

suspects were connected to Waleed, they would very likely have those abilities.

Evan pushed off the wall, his focus razor-sharp now. "Could be simpler. Someone in-house could've deleted it, or even Pilcher could've done so."

Singer shook her head. "If Pilcher uploaded that particular file to the server, there's no way he had access to it. And he would be put under review if he deleted it."

Kiley didn't want to waste precious time speculating. She wanted to act. "Give my team access to your network files, and we'll tell you where the modification came from. Depending on when the file was uploaded and when your department runs backups, we might be able to produce the video from a backup."

Singer pursed her lips. "I'll need to get approval for that."

"Then do it. Now. And we'll interview Pilcher." Not giving Singer time to ponder her options, Kiley stepped to the door. "Where will we find him?"

"Last door on the left," she said, sounding dejected. Either her spirit of cooperation was sagging, or she was worried about the deleted file.

Kiley left the office and hurried down the hallway, which reeked of burnt popcorn.

Evan caught up to her. "What's your take on the deleted file? Inside or outside job?"

"I'm leaning toward our suspects doing it. I can't see anyone in-house with a reason to delete the file. And as Singer suggested, Pilcher would be in big trouble if he did."

"Your team can really find out who did it?" he asked.

"We can track all changes to server files. Doesn't mean we'll be able to trace it to the source's location, though. If someone had the skills to hack the server, they'd also know how to bounce their connection through enough hubs that we might never find the end."

Evan shook his head. "Gotta love the internet, but man, it's made law-enforcement work so much harder."

She nodded and took out her phone. "I'll want Sean to take charge of tracking this hack. Give me a second to give him a heads-up that I might need him so we don't waste any valuable time."

Sean answered, and she made her request as succinctly as she could so she could get to questioning Pilcher. When she disconnected, she glanced at Evan. "Ready?"

He nodded and pushed the door open, then stepped back, giving her first access.

Pilcher jumped to his feet. The trim young guy with close-cut auburn hair and dressed in his uniform held out his hand. "Officer Dan Pilcher."

She took his firm grip, and while she would normally smile to relax an interview subject, she had little time to waste and wanted to impress a sense of urgency in him. She made introductions and gestured for him to sit back down.

She sat and crossed her legs, working hard not to swing her foot to release mounting tension. "Tell us what happened with the two suspects you talked with on Thursday night."

Pilcher took a small notepad from his vest pocket and rested it on his knee but didn't look at it. "I was on patrol around eleven-thirty—usually pretty dead at that time of night—when I see these two guys hurrying down the sidewalk. They had their heads down, and when I rolled up on them, they stepped into the shadows close to a building like they were trying to hide."

"And so you stopped," Evan said, dropping into a chair.

Pilcher shook his head. "I didn't have a reason to. Just a gut feeling that something was off. So I circled the block and found them at the bank ATM."

Kiley made a mental note to request the video footage and banking information from the machine.

"One of the guys points at my car, and they hurry off. So now I *do* stop them." He ran a hand over his military haircut. "They kept looking down, so I made them both take off their caps and hoods and look at me. I wanted to take a long look at them and get their faces on my body-cam."

Footage that they might or might not recover, and at this point, Kiley couldn't count on it. "Did you get a good enough look for a sketch?"

"Yeah, but my cam captured them, so that shouldn't be needed."

"You're sure about the footage?" she clarified.

His eyes narrowed. "Not positive, I suppose. I mean I didn't review the file, but it was definitely recording. I uploaded everything to the server at the end of my shift."

"Tell us more about the stop."

"Yes, ma'am," he said.

Kiley had to swallow a snort. No matter how old she got, she would never be a *ma'am*.

"One of them spoke pretty good English," Pilcher went on. "The other's was broken. A hint of Arabic, I think. I asked them what they were doing out so late at the bank. The older guy said they were waiting for their ride home from visiting friends in the area."

"Did you ask for the friends' address?"

He nodded. "They rattled off an address for an apartment complex in the area."

Kiley wanted to race out to visit the apartment but forced herself to remain seated. "Write down the address for me, please."

Pilcher scribbled on his notepad, ripped off the paper, and handed it to her. "Still, I asked for ID, and they forked over Washington State driver's licenses. I made sure to get a good shot of both

IDs with my body-cam. You can get the details there."

Kiley was now frantic to see the footage and prayed a backup existed with an intact file. "Did you run them through DMV?"

He shook his head. "Had no reason to do that."

"Do you remember the names?"

"Sorry," Pilcher said. "Once I determined they had a debit card for said bank, I didn't think much about them again."

"How were they dressed?"

"Typical attire for their age. Jeans. T-shirts. Sneakers and Mariners ball caps. And they each had a huge backpack, totally full. Can't tell you how much I wanted to get a look inside them, but I had no cause."

"Anything else you can tell us about them?" Evan asked.

"Both had dark hair. But then, with their names, you'd expect that."

"About the names," Evan said. "Did they seem comfortable saying them when you asked?"

"You mean like did they hesitate or look away because the IDs were bogus?" Pilcher's eyebrow went up. "Nah, they looked me square in the eye. Combative more than anything. And pushy. Like they had a right to be there. Which they did, so I backed off."

"Anything else you think we should know?" Kiley asked.

"Like I said, they were kind of combative. If I had to detain them, I would've called in backup first. You might want to be prepared for that."

Kiley had heard enough. "Do you have a card with your cell on it?"

He pulled one out of his pocket. Kiley took it and handed him one of her own. "In case anything else comes to mind."

He got to his feet. "I'm assuming since the Feds are interested in these guys, they have something to do with the big investigation at the port."

"Something like that." Kiley gave him a smile to preempt any additional questions and bolted for the hallway. She typed the address Pilcher provided in a text to Cam and added *Need name for apartment occupants.* She hit send and led the way back to Singer's office.

"Permission granted." The lieutenant waved them in and held out a piece of paper. "Our IT director's details. He'll be your contact."

Kiley shoved the paper in her pocket and shook hands with the lieutenant. "Thank you."

She nodded. "I hope you get your guys."

As Kiley stepped into the hall again, her phone rumbled against her leg. She looked at the message from Cam. *Apartment rented by a Zahra Yasdi. DL picture attached.*

Kiley looked at the woman's photo, excitement burning in her gut. She fired off a reply, *Need background check,* and at the last second added that she needed ATM video footage and account details for the bank, along with CCTV video for the area so they could track the movements of the suspects.

She turned to Evan. "You'll want to make a pit stop before we leave."

He nodded. "Will do."

"You're not going to ask why?"

"Nah, figured we'd be headed over to the apartment Pilcher mentioned to stake it out. Am I wrong?"

"No, you're absolutely right." She smiled at his uncanny way of knowing what she was thinking. "But hurry up. I want to get eyes on the woman our terrorists claim to have visited, and I want to do it, like, yesterday."

Eager to talk to this woman, Evan sped toward the apartment while Kiley communicated with Sean. He'd rushed over to the IT department and was updating Kiley on the information being uncovered. Of course, Evan didn't understand anything they were saying. Something about obfuscation techniques and blocked IP addresses. All of it geek-speak to him.

He parked his Tahoe down the street from Zahra Yasdi's apartment and grabbed his binoculars to glass the building and confirm they had eyes on the right apartment.

Kiley ended her call. "The police server was

hacked from the outside. Sean's deep in the files. Now we wait."

Evan nodded. "I'd like a copy of Yasdi's DL for my files."

"Of course. Mind sharing those binoculars?" she asked, even though it was more of a command.

He had to admit he found her ongoing bossiness attractive, which was weird because he was attracted to her when she was shy and insecure too. But that didn't mean he'd give in. "In a minute. Making sure we can have a clear view of the apartment from here."

"I knew I should've driven," she grumbled.

And he liked that too. Reminded him how determined she was to do a good job, and when she wanted something, no one could stop her. He'd once thought she'd wanted him, but then Olin died before Evan could find out.

She reached out and snagged the binoculars. The touch of her hand was a shock to his system, and he let the binos go so fast they almost fell to the floor. She grabbed them at the last minute and lifted them to her eyes.

"Kiley," he said.

She lowered the binoculars and glanced at him.

"I know I said I wouldn't mention Olin again, but I wondered if you've had a chance to think about our conversation."

She looked at him for a long tension-filled

moment before raising the binoculars again. "I'm too focused on this lead right now."

Nice one, Bowers. They'd been communicating pretty well today, and now he'd blown it. Even had a moment between them last night, and then he'd had to bring up the past. But what good did communicating or even sharing a moment do when underneath it all, the issue of how Olin died remained?

None in his mind.

He kept trying to think of what to say but couldn't come up with a thing.

She handed the binoculars back to him. "Would be great if Sean comes through with the body-cam footage before Yasdi comes home. That way we could show her pictures of the guys Pilcher stopped."

Evan looked at her. "What do you think the odds are of that happening?"

"Honestly, not good." She rubbed her eyes and rolled her head. "I have to think if the hacker was smart enough to delete the body-cam video, he was smart enough to find and delete a backup. It all depends on where the department backs up their files and if those servers are accessible through the same vulnerability the hacker exploited."

Her phone dinged. "It's from Philips. The sketches from the DNA." She tapped on the screen. "Wow, look at this. These are great." She held out her phone. "Know these guys?"

He studied the men's faces. Both had dark skin, ebony hair, and full beards. The typical features for ISIS suspects, yet he'd never seen them before. "Definitely not the Amaris."

"Yeah, they don't look at all like them."

Her phone dinged again.

"Sean?" Evan asked hopefully.

"Yasdi's background info from Cam." Kiley tapped her screen. "She's a U.S. citizen. Born here to Iranian immigrant parents. Thirty-five. Never married. No children. No criminal history. Not overtly a member of any extremist groups. Works as a social worker for the state."

Evan glanced at Kiley. "Doesn't sound like the kind of person who would host known ISIS terrorists, especially being of Iranian descent. But then I've run across people in the past who on the surface seem like the boy or girl next door, but a little digging proved they were radical terrorists."

"True. I'll have Cam dive deeper." She texted Cam, set her phone on the dash, and leaned her head back. "You mind watching the building? I'm getting a headache and need to rest my eyes."

"Go ahead. I've got it." In all honesty, Evan would rather be watching Kiley than staring at an apartment building hoping Yasdi came straight home from work today. As a social worker, she should be getting off work anytime, and the social services building was about a thirty-minute commute. Problem was, he never met a social worker who kept office hours. Most of them worked late into the night and on weekends. Especially the dedicated ones.

Kiley moved, and Evan glanced at her. She was rubbing her temples. Her headache was likely tension-driven. Or due to a lack of food, as they had skipped lunch again. He could massage her temples for her. Maybe her shoulders. And then what? Declare his feelings for her? Yeah, that would go over well.

Her phone dinged, and she shot up in her seat to grab it from the console. "No way! Sean retrieved the video."

"Yes!"

"Ready to watch it?" Her voice was nearly breathless with excitement.

"Are you kidding? Of course I am."

She fired off a text thanking Sean, then leaned across the console and held out her phone. Evan was wildly aware of her presence but worked hard to ignore it and focus.

"Okay, here we go." She hit play, and exactly like Pilcher said, he'd rolled up to the curb and told the two men to stop. Their faces were downcast.

"Caps off. Heads up," Pilcher demanded, his directive not optional, and the men removed their caps.

"Zoom in," Evan said. He could barely contain

his excitement over seeing their suspects' faces for the first time.

Kiley did so, revealing the men's faces. They were dark-skinned with slicked-back black hair and dark eyes. Both men were clean-shaven.

"They look like any Arab American might look," Kiley said. "Likely so they won't draw attention."

"Agreed." Evan glanced up at the apartment building. He was glad to see the video, but they couldn't lose sight of Yasdi coming home.

"IDs," Pilcher demanded on the video.

"Here we go," Kiley said. "We'll finally have names."

Evan looked back in time to see Kiley pause on a driver's license of the oldest guy. "Does this guy look like one of the phenotype sketches to you?"

Evan took a good look. "Totally."

"And the age matches one of the ages Philips provided from the DNA." She flashed Evan a big smile and zoomed in further. "Guy's name is Kahram Darzi. Ever heard of him?"

"No." Evan memorized the man's face so that if he saw him, he would be able to detain him. Long chin. Hook nose. Mole by his right eye.

Kiley moved to the next ID. "Ehsan Rostami."

"Never heard of him either." Evan took in the photo. This guy was good-looking. Big eyes. Long lashes. High cheekbones. Wide jaw. "Matches the other sketch."

"So these are the guys from the container. We finally have their names." Her smile widened as she looked back at the phone. "They have the same address."

Evan had noticed the same thing. "We know they're not living in the U.S., so the address is likely bogus."

"Or set up in case someone like Pilcher needed to confirm their IDs." Kiley started the video playing again, and they watched until Pilcher walked away.

"I'm going to run their licenses." Kiley reversed the video and got out her laptop to start typing. "DMV records look legit."

She grabbed her phone and tapped the screen. "Cam, good. I'm assuming Sean sent you Pilcher's body-cam footage. I need all the information you can gather on the two men he stopped. And I want Mack or Sean to get eyes on their apartment ASAP and keep them there." She pursed her lips as she listened. "If these guys are spotted, make sure I hear about it right away."

Evan quickly checked on Yasdi's apartment again but saw no sign of her.

Kiley ended her call and went back to her computer. "I'll take a screenshot of the licenses and crop the picture so I can show them to Yasdi without the identifying details." She worked for the next few minutes and then glanced up. "Any sign of her?"

"No. You put someone on the suspects' apartment. Do you really think we'll find them there?"

"Sounds like you don't."

"Honestly, I don't. Not after Pilcher checked their IDs. I would expect them to be too paranoid about the stop blowing their cover."

"You could be right," she said, not sounding as if she liked it. "We'll wait to talk to Yasdi, then head back to the office to plan a raid on their apartment."

As Evan nodded, Olin's face flashed in his mind. He touched the ugly scar that reminded him of his failure. Vivid images of the scene outside Sapin's house popped into his brain. Sapin barreling out the door, the automatic rifle in hand. Firing as he rushed them. Olin taking a bullet. Dropping. Blood pouring from his chest. His face paling. Dying.

Evan looked at Kiley, and his gut tightened.

If these men are in the apartment, don't let history repeat itself. Please.

CHAPTER 19

Kiley shot up in her seat and zoomed in on the woman's face as she slid a key in the lock for apartment 2B. Kiley glanced at her phone to compare this woman to Yasdi's DL picture.

"Looks like that's her." Kiley handed the binoculars to Evan.

Evan quickly focused on her, then lowered the binoculars. "Right. Let's go see what she has to say."

Kiley stepped out, and the cool wind blowing off Puget Sound washed over her body as the sun started its descent toward the horizon. She shivered and wrapped her arms around her midsection.

They waited for traffic to clear before rushing across the street. By the time they reached the second-floor landing, Yasdi had entered her apartment. Kiley approached the door and knocked loudly.

Yasdi opened the door a crack, leaving a chain lock in place. Curiosity mixed with caution in her gaze as she peered out the opening. "Can I help you?"

"Ms. Yasdi?" Kiley asked.

"Yes." Wariness coated the single word, which spoke to years of distrust.

Kiley held up her ID and identified herself and Evan, acting relaxed to try to put the woman at ease.

"ICE?" She lifted her hand to her chest and clutched her blouse. "I don't understand. I'm a U.S. citizen."

"Yes, ma'am, we know." Evan gave her a potent smile Kiley thought would disarm any woman.

At least it would do so for Kiley, but that could be because she had feelings for him. "We're here about another matter. May we come in and talk for a moment?"

Yasdi bit her lip and looked over her shoulder. "I . . . now's not a good time."

"It's a perfect time for us," Evan said, pressing on the door.

She held firm.

"Is there something you don't want us to see, Ms. Yasdi?" Kiley asked, getting a bad feeling from the woman.

"My place. It's a mess . . ."

Kiley forced a smile. "We're okay with that."

She looked over her shoulder again and, after a deep breath, pushed the door closed to release the chain. She stepped back, and Kiley brushed past the thin woman before she changed her mind. She was a few inches shorter than Kiley, and her black slacks and long blouse in vibrant purple spoke to a vivacious personality. A beige contemporary hijab covered her head and neck.

Her clothing looked high quality and expensive. Not the sort of woman Kiley imagined down in the trenches as an ISIS fighter.

As Kiley moved deeper into the apartment, she took a quick look at the furnishings—serviceable items, nothing fancy but in good condition. A beige sofa. Two gleaming glass end tables. A kitchen abutted the family room with a small dining area. All neat and tidy.

Kiley assessed Yasdi. They hadn't even gotten into the place and the woman had lied to them.

She gestured at the round dining table. "Please have a seat."

Kiley stepped to a padded gray chair and sat while Evan leaned his shoulder against the nearby wall and got out his phone. She was glad he was hovering over Yasdi, as she was taking furtive looks at the hallway, and Kiley believed she might be hiding something. Or someone.

Yasdi settled on the edge of her chair and folded her hands on the polished glass table, a slight tremor giving away her nervousness. "What is this about?"

Kiley shifted her chair so she had a clear view of Yasdi and the hall. "In the course of our investigation, we learned two men visited you here on Thursday night."

She shook her head hard, her expression baffled. "I did not have any men in my apartment that evening."

"You might know them by the names of Ehsan Rostami and Kahram Darzi."

"No!" Her head swung even wider. "I don't know them."

"Are you sure?" Evan asked. "Think carefully. They would have been here about eleven that night."

She looked around her apartment. "I was not here then. I was with my friend at . . . um, a meeting."

"What kind of meeting?" Kiley asked as Evan tapped on his phone.

"Just a meeting. You know. A meeting." She twisted her hands together. "It started at eight and ended around ten. Then we grabbed some dinner."

"We?"

"Um . . . well, a friend."

"Will your friend verify this?" Kiley asked.

Yasdi clasped her hands tighter and stared at them. "I . . . he—"

A noise sounded down the hallway. Yasdi jumped up, and Evan's hand shot to his sidearm.

"Is there someone here with you?" Kiley kept an eye on Yasdi and her hand on her weapon.

"Um . . ." She bit her lip. "Yes. My friend."

"The one you went to the meeting with?" Kiley asked.

Yasdi nodded, that nervous glint back in her eyes.

"What's his name?"

She didn't answer but bit her lip again.

"Please answer my question, Ms. Yasdi," Kiley said.

"Arash. Arash Sidiqi."

Kiley stood and walked to the opening to the hallway. "Arash. This is FBI Special Agent Kiley Dawson. Come out with your hands where I can see them."

She pulled out her gun and stepped back.

"Oh . . . but . . ." Yasdi rushed Kiley.

Evan intercepted her. "Stand back, Ms. Yasdi."

"No! No!" she shouted. "He's not a criminal."

A slight man Kiley placed in his early thirties stepped into the room, his hands held out in front of him. His eyes were terrified, his hands shaking. "I am Arash."

Kiley met his gaze and held it. "My partner will search you for a weapon. Do you understand, Mr. Sidiqi?"

He gave a swift nod. "You are no different from the police of Iran."

"Iran?" Kiley asked. She gestured toward the wall. "Hands on the wall."

The man spun and planted his palms on the flowered wallpaper. Kiley stepped back to Evan, his hand on Yasdi's arm, his stance battle-ready. Kiley didn't think the woman was a threat and believed Evan was overreacting due to Olin's death, but she appreciated his backup.

She kept her weapon raised as Evan frisked the man, who was wearing worn baggy jeans and a sloppy gray T-shirt.

"Nothing," Evan said when he'd finished. "Have a seat in the dining area with your hands on the table where we can see them."

His teeth gritted, he sat down at the table. Yasdi rushed over to sit next to him and take his hand in hers. "We have done nothing wrong."

Kiley holstered her weapon but remained standing and kept a firm eye on them. "Then why was Arash hiding?"

The couple shared a tense look.

"My visa has expired," he answered, lacing his fingers together on the tabletop. "My family is Afghan, but we were expelled from Iran. I made my way here and am seeking a better life, but I have faced much prejudice and have been unable to keep a job."

"He is an old family friend, and I'm helping him," Yasdi explained, her chin raised.

"As in hiding him from authorities," Evan stated.

She nodded. "And working with a local group to try to get his visa reinstated. That is where we were on Thursday night."

"Can anyone vouch for your whereabouts?"

"They would likely do so, but I would not ask them," Sidiqi said. "I do not want to get anyone else into trouble."

"Wait!" Yasdi cried out. "We went out for dinner afterwards. I have the receipt." She jumped to her feet and charged to her counter where she dug into a pricey leather handbag. She jerked out her wallet and returned to the table with the receipt.

Kiley studied the receipt, then took a picture of it. "This only proves you bought dinner, not that Sidiqi was with you."

Yasdi tapped the receipt. "But see here? Two meals. Two sodas."

"Still not proof Sidiqi was with you."

"Ms. Yasdi," Evan said, "can you think of why these two men would claim they were here if they weren't?"

She crossed her arms. "I have no idea."

His focus intensified, and Yasdi cringed. "What's your take on the current war on terrorism in our country?"

"Terrorism!" Her big brown eyes widened, and her gaze bounced between Kiley and Evan. "I don't agree with terrorists' methods, and I'm not involved in anything like that. Not at all."

"Nor am I," Sidiqi added.

Kiley kept watching the pair. Either they were superb actors and Yasdi had the receipt in place in the event someone came to question her, which was possible, or she was legitimately afraid and shocked.

Kiley lifted her phone and opened Rostami's

photo to display for them. "Do you recognize this man?"

Yasdi studied it carefully. "No."

Sidiqi shook his head.

Kiley swiped to Darzi's picture. "This one?"

"No. No," Yasdi said adamantly.

"I . . ." Sidiqi fell back in his chair, his face paling.

Kiley's warning senses started tingling. "You know him?"

He shook his head hard. "But I saw him. He walked past the restaurant and took a long look inside when we were eating."

Evan watched as a fellow ICE agent escorted Sidiqi and Yasdi from her apartment. Evan didn't much like having to take them into custody, but until the team could be sure neither of them were part of the ongoing plot, the couple had to be detained. At least Kiley had pulled strings with Eisenhower, and the pair would be held in a safe house, not a detention center. And if they were cleared, Kiley promised to work toward getting Sidiqi's visa renewed. If she hadn't offered, Evan would have because he didn't like that Sidiqi thought of American law enforcement the same way he did corrupt departments he'd encountered in the past.

"We should get over to the restaurant to check security footage so we can get tonight's op planned," Kiley said.

He led her to the car and drove the few blocks to the steak-and-seafood restaurant.

She pointed above the door. "Security cameras."

"Let's hope they're legit and not dummies set up as deterrents." He opened the door for Kiley and followed her into the dimly lit space.

He took a moment at the door to let his eyes adjust to the atmosphere and breathe in the smoky aroma of grilled beef mixed with savory fried onions. His mouth watered, and he wished they could sit down and eat instead of heading back to plan an op where someone could get hurt.

He noted another camera right inside the door, and despite the long day, he felt optimistic about their chances of catching not only Yasdi and Sidiqi on video but the container suspects as well.

"Let's check in with the bartender." Kiley, her look all business, marched toward a young male polishing a gleaming wood bar.

Evan still couldn't believe how confident she'd become. He'd seen no traces of the shy, awkward young agent he'd first met years ago. She'd once told him she'd spent so much time behind a computer in her room growing up that she was uncomfortable around people. But, and this was a big but for him, she'd always felt at ease with him. He'd felt the same way. Not awkward and shy, but comfortable.

She displayed her ID. "I need to speak to the manager."

The bartender's hand stilled. "She's in back. Can I tell her what this is about?"

Kiley smiled. "I'd rather do that."

"Okay." He dropped his rag and headed through a swinging door.

Evan heard steaks sizzling on the grill in the back, and his stomach rumbled.

"You should've had lunch." Kiley gave him a look much like his mother used to when he was in trouble.

"Yes, Mom," he joked.

She rolled her eyes and chuckled before she looked away. The last thing she probably wanted was to laugh with him, but it sure felt good to him.

"So, you think the suspects spotted Yasdi and Sidiqi and followed them to her place for some reason?"

"Seems like a good possibility," she said. "Who knows, maybe they were spooked and wanted cover in case they were stopped."

"If so, they did the right thing, because Pilcher bought the story."

She looked like she was about to add something when the bartender returned.

Behind him, a worried-looking redhead wearing black pants and a crisp white blouse approached, a half smile on her face. "Laney Wilder. Manager. Can I help you?"

Kiley showed her ID. "I need to get a copy of your security footage for Thursday evening."

"I . . . I'm not . . ." She shook her head. "I don't know protocol on this. Never been asked for it before."

"Businesses often willingly provide footage for our investigations, but we don't want to put you on the spot and can get a warrant if needed." Evan gave her a sincere smile. "It's just been a really long day, and I'd rather not have to go through the hassle of filling out the paperwork and finding a judge. I'm sure you understand."

She took a breath and glanced at the bartender, who shrugged. "Okay," she said. "Wait here. I'll make a copy for you."

"Thank you," Evan said.

She nodded and walked away.

Evan got out his phone, swiped to the photos of their suspects, and held it out to the bartender. "While we wait, maybe you can tell me if you've seen either of these guys."

The bartender gave each photo a long look. "Don't think so, but they coulda been here and I wouldn't have seen them. Most people don't come to the bar."

He returned to his task but kept his head cocked in their direction, so Evan knew better than to discuss anything with Kiley. Instead he recorded the manager's and bartender's names in his phone, then added details of the restaurant.

Laney returned and slid a flash drive across the counter. "I put the whole day on here for you."

"Thank you." Evan swiped back to the photos on his phone and displayed the pictures for her. "Have you seen either of these men?"

Laney frowned as she looked at the screen, then shook her head. "Not that I remember, but then we get a lot of people through here so . . ." She shrugged.

Evan handed his card to her. "Please call me if they come in."

Kiley looked sideways at him, probably wondering why he was handing out his card. But she couldn't deal with every person in the investigation, and he was perfectly capable of handling a phone call.

They left the restaurant and stepped into the fading sunlight.

"You put *everything* in your phone," Kiley said.

"You noticed?"

"Hard not to when you're constantly doing it."

"I don't want to miss any details. Might mean life or death."

She eyed him. "Is this because I'm here reminding you of Olin?"

He shook his head. "I've done it since he died. Just a precaution."

"Like the way you reacted to Yasdi at her place?"

"She could've been going for a gun." He met

her gaze and held it. "I won't let anything happen to you, Kiley. If that means I occasionally overreact, so be it."

She looked like she wanted to say something but then changed her focus to down the street.

"What now?" he asked as his stomach rumbled again.

"Now we grab something to eat on the way back to the conference room. And then we go take down a pair of terrorists."

Kiley forced herself to settle at the conference table when she really wanted to raid that apartment. Evan took the chair next to her, seeming far less eager to act. She gave him a skeptical look. He lifted his shoulders and fired a defiant look back at her.

Did his attitude arise from his earlier comment about protecting her? Because she surely didn't need protecting. Not at all. She was a capable agent and could handle herself on the upcoming raid.

She looked down the table and caught Mack watching them. He had to be noticing the tension between her and Evan. Hopefully, Mack was thinking it had to do with the investigation and not a personal connection that seemed to be growing despite her best efforts to stop it.

"Anyone hear from Sean?" she asked to get things moving.

"He's watching the apartment like you asked," Mack said.

"And I took over tracking the server hack," Cam said. "Though it's been run through so many hubs, the final destination might be in question."

She looked between the pair. "Where do we stand on gathering intel on the suspects?"

"We've gotten ahold of the apartment complex manager," Mack replied. "Rostami rented the place six months ago and signed a yearlong lease. Sean showed him a picture of our suspects, but he says neither of them looked like the guy who signed the lease. He has a DL photo on file."

"I'll put it up on the screen." Cam clicked around on his keyboard.

A Washington State driver's license flashed up on the wall-mounted TV, the name Kahram Darzi, yet the photo was different from the guy Pilcher stopped.

Kiley peered at Cam. "I assume you looked into this."

"I did, and the plot thickens." He grinned. "I checked DMV records. The photo they have is for the guy Pilcher stopped."

"They're all likely forged," she said, "and they probably hacked the DMV to create the files there so that they look legit."

Cam nodded. "I got a woman in IT at the DMV tracking down the source of the files."

Kiley shifted her attention to Mack. "What else did the manager say?"

"Darzi paid online each month and on time," Mack said.

"A year lease seems odd," Evan said. "When the container gets shipped again next week."

"Manager told me they only do year leases," Mack said. "He also mentioned that he never sees the guys around, and he's never had a complaint about them."

"I've requested a warrant for the rent payment details from the credit card company," Cam said.

"Please tell me we have something else on them. Anything." Kiley hated that she sounded so desperate.

"Nothing. Nada. Zip." Cam sighed. "And you know I've been looking. It's like they suddenly appeared with this apartment and these driver's licenses."

"Anything more on Yasdi?" Evan asked.

Cam's eyes brightened. "That chick was a piece of cake to research. She's squeaky clean. I mean *squeaky*. No signs of living beyond her means or taking money from anyone."

Kiley thought back to the visit. "When we met with her, she was wearing pretty expensive clothes, and the restaurant wasn't cheap."

"But her rent isn't high, and she makes good money," Cam said. "So she can afford extras. Sidiqi was a little more difficult, but he checks out too."

Evan rested his hands on the table. "For what it's worth, I believed their story, and the restaurant video confirmed their whereabouts at the time our terrorists claim to have been with her."

"Me too," Kiley said. "But to be thorough I have ERT processing her place for prints just in case Darzi and Rostami entered the apartment without her knowing it."

"Any signs of a break-in?" Mack asked.

Kiley shook her head. "And I don't think we should waste additional time on this unless we find suspicious prints."

"Agreed," Cam said as he looked at Evan. "FYI, the MIT social media accounts from your friend are returning data. The analysts are hearing about something big coming. No details yet, but the threat is obviously very real and 9/11 is the target date."

Kiley's gut cramped at the confirmation of the approaching deadline. "Okay, let's work on assignments until Sean calls in with recon info."

Kiley waited for everyone to get to work, then checked her email. She found a message from Quinn with the Amaris' background information. "Quinn sent me a report on the Amari brothers. They were model citizens and high school leaders. Bilal was a sports fanatic and soccer team captain, Gadi a high school class valedictorian who went to Georgetown majoring in economics.

Bilal didn't have top-notch grades and attended community college majoring in IT."

Evan's head popped up. "Means he could be the guy behind the Wi-Fi bomb in Pennsylvania."

"And as a member of The Righteous, behind who knows what else," Kiley said. "With Gadi's degree in economics, he could be securing funds for the group. I'll print the report for everyone in case I overlooked something." She sent the files to the printer, and as she distributed them the call came in from Sean. She put him on speaker.

"No movement on the apartment or sighting of the suspects," he said, "but I'm sending recon photos. Place is on the third floor. No elevator. Exterior door. One window facing the road. Blinds closed tight. Back patio door not accessible except from inside or by rappelling from the roof. Blinds closed there too."

"So we either stake it out or we go in now," Mack said.

Kiley thought for a moment. She had never been responsible for prepping for a raid, and now she understood the pressure Evan had faced when planning to keep everyone on the team safe the day Olin was killed. And that didn't include the safety of innocent bystanders. Which was why they went in so early in the morning to take Sapin down. No neighbors up and about.

"Since you have eyes on the place, Sean," she said, "I say we keep surveilling until later tonight when the suspects are most likely to be home. Plus we won't have civilians moving around and getting caught in potential crossfire. Ten o'clock sounds good to me."

Evan turned to stare at her, his finger running down the scar on his face. "We should take a better look. Plan."

Evan's telltale touch of his scar said he was freaking out due to Olin's death. Kiley couldn't let his worry interfere in their plans, but she might be able to ease his concern. "What if we cut a hole in the front window and run a camera inside? At least see the main living area that way."

"I don't recommend it," Sean said. "If we do, we risk alerting the suspects and put them in the wind."

Evan crossed his arms. "We need more. A full risk assessment."

"Sean's done one," Mack said before she could speak. "And I don't see as how this is your call. Kiley's in charge. She makes the decision. We follow. Simple as that."

Evan scowled at Mack.

"Sit out the op if the plan bothers you." Mack leaned back as if all of this was no big deal, but an uneasiness clung to him. "We got this covered."

Evan's scowl deepened. "No way."

"Then we go as planned," Sean said. "I'll stay here and report in if anything changes."

"FYI," Sean added, "the Amaris weren't on any flight manifests, and I also compared the dates from Firuzeh's journals to any known terrorist actions, and it was a bust too."

"If you have time, can you get back with the analysts who reviewed the SeaTac flight manifests to check for Darzi's and Rostami's names?" she asked.

"Sure thing." He disconnected the call.

Kiley set her phone on the table and looked at the others. "Be ready to go at a moment's notice. Mack, bring in vests so we can dress out quickly."

He nodded and closed his laptop.

Her phone rang. She hoped it might be CRRU with information on the letter, and she eagerly glanced at the screen only to be disappointed. "It's Vivian returning my call. I'll take it in the hallway. Keep us updated, Sean."

She pushed through the door for privacy and leaned against the wall down the hall as she put her mind solely on the Montgomery Three investigation.

"Vivian," Kiley answered.

"You screwed up again." Her shrill voice came over the line.

Kiley took a breath to make sure she didn't come across as surly. "I know it might seem like that to you, but you know how leads often don't pan out."

"How many times have I heard excuses?" Vivian's sharp tone cut right into Kiley. She could easily imagine the mother rolling her eyes, as she frequently did so for emphasis.

"I'm sorry, Vivian," Kiley said sincerely. "We're doing our best."

"Your best! Your best! Hah. Your best would be that stupid Eisenhower not shutting down the investigation."

Kiley didn't like that Eisenhower closed the case, but she also didn't like Vivian slamming him. "The investigation went cold. He had no other choice."

"If he had kids—if any of you had kids—you'd understand and would have found a way to keep it open."

"We can't begin to know your pain," Kiley said, thinking about her father and Olin dying. "But we all do have people in our lives we loved and have lost."

"Yeah." Her skepticism was rampant. "Like who?"

"My father and one of my partners to name a few."

"Really?" Her voice had softened.

"Yes, really. They didn't disappear and leave me without answers like you're facing, but I lost them from my life. So I know pain. We *all* know pain."

She sighed, the long breath going on and on.

"I'm sorry. I know you're trying to help. It was just another thing I had hopes for, and it didn't work out."

"Would you like us to stop telling you about what we find? That way if the lead doesn't come to anything, you won't have gotten your hopes up only to have them dashed."

"Nah, I want to know. Hope is the only reason I get out of bed in the morning."

Kiley understood. "Tell you what. After we close out the investigation we're working, I'll stop by your place and we can have a long talk. Would you like that?"

"Please. And, Kiley, I'm really sorry. I appreciate you all. Tell Sean I'm sorry I lost my cool, okay?"

"I will."

"Good luck on your current investigation." She fell silent for a moment. "It's not about anyone missing or someone dying, is it?"

"No," Kiley said and prayed right then and there that the investigation never became about someone losing a loved one. Not as long as she was breathing and could do her best to stop the loss of innocent lives.

Evan didn't know what he'd done, but Mack crossed the room, eyeballing Evan like he'd fired a .50 cal at Mack, hitting dead-center. Evan had to admit he was uncomfortable under Mack's glare. Still, Evan needed to know why Mack was so ticked off. "Something wrong?"

"Wrong?" Mack's eyebrows went up. "Yeah. Maybe. You tell me."

Evan tried to figure out what he might have said to offend the man but couldn't come up with a thing. "I don't understand."

"Kiley." Mack almost spit out her name. "You've got a thing for her. Got it bad, and I don't want to see her get hurt."

Obviously, Evan hadn't succeeded in hiding his emotions. He understood Mack's concern. But the guy was making a complete turnaround in attitude from thinking Evan was good for her to now being angry and put off. "Sounds like you have a thing for her yourself."

"Thing?" Mack scowled. "No, but having my teammate's back? Yeah, I got that in spades."

Evan stared at Mack and held on. "I don't plan to hurt her."

"See that you don't or you'll be dealing with me." Mack stabbed his index finger into Evan's chest. "That clear?"

"Crystal."

Mack's intense gaze lingered while Evan felt like squirming. Mack suddenly spun and headed for the door.

"Mack," Evan called out.

The big guy stopped and looked over his shoulder.

Evan smiled. "Thanks for caring enough about Kiley to have her back."

Mack's mouth fell open. He quickly snapped it closed, gave a terse nod, and walked out the door.

CHAPTER 20

Man, oh man. Kiley was hyperventilating.

She watched Mack march down the hallway. Thankfully he turned in the other direction and didn't notice her. She didn't want him to see her shell-shocked face after overhearing his conversation with Evan.

She slid down the wall and rested her forehead on her knees.

Why did she have to overhear their conversation? It did her or Evan no good. It just brought up everything she'd been trying to avoid admitting. Evan was a good guy. A man of honor. Hardworking. Dedicated. Cared about others. A team player. The man she was falling for, and still—still—he was the guy she wanted to blame for Olin's death. Maybe needed to blame.

She was caught between two opposing emotions, and she couldn't see a way out of it.

Father, please, help me here.

Forgiveness . . . the word sprang to mind as it often had in the early days when she'd prayed about coming to grips with losing Olin. Could she forgive Evan? Was he even at fault here, or was she unwilling to take her share of blame? Blaming Evan was much easier than admitting she could have done more to save Olin too. To accept that maybe all of it was one of those situations God allowed and yet made no sense to them.

God, please, I am begging. Help me see the right thing to do here.

Vivian's face came to mind, along with the anger and blame she'd just directed at the team. Kiley had taken the woman's wrath because she'd thought they deserved Vivian's anger, but did they? They worked as hard as they could. Did everything they could. Hadn't let go of the investigation even when they'd been ordered to do so and were still working on behalf of finding her daughter and the other girls.

No. They shouldn't feel guilty. And maybe Evan shouldn't either. Sure, he'd made a mistake, but people weren't infallible. Had she been wrong in blaming him? Was she clinging to his guilt these past few days so that she didn't have to face her feelings for him?

"Kiley?" Cam stepped into the hall. "You okay?"

She raised her head that felt as heavy as the battering rams they used to break down doors. "Just taking a quick break."

"Ready to get back to it?"

She nodded and whisked all thoughts unrelated to the investigation from her mind.

Cam stretched out his hand. "We've got this, you know? It won't best us."

Did they? Did they really?

She took his hand and stood. Mack came back down the hall, carrying bins and Evan's tote, his expression much calmer. She smiled at her friend, thankful he had her back, though she didn't appreciate him trying to scare Evan off. Still, now wasn't the time to talk about it.

At the doorway, her phone chimed, and she dug it out to see a text from Eisenhower telling them not to worry about stepping on Counterterrorism's toes when researching Malouf. The shipping company owner wasn't on Counterterrorism's radar at all. This told her two things. Since Counterterrorism wasn't looking at him, and the team hadn't found anything questionable on the guy, he was likely on the up-and-up, and she should back-burner looking into him and work on more pressing leads.

She stepped into the room, and Evan ran his assessing gaze over her. She did her best to hide her emotions and took a moment to cross off those action items on the whiteboard they'd finalized, and ran down the outstanding items she wanted to follow up prior to their op. But before she got to work on them, they needed to pin down tactics for the op. "Cam, can you put the recon photos from Sean on the screen for review?"

He nodded, and soon a picture of an older three-story apartment building popped onto the TV. He slowly scrolled through the photos of the entire complex and a sketch Sean had made of the layout, plus an apartment floor plan. They reviewed their basic breach drill, Evan paying full attention to the details.

"What's the stacking order at the door?" Evan asked with a hitch in his voice.

"Mack, me, Sean," Kiley replied. "And you take up the rear."

Mack angled his head as he peered at the screen. "Looks pretty straightforward."

"Agreed," Kiley said. "No rear exit, but we should still arrange for local SWAT to back us up." She shifted her focus to Evan. "Can you contact your Tacoma police connection and arrange that?"

"Absolutely." His enthusiasm didn't surprise her, as SWAT would bring added security to the raid. "Can I make one suggestion?"

"What's that, Evan?" Kiley was almost afraid to hear his suggestion. He had to be worried about the breach.

"We know these guys are potential bombers, right?"

Kiley nodded.

"I'd like to evaluate the door for any possible charges before we go barreling in."

Kiley might have passed his ongoing concern off as lingering guilt over failing on Olin's op, but Evan was right. She should've thought of making sure the apartment wasn't rigged to blow. "Sounds like a good plan."

"I agree," Mack said. "We've got all the tools you need in the SUV. I'll get them organized for you."

"Thanks." She looked back at Evan. "Will you start calling the people Waleed provided for his alibi for Firuzeh's murder?"

"Glad to." He reached for his phone.

She looked at Cam. "What about your algorithm linking Malouf, Barzani, Waleed, or Amari?"

"Still running, but no data. If it was going to return anything, I think it would've by now."

Kiley was getting more and more disappointed in their lack of progress, yet she made sure not to convey this to the others. "Let it run. You never know."

Mack looked up. "Just got an email from the analyst in charge of monitoring the video games. They've had chatter that makes no sense. Transcript's printing."

Cam shook his head. "I'll never live it down if Kiley's right and they communicated that way."

She mocked twisting the ends of an imaginary mustache as she moved to the printer. She reviewed the conversation. "It's every bit as senseless as the analyst said. Like the letter recovered at the Abeds' mailbox store. We need to have this evaluated for code."

She texted Eisenhower asking him to secure another code analyst. His affirmative reply came immediately.

"Eisenhower's looking for an analyst," she told Mack. "See what they know about where the game transmissions originated."

"I'll follow up on the information we need to obtain a warrant for Sony."

"You know that's gonna take some time to serve and get the information back," Cam said. "The suspects will likely have relocated by then."

Kiley nodded. "We still need to run it down."

"Yeah." Cam scowled. "No stone unturned. Because these slimy terrorists live under rocks."

"Got ATM and nearby businesses' video from Thursday night," Cam said.

"Put the first one up on the screen." Kiley closed her computer to put away the bulletin board pictures from The Righteous's office, the police reports detailing the convenience store manager's 911 calls, and the store security videos she'd been working on for the last three hours. Nothing stood out to her, but she forwarded the files to Counterterrorism to compare to known ISIS connections just in case.

"Okay," Cam said. "Here you go."

The ATM video played on the TV, and the camera caught Rostami's hand as he scratched his chin.

Kiley spotted a black blob near his wrist. "Zoom in on his hand."

The close-up revealed a black circle with white Arabic writing.

Evan moved closer to the screen. "It's the seal of Muhammad. The writing says 'of Allah is the prophet Muhammad,' and it's part of the jihadist black flag."

"No surprise there," Kiley said. "Start it running again."

Cam played the video that ended when Rostami stepped out of the frame. Cam opened a second file, this one of Pilcher stopping to talk to the suspects. At the end, the pair walked away from the officer, calmly strolling down the street. When they moved out of camera range, Cam changed to a video catching the corner of Pacific Avenue. A black Honda Accord pulled to the curb, and the men got into the back seat. Kiley held her breath, hoping the camera captured license plates, but the angle left a fuzzy image.

Evan slammed a fist on the table. "No way we can put out an alert without plates. Especially not with Accords being one of the most popular cars."

The car turned north and got onto I-705 heading south.

"That's as much video as I've located." Cam disconnected from the TV. "Now that they've gotten onto the interstate, I can request traffic-cam footage. If the Department of Transportation doesn't get back to me within the hour, I'll find another way to get the file."

Kiley knew he meant hacking into the system but would never say it aloud.

Her phone chimed, telling her of a new email, and she glanced at her laptop, surprised to find a message from the FBI lab so late at night. "Got an email from the Latent Print Operations Unit at Quantico." She eagerly read the first paragraph. "They confirmed five sets of prints, but two sets were lifted from items like dishes, toothbrushes, et cetera, where the others were found on the container itself."

"Suggesting the pair of prints were from the occupants just like the DNA results," Evan said.

Kiley continued reading, her pulse ratcheting up. "This is good. Really good. Unlike DNA, they got a match for the pair in Interpol's database."

"Don't tell me," Cam said, sarcasm rampant in his tone, "they're Pilcher's suspects. Darzi and Rostami."

Kiley kept reading and looked up, blinking hard to make sense of the news.

"Wait," Cam said. "Not them?"

She shook her head. "A Mohamed Nabi and Jangi Shah."

"Those aren't the guys Pilcher stopped." Evan sat motionless. "Not even the guys from the Pittsburgh bombing."

Kiley shook off her daze. "No additional details on the men, but they gave me a contact at Interpol to call—someone named Nigel Clark."

"Interpol's Command and Coordination Centre's located in France," Mack said. "But each member country hosts a National Central Bureau."

"And ours is in D.C.," Kiley finished for him. "I doubt Clark's in the office at this time of night, but I can leave a message." She quickly made the call and urged Clark to call her back the minute he got the message. "Cam, get going on digging up background info on those names."

"Already on it."

"What about Counterterrorism?" Evan asked. "They likely have a file on them."

"Good point." She thought about calling Eisenhower, only she needed to handle such an important lead directly. "I have a contact there. She usually works late."

Evan shoved a hand into his hair. "Let's hope she's true to form tonight."

Kiley dialed the agent and held her breath.

"Agent Debra Bessemer," she answered right away.

Thank you! Oh, thank you!

Kiley quickly asked Deb for information on Nabi and Shah. "I need what you have now!"

"I know we have a file on Shah," Deb said, not sounding put out by Kiley's demand. "Not sure about Nabi. Let me get Shah's file open and give you an overview."

"Mind if I put you on speaker for the team?" Kiley asked, her heart starting to race.

"Go ahead."

Kiley tapped the button. Unable to sit still any longer, she jumped up and set her phone on the table.

"Okay, so here we go," Deb said. "Shah's an ISIS lieutenant working toward taking over his faction. He's responsible for more brutal attacks than I can count. He favors bombs and is quite skilled at making intricate devices but is equally at home with weapons and beheading."

Mack scowled. "An equal-opportunity terrorist."

"That he is." Deb's tone was deadly serious. "He's known to have a temper and takes it out on anyone in his organization who makes a mistake. And he's got an ego the size of Texas."

"Hey, don't utter my home state in connection with this dude," Mack grumbled.

"Sorry," Deb said, "but his ego *is* that big. Each attack has to be grander than the last, which, by the way, was capturing an entire school of young girls he then gifted to his men."

Kiley couldn't fathom what made someone turn to such brutal actions. "He sounds disgusting."

"I'm not sure 'disgusting' is a vile enough word for him," Deb said. "But you must know, if there's a way to innovate a terrorist attack or pull off the impossible, he'll be behind it."

"Sounds like he could be our guy all right." Evan's expression said he didn't like the idea very much.

As much as Kiley didn't want to agree with his

assessment, she did, and they needed additional information to stop him. "What's behind all this rage?"

"A sad story," Deb said. "Almost makes you feel bad for him. Until you see what he's done."

"Tell us about it," Kiley encouraged.

"He lost his whole family in the war. Everyone. Parents. Siblings. Grandparents. Cousins. Aunts and uncles. They were at his sister's wedding." Deb sighed, giving Kiley time to picture the event. "Shah stopped at the market to pick up the wedding present and was running late when the bomb hit. He arrived to find only rubble. I think he lost his mind that day and is mentally unstable. He blames our country and gets revenge wherever and whenever he can."

"He's suffered a great loss, but it still doesn't excuse his behavior." Kiley detested wars and hated that innocent people died in them. "What about Nabi?"

"Let me look."

As Kiley paced the room, she heard the sound of Deb's fingers typing coming over the speaker, urging Kiley's feet to move faster. She neared the end of the table, and Evan snagged her wrist.

"You'll burn yourself out," he whispered.

He was right, but she just couldn't sit down. Not with what they were learning about these very dangerous men who were planning an unthinkable tragedy. Still, she appreciated Evan's concern, so as she extricated her wrist, she offered him the brightest smile she could manage at a time like this, then moved back to her phone.

"Yeah, here he is," Deb said, stilling Kiley's feet. "He's a long way down the totem pole from Shah, but he's climbing the ranks. Hmm . . . yeah, he was involved in the schoolgirl kidnapping with Shah. Together they could do some serious damage."

"Anything else on his background?" Evan asked.

"A little. He was a street kid when ISIS recruited him. Says his loyalty to them for feeding him when he was starving knows no bounds."

Evan frowned. "I've seen kids like that recruited during my Navy days. Breaks your heart. But seeing them starving and homeless is equally hard."

Kiley looked at him and found anguish in his eyes. She'd never really thought about the tragedies he'd seen in his military career. Starving kids was likely just the tip of the iceberg.

He sat up straighter. "Where was the last known sighting of these men?"

"I can't say for Nabi," Deb replied, "but Shah hasn't been seen in public for more than a year."

"Do you find it odd that we don't have prints on these two and had to go to Interpol to get a match?" Cam asked.

"No," Deb said. "They've never committed a crime in the U.S. They stick closer to home, targeting Americans abroad." She paused for a long moment. "But I guess if you're looking for their prints, they must have arrived here."

"That's for your ears only," Kiley quickly said, knowing Deb would heed the warning. "Can you send me their files right away?"

"I'll email them as soon as we hang up." Deb let out a slow, noisy breath. "I know you all are like this super team, but be careful, Kiley. These guys are bad news. Real bad news."

Stomach churning, Kiley swallowed. "I have a few more names I'd like you to check before you go. Starting with Ehsan Rostami and Kahram Darzi." Kiley spelled the names to be sure Deb got them right.

Deb's typing resumed, and so did Kiley's feet. She made a wide path past Evan so he couldn't stop her this time, and the urge to act was burning in her gut now.

"You sure on their names?" Deb asked. "I have nothing on them. No listing at all."

Kiley swallowed down her disappointment and moved on. "What about a Haval Barzani?"

"Let me check," Deb said, typing. "Sorry. Nothing on him either."

Kiley nodded. "Okay then, I have two sets of brothers. Nasim and Ibrahim Waleed, and Gadi and Bilal Amari."

Deb hummed as her fingers clicked over her keyboard. "We have the Waleeds tied to The Righteous. You familiar with that group?"

"Yes," Kiley replied. "Any actual terrorist activities on file?"

"No, just suspicions. Nothing else except that Nasim was a former sniper and is suspected of committing several murders. And the Amari brothers have a short listing. Members of Waleed's Righteous group, but that's it. No terroristic activities tied to either of them."

"If any of these names come up on the radar, will you contact me?" Kiley asked.

"Sure thing."

Kiley thanked Deb and tapped her screen to end the call.

"Well, that was a blast." Mack shook his head and took a long pull on his can of Red Bull.

"You won't believe this," Cam said. "I just did a quick internet search on Nabi and Shah. Take a look at the screen."

They all looked up at the TV. A grainy picture of two men filled the screen.

"That's Darzi and Rostami." Kiley shot a confused look at Cam. "The guys Pilcher stopped."

"No." A smug grin crossed Cam's face. "You're looking at Nabi and Shah."

"Son of a gun." Mack set down his can and leaned closer. "Darzi and Rostami are aliases.

Explains why the wonder boy here couldn't find anything on them."

"Then we need to rethink the apartment breach," Evan stated. "These guys are extremely dangerous."

"They were dangerous under the other names too," Kiley said. "The plan stands. They should've settled by ten. We go in then."

CHAPTER 21

The alarm Kiley had set for the raid sounded, bringing her to her feet, her heart pounding. She looked at Mack. "Weapons loaded in the vehicle?"

Mack nodded, and Kiley rushed to the bins he'd delivered to get out ballistic vests. She tossed them to the team. Evan grabbed one from his tote bag, and tensions mounted as the ripping sound of Velcro cut through the air.

She secured the last tab on her vest, catching Cam's longing gaze following their movements. She wished he could come along, or even achieve his dream of becoming an agent so he could be a part of their ops.

She smiled at him. "Thanks for holding down the fort. I appreciate everything you do."

"Doesn't make it easier, you know." He shook his head. "Maybe I need to start doing a bad job so Eisenhower will let me apply."

"Probably not the best plan," Mack said.

"Yeah, probably not." He slumped down in his chair. "FYI, I got the Washington DOT files. Nabi and Shah got off I-5 in Olympia, and I lost them there."

Kiley loaded extra ammo magazines in her vest pouch. "It was inevitable that we'd run out of camera coverage and lose them at some point. Any thoughts on why they stopped in Olympia?"

"Nothing there target-wise, so maybe a pit stop." Cam got up and headed for the door.

She thought to call after him, but there was nothing she could do to ease his mind and she had to move on. She grabbed a marker and crossed the video lead off the board, then turned back to the others. "Okay, let's go meet with SWAT and get this op going."

Mack marched for the door.

Evan hung back. "Kiley, a word before we go."

She glanced at him, then at Mack. "We'll meet you at the car."

He arched an eyebrow and didn't move.

She waved him on. "Go. Be there in a sec."

One last lingering look and he departed.

She faced Evan. "What is it?"

He furrowed his brow. "You're an agent. A good one. I get that. Respect it even, but I don't like you going in before me. So I wanted to tell you to take care. Don't be a hero or cowboy."

He looked so forlorn she had to do something to change his mood. She forced a smile. "No worries. Cowboy is Mack's job on the team."

She hoped he would laugh. Instead he closed the distance between them in five long strides. "I'm serious here."

His intensity scared her, and she knew she couldn't make light of his concern again. "I'm always careful, and I don't want you to worry."

"Hard to do after Olin."

"I'm sure you've been on lots of ops since then. Do you worry this much every time?"

He widened his stance. "This is different."

"How so?"

"You. You're here. I . . . Oh, what the heck." He grabbed her upper arms and pulled her close.

He wove his fingers into her hair, looked deeply into her eyes, and she was a goner. His head descended. She barely had time to register the fact that he was going to kiss her before his lips settled on hers.

Shock traveled through her body, emotions radiating like beams of bright sunshine. Warm. Intense. Spellbinding.

She should step back. Should but couldn't. Couldn't get enough of him. Of his touch, the warmth. The joy and intensity.

She wrapped her arms around his neck and pulled him closer. Put all her feelings from years ago, from the past few days, from everything, into her kiss.

Nothing else mattered right now except Evan. Nothing.

Evan's heart soared, his pulse roaring as Kiley returned his kiss with a passion he never expected. He was lost. Totally and completely lost. For now and forever. The way he knew it would be when he finally locked lips with her. The woman he found so captivating for so long. Now he'd finally done what he wanted to do all these long years.

"Kiley, come on." Mack's deep voice barreled down the hall, hitting Evan like a bullet to the chest.

They were heading into danger, and Evan's gut clenched. He released Kiley and sucked in air. He noticed her breathing was just as ragged, and she was trying to gain control. It was a heady feeling to know she was feeling the same way, but he didn't want her distracted on the op, so he took a step back and gave her forehead a gentle kiss. "Let's get going."

She clutched his hand for a moment. "You don't be a cowboy either. We don't have a bomb suit, so if the place is rigged, we call in the bomb squad."

He really didn't need a suit, but if he expected her to be careful, he had to do the same thing. "Understood."

She spun and charged down the hall as if racing away from him or her feelings. He took several breaths and blew out his emotions. He'd let her get to him. Let her kiss blind him. Now he had to be alert. Had to be ready for anything. To protect her if needed. Give his life for her if needed.

When they stepped into the cooler evening air, Mack eyed them from the SUV. Kiley seemed to ignore him and slid into the passenger seat. Evan climbed in back, remembering Kiley's comment about Mack being the team cowboy.

He didn't say what was on his mind, and tension permeated the vehicle all the way to the grocery store parking lot where they met with Tacoma SWAT and reviewed logistics. Then in the shadows of the apartment complex, well out of view of the suspects' apartment, they brought Sean up to speed on the plan.

Kiley locked her gaze on Evan. "Time to scope the door for any charges."

He nodded and opened the SUV's rear hatch.

"Mack, you assist Evan. Sean, come with me to check nearby vehicles. I don't want anyone waiting with an electronic device ready to explode the apartment." Kiley tossed the strap of a Heckler & Koch MP5 automatic rifle favored by the FBI over her shoulder and strode off with Sean.

Mack popped open a bright red bin. "Everything you'll need is in here."

Evan sorted through the tub to gather items, including an endoscopic camera that looked like a black snake with an eye at the end. He would insert it under the door for a good look at the inside framing. He pocketed it and looked up to find Kiley and Sean returning.

"We're clear," she said.

"Then it's go time." Evan grabbed a rifle as

a spark of adrenaline lit in his body. He willed himself to calm down, but the fire sizzled like ignited detcord. "You all wait here while I creep up there."

"You're not going alone," Mack said, shouldering his own weapon, but his expression was uneasy. "I have your six."

Kiley appraised Mack quickly, then looked as if she'd decided something. "We'll keep eyes on the place from down here and let you know if there's any movement."

Evan evaluated the parking lot and decided she was far enough away from the building in the event of an explosion, but still, he looked at Kiley. "I'd prefer it if the two of you moved behind the vehicle. Just in case."

She frowned. "Remember, Mack's the cowboy."

Mack eyed her. "What's that supposed to mean?"

"Just telling Evan not to take unnecessary risks. You two find a device, we call in the bomb squad. Understood?"

"Aye, aye." Mack saluted her and grinned, but Evan could tell he would listen to her directive.

One last look at Kiley, and Evan lifted his rifle to set off. He heard Mack's nearly silent footfalls behind him, reminding Evan of his days as an EOD tech in the Navy.

They climbed the exterior stairway. Step by step. Silent. Efficient. Lethal.

Outside the door, Mack took a stance with his back to the building, his rifle pointed at the parking lot.

"Do your thing, man," he whispered, his eyes wild and intense at the same time.

Evan squatted in front of the door and got out the camera. He found an opening in the weather stripping and threaded the snake inside. He turned on the endoscope and gently eased the camera around the doorframe.

He jerked his hand to a stop and sucked in a sharp breath.

"What is it?" Mack asked.

"A pressure device, and enough explosive material to blow this entire building."

CHAPTER 22

Evan loved seeing how Kiley was holding her own with the local bomb squad leader, a tall, lanky sergeant with an intensity that fit his extreme position. But Evan wished she'd give in and let him take over rendering the bomb safe.

"I'm not about to tell you how to do your job," he said loudly to be heard over all the commotion in the parking lot, set up as a staging area for equipment and personnel. "That said, I really think you should consider it."

"No." Kiley planted her hands on her hips and stared at the sergeant.

He cringed at her vehemence.

"Your tech can take care of it," she added.

"Begging your pardon, ma'am"—the sergeant tipped his head toward Evan—"but your guy has far more experience with this kind of device than mine does. No better bomb techs than the Navy's EOD guys."

Kiley shifted her focus to Evan, and he felt like a kid on the playground where leaders were evaluating his merits before deciding if he could join their team.

She turned back to the sergeant. "But it's your responsibility."

"And I'm not trying to shirk that. My job,

however, is to minimize loss of life and property. Your guy would make that more of a reality."

"I can do it, Kiley," Evan cut in. "I'll even wear the suit."

She looked at him again. He tried to fire back the confidence he felt in doing the job he'd been well trained to handle.

She bit her lip, then suddenly something changed in her expression and she gave a sharp nod. "He's cleared to help."

"Thank you," the sergeant said. "We'll get the suit ready."

Kiley stared after him, still gnawing on her lower lip. Evan understood her angst. As the leader, she'd made the best decision for the team, for innocent civilians, yet it wasn't a decision she wanted to make.

She stepped over to him and locked gazes. "You'll wear the suit, and no cowboy maneuvers."

Despite the danger awaiting him, Evan smiled. He liked seeing her so confident and in charge and respected her all the more for putting aside her personal feelings for the greater good. "I'll just go get suited up."

"You *do* know the risk, right?" she asked. "We've jammed cell signals, but our suspects could be in there with a manual trigger waiting to blow the place."

"Could be, but RANGE-R didn't pick up any movements." They'd run the handheld radar device that looked like a large stud finder along the exterior wall. Using Doppler radar technology, the device had a ninety-five percent probability in detecting the slightest human movement, as slight as breathing, within fifty feet.

"I know, but . . ." She shuddered, likely over the unknown five percent.

"But it'll be okay."

"Ready for you, Bowers," the sergeant called from the back of his vehicle.

"Time to get after it." Evan inconspicuously squeezed her hand and gave her a smile. She returned it with a trembling one of her own. Reluctant to leave her feeling so upset, he took a breath and marched over to the truck, where the tech helped him into the eighty-pound suit. Evan purposely avoided looking at Kiley as they affixed the many Velcro tabs, tugged up zippers, and lifted the helmet over Evan's head.

When he was ready, he gave a thumbs-up in a bulky glove and headed up the steps with a tool bag in hand. A lumbering task, and sweat beaded up on his forehead before he even reached the stairs.

It had been years since he'd strapped on the heavy bomb suit, and his steps faltered. Not for long. The briefest of moments, but long enough for the memory of Olin's death to come rushing back.

No. Stop. No one's going to die here. You got this.

He started off again. Calmly. Rationally.

At the top, he glanced back at Kiley. A lump formed in his throat, and he swallowed hard as he turned toward the bomb. He wouldn't disappoint her. Put her at risk. Or anyone else for that matter.

He carefully set down the tool bag and knelt on one knee by the window nearest to the door, working hard to maintain his balance. He grabbed a glass cutter and pressed it against the window. Each movement calculated. Exact.

He lifted out the circular shard carefully and threaded in the camera to take a better look at the wiring and track it back to the C-4 explosive. Then he scoped out the device, a pressure trigger that released when the door opened and the lack of pressure activated the bomb. While it was a relatively simple device to render safe, he had to get his tools inside the building to accomplish the task.

Showtime. Just him and the bomb.

Alone.

Tick. Tick. Tick. He could almost hear a detonator ticking down when in fact there wasn't one. Just the switch that he needed to disarm.

He pulled out his camera and broke the glass, then swept the sharp shards out of his way. He set the bag of tools inside and paused. If anyone was going to come out laying down fire, he wanted it to be now, not when he was hunkered down near stacks of C-4. But his actions were met with silence.

Now the truly hard part. Getting the suit through the window.

He lifted a bulky leg over the sill, then scooted in feeling like a blimp squeezing through the eye of a needle. He grabbed the bag and bent before the device. He withdrew a Leatherman from the pouch. The multipurpose tool felt familiar in his hand as he still carried one in his pocket every day.

He raised it. Prepared to cut. Took a deep breath in the stifling helmet. Held it and paused to lift his eyes.

If any situation called for prayer, this one did.

He offered a quick request to keep everyone safe. To make his movements sure and true.

He made the cut, a quick snip.

Nothing happened. What he expected. Still. He held fast for a moment. Waited.

Silence.

He eased out a breath and lowered the Leatherman. A simple and anticlimactic ending for all the prep and discussion on how to handle the device.

He pictured Kiley waiting. Looking up, fear in her eyes. He wanted to report to her, but before that he had to go the extra mile. Look for additional booby traps while suited up. He grabbed a flashlight and swung it over the main room.

The first thing he noticed were lawn chairs serving as the only living room furniture. He stepped down a hallway, searching for any signs they'd drilled into walls or the ceiling or had run wires along carpet or through vents. He stopped to check a bathroom. Nothing,

In the bedroom at the end of the hall, he spotted a sleeping bag, prayer rug, and trash bag. The closet door stood open, revealing an empty interior. He ran the flashlight over the space to check for wires.

He crossed back through the living room and found another bedroom holding similar items. Finally he checked the kitchen and went to open the front door. But first he pushed the buttons on the side of his helmet to lift the face shield. He stepped onto the balcony and gave a thumbs-up.

Mack, Kiley, and Sean came charging across the street from the staging area and stacked at the stairs in the same order. They pounded up the concrete steps toward Evan. He moved out of their way, giving them access to the apartment and prayed their sweep produced a lead. Even more, they needed to find the whereabouts of these men. Men who'd somehow obtained and rigged enough explosives to flatten a city block.

After clearing the apartment, Kiley looked at the tall stack of C-4 bricks and shuddered. Her heart was still pounding. Had been racing, threatening to escape her chest since the second she agreed to let Evan render the bomb safe and he'd put on that suit and trudged up the stairs. Then that pause at the top, and she could swear he was looking right at her, and her heart felt like it stopped.

But he was safe now. They all were. And she never wanted to see him put on a bomb suit again. Never wanted him to face another explosive. Never wanted to see him in harm's way of any kind. And with the extreme fear she usually kept below the surface now fighting to take her down, she knew he'd come to mean something more to her than she'd thought possible.

She couldn't have picked a more untimely moment to realize it. She was in charge, the RED team awaiting directions. Two local squads were waiting on her too. She had to let it all go and put on her professional persona.

She marched to the balcony and gave the all-clear signal. The tough bomb and SWAT officers visibly relaxed, but she couldn't. Not after seeing the bricks of C-4 by the door. If Evan hadn't suggested checking for a bomb, her decision could've killed everyone. She'd had the intel right in front of her, yet she failed to factor it into her plan. Much like the way Olin died. And just like that, she knew she could forgive Evan. Now was not the time to tell him, but she would make time to talk to him, and soon.

Determined to resolve that issue, she stepped inside. Mack flipped on the overhead light and eased out a nearly silent breath. The op had shaken the guy who was nearly unflappable, and she had to wonder if past memories were bothering him.

He looked at her, his eyes clear of turmoil. "Let's check this place out."

Kiley studied a pair of old lawn chairs, a cardboard box tipped over to serve as a side table, a TV, and a PlayStation console.

"Not much here, but there are sleeping bags and prayer rugs in the bedrooms," Mack said.

"A bag of trash in one of them too," Evan said as he pulled down protective flaps that went around the helmet area of the bomb suit.

Sean went to the adjoining kitchen and opened the refrigerator. "Some water and Gatorade. That's it." He jerked open a few cupboards. "Protein bars. Chips."

Mack looked in a trash can. "Fast-food wrappers."

"With their personal belongings gone, they obviously skated." Evan ripped Velcro tabs free on the bulky suit, the sound echoing through the empty apartment. "Doesn't look like they spent much time here."

"So why did they come here at all?" Kiley frowned. "No need for an apartment when they could've stayed in a motel for a night or two."

"Which supports your theory that they rented this place for potential inquiries," Evan said.

Kiley turned to Sean. "Get ERT out here. Mack, give the kitchen trash a thorough search."

"Great, thanks for trash patrol." He rolled his eyes and put on gloves as he squatted by the can.

"I'll grab the bag from the bedroom and check out the bathrooms," she continued while looking at Evan. "I assume you'll want to get out of that suit."

"You know it. It might have a fan inside, but it's still sweltering." As he passed toward the door, he brushed against her hand, and with the intense look he flashed her way, she thought the touch was on purpose.

She'd forgotten all about the kiss during the op, but now the memory played in her mind, and she was very aware of him. The kiss was amazing. Beyond what she could have imagined. A connection she hadn't felt before. Ever.

Forget it.

He disappeared through the open door, and she put on gloves to search the bathroom cabinets and grab the bag from the bedroom. Task complete, she hurried past the front door before he came back inside and spoke to her. Here she was running from him as if *he* were the terrorist bent on hurting her when in fact, if his kiss said anything, it said he only wanted to love her. Now that there was no unforgiveness between them, the thought was far scarier than facing down a terrorist, as the sentiment could carry a lifetime of commitment if she let it.

She forced her attention on the bag and dumped it out onto the counter. Several candy and protein-bar wrappers lay in the pile. A couple of water bottles bounced on the Formica countertop and rolled to a stop. Underneath it all she found a wadded-up scrap of paper. She unfolded and pressed it out on the counter. A website address for a hotel reservation company was printed on the top of the page. An *L* came after the main website, but the rest of the URL was torn off.

"That for a login page?" Sean asked, looking over her shoulder, his phone to his ear.

"Maybe," she said. "But why would these guys book a hotel when they have this apartment?"

"They'd need a place to stay if they left town," Sean said.

She thought for a moment about the information, recalling everything she knew about this reservation company. "Using the hotel site is a smart move. They could use gift cards and PayPal so they would remain anonymous when they checked in."

"We should see if there are any internet providers associated with this apartment. If so, we could get the full link."

"Agreed." She texted Cam, updating him on the op and asking him to begin looking into it.

Sean stepped back, greeted ASAC Stadler on his phone, and made their request for ERT.

Kiley checked the other bathroom and then helped Mack go through the kitchen trash. The can held nothing other than bags and wrappers from McDonald's and Wendy's.

"It'll all be good for forensics," Mack said. "Prints. DNA."

She poked at the wrappers. "I'll have Cam request security video for these nearby restaurants. Maybe we'll find out if they're driving the same car we saw on video and get a plate." She texted Cam the additional request.

As she set aside the items she wanted the evidence tech to take, Cam texted back, promising to get right on warrants and a search for the internet company. His texts didn't convey his tone of voice, but she imagined him still being disappointed and vowed to find a way to help him achieve his dreams of becoming an agent.

Mack stripped off his gloves. "I'll take Sean over to pick up the other car."

The pair departed, and Kiley stepped outside to wait for ERT. She leaned on the railing, breathing in bacon-scented air and trying to remember when she'd last sat down for breakfast, or any meal not eaten on the job. She couldn't come up with a day. Like Evan had said, she worked all the time. Her job demanded it. He might be transmitting his interest in her and perhaps thinking about seeing where this thing between them might lead, and she now forgave him, but they still had a big obstacle between them. They both worked far too much for a relationship. And lived on opposite coasts too.

She ignored the special-ops teams packing up in the parking lot, the residents filing back toward their homes, and stared at the city skyline reflected in the water, her mood so contemplative she couldn't focus her thoughts and simply stared for what felt like hours.

Is this you, God, telling me to consider my life? To look at it through fresh eyes? Maybe make some changes? Or is it wishful thinking on my part?

Mack pulled into the parking lot and maneuvered around residents to park at the base of the stairs. She stowed her wandering thoughts as he climbed the steps and joined her on the balcony.

"Sean went back to the office," Mack said, taking a position next to her and facing the water in the distance. "Evan take off?"

"He's still here somewhere."

"Avoiding him or arguing?"

"Avoiding," she admitted.

After not speaking for a long moment, Mack shifted to look at her. "You still blaming him for Olin's death?"

She kept her focus pointed ahead and explained her recent realization.

"Ah, so now you're avoiding your feelings for him."

She swiveled to look him in the eye. "Speaking of feelings, I overheard you warning Evan off."

A sheepish look crossed his face. "I might've gotten a little overprotective."

"You're a great friend, Mack, but I can fight my own battles."

"Can you?" His eyebrow arched, and he looked like a pirate in the dim light. "Because if you can, you wouldn't be avoiding Evan."

She opened her mouth to argue, then closed it. He was right. She was running from her feelings and couldn't argue the point.

The ERT van pulled into the lot, and she started for the stairway. "I'll head down to meet them so we can get going."

"Kiley . . ." Mack said.

She glanced over her shoulder at him.

"I avoided personal things for too long and it cost me my relationship with Addy." He met her gaze and held tight. "Try not to do the same thing, okay?"

This was the first time since he split with Addison that he'd mentioned anything about her, so Kiley knew it took courage for him to bring it up, and she wouldn't blow it off.

"I'll do my best."

"Promise?" he asked.

"Promise," she said, and jogged down the steps.

She gave the ERT leader instructions and her business card. By the time she thanked him for coming out so late at night, Mack and Evan were headed for the SUV. The three of them rode in silence back to the office. She knew her thoughts were on Mack's comments, but she had no idea what the guys were thinking.

They found Cam and Sean in the conference room. Kiley updated Cam on their lack of progress in capturing the suspects.

"Then I guess it's a good thing I know where they are." He grinned. "Or at least where they were when they hacked the Tacoma police server."

Kiley gaped at him and ripped off her vest. "Seriously, that panned out?"

"I know, right?" he said. "Rarely does. But I tracked the hack to a dive motel in Los Angeles."

"L.A.," she and Mack said at the same time.

"I thought the URL I sent you was a hotel login page, but it might've been the beginning of Los Angeles."

Evan grimaced. "L.A. makes sense. According to the team reports, we have a double threat there. The Isabella Dam undergoing retrofitting, and a bunch of chemical plants."

Mack fired a sharp look at Cam. "You know which room we're looking at?"

Cam's grin widened. "I might've taken a peek at their reservation system. Our suspects booked under their aliases in room 104."

"We need to get to L.A. now!" Kiley's thoughts immediately went to logistics.

"I already checked, and there's a Joint Forces base south of L.A.," Sean said. "Eisenhower should be able to get a flight scrambled."

"We'll still need our L.A. SWAT team to watch the place until we can get there." Kiley grabbed her phone. "I'll call Eisenhower to arrange the flight and SWAT while you all pack and load the gear. I doubt we'll get another chance to get any sleep before this all comes to a head, so take advantage of the flight for that."

Evan touched the scar on the side of his face. "What can I do now?"

Stop worrying so much. "Pack your personal items and help load the vehicle."

Everyone shot into motion, and Kiley made the call, her heart pummeling against her chest at the thought of finally facing down the terrorists.

CHAPTER 23

Sean pulled the SUV into the seedy motel lot, and Kiley glassed the area with her binoculars. Bright moonlight shone down on the dingy one-story motel with pale-pink stucco walls and bright aqua trim.

This could be the moment they'd spent days anticipating, and her nerves raced as she scanned the parking lot filled with older-model cars and littered with trash. "No black Honda."

"They could've ditched that car by now," Evan said, "or taken public transit to get here. Or it might not be Nabi and Shah."

She searched the rest of the lot, glad to see SWAT hadn't parked their assault vehicle near room 104, but had taken stealth positions behind two large, rusty dumpsters across the lot.

Kiley stowed her binoculars. "We'll check in with the commander, then come back for our gear."

"I'll grab a key from the front desk." Sean slipped out and went straight for the motel office.

Evan ran a hand over his hair. "It would be a good idea to at least put vests on now."

She knew he would be concerned for her safety again, but she was shocked to see a slight tremble in his hand. Still, his suggestion wasn't a bad one.

She got out and opened the hatch to distribute the vests. By the time Sean returned and the team crossed the lot, the SWAT commander had stepped out to meet them.

He was a giant of a man wearing a green tactical suit, body armor, and a helmet, and he held an assault rifle under his arm. He shoved out his massive hand. "Commander Bart Hawke."

Kiley shook hands and made the introductions. "Any sign of life in 104?"

"None." He eyed Kiley. "These suspects must be high up the food chain to get my team out in the middle of the night for babysitting duty."

She nodded but didn't explain and lifted her binoculars to zoom in on the room again.

"So you're out of D.C.?" Hawke asked.

"We are."

"RED team, right?"

"You've heard of us."

"Not many agents who haven't."

Kiley had enough of the small talk, so she looked at Hawke. "We'll get our gear for the breach, and I'd appreciate your team providing backup."

As she turned to leave, the door to room 104 opened, and a dark-skinned man with black hair poked his head out. He caught sight of them and bolted back inside. The window shattered, glass flying everywhere, and a rifle barrel slid out.

"Gun!" Kiley started for cover behind a car.

Evan launched himself at her, grabbed her up in his arms, and dove behind the vehicle. He took the brunt of the fall on his shoulder. They still landed with a thud. It happened so fast she couldn't think of what to say while she tried to scramble out of his arms. He covered her body and held fast.

"Let me up," she demanded as gunfire sounded from the motel room.

He met her gaze, and she'd never seen such determination in his eyes before.

"Get off me," she demanded.

He waffled for a moment.

She seized the opportunity to push against his chest. "Let. Me. Up."

His expression softened and he eased back.

She scooted to her feet and checked to see if her team was safe. Sean and Mack had crouched behind a dumpster, their sidearms raised. Mack glanced at her, his expression wild and unfocused. He was such a strong guy, and he looked like he might be freaking out. She'd never seen him like that and worried he was remembering something from his past days in the military.

She tried to communicate with her eyes that everything was going to be all right. He suddenly shifted, clearing his gaze, but she would definitely ask him about it. Once she got over her mortification for being tackled like a helpless woman. Would be even more mortified when she looked into Hawke's face if he'd seen what happened.

She drew her weapon and slipped around the dumpster to come up beside the commander. "We need the shooter alive."

"Might not be possible," he said, keeping his focus on the building. "I'm dispatching a phone to him now, but if he doesn't stop firing to pick it up and negotiate, we might have no choice but to take him down before innocent civilians get hurt."

He lifted a bullhorn to his mouth. "Put down your weapon. I'm sending our robot with a phone so we can talk."

One of his men holding a laptop deployed a small robot that hummed across the lot. The gunman fired on the bot, tumbling it over. The tech righted it, but the gunfire continued, sharp reports with bullets pinging off the dumpster and ground nearby.

In a momentary lull, Hawke shouted, "Come on! Pick up the phone and we can talk about this."

The shooter kept firing.

"Sorry, Agent Dawson," Hawke said. "People are starting to come out of their rooms, and we need to end this before any of them or our people get hurt."

She didn't want the standoff to end this way. Not only because she needed Nabi and Shah's information but also because she didn't want any casualties. Hawke was right. The situation was extremely volatile, and he had protocols to follow. They had no other option. Protecting innocent lives was the most important thing at all times in law enforcement.

And it didn't matter what she thought. He didn't need or require her approval, but he did get out his phone and run the situation down for one of the special agents in charge of the big L.A. office. He was calm and steady while they continued to take fire, and Kiley's respect for the man grew.

"Affirmative. We're cleared to take the shot." He gave a firm nod and pocketed his phone. He looked at Kiley. "We're a go."

She nodded, but her heart sank into her stomach. She didn't like this. Didn't like it at all. Still, she knew what was coming.

SWAT prepared for this very situation and had at least one sharpshooter in position, likely on overwatch this whole time. Focus pinned to his scope. Waiting for the word to do his job. Willing to take action, but not liking the consequences either.

"Take the shot," Hawke said into his mic and listened. "Affirmative. You're cleared to take the shot."

The L.A. office supervisor had needed to affirm the plan to take a life with Hawke, and in turn his shooter needed the same confirmation so that no mistaken shots were fired.

Kiley held her breath. Waited.

A single report sounded from the distance, and the gunfire from inside the room stopped.

"This is the FBI!" Hawke bellowed through his bullhorn. "Everyone back in your rooms now."

Guests poking their heads from out their doors scrambled back inside.

"Sit tight," Hawke said to her and then bent to his mic. "Move. Move. Move."

The SWAT guys swarmed out of hiding to secure the area, their boots pounding over the pavement as they rushed the room. Evan stepped cautiously along the side of the car, and her thoughts turned to his football tackle. Anger consumed her adrenaline, and she could hardly look at him. He'd let his personal feelings color his actions, and she couldn't have her authority challenged that way in front of another team of agents.

"We're clear," Hawke called from in front of the room. "One suspect only."

Holstering her weapon, Kiley went to join Sean and Mack, as did Evan, but she kept her gaze pinned on her teammates.

Sean glanced around the lot. "C'mon, Bowers. You can watch the entrance with me to see if this guy's buddy shows up. On the way we'll take pictures of license plates and run them for IDs."

Evan nodded and gave Kiley a long look she ignored. He followed Sean toward the entrance. She made a mental note to thank Sean for getting Evan out of her sight and for thinking to cover the entrance and run plates.

"Let's get gloves and booties so we can check out the room," she said to Mack.

She marched toward their SUV, putting her anger into each step. Mack kept up with her, and she glanced up at him. "You okay? You looked freaked out back there."

"Fine," he said, his tone shutting down the questioning. "And you?"

She'd let him get away with it for now but would watch for that unsettled look in future ops. "I'm mortified. I'm supposed to be the leader on this op, and Evan tackles me."

"There was nothing you could do anyway," Mack said.

She gritted her teeth. "He'll be off this investigation as soon as I can have a civil conversation with him. I can assure you of that."

"Don't be too hasty. We might still need him."

"Are you kidding me?" She gaped at Mack. "You're taking his side?"

"No, but I understand wanting to protect someone you love. I once did the same thing with Addy." A fond smile, speaking to his love for Addison, claimed his mouth. "She was just as mad at me, but I didn't care. I love her and would do anything to protect her. *Anything,* even if it embarrassed her in front of other agents."

She didn't miss the fact that he said love in the present tense, and Kiley hoped it might mean they would get back together someday. "Big difference here is that he did it because Olin's death freaked him out, and now he's trying to make sure no one gets hurt on his watch ever again."

"Are you sure?" Mack pulled her to a stop. "He's in love with you, kid, and you're too blind to see it. Or maybe just unwilling."

She sputtered, trying to come up with a rebuttal, but how could she refute Mack's statement? He was a keen observer of people. Her, not so much. Was he right? Was Evan in love with her? Sure, they had a connection and that kiss, but love was a whole different thing, wasn't it?

Thinking about Evan right now was only getting in the way. She shook her head to erase her thoughts and started off again.

"You can't run away from it," Mack said, catching up.

"I'm not running. At least not this time. This could be our best lead yet, and I need to get my head back in the game." At the SUV she grabbed a box of booties and gloves and spun to go to the room.

Mack fell in step next to her. "Besides, the SWAT guys were the right ones to handle the shootout. They were prepared for an altercation. Dressed for assault and had sharpshooters on the team."

He was right. Of course he was.

If Evan hadn't taken her down, what might she have done? If not for his interference, maybe she would've taken over from Hawke and gotten someone hurt in the process. She would have to give her actions some serious consideration when they debriefed. She wouldn't think about Evan being in love with her. Those thoughts would wait until the wee hours of the morning when she was ready to drop from exhaustion and didn't have the strength to block the crazy idea.

They approached Hawke, who was standing outside the door, his assault rifle still in his hands. "Suspect's dead."

She'd expected as much. "Would you mind calling your supervisor and getting ERT out here?"

"Sure."

"Thanks for handling it," she said, and hoped she sounded stronger than she felt as her subsiding adrenaline brought on a heavy dose of fatigue and threatened to give her a headache.

"Thanks for letting us." He lifted his shoulders. "I'm impressed that you knew we were better equipped and took a back seat."

If he'd seen Evan tackle her, he didn't let on, so she gave a nod, though she had to wonder again what she might have done if not for Evan's interference. She put on the gloves and booties and stepped into the room. The metallic smell of blood mixed with spicy pizza lying in an open delivery box. The suspect had come to rest on his back between the window and a double bed, his lower body twisted at an odd angle. She'd hoped to make a visual ID, but a direct hit to his head prevented any possibility for facial ID.

She spotted his wallet and phone on the nightstand. She bagged the phone so they could image the device and search it the minute they got to the local office, then grabbed the wallet and withdrew a Virginia driver's license. "This isn't Nabi or Shah. It's Gadi Amari."

Mack's mouth dropped. "We'll need to grab the portable print scanner and try to get his prints from Interpol to confirm."

Kiley nodded. "I need to follow up with Nigel Clark anyway."

Mack stared at Gadi. "So if the police hack originated here like Cam said, the Amaris are connected to Nabi and Shah, which links the Pittsburgh bombing to our investigation."

"Looks like it," she said, her thoughts spinning. "Question now is, what role were the Amaris supposed to play in the upcoming attack, and can they still carry it out without Gadi?"

Sean had gone inside to run license plates, leaving Evan to stand guard duty alone. But now

376

a local team of agents arrived to set up a stakeout, and Evan gladly turned over the job and jogged across the parking lot. He couldn't quit thinking about Kiley and wanted to find out if she was still mad at him. Clearly in the heat of the moment, she hadn't been glad of his interference.

In hindsight, he felt a bit foolish. But the second that rifle poked through the window, he could do nothing less than get her out of the line of fire. Maybe he should have stopped there and let her get up right away, but at least he'd come to his senses and finally moved.

Fully expecting to be kicked off the investigation, he put on booties and gloves and stepped into the motel room. Sean sat on the bed engrossed in his laptop, likely still running plates. Evan expected the stink eye from Mack. Surprisingly he didn't say a word or even look angry. Kiley refused to acknowledge him, or maybe she found the dresser search more interesting.

If he had any hope of remaining on this team, he needed to make himself useful and not stand around waiting for her to tell him what to do. He stepped over to the victim they would officially be identifying from DNA or prints, since facial recognition obviously wasn't possible. Striped cotton pajama bottoms were his only clothing, exposing his flabby middle. He'd likely just woken up in the middle of the night, found his partner missing, and stuck his head outside to look for him.

"We find any ID for this guy?" Evan asked.

"Virginia DL says it's Gadi Amari," Mack told him.

"Really? Gadi." Evan took a moment to process the surprise. "Any thoughts on why his brother wasn't here at this time of day?"

"Maybe he went out to get supplies or food," Mack said.

"If so, he should've been back by now," Sean said. "And there's been no sign of him."

"He could have returned during the gunfire and bolted," Kiley said. "Or maybe he's not even in LA. I should text Cam to look for CCTV footage in the area."

Surprised she hadn't thrown him out of the room, Evan watched her get out her phone. Because she let him stay now didn't mean she didn't plan to kick him off the team. Maybe if he found something of importance in this room, she'd realize his value and keep him around.

He looked back at the body and remembered the tattoo from the bank video. Maybe Gadi had one too, tying him to the suspects from the container. Evan squatted down to get a closer look at his hands.

"Something of interest?" Kiley asked from above.

He looked up. "Checking for a tattoo like we saw in the bank video. He doesn't have one."

She gave a quick nod, which he took to mean *carry on.*

He turned his attention back to Gadi and knelt down by his torso. He might not have a matching tattoo on his hand, but he had a larger tattoo on his upper arm, and Evan wanted to get a look at it. He shouldn't touch a body before the ME arrived, much less move it.

He turned to Kiley. "He has a tattoo on his arm. Okay if I nudge him to get a better look?"

"Go ahead." Kiley's phone rang, taking her attention. She answered and nodded. "Perfect. Thanks for letting me know."

She stowed her phone. "Prints lifted at the apartment in Tacoma matched the container prints."

Mack looked up from the backpack he was pawing through. "Then we were right. The container guys were both there. Hopefully we'll get some good prints from this place proving they were here too."

Kiley nodded. "And get the information we need from Interpol to match it up to Nabi's and Shah's prints."

Sean closed his laptop. "Finished the last plate from the lot. All but two check out. They're for rentals, so I have Cam tracking them down."

Evan lifted Amari's shoulder, but the lamp cast a shadow on the arm. "I can't see the tat clearly. Too dark. Can someone help me lift his shoulder so I can take a picture of it?"

Kiley moved around the body and squatted next to him to pull up the dead man's shoulder.

Evan snapped a few pictures and looked at the screen. "Wow. Oh, wow." He held out his phone to Kiley.

"A Soundwave tattoo." Excitement burned in her expression.

Mack stepped over to them. "Never heard of it."

"Sounds and messages are embedded in the tattoo, and you can listen to them with a special app," she said, grabbing her phone from her pocket and tapping the screen.

"Sounds. Like what kind?" Sean got up to join them.

"It's usually used for personal things," Evan said. "Like a spouse's voice saying I love you, or a child's voice or laughter."

"Where do we get the app?" Mack asked.

Kiley held up her phone. "I've got it downloading now. I'll have to hold my phone over the tattoo, so we'll need to turn the body."

"Could mess with forensics trajectory calculations," Mack said.

Kiley looked at her team. "Are we in agreement that moving him is the right thing to do?"

"It's not like we don't know the cause of death," Mack said. "And we shouldn't have to lift him much more than you did for the picture and won't alter his position."

"Agreed," Sean said. "This isn't a homicide investigation, and we have millions of people counting on us figuring this out."

Her phone dinged. "App's ready." She eyed the team in a dramatic pause.

Evan felt the tension in the room skyrocket.

"I'll help stabilize him so he doesn't move." Mack bent over the body.

Evan lifted the shoulder, concentrating on revealing the ink while keeping the body stable.

Kiley placed her phone over the tattoo. A deep male voice came from the speaker, the words in a foreign language.

"Anyone catch that?" Kiley asked. "Sounded like Arabic to me."

"Play it again," Sean said. "I'll record it on my phone so we can get a translator working on it."

Evan positioned his phone over the tattoo again while Sean held his phone close. He played back the recording. "Got it."

Mack looked at Evan. "Great job, man. This could be the thing to bust this case wide open."

Evan nodded as he thought the same thing. Selfishly he also hoped it was enough to get Kiley to forgive him for his hasty tackle and keep her from sending him out of her life and away from the most important investigation of his career.

CHAPTER 24

Kiley joined the team in the large conference room at the FBI's busy Los Angeles field office. A perfect place to work on the threat, as the staff in one of the biggest offices in the bureau offered unlimited resources. She'd already taken advantage of that, requesting an interpreter for the tattoo message on the way in.

Her phone rang, and seeing Nigel Clark's name on the screen, she snatched it up with a frenzy. "Agent Dawson."

"Yes, Agent Dawson. Nigel Clark here. You're looking for information on Mohamed Nabi and Jangi Shah."

"Thanks for calling back. My print examiner said you gave him their names." She thought for a second on what to tell him and decided he needed to know the severity of the threat so he would adopt her sense of urgency for the request. "We have reason to believe they've entered our country and are planning a horrendous attack. I need additional information on them ASAP."

"That doesn't sound good," he said, a hint of worry in his tone. "I can email a detailed report, prints, and DNA profiles for the pair."

"I'm also looking for information on Bilal and Gadi Amari. Especially prints for Gadi."

"Hold on while I look at what we have."

Kiley had no time to stand around and wait for him to come back on the line. She moved to the end of the table to set up Gadi's phone to image where she could keep an eye on it.

"Okay, yeah," Clark said. "We have Gadi's prints. Brother's prints too. They're new to the terrorism scene so not much additional info, I'm afraid."

"Send everything you have on all four men. Don't delay. It's urgent." She gave him her email address and warned him to keep the fact that these men were in the U.S. confidential.

"Understood. I'll send the email right away." He disconnected.

Hoping she'd set a fire blazing under him, she opened her email on her computer. She kept one eye on it and the other on the team. "He's sending DNA, prints, and details on Nabi and Shah. Plus he has the Amaris' prints."

Evan dropped into a nearby chair. "Seems like we're finally making some progress."

"But we need more. Much more. And faster." She shot a look at the wall clock. "We have a little less than twenty-four hours until 9/11. Give me an update so we can get moving. Anyone. Go. Toss it out there."

Cam looked up. "No CCTV at the motel, but I've got calls out to nearby businesses."

"Since we totally struck out on cars in the motel

lot," Mack said, "hopefully the CCTV will catch Bilal's car if he's in town."

"Agreed," Cam said. "Clark's data might give an idea of the role the Amaris are assigned in the attack. If not, I'll work on expanding our information on them."

Kiley scribbled the words *cyber* and *bomb* on the whiteboard. "We still need to nail down the threat. If it's cyber in nature, Bilal's IT skills could come into play. If a bomb, he could be in charge of the Wi-Fi backup."

A knock sounded on the door, and a woman poked her head in. "I'm Agent Haddad. You needed a translator?"

Kiley rushed to the door. "Come in. Come in. We recorded a message and need to have it interpreted immediately."

The woman wearing a black pant suit and white blouse cautiously approached the table, and Kiley had to resist the urge to get her moving faster.

Sean had connected his phone to a Bluetooth speaker and started the recording playing.

Haddad frowned as she ran her hand over gleaming black hair pulled back in a ponytail. "Would you please turn up the volume and play it again?"

Sean tapped a few buttons, and the voice sounded louder.

"Okay," she said. "He's saying, 'work hour wait win yesterday.'"

Kiley didn't know what to say or do. She'd counted on the message providing that all-important lead, but Haddad's interpretation was just nonsense. "Are you sure that's right?"

"I know it doesn't make sense and that's why I had you play it again." Haddad shrugged. "But that's what he's saying—'work hour wait win yesterday.' "

Kiley nodded. "Thank you, Agent Haddad."

Her eyes narrowed, and she backed out of the room.

Kiley turned back to her teammates. "Any ideas?" She frantically searched for an explanation from the team as the pressure of their short deadline built. Sean and Mack shook their heads. Cam and Evan frowned. This was up to her, but what did it mean?

An idea popped into her brain then. "The letter we intercepted at the Abeds' mailbox place seemed to be in code. Maybe this is code too. It could even fit with the information in that letter. Or something in Firuzeh's journals. Or files at the shipping company."

"Or even communications they might have made via the video games," Mack added, catching her enthusiasm.

"Okay. Yeah. Yeah. This is sounding more possible." Kiley wrote the words on the whiteboard in red marker, then grabbed copies of Firuzeh's journal from her backpack and slid them across the table to Cam. "You and Evan start reviewing those. Look for anything that might fit with the words *work hour wait win yesterday*. Sean and Mack, start on the shipping files."

Kiley snatched her phone from the table. "I'll call Cryptanalysis to ask about the letter and give them these details and the PlayStation chat information. Then I'll get started reviewing the game files." She sent the game files to the printer and dialed the FBI's Cryptanalysis Department. She had to go through a few people, growing more irritated with each one, until finally connecting with Ulrich Lane, the person handling their letter.

"Agent Dawson," he said. "I assume you're calling for an update on your letter."

"Tell me you have something for me," she nearly shouted at him.

"I've been working on the letter and believe we have a masonic cipher here."

"Seriously, it really is code?" She looked at her team, whose heads came up. They were watching her intently. She was glad to see they'd caught the enthusiasm, but they had no time to waste so she twirled her finger, telling them to get back to work.

"Yes, it's a centuries-old cipher with two X patterns and two tic-tac-toe diagrams to represent the letters of the alphabet," Ulrich continued. "I use the patterns formed by the intersecting lines and dots to decipher the message."

She could barely contain her excitement and wished she could jump through the phone and speed up his work. "How long before you finish it?"

A heavy sigh came over the phone. "If all goes well, and I'm not interrupted, by the end of the day."

"This is top priority," she said emphatically. "I'll make a few calls and ensure you're not interrupted."

"Thank you. I appreciate it."

"Please add the following words to the end of the letter to see if it makes sense." She shared the odd words from the Soundwave tattoo.

He repeated them back.

"That's right. Call me the minute you finish, no matter the time of day. Understood?"

"Will do."

"Millions of lives are counting on this, Ulrich," she said. "Please do your very best work here. Don't let your country down." Kiley ended the call and shared her conversation with the team. "We could have something by the end of the day."

"And what about the video-chat information?" Evan asked.

"I already asked Eisenhower to get another analyst assigned to it." She took a seat and sent a text to Eisenhower, updating him and asking him to pull strings to make sure Ulrich Lane's time was fully committed to the cipher.

He responded, promising to act on Ulrich. *FYI, warrant is in the works for Barzani's customer numbers. Should have it today.*

She glanced at her email, disappointed in not seeing a message from Clark yet and willing it to appear.

"Gadi's phone is done," Sean announced from the end of the table.

"That completed way too fast." Kiley raced for the phone and looked at the files. Shocked, she dropped into a chair. "Someone wiped the phone while we were imaging it."

Sean met her gaze. "Seriously?"

She gave a solemn nod.

He paled. "I've only seen that happen once."

She felt sick to her stomach. "Encrypted phones from Phantom Shield."

He nodded.

"Who's Phantom Shield?" Evan asked.

Kiley hadn't really looked at him since he tackled her. Too many loose ends needed her immediate attention, and she couldn't even begin to deal with his actions. She shoved it away and focused on answering his question. "The company offers encryption services to businesses and executives, or so they claim. In reality, they're a criminal enterprise providing gangs and drug traffickers with mobile devices that hide data and mask communications. And if the user's apprehended, the phones can be completely wiped on command."

"Is that legal?" Evan's mouth formed a tight line.

"Not definite at this point," she replied. "They're currently under investigation by the bureau. The theory is that it's against the law if a company purposely provides criminals with the means to evade law enforcement through special encryption and destroy evidence."

Evan grimaced. "Looks like they expanded to include terrorist cells."

Kiley thought about the development, trying her best to find something positive. "If we access their company files, we might be able to download information for both of the Amaris' phones."

"Permission to do that will take time we don't have," Sean pointed out.

Kiley planted her hands on the table and gazed at the team. "We're less than a day away from an attack on millions of people and no solid leads. We have to do this however we can. Even hacking them."

Mack eyed her. "And if we get caught?"

"C'mon, man." Cam waved a hand. "You know we won't get caught."

Evan shot a questioning look at Cam. "How can you be so sure? They're providing phones and service to the worst of the worst. So they must have the worst of the worst in charge of their network, which means it's highly secure."

"We can do it," Sean said. "More likely Cam and Kiley can do it. They both have on-the-job experience in network management in addition to their FBI experience."

Kiley looked at Cam. "You in?"

"Heck yeah, I'm in." His lips cracked in a mischievous grin. "No way I'd say no to this."

She changed her focus to Evan. "And to keep them from locating us if for some reason we mess up, we do what all exceptional hackers do."

Cam's smile widened. "We buy fresh machines, check into some cheap motel, and we bounce our transmissions around the globe so it won't lead back to us."

The excitement of the hunt built in her gut, and she looked at Mack. "You and Sean get the machines. Pay cash."

"You sound like a criminal," Evan said.

And she felt like one, but desperate times called for desperate measures. Her phone rang. "Everyone hang tight for a second. It's Agent Quinn and I gotta take the call."

"Glad I caught you." Quinn's tone was packed with angst. "Nasim Waleed hopped a plane to Sacramento ten minutes ago."

Sacramento?

"No idea why he's headed to California,"

Quinn continued, "but my team confirmed he boarded the flight, and I have the best local agents meeting it on the other end. Hopefully we'll figure out his plan."

Could they be coming cross-country to meet up with Bilal Amari? "Did you question Waleed about the Amaris?"

"Yes. He claimed he doesn't know them, and they just started supporting The Righteous out of the blue." Quinn's disgusted tone said just what he thought of that claim. "But we got a warrant for Waleed's files, and our review proves the Amaris are officially on the membership roster."

"Get me a copy of that roster ASAP," she said, not caring how demanding she sounded.

He didn't answer right away, and she was about to say please when he said, "I'll email it to you."

She might be anxious for information, but she didn't have to be rude. "Thank you."

"Are you still thinking our investigations are connected?" he asked.

"Yes," she said and clamped her mouth closed. She felt bad about not updating him about Gadi, but Quinn didn't have clearance for that information. And besides, she still hadn't gotten prints from Clark to confirm Gadi's ID. "I'll be watching for your email."

She quickly disconnected before he asked additional questions. "Nasim Waleed is on his way to Sacramento."

Evan glanced up. "Isn't there a dam near Sacramento?"

"Oroville Dam," Sean answered. "Are there chemical plants there?"

"It's not on my list, but I can look into it," Mack offered.

"Maybe Waleed's trip has nothing to do with Sacramento," Evan said. "Maybe he flew in there and is driving to the target location. Or even on his way to meet Bilal Amari."

Kiley nodded. "Leading agents on a wild-goose chase would be the best way to lose his tail."

"If the attack is to take place before 9/11, then he has about nineteen hours to be in position," Evan said. "Means the location would have to be drivable in that time frame."

Cam lifted his head. "With nonstop driving at sixty mph, he could be anywhere. He could just drive to the nearest airport and hop a plane under a bogus ID."

Mack scowled. "Then if he's involved in this upcoming attack, we better hope the agents don't lose him."

Kiley quickly calculated Waleed's flight time and how long it would take for the team to get to Sacramento. "This is too important to leave up to other agents. If Eisenhower can arrange transport, we should tail them ourselves."

Disappointment crowned on Cam's face. "What about the hack? I thought it was top priority."

He was right. Getting information on the Amaris' phones was also a priority she couldn't lose sight of. Nor the email from Clark. She was going to have to juggle many balls in the next few hours, but she was amped and up for the challenge.

"The hack is still on." She met Cam's gaze. "You can do that from anywhere. You just might have to do it on your own."

Evan pulled the small white Corolla to the curb at the Sacramento airport passenger pickup area, making sure to leave several cars between them and the beige Buick holding Mack and Sean. Waleed would recognize Evan and Kiley, so Mack and Sean took lead in the op while Kiley joined Evan. Cam was on his way to a motel not only to run communications for the team but also to start hacking Phantom Shield.

Kiley moved in the passenger seat, her shapely legs grabbing his attention as he shifted into park. They'd made a quick stop before leaving L.A. to buy casual attire so they could blend in better. She'd chosen khaki shorts paired with a T-shirt and a flowery blouse worn to hide her sidearm. He'd grabbed gray cargo shorts, a navy T-shirt, and a plaid button-down shirt to hide his holster.

A text came in from Eisenhower, and Kiley had the infotainment system read it aloud: *"Finlay Brooks assigned to your video-chat conversation.*" The message ended with Finlay's phone number.

Kiley issued a thank-you text to Eisenhower. He replied, *"Warrant came in for Barzani. With you out of town, I'm having a Seattle agent serve it. Will update you soon."*

"Let's hope Barzani's numbers lead us to whoever booked that container," Evan said.

Kiley held up her phone. "I'm gonna give Finlay Brooks a call."

Evan leaned back to listen in, but she didn't put the call through the system or on speaker, so he only got a one-sided version, where Kiley impressed upon the woman the importance of cracking the code and quick—if indeed it was code.

She ended the call and stared out the window. "I wish we had a concrete link between Nabi, Shah, and the Waleeds, so we'd know if coming here is a waste of time."

"It'd be better if the email you got from Clark pointed to a connection, but it didn't so we have to follow the leads where they go and hope they connect at some point."

"Yeah," she said, as she'd received Clark's email on the flight. "But I'd hoped for more from Clark. He didn't tell us anything about our suspects' backgrounds that we didn't already know."

"At least he confirmed prints for Gadi, and we know he's the motel victim."

"Right, that helps," she said and looked like

she appreciated that Evan was trying to keep a positive attitude. She pointed out the front window. "Mack's headed our way."

Evan lowered his window, the steamy warm air drifting in.

Mack planted his hands on the door and leaned down. "Plane's on the ground. Agents will follow Waleed out and keep us updated, so we wait here. I'll get the security officer to relax and let us stay put." He strode toward the female officer waving traffic forward, his cowboy boots barely heard above the passing cars and planes overhead.

Evan raised his window and cranked up the air conditioner. "He seems pretty confident he'll convince her to let us sit here."

She nodded. "He turns on his Southern charm and women are putty in his hands."

"You too?"

"What?"

"Are you putty in his hands?"

"I'd like to say after years of working with him that I'm immune, but I still fall for it at times. Then I find myself saddled with a task I had no plans of agreeing to take on." She gave a genuine smile, her eyes glinting with fondness for Mack.

Evan had once been on the receiving end of such smiles, but that was long ago. Now he was just happy that she wasn't overtly angry with him over his foolish tackle, though it had lingered under the surface when he'd caught her looking at him on the helicopter ride to Sacramento.

They could be stuck together in this small car for hours, and it would be best if they got everything out in the open and moved on so they weren't distracted. "We never talked about why I tackled you."

She was stowing her phone, and her hands stilled. "No."

"I know you didn't like it," he rushed on before she shut him down. "But the only way I could breathe was to be sure any bullet would have to go through me first. You didn't need me to do that. I get that. You're beyond capable, and I'm sorry if I embarrassed you."

The moment came rushing back. The gunfire. Bullets pinging everywhere. Her body a sure target. He could have lost her and couldn't bear the thought. Nor could he bear the thought that she was still angry.

He reached out to cup her cheek and waited for her to flinch. To recoil. She just sat staring at him. But what did he expect? That she would instantly forgive him?

"I know you still blame me for Olin too, but . . ." He couldn't keep babbling on. Not when emotions he couldn't put a name to swam in his gut. He slid his hand around the back of her neck and drew her closer.

She made a sound of surprise but didn't tell him to back off.

He forgot about the job. About the people rushing around them and cars honking. He pressed his lips against hers, setting a fire inside his body he knew only she could douse. He let go of everything but the feel of her lips on his and deepened the kiss.

Warm, wonderful emotions swam through him. Love. This was love. He knew it in a heartbeat. He was in love with her.

Her hands went up around his neck, tangling in his hair, drawing him closer. She kissed him back, his heart lurching.

A horn honked. The sharp sound echoed through the air and brought him down to earth again. He pulled back, got control of his breathing, but kept his gaze locked with hers.

"I know you're attracted to me," he whispered, fighting desperately hard not to tell her he loved her and send her running away, "but I hope you can forgive me for everything, and we can see where this might lead."

CHAPTER 25

Mack walked up to the car, and as he talked with Evan, Kiley touched her lips. Evan had kissed her in front of her teammates. And she'd let him. Not only let him, but there wasn't a single moment when she thought to tell him to stop. She couldn't believe she'd let it happen. Encouraged it even. And that was the last place her focus should be directed. The very last place.

Evan looked at her. "What do you think?"

Case in point, she had no idea what they'd been discussing.

Mack peered at her. "You okay? You look flushed."

"Fine," she said quickly and hoped he thought the heat had put the color in her face. "What did you say?"

Mack tilted his head, his eyes assessing. "Ibrahim Waleed flew in on a different airline."

She couldn't believe she'd tuned out such an important discussion, but she was determined to focus now. "If the brothers go separate ways, we'll tail Ibrahim. Our comms will only work for two hundred miles or so. If it bugs out, we'll stay in touch by phone."

Mack's eyes narrowed. "Be careful. Ibrahim

is more dangerous than Nasim, and we know Nasim's no saint."

She nodded, and Mack headed back to his car. She connected her phone to the USB port, not only to keep the battery charged but also to allow easier communication if needed, then fixed her earbud in her ear and turned on her comms unit. Evan put on his device too, and she mentally prepared for conversing this way with Sean and Mack. They would all be using push-to-talk on their mics to keep the chatter to a minimum, allowing private conversations in the vehicles.

"Goldilocks picked up baggage and is headed our way." Mack's voice came over the earbud. "Brother Bear not with him."

Kiley rolled her eyes at the code names Mack had chosen in the event someone overheard their communications. In the helicopter, they'd decided on Goldilocks, but Mack had obviously called an audible and added Brother Bear.

"We should take a good look at Ibrahim's photo so we recognize him." She pulled up his picture and held out her phone.

"I'd rather look at him than his brother," Evan said. "Nasim hides his ugly two-faced nature, while Ibrahim's glare says it all."

She had to agree. Ibrahim displayed his meanness for all to see. Even so, she sure didn't like looking at his picture. She put on a baseball cap and got out of the car. She pretended to be looking at her phone when she was actually watching the crowd. She wished she could use binoculars to scan the area, but she couldn't draw attention to herself.

"Goldilocks exiting middle door by you, Mack," she said into her mic. "Scanning the vehicles."

"Got him," Mack said.

Nasim suddenly bolted through the crowd, and she could no longer see him. "Goldilocks on the move."

"Getting in a silver SUV. Run the plate, Cam." Mack rattled off the license plate number. "Vehicle's departing. So are we."

She heard a car door slam and saw Sean pull out of their space. She watched them drive off, leaving her feeling vulnerable, and also feeling extremely thankful for Evan. She waited for anger over his behavior at the motel to surface.

It didn't.

Not because of his apology, though that did help. But on the chopper ride, she'd given her conversation with Mack some consideration. It was looking like Evan's actions could be motivated by more than fear of someone dying on his watch. The kiss and his comment told her that much.

He would give his life for her for a myriad of reasons. His oath to protect others. His desire to do the right thing. That fear too.

And she would do the same thing. She would rather die than let him be harmed.

Oh, man. She had feelings for him too. Love? She'd never been in love. Sure, she'd had crushes before. But love? No. She'd never allowed herself to fall for anyone. Or maybe she had when she and Evan first met. Still, this achy, wonderful feeling had to be love. It could be nothing else. The thought left her breathless.

"Car's a rental." Cam's voice came over the earbud. "I'll track down the contract."

"Brother Bear is on his way out the same door," Evan said.

Kiley looked down the way and spotted Ibrahim. He wore jeans, hiking boots, and a tan T-shirt, making her wonder what he might be planning. "Got eyes on him," she said.

A black sedan darted to the curb, and he tossed a small bag in the back, then climbed in.

Kiley jumped into their Corolla. "Black sedan pulling from the curb."

"Got it," Evan said.

He waited a beat before merging into traffic, hanging back so that Ibrahim or his driver didn't spot them. As an ICE agent, Evan likely did his fair share of surveillance, and she was immediately impressed with his skills in tailing them without being discovered.

They trailed Ibrahim out of the airport, and Kiley gave Cam the plate number to run, then pulled up a map on her iPad to track their progress.

"Goldilocks headed north on Highway 99," Mack reported.

"Brother Bear going the same way," Kiley said.

"Brother Bear in a rental car too," Cam said. "Working on getting both contracts now."

The miles passed while Kiley kept her focus riveted to the black sedan, and as traffic thinned, Evan backed off even more.

"Goldilocks merging onto Highway 70," Mack announced.

"Roger that." Kiley looked at the map and then at Evan. "Looks like they're heading to the dam."

"Brother Bear remaining on Highway 99," she told Mack and Sean. "Do you think Goldilocks's driver made a mistake and missed staying on 99?"

"Maybe," Mack replied. "Or maybe they're both on the move as decoys to distract us from the real targets. Or they could know they're being tailed and they're splitting up to confuse us."

"Nasim has to know he's under surveillance and suspect he'd be tailed," Evan said.

"Likely true for Ibrahim too," she said, watching him take the dam exit and reporting his movements to the other team.

"I don't like this," she said to Evan as he followed Ibrahim down winding roads through the Oroville Wildlife Area.

402

Evan's sharp focus didn't leave the road. "He could simply be tasked with surveilling the area."

"I hope that's all they're up to." She leaned forward and watched as Ibrahim pulled into a launch area and drove straight toward the water.

Evan stopped their car where they overlooked the ramp running downhill toward the lake. Kiley quickly updated the others on their location.

Evan glanced at her. "This location makes no sense."

Her heart pounded against her chest, her mind racing to come up with a plausible explanation as Ibrahim slipped out of his car. He grabbed his bag and strode toward a large boat being off-loaded from a trailer attached to a gray pickup truck. He climbed into the boat, slowly turned, and lifted his hand in a salute.

Kiley couldn't see the guy's face, but could imagine it held a cocky or malicious smile.

"Clearly he knows we're tailing him." Evan shoved the car into park. "Since we're blown, I'm going to take some pictures of his friends."

Before she could warn him to be careful, he jumped out and jogged toward the lake. Her heartbeat ratcheted up, and she bolted out of the car after him, taking a stance by a tree for cover and drawing her weapon.

She aimed at the man nearest to Evan as he pointed his phone at Ibrahim and his pilot. The man glared at Evan but remained by the truck.

Evan swiveled to face the guy, and he issued a guttural warning that Kiley couldn't make out.

He started for Evan, and she lowered her finger to the trigger, her eyes pinned on the pair.

Evan held up his hands and backed off toward the car. She stepped out, easing closer to him.

"That was a risky move," she snapped, her fear for his life lingering in her tone. "Five against one are not good odds."

"No biggie. I didn't even need to draw my sidearm." He cast her a look she couldn't read and got behind the wheel.

She waited for him to close the door, then slipped inside and holstered her gun.

He met her gaze. "Thanks for having my back, but I think you might've taken a play out of my book and overreacted."

He was probably right, but she wouldn't spend valuable time discussing it now. "Recognize any of the men?"

He shook his head. "And I was disappointed that Bilal wasn't in the group."

"Obviously there's no way we can follow Ibrahim." Kiley watched the boat pull away from the shore, then looked at her iPad, her heart rate starting to slow now. "Nearest boat rental is thirty minutes away. By the time we get a boat and go after him, he'll be long gone, and this lake is far too big to track him."

Evan's eyes remained on the shoreline. "We

need a drone. You don't happen to have one of those in your trusty bins, do you?"

"Actually we do, but it's in Sean's car. Doesn't matter anyway. This lake is much larger than the drone's max range." She clicked on her mic and gave Mack an update. "What's happening with Goldilocks?"

"We're turning off on Highway 162," he said. "Don't know where Goldilocks is going, but he's bypassing the dam."

She looked at her map again. "You have Lake Oroville coming up soon. He might be up to the same thing with you. Maybe they plan to use another ramp to leave the lake and lose any tails."

"If so, it's clever, I'll give them that," Mack said.

"I'll call Eisenhower to see if we can get a chopper out here to monitor Brother Bear. Let me know where Goldilocks settles."

"Will do."

Kiley selected Eisenhower's name on the dash screen. After she explained their predicament, he agreed to call in air support if he could arrange it in a timely manner.

Evan continued to look in the boat's direction while holding on to his phone. "I can text the pictures I just took to Cam for a facial recognition search, but then what do you want to do?"

Yeah, what should she do, other than lose her cool as she was fast doing? She wiped sweaty palms over her shorts, took a breath to calm her nerves, and traced the map on her iPad. "Let's plan on Eisenhower coming through with the helicopter and take a strategic position so we're ready to go after Ibrahim if he makes a break for the dam. Take Route 167 and head south."

"Roger that." Evan sent his text and got them going, circling past the pickup truck where the men stood facing them.

They glared at her, and the evil vibe emanating from the men sent her heart racing again. She forced up her chin and stared them down. Easy to do when behind locked doors, but facing them earlier gave her a preview of how vicious the final showdown with Nabi and Shah would likely be.

"With those looks, it's not hard to imagine the terrible things they've done," Evan said, a tremor of unease in his voice.

She glanced over her shoulder. "Let's keep watch to be sure they don't tail us."

They both continued to check the mirrors for the next few miles.

"Looks like we're clear," she said, but remained unsettled, her heartbeat still faster than normal as adrenaline continued to course through her body.

The infotainment system announced a text from Eisenhower. *"Sacramento Police Department chopper in the air soon. Contact Lieutenant Jamison."*

The message ended with a phone number,

and Kiley quickly called Jamison via the car's Bluetooth so Evan could hear the conversation while he drove. "Agent Kiley Dawson checking in on the helicopter."

"We'll need a description of the boat and passengers." Jamison's deep baritone sounded over the speakers.

"I can send you a picture."

"I'm on my cell. Send it now."

Evan handed his phone to her before she had to ask him for the photos, and she sent the text. "Text is coming from a different phone number."

"Okay, got it," Jamison said. "And they put in where?"

She gave him the location.

"Okay. We're cleared for takeoff. I'll contact you when we're over the lake. Should be about fifteen minutes."

"Hurry," she said, the adrenaline still gushing through her body and making her hand shake.

"You were right, Kiley." Mack's voice came through her earbud. "We're at Oroville Lake. Goldilocks climbed into a boat. Sean's commandeering a boat, and we're going after him."

"Keep in touch." Kiley released her mic and swiveled to face Evan. "Do think this is really about the Waleeds losing us, or do you think it still has something to do with the dam?"

"Honestly, I don't know. These guys are clever,

so maybe it *is* about losing us so they can meet up with Bilal or the container guys."

"Do they even know that Gadi's dead? Or maybe the Waleeds didn't plan to connect with the Amaris and they have nothing to do with the threat."

"Or they could simply be decoys to keep us from looking for Nabi and Shah," Evan said. "The Waleeds know Quinn had them under surveillance, so maybe they're meant to pull him and us off course."

"We don't know enough to take any action." She sighed and worried her fingers together.

"Still waiting on rental contracts." Cam's voice cut in on her thoughts. "Evan's pictures sent off for facial recognition too. Now, if you all don't need me, I'll get started on the hack."

"Be sure you don't get lost in your own world and don't respond if we *do* need you again," Kiley warned.

"Me?" He chuckled. "Seriously, I got your backs."

"See that you do," Kiley said with force to make sure he got the point, or maybe because she needed to blow off some of this pent-up worry.

Evan pulled over and looked at her. "Sounds like the pressure's getting to you."

"Don't tell me you're not feeling it too."

He shifted into park. "Oh, I am. I just wish I could do something to help."

"The only thing that will help now is for this to start making some sense and we can at least figure out the target."

He opened his mouth as if to reply, but a call came in from Jamison. He quickly tapped a button on the steering wheel to answer the call.

"Found the boat anchored in the middle of the lake." Jamison's voice could barely be heard above the helicopter rotors. "Guy's just sitting there."

Evan shot Kiley a questioning look.

She shrugged. "Lieutenant, can you get closer and take pictures of the suspects and boat for us?"

"Will do." The screen went dark.

Evan looked at her. "Maybe the Waleeds really *are* a distraction."

"We don't have time to waste on a distraction." She focused her thoughts and formed a plan. "If the pictures from Jamison are innocuous, we'll get a boat and agents out there to keep an eye on him. Then we'll head back to Sacramento where we can check in with Cam and work other leads."

Her phone chimed. Expecting the pictures, she was surprised to see a text from Harrison.

"Harrison says the DNA on the letter sent to B. Amari matched the DNA on Nasim's drink cup."

"Another solid connection between them," Evan said.

"And with having Nasim's DNA now, I can ask

Veronica Jennings to compare it to the slugs and casings from Firuzeh's murder." Kiley replied to the text, giving Harrison contact info for Jennings and instructing her to have the comparison made.

Kiley just finished the text when the pictures arrived from Jamison. She grabbed her iPad so she could display larger photos.

She held the device and flipped through photos of Ibrahim and the man operating the boat, sitting and looking up at the helicopter. She zoomed in on each photo to search every visible inch of the boat. "I don't see any weapons or a bomb, but they could be hiding things in the cabin."

"It needs to be searched, yet we don't have probable cause for a warrant, and Ibrahim would know that."

Kiley called Jamison. "Can you keep up surveillance until we get a boat out there?"

"Can do so long as our fuel holds out."

"Which is how long?"

"Too many factors to predict. Especially if we have to hover for a long time. But I can give you a heads-up if we have to leave."

"Thanks," she said and disconnected.

"Now what?" Evan asked.

"Now we sit tight until Eisenhower arranges for a boat and agents to watch Ibrahim. Then we do something, *anything* to move this investigation forward for once."

CHAPTER 26

In the Sacramento office conference room, Kiley set down her backpack, her stomach swimming with acid. She and Evan had just returned, and she felt like she was failing big-time—missing something obvious. Something that was just within reach, but like in a nightmare, she couldn't grasp it.

She'd checked in with Cam. He'd ruled out all the cars from the motel, had gotten the rental agreements for the Waleeds' driver, and he was on target with the hack. She'd had agents dispatched to watch these addresses in case the Waleeds showed up and to take over watching Nasim, as he too was just sitting out in the lake. Mack and Sean were far too valuable to be bobbing in a boat and were on their way back now.

Her phone rang, announcing a video call from Eisenhower, something rare, speaking to the importance of whatever he had to say. She ran her fingers through her windblown hair, twisted it up in a bun, and stabbed in a pencil. After taking a deep breath, she accepted the call. "Sir."

He had on one of his many gray suits and crisp white shirts. He sat behind his neat desk, looking fresh and professional as usual. "The team with you yet?"

"Just Agent Bowers." She explained that Mack and Sean were on the way but didn't mention Cam.

He gave a sharp nod. "Go ahead and get Bowers on this call. I'd like him to weigh in here."

She didn't like the sound of that. Not when Evan's experience with explosives was the likely area of expertise Eisenhower might want an opinion on.

She attached her phone to the TV and made sure she and Evan were both in the video frame from their end. "Go ahead, sir."

Eisenhower laced his fingers together on the desk, looking calm and unflappable. "First, I received Barzani's customer information. Ibrahim Waleed ordered the container shipment."

Kiley's mouth dropped open and she glanced at Evan, who looked equally surprised.

"So, the Waleeds *are* involved," she said once she recovered, "and we have a proven connection between them and Nabi and Shah."

Eisenhower pursed his lips and didn't speak for a long, uncomfortable moment. "Okay, now the big news. Tooele Army Depot in Idaho reported the theft of an extremely large quantity of RDX."

"RDX!" Kiley cried out, and Eisenhower flinched at her tone. "But that's a crazy powerful explosive and should've been guarded."

"Agreed," Eisenhower said. "Only excuse they gave was that it happened on Saturday when staffing levels were down."

Kiley shook her head and hoped someone would be disciplined for this breach. "That was days ago. Why are we just hearing about the theft now?"

"You know how the military likes to keep things under wraps and work out their own problems."

Kiley looked again at Evan. His forehead was furrowed, and he fidgeted with his hands. He was clearly as worried as she was.

"I don't yet have any information on who stole the RDX," Eisenhower continued. "But as soon as I have more, I'll get back to you."

"Any idea on how long that will take?" she asked, mindful of the little bit of time she had remaining to find the threat and neutralize it.

"No, but I have agents babysitting them to give me information as it becomes available." He reached for an iPad to slide down the screen. "I'm also calling about the Idaho National Laboratory's new Cybercore Integration Center. They're charged with helping to protect our critical infrastructure. I've made contact with a Sam Olsen there, and we've been looking for a target-rich environment where a terrorist might launch a cyber attack."

Kiley didn't know where he was going with this and was half afraid to find out. "And have you found something actionable?"

He frowned. "Unfortunately, the U.S. is

rushing to catch up to threats by hackers on all infrastructure, and Olsen's team is concerned we're already behind the game. Like many businesses, these old infrastructure systems have already been infiltrated by malicious entities waiting for the opportune time to strike."

"Specifically what kind of things are we talking about here?" Evan asked.

"Systems operating energy pipelines, hydro-electric projects, drinking water systems, nuclear power plants. All across the country. As you can imagine, this gives us an unbelievably large list of target-rich environments that we should be considering. So I asked Olsen to narrow it down to an attack that would endanger millions of people. He suggested we focus on dams."

With the Waleeds so close to a major dam, Kiley didn't like the sound of that. "Did he name a particular dam that would top the threat list?"

"He did. The Glen Canyon Dam in Arizona."

Arizona. A niggle of worry formed in Kiley's gut. Her mother and grandparents had moved there for her grandfather's sake, who suffered with arthritis. They could be in harm's way. She might be at odds with her mother, but she couldn't fathom losing her. Particularly when they were on the outs. Kiley needed a chance to talk to her. Make things right. And she couldn't lose her grandparents either.

She swallowed hard so she could get out her next question. "And is this dam vulnerable?"

"Extremely so." His dire expression left Kiley wanting to hop a plane to talk to her mother before it was too late. "It doesn't have the infrastructure to survive a malicious attack that would quickly release excessive amounts of water."

"How's that?" Evan asked, looking as horrified as she felt.

Eisenhower made strong eye contact. "It's not the tallest dam in our country, yet it holds back the largest body of water and was built on totally unsuitable sandstone."

"Meaning?" Evan asked.

"It's deeply fissured and constantly leaks water. Large pieces of canyon wall abutting the dam routinely break away. Increasingly longer rock bolts are installed in hopes of stabilizing the dam, but this looks to be a losing battle. If a terrorist took control of the dam, everyone near the Colorado River would be at risk."

"Which means what exactly?" she asked, but as she thought about her family in harm's way, she really didn't want to know.

Eisenhower took a long breath and glanced at his iPad. "If it failed, it could set off a series of catastrophic events with enormous human and economic impacts extending from Utah to Mexico. Downstream communities and perhaps every dam along the Colorado River as well as lowlands would be flooded or irreparably damaged. The Hoover Dam is the only one that might survive, but it would overflow, causing destruction too. The possible domino effect could destroy water systems for more than twenty-five million people in the lower Colorado River Basin."

Worry for all of these people and for her own family made Kiley sick to her stomach. She desperately wanted to warn them. But she couldn't. Not without violating her security clearance.

So what should she do?

The only thing she could do. Remain positive that she and her team would stop any such attack before someone died, much less her family. But how they were going to do that was totally beyond her right now, and panic was threatening to take her down.

Eisenhower hung up, but Evan couldn't stop staring at the screen as the news of the stolen RDX mixed in his brain with thoughts of destroying a monstrous dam. Could the terrorists they were hunting really be thinking this big? From what Deb at Counterterrorism said of Nabi and Shah, Evan thought it a very good possibility.

"My mom and grandparents . . ." The words whispered out of Kiley's mouth before she clamped her hand over it, her terrified gaze flitting around the room.

He swiveled to face her. "What's wrong?"

"Nothing."

"No. It's not nothing. You're spooked."

She clasped her hands tightly together on the table, her eyes glistening. "My mom and grandparents moved to Arizona a few years ago. The dry heat there helps my granddad with his arthritis. They're in the Colorado River Basin."

"And you're worried about them," he stated, feeling helpless to do much more.

"Yes." Her hands started trembling.

He rested his hand over hers. "We'll stop this."

"How?" She gaped at him. "Just how? We're less than thirteen hours out and we don't have a solid lead to find suspects driven by such horrific personal tragedies that make them so very dangerous."

She had a very valid point, though he didn't want to admit it. "Maybe you should call your family. Tell them to take a trip out of the area."

"But we don't even know if it *is* the Glen Canyon Dam. Or any dam." She pulled her hands free, her expression like that of a frightened child who'd lost her parents and had no clue where to find them. She got up. Started pacing, a sob tearing from her throat.

She paused by the window, her back to him and her shoulders shaking.

He'd never seen her cry and couldn't sit here while she fell apart. He crossed the room and turned her to face him. "*Shh.* Hey, it'll be all right."

"Will it?" she got out between sobs and took a long breath. "I'm not qualified to run such a huge investigation. What was I thinking? Eisenhower should replace me. Maybe Sean or Mack could take over."

"You're doing a great job."

She sniffled. "You're just saying that because we have this connection."

Another good point, but . . . "Well, yeah, of course my feelings play into it, but putting them aside and looking at this objectively, I can see how successful you've been."

"Really? Then why didn't I think of contacting the Cybercore Integration Center like Eisenhower did? We might've had this information sooner, and it could've informed my decisions."

"Or not. As you said yourself, we don't know for sure if it's the target. Besides, the rest of us didn't think of it either, and you respect your teammates' skills, right?"

She nodded.

"You've led them fearlessly through this investigation," he rushed to add. "Not a one of them has complained or questioned your leadership. I don't know them as well as you, but if they thought you were failing, wouldn't they call you on it?"

She gave another hesitant nod.

"And you've kept so many leads going. Following up. Assigning tasks. Communicating. *You're doing a great job,*" he repeated, this time emphasizing the words.

She still looked skeptical, but at least her tears had dried up and she was no longer shaking. A win in his book.

Her phone rang. She hurried back to the table to grab it. "It's Ulrich." She answered it on speaker. "Please tell me you've finished the letter."

"I did. I've emailed the information to you."

"Let me look while I have you on the phone, in case I have any questions." She brought her email up on the large TV, and Evan looked at the deciphered letter that told of the Pittsburgh attack.

His heart sank. It wasn't the information they'd hoped would move the investigation forward.

"Is this what you were thinking the code might reference?" Ulrich asked.

"No." Just one word from Kiley, but it carried a heavy weight of despair.

"Then I guess that's why the last information you gave me doesn't fit."

"You mean the *work hour wait win yesterday?*"

"Yes. It's not part of the letter code."

Kiley shoved a hand into her hair, loosening the knot in back, and the pencil clattered to the floor. "Finlay Brooks is working on another conversation. I need you to take the code that didn't work and give it to her."

"Sure, yeah. I can do that."

"And then I need you to work with her." Kiley was sounding stronger now. More in control. "To get this second item done faster."

"I don't know. My in-laws are coming to dinner." His whiney tone when so many people were counting on them grated on Evan.

"I appreciate that you want to be there, but your country needs you, Ulrich. Needs you desperately. So many lives are depending on this." Her impassioned plea brought a long silence.

"I don't know," Ulrich finally said. "My wife will kill me if I bail."

"This is your chance to be a hero," Kiley rushed on, sounding patriotic. "Your chance to stop a terrible thing from happening. To save lives. So many lives. Please. For your country."

After her emotion-filled plea, Evan would do anything she needed to have done, but would Ulrich?

"Okay. Fine. But I might need you to talk to her and smooth things over."

"I can do that. And thank you, Ulrich. You're already a hero in my eyes." She ended the call.

Evan went to her and took her hands in his. "See. This is a perfect example of why you're doing an excellent job leading the investigation.

You got him to buy in and do his very best. Take confidence in your abilities. You've got this, and we will stop this attack. Together. You and me."

She looked down at their hands and then met his gaze. "Thank you for being there for me. For being my cheerleader. I needed a pep talk. Needed it badly."

"Rah, rah," he laughed, wanting to lighten the mood.

But instead of laughing, she looked deep into his eyes. "You're a good man, Evan. A very good man, and I'm sorry I blamed you all this time for Olin. You weren't responsible for his death. I needed someone to blame, and you were the only person there."

"It's okay, really. I blame myself and deserved it."

She pulled a hand free and gently cupped the side of his face. "You made an honest mistake, and you have no reason to feel guilty. Let it go. Please. Promise me you will."

The gentle touch of her warm fingers on his skin nearly had him losing his concentration, but he worked hard to keep his focus. "I'll do my best if you promise me you'll give us a chance."

"I'll try."

He pulled her to him, tight against his body. He thought he cared for her before, but man, the rush of emotions flooding him now were beyond anything he'd ever felt, and he would do anything to make sure she stayed safe. That her family stayed safe. That the country stayed safe.

He released her and stepped back. "As much as I want to kiss you right now, I think it would be a good idea for us to put whatever this is going on between us on the back burner."

"So we can focus on the investigation," she said, readily agreeing with him.

Evan nodded and would do his best to honor the agreement. He knew she needed to succeed so she never had to live with the guilt of failing to stop the most deadly terrorist attack ever perpetrated on American soil.

CHAPTER 27

Kiley's phone rang with a call from Veronica Jennings as the conference room door opened and Special Agent in Charge Charles Kagan poked his head in. Kiley assumed he'd come to update her on his agents who'd taken over for Sean and Mack. But right now, Jennings's call took precedence, so Kiley gestured at Kagan to hold on as she took the call.

He stepped into the room, pausing just inside the door and running a hand over his short black hair.

Kiley ignored him and turned her attention to Jennings. "I take it you got Nasim Waleed's DNA."

"Yeah." Jennings sounded pumped. "It's a match. A one hundred percent match. Every allele."

Kiley shot to her feet. "You're sure? He touched the slugs or casing?"

"Positive for both. This guy's DNA was all over them."

"Thank you, Jennings. Email me the official report." Kiley disconnected, and with Kagan watching her, she couldn't take the time to savor the fact that this meant they had Nasim for murder. But—a huge but—she had Nasim right where she wanted him. Under surveillance by this man's team.

She forced herself to calm down and look at Kagan. "I need your agents to move on Nasim Waleed and take him into custody for the murder of my confidential informant."

He frowned, and his tight look as he ran a nervous hand down his slate-gray tie raised Kiley's concern. "Actually, that's why I stopped by," he said. "I've got bad news for you. The Waleeds are in the wind."

"What?" Kiley planted her hands on the table and glared at the man. "How on earth did that happen?"

"They both went for a swim. As they got back in the boat, the other guy dropped a towel over their heads, blocking any view of their faces. My agents had no reason to believe it wasn't the Waleeds, so they didn't investigate. Hours later, one of my agents caught a glimpse under Nasim's towel. It wasn't him."

"A diver switched places," Evan said.

Kagan nodded. "We immediately checked on Ibrahim. Same thing."

Kiley slammed a fist on the table, thankful for the pain to keep her from railing even more at this senior agent.

Kagan solidly met her gaze. No backing down or cowering. "We're mortified this happened."

"Could've happened to us just as easily," Sean said.

Kiley shot Sean an irritated look and didn't want to admit he was right, but he was.

"I've already put out an alert for the Waleeds and have additional agents headed out there to interview people. We'll thoroughly canvass the area. Let me know if there's anything else I can do."

Kiley nodded and waited for the door to close behind him. "This is the last thing we needed."

"So Nasim's DNA matched the slugs or casings?" Evan asked.

She nodded. "Fat lot of good it does us, as we have no idea where he is right now."

"We'll get him," Evan encouraged.

Kiley gave him a nod and dropped into her chair to regroup for about the thousandth time. Before Jennings called, Kiley was planning to update Sean and Mack on Eisenhower's information, so she proceeded to do so.

"Man," Mack said, "that doesn't sound good at all."

"We have no proof Olsen's theory holds any weight," Kiley continued, "but the Glen Canyon Dam is the best target we have right now."

"Since the Waleeds showed up here, I think we should look at Oroville Dam too," Sean suggested. "They had recent issues with a damaged spillway and had to evacuate two hundred thousand residents downstream. I have to think it would be a target."

"Your report said they made the necessary repairs, though," Kiley said.

"To one of the spillways, yes," Sean said. "But what about the others? Are they in good condition? Questions I can't answer, but I can research it."

"I think this lead is strong enough to at least do additional research on both dams." Kiley looked at her watch. "I'll get back to Eisenhower to see if they want to take any precautions at Oroville or Glen Canyon. But we should all be prepared to spend the night gathering intel."

She didn't bother saying why. Didn't say tomorrow was their last day to find the target and neutralize the threat. She didn't have to. Everyone in the room knew the clock was ticking down faster than their answers were appearing, and the pressure was nearly unbearable.

Seven hours. Only seven hours until the clock hit 9/11. And Kiley was jumpy. She got up from the conference room table to pace. The Waleeds were still in the wind. Not even a hint of where they were hiding out or what they were doing. The team was no closer to determining the actual target than when they'd started gathering details last night, and she was more tired than she'd ever been.

And the pressure. Man, the pressure was beyond bearable at this point. Her skin crawled with it. They'd worked all night, and she had to admit Sam Olsen's take on the Glen Canyon Dam was seeming to be the most logical target. If so, were the terrorists planning a cyber attack or actual bombs? Sure, there'd been a big theft of the RDX, but Eisenhower had yet to gain any additional information connecting the break-in to the container suspects. So with the Waleeds missing, she was leaning toward a cyber attack, though she had nothing to base that on. Just a gut feeling, and she didn't know what to do next.

Should they head to the dam or sit tight?

She needed to make a decision soon but kept hoping God would reveal the lead they needed. Kiley didn't know if they could even find the target, but God knew, and Kiley closed her eyes to pray for divine intervention in a situation that seemed impossible.

A text sounded on her phone. She looked at it to find the message was from Deb Bessemer. *I emailed updated files on Nabi and Shah to you.*

Thank you, Kiley replied and opened her email.

"Got facial recognition results back on the guys from the boat ramp," Mack said, taking Kiley's attention. "They're on The Righteous list, but no terrorist activities attributed to them."

"Go find Kagan and have him assign local agents to visit them too," Kiley instructed. "Maybe we'll get lucky and the Waleeds will be at one of their homes."

"You got it." Mack headed out of the room.

Kiley was starting to read the report from Deb when her phone rang and Ulrich Lane's name popped onto the screen. She eagerly answered, the desperation in her tone scaring her and had to be unsettling for Ulrich.

"We cracked the code," he said, sounding more tired than excited. "I'll email the information to you."

"Do it now! Don't waste a second."

"Will do, but FYI, you should know the extra code you gave me was the key to making sense of this one."

"Glad to hear it," she said and disconnected. "Ulrich deciphered the code." She looked at Evan and smiled. "And the words from Gadi's tattoo were the key. Good work on figuring that out."

He returned her smile but didn't let it distract her. She shifted her attention to her phone, waiting for the email from Ulrich.

C'mon, C'mon, C'mon. Send it already.

"You think this is finally it?" Evan asked. "The location we need."

"We better hope so," Sean said.

Kiley shook her hands and danced in place to displace her anxiety. Her phone chimed. She snatched it up and read the message aloud.

" *'Never forget 9/11,' the infidels say. We will not forget either. We will remember and inflict more pain than they could ever imagine. When the clock strikes midnight on 9/11, we will strike. Allah be with you on your travels to the GC Dam."*

"GC has to stand for the Glen Canyon Dam," Evan said.

Kiley's heart dropped, and she thought of her mother, her grandparents. Her only relatives on this earth. In the path of assured destruction if she didn't stop the attack. She had to stop it. For them. For everyone, so when this was all over, she could visit her mother and clear the air once and for all.

"We finally have our target," Evan said, bringing her back.

She was in charge of this investigation, and she had to let go of her fear for her family so she could lead the team. Let go of every emotion except the desire to find the terrorists and bring them down. She couldn't do it alone. Not at all.

Father, please show me the way to stop this attack. Watch over my family. Don't let them or anyone be harmed.

"Kiley," Sean said, "what do you want to do?"

"I'll put a visual of the dam on the TV." She clicked around on her computer, her fingers shaking as she brought up an aerial shot of the Glen Canyon Dam.

The door opened, and Mack along with Cam sauntered into the room. Cam looked tired and was wearing the same clothes as the last time she'd seen him. He ran his gaze around the table. "Hey, what's up? Why so tense?"

Kiley updated him and Mack on the message. "We've researched this dam, but we need every bit of information you can find on the place."

Cam nodded. "Thought you might want to hear what I discovered in my hack."

"What?" Sean's eyes widened. "You honestly got something?"

"Now, that hurts my feelings." Cam feigned pulling a knife from his chest as he dropped into a chair and put two laptops on the table.

"Just tell us what you have," Evan snapped, a testament to the pressure they were all under. "Sorry, man. Stress."

"No worries." Cam leaned back in his chair and clasped his hands behind his head. "So Nasim Waleed must have felt very secure in his phone communications as he texted openly with Gadi regarding the Pittsburgh bomb. They analyzed the failure and talked about how to correct the timing in the big event."

"Did they name the event?" Kiley asked, holding her breath while she waited for a reply.

Cam shook his head. "But he confirmed that he and Ibrahim were decoys meant to keep us busy. And he confirmed the Amari brothers, along with Nabi and Shah, are to be involved in the attack, but no details."

"You think they planned a bomb or a cyber attack?" Kiley asked.

Cam shrugged.

Evan stood and went to the TV. "They *could* be doing both."

"There'd be no point in targeting the computer system if they planted bombs," Mack said.

Evan tapped the image of the high bridge leading to the Glen Canyon Visitor Center and pointed to another bridge near the back of the dam. "If I planned to hack or even bomb this dam, I would want to make sure help couldn't arrive to fix the hack."

"You'd bomb the bridges," Kiley said.

"Exactly. Keep emergency responders away."

Kiley brought up a 3-D picture of the main bridge on the screen and used her mouse to review all angles. "How could anyone get under that bridge without being seen?"

"My question too," Cam said, looking at his computer screen. "Says here the bridge is one of the tallest in the country, rising seven hundred feet above the river."

Evan clenched his jaw. "Only two ways. They could be planning a suicide bomb in a vehicle. Or placing a device under the area of the bridge that's accessible from the road. This would have to occur at night, and the bombers would likely need to have one person or more on the dam security team to act as a lookout or disable cameras if they exist."

"If that's the case," Mack said, his tone grim, "then the bombs are already in place."

Kiley's stomach roiled at the thought. "We need to get there. Now!"

She tapped Eisenhower's number on her phone and looked at the team as she waited for the call to connect. "Cam, gather the intel on the dam so we can review it on the plane. Sean, call Sam Olsen at the Cybercore Integration Center and pick his brain on the cyber vulnerabilities of this dam. Mack and Evan, get packing and load the vehicles. Eisenhower is sure to get us a military flight, and I want wheels up within the hour."

CHAPTER 28

The team scored a military flight, followed by a helicopter ride to the dam. Problem was, a raging thunderstorm was tossing them all over the place. The pilot had hoped to arrive before the storm hit, but it rolled in fast thirty minutes ago. At least they were the only passengers, so with headsets they'd been able to talk through their plan.

The rolling and jerking motions didn't bother Evan, but Mack's face paled. Either he had motion sickness or issues with a prior chopper ride that hadn't ended well. Knowing Mack used to be a Night Stalker, Evan wondered if the guy had been forced to leave the military due to PTSD.

A bolt of lightning cracked the air. Kiley jumped, then quickly settled. "So the local authorities have pictures of Nabi, Shah, Bilal, and the Waleeds, and the sheriff has set up roadblocks and stopped all incoming traffic. He's also working on jamming cell signals to prevent them from setting off bombs on the bridges. Meanwhile, he's getting the right equipment in place."

"And he can't jam Wi-Fi," Cam said.

Everyone knew the danger facing them even without Cam's statement, Evan more than the others. If there was a bomb on either bridge, he'd be in charge of rendering it safe. "And the dam evacuation?"

"The head of security took care of that. FYI, he works for the Bureau of Reclamation and manages a contracted staff of armed guards."

"Rent-a-cops?" Mack scowled. "We have millions of people counting on rent-a-cops?"

Kiley gritted her teeth, and Evan wanted to deck Mack for pointing out something that only made things worse for Kiley.

"The sheriff is calling in additional help, but it'll take time," she said. "The visitor center is closed for the day, and dam security evacuated all nonessential personnel and locked the place down."

"That's a start," Mack said grudgingly.

"Also, a few of the most trusted officers are sweeping the dam for bombs. They already confirmed the back bridge is clean."

Evan imagined one of the rent-a-cops trying to be a hero. He didn't want to comment but had to. "They know not to touch anything they find, right?"

She nodded. "The closest bomb squad and dog have been deployed too. They won't arrive until after we put down."

Kiley sat up straighter, her focus intense. "They'll blow the bridge before the dam. Evan, I want you to start by sweeping the bridge for devices."

"Depending on the timers I find, I can diffuse them, or we let them blow to make sure we're on-site to get to the computers."

"Right, we'll have to play it by ear," Kiley said. "And while you're assessing the bridge, Cam and Sean will go straight to the server room. Mack, I want you with Evan to get him everything he needs. I'll coordinate all our efforts and keep in touch with Eisenhower, who's on his way."

Everyone fell silent. The tension was so thick, Evan wondered how they were all sitting there so calmly, although he suspected their insides were churning in a tornado of acid just like his were doing. If the terrorists had set a bomb under the bridge, he would immediately be facing a life-threatening situation, not only from the bomb but also from a potential lightning strike.

People often thought bomb techs didn't feel the intensity of the situation. *Hah. Right.* He felt it. Oh, how he felt it. He'd just learned to deal with it in a way that left his hands steady and his brain alert. Part of it came from his training, the other part from the sheer desire to help save others.

Tonight, though, the stress was getting to him and he was struggling. So much pressure. He closed his eyes to take calming breaths and pray.

"Three minutes to touch down," the pilot announced.

Evan opened his eyes and tried to see through the pelting rain as they flew over the dam. Its wall was lit from below, and he watched as water spilled out over the lake. Bright lights lit the bridge as well. They were both far more magnificent in person than in the pictures he'd seen, but he had to admit the height of the bridge put a hitch in his heart. He would feel better if he had the time to inspect the equipment. Instead he had to trust the local bomb squad to have everything in tiptop shape.

The chopper lunged through the rain, started a wobbly descent, and touched down with a hard jolt in the parking lot across the road from the dam. The county command and bomb squad trucks were parked in the lot close to the dam entrance.

Kiley looked at him. "I'll meet with the sheriff to give him a comms unit and get Cam and Sean access. You and Mack grab whatever gear you need from the bomb squad."

"Roger that," he said and wished he could give her a hug, maybe a kiss before heading out, but they'd agreed to focus on their jobs.

Mack whipped the door open, and rain cut a sideways path into the chopper, instantly wetting them. As they hopped down onto the pavement, Evan wished for some sort of protective clothing against the deluge. The downpour didn't seem to bother Kiley, who marched straight for the sheriff with slicked-back hair and a poncho over his uniform. Sean and Cam followed her.

Evan nodded at Mack, and they jogged to the bomb squad's vehicle. Lightning split the sky, briefly illuminating the area around the dam. Evan's heart rate kicked up, and he had to breathe deeply to calm his nerves. He shook hands with the tall sergeant in charge of the team as a waterfall of rain poured from the man's hat.

The sergeant led the way to the back of his truck and jerked open the doors. "Help yourself. I've already got the rigging on the bridge for you. When you're ready, I'll show you the way."

Evan grabbed a tool belt and loaded it with a multipurpose tool, shears, mirror, screwdrivers, tape, and wire strippers. Not everything he might need, but for now it didn't matter. He'd figure it out. When he was an EOD tech, he didn't always have what he needed on hand, which was where the major part of the Navy's stellar training came into play. It taught him to think outside of the box. And taught him to perform these skills when tired or cold, at night or during the day, no matter the environment. Worrying about the woman he loved or the thunderstorm raging around them didn't matter either. He would handle it.

He grabbed a helmet and gave a firm nod to the sergeant, then took off across the road, his boots sloshing through deep puddles. He stopped in a soggy grassy area by the bridge. The rigging had been secured, just as he'd been told. Still, Evan checked it to be sure. Mack followed behind to confirm, beads of worry dotting his forehead.

Evan donned the rigging and secured the belt, noticing through the rain—now coming down in a sideways wave—that Sean and Cam were heading inside with the sheriff.

Kiley sprinted over to him. Her hair had come loose from its knot and now hung like limp spaghetti over her shoulders. Her clothes were plastered against her body, and she swiped rain from her face. Beautiful . . . Evan pulled his gaze free and fixed the tactical rope to the harness.

Kiley marched up to him, her eyes clouded, but she didn't speak. He settled the helmet on his head, careful not to dislodge the team comms unit. They'd set the system to a different frequency to keep their signal from being jammed. It would be his only line of communication once he rappelled off the side.

Kiley moved closer to him, worry darkening the eyes he loved looking into. "Promise me, Evan, you won't take any unnecessary risks."

He wanted to talk more, but every second counted now. "You go do your thing, and I'll do mine."

She nodded and turned to head to the building. Her thing normally wasn't dangerous, but if the dam blew, he had no idea what the explosion would do to the server room where she'd be directing operations with the team. He wanted to go with her. To be her bodyguard. Yet he couldn't, not when others were counting on him. The thought didn't sit well with him, and he offered another prayer as he double-checked his rope and tightened the tool belt around his waist. He gave a thumbs-up to Mack, who would manage Evan's descent.

"I'd rather not go boom," Mack said, his tone lighthearted, his expression troubled. "These are my best boots, and the rain's already doing a number on them. Don't want to ruin them completely."

Evan chuckled and held out his hand for a fist bump. Evan appreciated the levity to help ease the tension, but after the bump he let the humor go and pinned his focus on the mission ahead.

He rappelled down the sandstone near the end of the bridge. Sharp flashes of lightning illuminated the stone of vivid red and orange striations. He swung away from the wall, hanging seven hundred feet over churning water. Most people would freak at the height, but after jumping from a plane, this distance wasn't scary at all.

He got his body swinging and hooked a leg over a heavy steel girder.

"Hold there," he said into the mic, telling Mack to tighten the slack.

Evan pulled up on the girder and searched the area around him. Ahead about six feet, he spotted the blinking red lights on a digital timer strapped to explosives.

"I have one," he said, swallowing hard and offering a prayer as he inched over the slippery steel toward the device. "And it contains the white phosphorus."

White phosphorus. Super dangerous. Kiley stared at the computer monitor and could barely breathe in the cool server room. Her hands were trembling as she reached for her mic to activate it. "Be careful, Evan. Please be careful."

"Wish we had video on him." Sean looked over his shoulder from his seat in front of a terminal.

She nodded, but she didn't know which was better, seeing the man she loved working on a bomb in a lightning storm or living with the cold dread of not knowing what was happening. And her family? What about them? They were downstream from the dam, and she hadn't called to warn them.

"Need some slack." Evan's voice came over the mic, and she heard him grunt with exertion. She could easily imagine him gripping the wet steel with his muscular legs.

"Okay," he said, his voice steady and confident. "At the device now."

Kiley offered an emotion-packed prayer. Surely God didn't bring them together—with her coming to realize she *did* need a partner like Evan in her life—only to end it all, did He?

She looked at the timer she'd set on her phone,

the numbers counting down until midnight. One hour, five minutes, and fifteen seconds. They only had a little more than an hour to figure this out.

"How much time on the timer?" she asked Evan and held her breath.

"It's set to blow in sixty minutes."

"Be careful," she said again.

"Will do."

"You seeing this?" Cam asked.

Kiley jerked her gaze back to the monitor. "No signs of an external hack in the recent past."

Cam swiveled in his chair to look at her. "Okay, so these guys are either very good, and we need to dig deeper, or they didn't hack the system from the outside."

"You think it's an inside job?" Sean asked.

"I think we need to look at both possibilities." She faced Sean. "You concentrate on finding any internal changes. Cam, you take an external approach, and I'll go through the notes I took from my interview with the system administrator when we arrived."

She sat to take out her notepad, but her nerves propelled her back to her feet. She read the notes and paced the small room, fielding incoming requests and concerns from the sheriff and dam staff as she read.

"This thing has a timer, and it's also cellphone- and Wi-Fi-enabled," Evan said over her earbud. "Same switch as the Pittsburgh bomb."

"Makes sense." She didn't like that the terrorists had multiple chances to detonate the bombs, also making it more difficult for Evan to disarm them.

"Sheriff got those cell signals jammed yet?"

"Not yet," she replied and hated to tell Evan that with a bomb staring him in the face. "He said five or ten minutes."

"Assuming he manages it, the bombers will have to be close enough to detonate if they plan to use their backup method," Evan said.

Kiley ran through the Wi-Fi details she'd learned earlier. "Unless they have better technology, we'll assume they can't do more than a third of a mile on Wi-Fi. I'll get the sheriff to patrol out to that range."

"This may not be a remote attack," Evan said, "but one carried out from the inside."

Kiley considered the possibility of there being someone in the building who could set off the bomb. "We can't stop a cellphone detonation, but, Sean, make sure the dam's Wi-Fi is offline."

"Already took it down, but I'll check again."

"FYI," Evan said, "they're using RDX. As powerful as it is, it would spray this phosphorus in a wide path."

"So we were right. They must've been the guys who stole the RDX."

"Yeah. I'm pocketing the glass jar containing the phosphorus to bring it in for safety's sake."

"Evan, I don't like the thought of you carrying it."

"It's fine as long as I don't break the glass."

"But you're climbing over steel girders. That could happen." Kiley was shocked at the panic in her voice.

"I'll make sure it doesn't."

He sounded so calm and confident. She had no idea how he could be, yet she was impressed by his determination. "Be extra careful, Evan."

"Roger that. But you should know," he added, "I just spotted a second device on the other end of the bridge."

"Abort," Kiley said. "If we lose the bridge, we lose the bridge."

Evan heard her panic but couldn't obey. "No way. At the very least I can remove the device and drop it below."

"No, Evan."

"As much as I like hearing your voice, I'm signing off so I can concentrate."

"Evan," she said, "please . . . be careful."

"Always." The driving rain made the steel girders slippery and nearly impossible to hold on to. He'd taken his gloves off to work on the bomb and could put them back on, but he had a better idea. "Haul me up, Mack. It'll be faster to hoof it across the bridge than to try to cross on the girders."

"Roger that," Mack replied.

Evan glanced at his watch and swung free from the steel and into the pouring rain, making sure to keep the phosphorus from connecting with a massive beam.

Mack hoisted him up. "Sergeant's already headed to the other side to secure new rigging."

Evan disconnected his rope. "Let's move."

He set the jar of white phosphorus in an out-of-the-way spot and hurried across the bridge. Mack kept up, cowboy boots and all. They covered the quarter-mile span, and then Evan put on his gloves. The sergeant had the rope secured.

Evan shared the location where he'd placed the jars of phosphorus. "It will remain stable as long as it's in water. Make sure it stays that way."

The sergeant nodded, then started for his truck.

Evan connected the rope and was soon swinging down over the side of the bridge, thankful not to have the skin-eating chemical in his pocket. He climbed onto the girders and got eyes on the other device.

It was identical to the first one, along with another jar of phosphorus. Timer was set for forty-seven minutes. He removed his gloves and grabbed a small screwdriver to open the waterproof housing. He let the screws and cover fall into the sharp wind to save time.

He got a look at the bomb.

Man. Oh. Man.

He was wrong. This bomb was different. It had an anti-removal device. He couldn't quickly disarm it like the other one. Likely the reason they'd brought Shah into the country, as he had the most advanced bomb-making skills.

"Evan," Kiley said over his earbud, "where are you at on disarming the second device?"

"This one has an anti-removal device. It's gonna take longer."

She gasped.

"What is it? What's wrong?"

"Bilal Amari and Nabi are here. A deputy's got eyes on Amari, but Nabi bailed from their vehicle and could be anywhere sending a signal to the bomb."

CHAPTER 29

Evan had to keep his focus. He couldn't think about Nabi, phone in hand, racing toward the dam. His mind screamed to start with the phone connection, but he had to render the bomb safe in a certain order, and that meant starting with the anti-removal device.

He swallowed, but his mouth was bone-dry.

C'mon, you can do this.

He willed his hands to remain steady and slid his fingers along the wires, tracing them back to the RDX. Each movement calculated. Precise.

He grabbed his wire cutter. A heavy gust of wind buffeted his body, and he lost his grip. His leg slipped. His body swung out from the girder. He dropped. A free fall toward the river, swinging like a pendulum.

The rope caught and held, his wild swing through the slashing rain slowing. The rope jerked, and he was hauled upward.

"Thanks, man," he said to Mack.

"How about not doing that again?" Mack asked, sounding shaken.

"Yeah. Why didn't I think of that?" Evan made light of the accident, but he swung his leg over the thick steel and let out a breath as he grasped it tightly between his thighs.

He flipped open his Leatherman.

Forgot about everything else.

Forgot about Nabi potentially standing nearby with a phone. Or Bilal with a Wi-Fi router, ready to set off the bomb.

Forgot about Mack waiting at the bridge. Even forgot about Kiley.

It was just him and the device, and the harsh rain pelting the bridge.

He sent up a quick prayer. Took hold of the wire. Held his breath. Tightened his legs. Snipped.

Silence save the pounding rain.

He sighed. But this was only the first step. He located the timer wire. Cut it. The bright letters continued to count down on the phone, flashing into the dark, but the clock was now disconnected and didn't matter.

He moved on to the detonator, carefully removing it from the RDX, moving it well away from the explosive, and taping it in place. The timer continued counting down, ineffective numbers flashing into the night.

He let out a long breath and hung there for a moment to still his racing heart.

"Device disarmed," he said.

"Thank goodness," Kiley said.

He turned his thoughts to the main event. "We any closer to finding the hack?"

"No."

The finality of the word resounded in his head. He looked at his watch. Thirty minutes until midnight. "Bring me up, Mack." Evan let go of the girder and relaxed, working out the tension in his shoulders while making sure not to bang the second jar of phosphorus as Mack hauled him up to the bridge.

He handed the jar to the sergeant, stripped off the harness, and looked at Mack. "I'm heading to the server room."

Mack nodded, his eyes filled with concern. "I'm right behind you."

The door burst open, and Kiley spun to see Evan rush into the room. She'd never been so glad to see someone in her life. She ran her gaze over him and sighed a long breath of relief. His clothing and hair were drenched, but he looked as ruggedly handsome as ever. Maybe more so with the tool belt slung around his trim waist.

"Nice to be inside." He ran a hand over his face and shook off the rain. "Mack stopped to talk to the sheriff. What did the bomb squad and dog find?"

Kiley stared at him, hating to answer, yet he deserved to know how dire the situation had become. "They've swept the whole facility and located nothing."

He frowned. "So this is definitely cyber then."

She clenched her hands together. "We haven't found anything there either."

He gaped at her. "Seriously? Nothing?"

"Nothing." Her stomach clenched.

"Well, if it existed, you all are the ones who would find it."

"Exactly," Kiley said. "These terrorists might be good, but there's no way they're better than our combined skills."

"The bombs on the bridge say we definitely have the right target." Sean clamped a hand on the back of his neck and looked up at them. "We have to be missing something."

"But what?" Kiley asked, that elusive lead that she knew was at the tip of her fingers but couldn't find still nagging at her. The only thing left to do was to review everything as a last-ditch effort before the clock hit midnight. She stepped up to Sean and pointed at his computer. "I know we're missing something. Pull up the information we have on all the suspects again."

Sean clicked his mouse, and Bilal's background report filled the screen. Kiley leaned closer to read over Sean's shoulder, and Evan joined her. She kept up with Sean as he scrolled down the screen, but nothing jumped out at her. "Move on to the next one."

Shah's updated information from Deb Bessemer loaded on the screen that Kiley had failed to read when Ulrich's call came in. She scanned down the report. Her heart sank. "No. No. No. No! It was so obvious, and we missed it."

She grabbed her radio and called the sheriff. "Evacuate everyone now! Hurry! The dam's rigged to blow."

Evan locked gazes with her. "How?"

She tapped the screen as her brain raced for a way to stop the explosion. "Shah became a certified diver."

Evan paled. "The RDX is underwater."

"Oh, man," Sean said.

"No time to waste." Evan bolted from the room.

Sean shot to his feet. "He's got to be going for scuba gear to stop it."

Panic swamped her, and she could barely breathe. But she was in charge and had to get control. Run this op. Stop the threat. She pressed her mic and ran for the door. "Mack. The explosives are underwater. Get the harness and rope and head to the base of the dam. Meet you there."

"Roger that." She appreciated his calm response.

"Which way did he go?" she asked the security guard outside the door.

"Maintenance. Bottom floor all the way to the back."

She sprinted for the elevator. The numbers above one of the doors blinked down. She jumped in the other car and punched the button for the lowest floor.

Father, please. Please let Evan disarm this bomb before the threat to millions becomes a horrific reality.

Kiley appeared in the doorway, and Evan jerked the wet suit over his shoulders and forced himself to ignore her presence. He had to be on top of his game. Underwater explosives were different from a surface bomb, and this was a suicide mission for Shah. Losing his life was the only way he could shatter the massive dam.

If Evan failed to stop Shah, Evan's life would be lost too.

Right there. In the water. Tons of concrete crumbling down around him.

He couldn't think about that. Just had to act.

"What can I do to help?" Kiley asked.

"Pray," he told her as he checked the oxygen tank on the scuba gear to make sure the O-rings would make a good seal with the regulator, then connected his buoyancy compensator that looked like a bulky vest to the tank. He pulled the tank straps tight as he ran through the most likely scenario he would find.

There wouldn't be a bomb and timer waiting like the bridge devices. He would find a double waterproof firing assembly—DWFA—near the dam. The rectangular piece of wood was six inches wide by eighteen inches long and floated like a tiny kickboard while holding two timed detonation cords or fuses. Shah would either be below the surface placing the explosives or diving the blasting caps down to the explosives and attaching the cord. Or he could already be coming up to the surface to pull the igniter cords on the DWFA. Evan hoped for the former but prepared for the latter. And he sure wouldn't tell Kiley about the added danger.

"What else can I do?" Kiley pressed.

"Evacuate. Now!"

She crossed her arms. "If you're staying, I'm staying."

"I need to be here. You don't." He slipped into the BC. "So go. Get out of here."

Her feet remained planted in place, her stance firm. He couldn't force her to leave so he loaded the BC accessory pockets with tools, covertly adding his folding tactical knife to keep her from worrying. He strapped the dive computer to his wrist and was thankful for the lighted screen so he could mark his dive depth without turning on a light. He grabbed lights, mask, and fins and marched to the door, glancing at the clock above it.

Twenty-one minutes until the clock rolled to 9/11. Twenty-one minutes to stop Shah from killing countless people. Evan wanted to stop and sweep Kiley into his arms, but time was of the essence.

"C'mon. You can head out while I go to the

dam." He eased past her and jogged for the elevator.

Her footsteps rang out behind him. "Mack's meeting us at the dam with the rope so we don't lose you."

No need for that. With Shah in the water, Evan couldn't be encumbered by a rope, but he said nothing as he didn't want to raise her concerns. He entered a different elevator car that led even deeper into the earth, and she followed before he could get the door closed. The car jolted into action.

"You've done this before, right?" She searched his gaze, hers laced with terror. "Underwater, I mean."

"Plenty of times."

"But each time is different."

"Yeah, that's true." He tried to smile but couldn't manage it. "I've got this. I can do it. Trust me. And trust God. He'll bring us through."

She frowned and twisted her hands together.

"This is the time to let go of that fear your mother heaped on you," he said. "You can do nothing about what's going to happen next. You've done all you can do, and it's time to rest on God's promises."

She nodded, but skepticism lingered in her expression, and her body trembled. Aw, man, he desperately wanted to hold her.

The doors opened.

Looking like a drowned rat, Mack was waiting for them in the driving rain with the harness and rope.

Evan sloshed through puddles to lead Mack away from Kiley and quickly explained what he would face in the water and that Shah had come to die and wouldn't give up easily. "There's a good chance this thing could blow. You need to take Kiley to higher ground or I'll be worried about her."

Mack grimaced, perfectly reflecting Evan's thoughts. "She'll fight it."

"Then tell her about the dive once I'm under so she goes."

Mack gave a sharp nod. "Be careful down there."

Back by Kiley, Mack held out the harness.

Evan waved a hand. "That might not be long enough for this dive, and I can't stop to take it off once I'm underwater."

Kiley gnawed on her lip. "I hate to think of you diving so deep."

"I know my limits." This might be the last time he saw her, and he wanted to kiss her, but millions of lives had to come before his feelings. He put on his fins and mask, then strapped the dive light on his free wrist and put on a headlamp.

He backed to the edge of a ramp and took the plunge into the cool depths. The last thing he saw was Kiley, hand over mouth, her eyes wide with fear.

And when he bobbed to the surface, the next thing he saw was the DWFA with the detcords running into the water.

Shah had started his work.

CHAPTER 30

As Kiley watched Evan disappear under the water, her heart constricted. She'd never felt such terror. Ever. Not for herself, but for Evan. Tears burned in her eyes, and she had to blink hard to stop them from flowing.

"C'mon." Mack took her elbow and tried to lead her away.

She shook free. "I'm not leaving here until Evan comes back up."

"He asked me to make sure you evacuate."

She shook her head. "I'm not leaving him."

"He didn't tell you everything." Mack frowned. "Underwater devices are different. No timers. There's a floating board that holds the fuses. Shah still has to be in the water to connect the detcord and then come up to trigger the explosion."

She spun to look at the water again. "Here? Shah's here? In the water?"

"Yes."

"But he could kill Evan."

"He could, but Evan has surprise on his side. And close-combat skills. Shah doesn't have either of those."

"Then why does Evan want me to leave? There would be no need unless he thought there was a good chance the dam could blow." Her heart rate sped up. She didn't know what to do.

Sean and Cam came barreling out of the elevator. She explained the dire situation, nearly buckling under the weight of the threat. But she couldn't. It was her job as lead to protect them. Yet she could do nothing to help Evan. He was the expert here and needed no direction from her.

But these guys? Men she respected and loved? She could direct them away from the blast area. "I want all three of you to go back to the main entrance and make sure everyone evacuates. Ensure this place is empty."

They didn't budge.

"Now!" she shouted. "Go! That's an order."

Looking reluctant, they departed.

Her fear threatened to take her down, but she had to keep working the investigation. She got out her phone and called the sheriff. "Where are we at in apprehending Amari and Nabi?"

"Amari's in custody, and my men are still in pursuit of Nabi."

"Do they have eyes on him, or is he still in the wind?"

"Eyes," he said. "The guy's hoofing it through the park. Just a matter of time before we grab him."

Kiley had to make sure the terrorists didn't escape to hatch a future attack. "I want to know the minute they're in custody."

"Roger that."

The call ended, and her thoughts went back to Evan. She moved to the edge of the concrete and stared down into the water. She spotted the floating board Mack had told her about.

Fear razored along every nerve ending, and she started to shake. Evan's words came rushing back to her. *"Trust God. He'll bring us through."*

She wanted to trust Him. How she wanted to take comfort in her faith. Then it hit her. She had no practice in doing so. Since her dad had died, she'd simply been going through the motions of faith. Her mother's constant fear had written the same fear in Kiley's heart as if with permanent ink, and the anxiety never washed away. No matter how many times she'd asked God to free her from the fear. It had informed everything she'd done since then. On top of that, she'd let Olin's death cement it in place. Now it needed an explosive of its own to blow it free.

If she wanted to be with Evan, she would have to face her fear head on. Talk to her mom and let it go. Exactly like Evan said. And she would try her best to let go. Being with him was worth the effort and so much more.

That was if they all survived this terrible threat.

The water was mottled at the surface from the rain but turned dark and murky as Evan descended. Blackness enveloped him, and he stayed near the edge of the massively thick dam wall and wished he could turn on his light. But there was no way he was alerting Shah that he was coming for him.

Evan felt around until his fingers connected with the detcords. He followed the cord, sinking down. Down. Down.

His gut churned as he breathed deeply, the sound of his rebreather comforting. His dive computer declared he'd reached eighty feet, and he spotted Shah with his headlamp fixed on the explosives near a cluster of the bolts the Bureau of Reclamation kept replacing.

Evan released a few bursts of air with his pressure inflator, allowing him to hover in place, his bubbles rising up. Even from this distance Evan could see the RDX. He couldn't miss it. Not with the massive number of bricks attached to the dam. Would have taken days to bring down this quantity of explosives. Shah would've needed an accomplice on the inside to get all the bricks into the building and down here.

At this quantity, if the RDX was detonated, it would tear a huge hole in the dam. Four and a half trillion gallons of water in Lake Powell would go coursing down the Colorado River, wiping out everything and everyone on its way.

And only Evan could stop it.

Keeping her focus on the water, Kiley made her final call to the sheriff. "Update."

"Your suspects are in custody, and the place is a

ghost town," he replied. "Just like you instructed. The last men are climbing into my vehicle, and we're heading over the bridge before the dam blows."

She didn't like his assumption that Evan would fail, but she did like that the sheriff was following orders and that Amari and Nabi could no longer hurt anyone else. "See you on the other side of midnight."

She disconnected and called Mack. "Head out with the sheriff."

He didn't say anything for a long moment. "We'll join you."

"No. If this thing blows, you're better off on the other side where you can assist in the recovery," she said, playing to his need to protect others to get him to leave.

"Kiley, I . . ."

"I know. See you soon, Mack." She'd done everything she could as the team leader and ended the call.

She swiped the rain from her eyes and searched the dark water for movement. Any sign that Evan was okay. That if he encountered Shah, Evan was winning in the fight. Plenty of drops pelted the surface, but no bubbles from a respirator.

She checked her watch. Five minutes until 9/11. *No. No.* Time was running out.

Was Shah going to win and they would all die? Just minutes to die.

Oh, God, please. No.

Her heart raced. Her palms perspired. She couldn't even think straight. "C'mon. C'mon. C'mon. Please, Evan."

Her leg muscles gave way. She dropped to the concrete and bowed her head. The words wouldn't come. She didn't know what to say. But God knew her heart. He knew she wanted to change. Wanted to trust. And so she simply knelt in His presence. Waited and trusted.

Evan withdrew his knife and slowly descended.

Shah looked up, his light catching Evan in the face.

Shah suddenly spun and swam away. Not toward the surface but along the side of the dam.

Another explosion planned?

Evan had a split-second decision to make. He could pull the blasting cap or he could go after Shah. He couldn't do both.

Sure, pulling the cap for this batch of RDX would disable this explosion. But what if there was another one? Shah would reach it before Evan could.

He stowed his knife to swim faster, kicked hard, and went after the fleeing terrorist, praying with each kick of his fins that he was a stronger swimmer.

He kicked hard. Furious. His muscles burning. His heart pounding.

461

He gained on Shah. Inch by inch. Second by second.

They neared the surface. Twenty feet down. He caught up to the terrorist. Grabbed a fin and pulled with all his strength.

Shah kicked free. Spun. Knife in hand.

He lashed out.

Evan flailed, dodging the first sweep. Shah lunged through the water. A second slash caught Evan across the arm. He jerked back.

Shah plunged toward the surface, moving at rocket speed. Pain radiated up Evan's arm. Too bad. He wouldn't let the injury stop him.

He swam after Shah. Lancing pains cut through his arm, slowing him.

He lost the terrorist in the murky blackness. Frantic now, he flashed his light. Searching the black void.

Nothing. No one.

What do I do, Father?

If Shah was setting another explosion, he would have to surface to ignite it. Evan kicked toward the surface, hoping, praying he was close enough to the other DWFA to intervene before Shah pulled the igniter pin.

A hand clamped around Evan's ankle, dragging him down. He reached for his knife and started a somersault.

Shah kicked around Evan, yanked on his regulator hose, and took off for the surface.

Evan kicked after him, taking a breath. No air.

Shah had cut Evan's hose. He reached for his alternate air source and clamped his lips on the mouthpiece. Took a breath. Nothing. Shah had cut both hoses. Without oxygen, Evan had a couple of minutes at best.

He shot toward the surface, thankful they hadn't gone deep enough to require a safety stop to prevent decompression sickness. He might be exceeding today's recommended ascent rate, but not the Navy's table.

He shone his light ahead. Spotted Shah's fins.

Evan kicked harder. They rose toward the surface. The dam's light shone above and cut through the water, illuminating Shah.

Lungs burning, Evan gained on the terrorist. Evan grabbed the man's leg. He kicked free.

Evan moved faster. Faster. His whole body fighting the strain of zero air and extreme movement. He surfaced. Gulped in air. Searched around. Zeroed in on Shah by a DWFA.

"Evan!" he heard Kiley scream.

His gut tightened. She hadn't left.

He couldn't think about that now. He crawled in Shah's direction, a parallel swim to the dam. Arm over arm he carved through the water, pain cutting through him like a repeated stabbing. He lunged for Shah. Grabbed his arm as he was reaching for the igniter pin.

His fingers mere inches away, Evan jerked the

guy back. He was strong and fought. Breaking free.

Evan didn't want to kill the guy, but he had to end this. He got hold of him and slashed at his arm with the knife. Didn't stop the man. Again he surged toward the DWFA.

Evan lunged onto Shah's back and pulled him under. He still had his regulator in his mouth and would survive, Evan not so much.

Shah squirmed free and faced Evan.

He aimed his knife at Shah.

The man clamped his hands around Evan's throat. Evan brought the knife home in Shah's belly. Surprise flashed on his face, and his hands went slack.

Evan burst to the surface to breathe. Adrenaline coursed through his body. He swam to the DWFA and removed the ignitors.

He put them in a pouch and turned to give Kiley a thumbs-up.

Her eyes opened wide and she screamed.

CHAPTER 31

"Behind you!" Kiley shouted to Evan, but her warning came too late.

Shah lunged forward and got Evan in a chokehold. They tumbled and threw punches. She had to help Evan, but how?

Get closer. Now!

She ran along the slippery walkway.

The pair went under the water. She reluctantly pulled her gaze away to watch the ground before she slipped and fell. She heard a splash. Looked to her left.

The pair came up. Evan was coughing and sucking in great gulps of air. Shah still had his respirator.

Evan whipped around. Faced Shah. The terrorist lifted an arm, water cascading down his wet suit. A knife glinted in the dam light.

"No!" She ran faster and drew her gun.

The knife came down. She aimed at Shah and fired. The bullet caught his body, and he fell back seconds before the blade plunged into Evan's chest.

He glanced back at her. Only for a flash of a moment. Then he grabbed Shah in a chokehold and swam toward the ramp. She ran after him, her legs shaking. He dragged Shah up the incline and out of the water. Blood instantly soaked the concrete and ran down in rivers of red rainwater.

"Is he—?"

"Dead?" Evan ripped off the guy's hood and rested his fingers on his neck. "He's got a pulse."

"I'll get an ambulance down here." She dialed the sheriff and put in the request. He assured her medics would be there soon.

She ended the call and allowed herself the chance to breathe deeply and look Evan over from head to fin. His wet suit was cut open, blood oozing from his arm.

"You're bleeding," she said as she dropped next to Shah to determine how to stem the flow of blood. "Let me look at it."

"It's just a scratch." He removed Shah's respirator from his mouth and the tank.

"A scratch doesn't bleed like that," she said, watching him as he took off his hoses and put Shah's hoses on his own tank.

He didn't respond to her comment.

Blood spurted from the hole in Shah's chest. She pressed her hands over the gaping wound and looked up at Evan. "What are you doing?"

"Going back in."

"What? Wait. You gave me a thumbs-up. Is there still a risk?"

"Not likely." He slipped into his vest. "But I need to swim the length of the dam to look for other DWFAs. And then I want to remove the blasting caps from the explosives. Just in case."

She understood his need to be thorough, but she didn't like it. "And you're sure you can use that arm?"

"Yes." His focus was pinned on the mission ahead. He secured the vest and gave her a tight smile. "Be back before you know it."

"Be careful."

"Always."

Right. Always. In her book, being careful meant running from a potential bomb, not running toward it. But then in her job she often ran toward danger, so she should understand. Problem was she loved this man with every fiber she was made of. She'd never been in love with a man before, and it was one thing to run into danger yourself. Quite another to have your loved one do so.

She watched him disappear into the water and then turned her attention back to Shah, pressing hard on the oozing wound.

She heard footfalls pounding down the ramp. Mack and Sean rushed toward her, guns raised.

"Heard the gunshot," Mack said.

She looked down at her hands covered in this terrorist's blood. "I shot Shah. He was coming at Evan with a knife. Medics are on their way."

"Where's Evan?" Sean asked.

She explained, and her voice hitched as tears burned in her eyes.

Mack knelt by her. "Let me take over."

She lifted her hands, and Mack slipped into place. She checked Shah's pulse. "He's still with us."

A pair of medics came running down the ramp, the rain sloshing under their feet and the wheels of their gurney. She moved out of the way and stood back by Sean and Cam. A medic took over for Mack, and he joined her.

The four of them stood for a time, staring at the dam as the rain washed over them and adrenaline pumped through her veins.

Mack put his arm around her shoulders. "Evan being on the team was the best thing that could've happened to us."

"Yeah," she said, still choked up.

"And he's on the team because you let him be. Despite your differences. So your level-headed thinking saved the day."

"No. It was you, Mack. You convinced me to keep Evan around."

Sean eyed her. "Seems like you might be glad on a personal level too."

"Maybe. Yeah. Not sure." She looked at her watch, seeing that the clock had ticked into 9/11 and they were all still standing. "Would one of you find Eisenhower and bring him up to speed?"

"I'll go," Sean offered.

"And I'll tell the sheriff," Mack said.

"What do you want me to do?" Cam asked.

Kiley had so many unanswered questions

swimming through her brain, but this was an easy one to answer. "Review the firewalls for the dam. I want to make sure it's locked down tight before we leave this place so it's not vulnerable to future attacks."

He nodded and followed the others up the walkway. Her team. The men she would go into battle with if need be, and tonight it felt like they'd done just that.

The medics strapped Shah onto the gurney.

"Will he make it?" Kiley asked as they rolled past her.

"He's lost a lot of blood," one of them answered.

A vague answer that told her nothing. She'd never shot a person before and didn't want to be responsible for someone's death, even a terrorist who'd planned to harm millions. She offered a prayer for him, and a prayer of thanks for being able to stop the terrible threat, then turned her attention back to the water.

Finally, Evan came to the surface. Fins in hand, he strode up the incline. Water slicked down his wet suit, highlighting his strong thighs and powerful shoulders. But she couldn't quit looking at the slice on his arm.

She might have lost him.

That fear—that ages-old ache that often bit into her deepest recesses—surfaced again. She could have lost him. Truly lost him when she'd just recognized her feelings for him.

He pulled off his mask and set it along with the fins onto the concrete. He locked eyes with her as he slid off his vest and tank.

Barefoot now, he crossed over to her, his focus pinned on her face. The heated look in his eyes make her heart skitter.

"Are we safe?" she asked, trying to keep them on a professional level.

He nodded. She heard footsteps behind her and turned to look. Sean and Eisenhower marched down the ramp. Her supervisor carried an umbrella, and his suit looked perfectly dry next to Sean's soggy clothing.

"Good work here, Dawson," Eisenhower said. "And on making sure we got Amari and Nabi in custody. DNA from the container was matched to Nabi and Shah, so we've got them for entering the country illegally too."

She wanted to sag with relief but instead held her shoulders back. "They'll go away for a long time."

Eisenhower shifted his attention to Evan and held out his hand. "Barry Eisenhower—ICE Special Agent in Charge of the Cyber Crimes Center. I hear we owe you a great debt of gratitude."

Evan shook the man's hand. "Just doing my job."

"Don't downplay it," Eisenhower said. "Not sure the last time I heard of an ICE agent saving the day quite so dramatically."

Kiley was so proud of Evan, but . . . "He's injured, sir, and should get to the medics."

"It's only a scratch," Evan said, downplaying again.

Eisenhower's eyes narrowed. "Go get checked out, and out of the wet suit, and then join us for a debrief."

"Will do, sir." Evan started to leave but then paused to look Kiley in the eye. "To be continued," he said.

Evan thought the debrief would never end. Eisenhower led the meeting, which included a look at employee files for the dam. The dam security manager had hired Nabi and Shah under the aliases of Rostami and Darzi. They must have spent the night in the apartment, drove straight to the Army depot to steal the RDX, then on to the dam to bring in the explosives brick by brick.

"And in closing . . ." Eisenhower said.

Evan almost shouted hallelujah, as all he could think about was getting Kiley alone for a few minutes. He still needed to get his arm evaluated at the ER, but the medics had bandaged the wound, stopping the bleeding.

". . . the Waleed brothers were also apprehended a few miles from here," Eisenhower continued. "We found phones with calls made to Gadi and Amari. We believe that in addition to facilitating the container shipment, they were also backup in the event Nabi and Shah survived the blast and needed a return ride to the container."

"And," Mack said, "Sony came through with the transmissions for the video-game chat. Nasim Waleed was in on the plot. That'll help keep him locked up."

"Great news." Kiley smiled. "I'm glad you kept after that."

"What about Shah?" Sean asked. "Did he make it?"

"He's in surgery, but it looks like he'll pull through."

Kiley let out a relieved breath. Evan knew what it felt like to take a life, and he was glad Kiley would be spared from knowing the pain of such a thing.

"And finally," Eisenhower said and looked straight at Kiley, "we recovered a Dragunov rifle in the Waleeds' vehicle. We'll be sending it to FTU to compare the rifling to the slugs from Firuzeh's murder investigation."

If anyone could find a rifling match, it would be the Firearms/Toolmarks Unit at the FBI's Quantico lab.

Kiley's face lit up at the news. "Adam Garvin evaluated the slugs and casing, so he's our guy at Quantico."

Eisenhower wouldn't be the one to send in the rifle. It would likely be Kiley, but Evan suspected she was so overjoyed and exhausted that she was saying whatever came to mind.

Eisenhower smiled at the group. "I want to commend everyone on the fine work. Especially you, Agent Dawson. You really stepped up to the plate as lead. Well done."

The others applauded her. A flush of red washed over her face, and she waved a hand. "A leader is only as good as her team."

"Okay, people," Eisenhower said with a clap of his hands, "let's get back to work and wrap up this investigation."

The meeting broke up, and Kiley's teammates congratulated her. Though everyone was exhausted, they would still need to write reports before they got any sleep, and that included Evan. But before he started on his account of the terrifying night, he was going to talk to Kiley. Alone.

He stood and, without a word, grabbed her hand to lead her from the building before anyone else asked for her time or attention.

"Where are we going?" she asked but didn't try to stop him.

"For a walk."

"I don't have time for a walk. I need to—"

He pressed his finger against her lips. "It'll only take a few minutes, and it'll help to clear your head before you spend hours getting your thoughts down on paper."

He led her outside and through the crazy number of people working the crime scene. He stepped onto the walkway at the top of the dam. The storm had broken and the night was clear now, the stars sparkling overhead.

She slowed. "This is . . . I don't like being up so high."

He wrapped his good arm around her waist and pulled her close. "We're perfectly safe."

"Says the guy who rappelled off a bridge seventy stories high."

He grinned. "You should try it sometime. It's a rush."

"No thank you." As if trying to prove her point, she planted her feet on the concrete.

They'd moved far enough away from the big lights illuminating the crime scene and had a bit of privacy, so he didn't force it. He slipped behind her and circled his arms around her waist, drawing her back against his body. His injured arm ached with the movement, but he didn't care. He needed to hold her. "Look up, not down."

She raised her head. "Hard to believe we were in a torrential downpour a couple of hours ago. The sky is so clear. The stars so bright."

"You don't see this in the city much."

"No, you don't."

A sense of peace—a rightness with the world that he hadn't felt since before losing Olin—settled into Evan's soul. "I'm always reminded of

God when I do. And when I jump out of planes or rappel or even approach a bomb. But tonight. After everything. Minutes from death. It reminds me He's infinite when life is finite. We don't ever know from one minute to the next what will happen." He tightened his arms around her and inhaled a deep breath. "We have to embrace every minute of every day."

Kiley turned in his arms and looked him in the eyes. "I am so thankful you don't diffuse bombs for a living anymore. I didn't like you being the one to do it today. Not one bit."

"Agent Dawson," Eisenhower called from the shadows at the end of the walkway.

She shot out of Evan's arms.

"Yes, sir!" she yelled.

"You're needed inside."

"Be right there." She looked back at Evan, and he could see she planned to leave him behind and go back inside.

"Eisenhower's a real taskmaster," Evan said.

"Yeah, but he's fair and a great boss. I respect him tremendously." She started to leave.

"Good to know," he called after her.

She glanced over her shoulder. "Why's that?"

"He offered me a job in D.C."

She spun. "He what?"

"He said he sat on the advisory board for a JTTF there, and they'd recently had an opening come up. Said I'd be perfect for the job."

"And what did you tell him?" She took a few steps closer to him.

"That I thought it's colder in D.C. than in Seattle."

She swatted her hand in his direction. "Seriously?"

"Seriously, I did tell him that. And also that my moving to D.C. was totally up to you."

She gaped at him. "You didn't."

He nearly laughed at her comical expression, but although he was making light of this to save his pride if she rejected him, he was dead serious. "I did. Thought it would be good for him to know we're a thing *before* I took the job than after."

"And are we?" She bit her lip, her eyes alight with questions. "A thing, I mean?"

"You better believe we are," he said adamantly, letting a slow, daring smile slide across his face, ensuring she knew how he felt.

She grabbed his shirt and tugged him close, her eyes warm and sumptuous, urging him even closer.

He peered over her shoulder at Eisenhower, who was still standing at the end of the walkway.

Evan didn't care if Eisenhower or even an entire cadre of FBI agents waited. He had to get this out now or burst. "I love you, Kiley."

Her mouth formed a small O of surprise before she whispered a soft breath that fanned his face. "And I love you too. So much. I—"

He tugged her into his arms and kissed her hard, his lips sealing anything else she planned to say. He gripped her tight against his body and deepened the kiss. Holding. Clinging. Never planning to come up for air again.

CHAPTER 32

Kiley had never been to the mobile-home park, not once since her mother moved to Arizona three years ago. She stopped on the sidewalk to take in the double-wide trailer with lattice covering the open space underneath. It looked like every other trailer in the retirement community, with its token cactus bed ringed by white rock and an older-model car parked in a matching white-rock driveway.

She tried to get her feet moving but couldn't bring herself to walk up to the small porch.

"You can do this, honey." Evan squeezed her hand. "You faced down terrorists who were going to blow up a dam. You can face your mother."

"She's scarier." Kiley laughed, but she honestly meant it. Confronting her past and letting it all go was super scary.

Evan turned her toward him. "You want to do this, right? If not, say the word and we're out of here."

She looked into the shining eyes of the man she loved more than she could ever imagine possible. She'd fought her mother's dominance to become independent and vowed never to need anyone. But in the past week she'd discovered she liked needing Evan. Liked having him in her life. And if she had to hash out the past with her mother to free herself from the fear of commitment, then she would confront her mother.

She circled a hand around the back of his neck and drew him close. "I will do almost anything to be with you. And you're right. With you by my side, and God with me, I can do this."

He kissed her, and his strong arms went around her to softly cradle her against his firm chest. A flash of love went straight to her heart, and she basked in his touch. She circled her arms around his neck and pulled him closer, urging him to tighten his hold. She lost herself in the feel of his lips. Reveled in her newfound love. And she didn't care if anyone was watching them. She loved this man and would shout it from the rooftops if she could.

Her phone rang in the tone she'd assigned to Mack. She opened her eyes. Blinked a few times. Reluctantly pulled away to answer it. He and the team had stopped off in Alabama to check out the leads for the Montgomery Three investigation that Evan suggested, and he could be calling with good news.

"Hi, Mack," she said on a ragged breath while trying to catch another one.

"You with Evan?" he asked.

"Yes."

"Put him on speaker."

"It's Mack," she said to Evan, who was

breathing hard, his eyes locked on her, love burning from his gaze.

She nearly wilted under the intensity of it and looked down at her phone, because if she kept focusing on Evan she would be lost. She tapped the speaker button. "Okay, Mack. You're on speaker."

"Hey, man, thanks," Mack said enthusiastically. "Your idea panned out."

Kiley shot a look at Evan.

He arched a brow. "Panned out how?"

"We found the van in a cave north of Birmingham."

"Seriously?" Kiley cried out. "You found it?"

"We did."

"That's wonderful," Evan said, looking proud of himself.

"Before you get too excited," Mack went on, "you should know they torched the van, and it doesn't have any plates."

"You can still get a VIN number, right?" Kiley asked, her hope starting to deflate.

"We did. Led us back to a flower shop in Birmingham, but the van was reported stolen nearly six months before the girls went missing."

Kiley tried not to get discouraged, but . . . "So, another dead end."

"Maybe not," Mack said, though he didn't sound convinced. "We have a few more days off. We'll get started interviewing people in the area and follow up with local detectives who took the stolen vehicle report. Hopefully it'll lead somewhere. And Cam is looking into the female connection."

Kiley let the news settle in and thought about their next step. "Is it time to tell Eisenhower what we're doing?"

"Sean wants to do the interviews first, then decide."

She wanted Eisenhower to reopen the investigation, yet she wasn't lead on this investigation. Sean was, and after heading up her first investigation, she wanted to be sensitive to that. "I'll call you when I'm done here, and you can tell me if I should join you or head home."

"You got it."

"Thanks, Mack." She ended the call and smiled at Evan. "Good job, Agent Bowers. I knew you were something special, and this proves it."

His face colored, and she loved that about him. He was a super agent but didn't let it go to his head.

"So, my mother." Kiley straightened her shirt and, having exhausted every excuse not to go inside, marched up the steps to knock on the door. Her heart thundered in her chest as she tried to remember the last time she'd actually seen her mother in person. It had been years, and as she heard footsteps coming to the door, she felt like bolting.

"You can do this." Standing behind her, Evan

placed his hand on the small of her back, giving her the confidence not to run. They'd agreed that he would come in and meet her mom to break the ice, and then when Kiley was ready to get down to discussing her past, he would step out and let them hash things out alone.

The door opened, and her mother looked at her, her eyes wide as she blinked lashes coated in thick black mascara. "Kiley? What are you doing here?"

"I need to talk to you," Kiley said bluntly.

"You should have called." Her mother ran a hand over her graying hair and glanced at Evan. "I'm a mess."

Leave it to her mother to be more aware of the man standing behind her than the fact that her long-lost daughter had shown up to see her. She propped a hand on her hip. Her skinny jeans emphasized her curvaceous figure. She'd paired them with ankle boots and a blouse in a rainbow of colors. Her mother looked ultra-feminine, while Kiley was wearing her usual tactical pants and shirt. They were such opposites, and her mother had always tried to get Kiley to be more of a girly girl but had failed.

"And who is this handsome man?" her mother asked.

Kiley looked at Evan. "He's my . . . uh . . ."

"Evan Bowers." He stuck out a hand, rescuing her.

"Lana Dawson." She shook Evan's hand. "Are you two an item?"

A broad smile crossed Evan's face. "We are."

Kiley warmed at his enthusiasm, but her stomach remained tied in a knot. "Can we come in?"

Her mother stood back, yet she didn't look happy about giving them access.

Kiley stepped into the space that smelled like fried onions. She took a quick look around the plain living area that held a plaid sofa, a coffee table, and a worn leather recliner. "Where's Wally?"

Her mother crossed her arms. "Gone, and good riddance."

Kiley wasn't surprised to hear her mother had broken up with yet another boyfriend and assumed it wouldn't be long before another man replaced Wally.

"Want some coffee?" her mother asked.

Kiley shook her head.

Her mother turned a dazzling smile on Evan. "How about you, handsome? Coffee?"

"No thank you, ma'am."

Her mother cringed. Likely at a good-looking man calling her *ma'am*. She was a beautiful woman and had always resented the fact that she was aging and her looks weren't as perfect as they'd once been.

"Go ahead. Sit." She waved a hand, her sparkly

pink fingernails glinting in the hot Arizona sunshine pouring in through the bay window.

On her way to the sofa, Kiley stopped to straighten an old landscape picture that had hung in their hallway for as far back as Kiley could remember. She concentrated on breathing normally when her heart was beating like a conga drum.

Evan sat next to her. His knee touched hers, sending a jolt of awareness through her, but he didn't move away. She assumed he was showing his support, and she would accept all the encouragement he wanted to give.

"So . . . what's up, Kiley?" Her mother perched on the armrest of the recliner and crossed her ankles. "Why the surprise visit?"

"I was in Arizona on an investigation and had a few days off so wanted to stop in." *Chicken.*

"And that's it? You just wanted to stop in?" Her mother's suspicion was tinged with sarcasm.

Kiley winced. "I wanted to talk about our past."

Evan stood. "And that's my cue to give you two some time alone."

Kiley didn't want him to leave, but they'd agreed she needed to do this alone. She smiled up at him and nodded. He squeezed her hand and stepped out the door, the latch closing solidly behind him.

Alone. She felt alone. So odd when just a week ago she'd been on her own and thought she liked it that way. Now she knew she needed Evan in her life. And her mother too, if they could patch things up.

"Okay, the big dramatic exit's over." Her mother crossed her arms again. "So, what about our past?"

Kiley took a long breath and blurted out, "After Dad died, you changed."

"Well, of course I did." She looked at Kiley for a long, tense moment, her eyes rimmed in thick makeup. "You try losing the love of your life and see if it doesn't change you."

Of all the things Kiley imagined her mother saying, she didn't expect this answer and had never really thought about her father's death from a wife's perspective. Never having been in a serious relationship, she had no frame of reference. Now that she had Evan in her life, she could better understand how her mother felt back then. Still . . . "I lost my dad too. You didn't seem to notice."

She raised her chin and sniffed. "Maybe I handled things badly, but there I was. No income with very little money in the bank. And I had a kid to take care of. I couldn't dwell on how you were handling things."

This was the first Kiley had ever heard of any money issues. "What about Grandma and Grandpa? If money was so tight, couldn't we have moved in with them?"

"I was far too old to run home to my parents."

"Instead you took up with the first man who came along."

Her mother gasped.

"I'm sorry, Mom." Kiley swiveled the glass bowl filled with fake apples on the table. "That wasn't nice, but it's how I felt at the time. That it was easy for you to replace Dad."

"I could never replace your father. Never." Her vehemence shocked Kiley. "Which is why I've never remarried. I keep looking for what I had with your dad. I know now I might never find it and have to be content to be on my own until something real comes along."

She sounded so sad, the anger in Kiley's heart thawed a fraction. "I'm sorry about that, Mom. I really am."

"I hear a big old *but* coming."

"But you knew some of those guys came on to me, and you still let them stay."

"They were paying the bills." The words flew from her mouth. "I couldn't throw them out. Did any of them hurt you? Do more than make a few suggestions and winks?"

"No, but I was just a teenager. Impressionable and vulnerable. On top of that, we lived our lives in fear. You basically confined me to the house outside school hours."

"I couldn't risk losing you." She cast a pleading look at Kiley. "Besides, seems like you turned out fine to me. You have a big FBI job. Tops in your field. Hours at a computer gave you that job, you know."

Kiley resisted sighing. "I'm not fine. I let fear color everything I do. I refused to ever make a commitment to a man because of fear."

"Then why bring that guy here?" She flicked a hand at the door.

"Because I love him enough to confront my fear once and for all."

"What exactly does *that* mean?"

"Means I needed to come see you, to tell you how I feel so I can let go of all this anger and fear."

Her mother looked down at her lap for a long time before lifting her head. Tears swam in her eyes. "I know I made a mess of things for you. For me. Your grandparents told me often enough. How could I not know?" She took a shuddering breath. "I can't change the past, but I can tell you how sorry I am. Can you forgive me?"

Kiley was stunned. This was the first time in years that she'd seen any real sincerity coming from her mother. She wasn't blowing smoke— she really meant what she said.

One of God's promises came to mind. *Remember, you have been set free.* God did that for her. She could do the same thing for her mother. She could forgive. Apparently she just needed to hear her mother acknowledge her mistakes and apologize. Didn't mean they would be instant buddies, but it was a huge step nonetheless.

She reached for her mother's hand. "Of course I can."

Her mother gave a sharp nod.

"I'm sorry I didn't talk to you about this sooner," Kiley said. "We've wasted a lot of time."

"Honestly, I'm not sure I would have heard you." She squeezed Kiley's hand and let go. "I had a little scare last month. Cancer. Turned out to be nothing, but it made me look back on my life. Look at my life now. That's why Wally's gone. I got a job, and I'm paying my own way for the first time ever."

"Good for you, Mom." Kiley choked up at the thought of her mother finally coming to grips with her life. "Maybe we can see each other more often."

Her mother's back went up in her age-old defensive posture. "I can't afford to travel."

"But I can."

"And you'd come out here to visit me?" Her timid voice cut through Kiley just like it would have if she'd shouted.

"I will," Kiley said adamantly, then glanced at the door where she knew Evan would be waiting for her.

Her mother waved a hand in that direction. "Go ahead. Bring him in so I can get to know him."

Kiley didn't have to be told twice. She jumped up and charged for the door. He was waiting right on the stoop where she thought she'd find him.

"Everything okay?" he asked.

She cast him a glorious smile and took his hand. "Wonderful. Mom wants to get to know you a bit before we leave."

She led him back to the sofa.

Her mom met his gaze and chuckled. "Don't look so afraid. I won't bite."

"Yes, ma'am," he said, not at all sounding certain.

Kiley had to resist laughing. Next to her sat a man who'd just faced down bombs and a ruthless killer, and here he was afraid of her mom. She smiled at him and squeezed his hand to get him to relax.

Her mother's eyebrows rose, and a soft look Kiley hadn't seen since childhood took hold of her mom's expression. "Looks like the two of you might need some help planning a wedding in the not-so-distant future."

"You never know. A wedding *could* be in our future." Kiley watched Evan.

Instead of shock or surprise, an intimate smile just for Kiley crossed his face, and her heart somersaulted. She couldn't believe she'd spoken the word *wedding* in conjunction with herself. This man—this marvelous, amazing man—had changed her life for good.

• • •

Evan grabbed Kiley's hand and ducked under the mobile home's awning to escape the blazing sun. He'd sat in the trailer waiting and waiting and waiting for this moment since Kiley mentioned the word wedding. Her mother insisted on serving coffee and cookies and reminiscing with pictures of when Kiley's dad was still alive. As much as Evan liked hearing about Kiley's younger days, he liked the grown-up woman facing him so much better.

He slid his hands into her hair, tilted her head, and kissed her. Kissed her hard and thoroughly, letting years of pent-up emotions fuel him. She circled her arms around his neck and drew him even closer. She deepened the kiss, and he wanted to hold on to her forever.

She slowly pulled back, and he stared down into her eyes. The loss of her touch shocked him, and he curled his arm tighter to keep her close. She gave a soft, enticing smile that he'd always imagined was just for him. "My mom's probably looking out the window and wondering why our car is still sitting in the driveway."

"Let her look." He gently lifted a strand of hair from her face and tucked it behind her ear. "I've been wanting to kiss you since you mentioned a wedding."

"I can't believe I even said that." She blushed crimson red. "You have a crazy effect on me."

"In a good way, I hope."

"Most definitely." She pressed her hands against his chest and stepped out of his hold.

He felt the loss acutely and thought to reach out again, but she took another step back. "We should get moving or we'll miss our flight."

Resigned to this wonderful moment coming to an end, he took her hand and clasped it tightly. "Where are we going—D.C. or Alabama?"

She cocked her head. "I like that."

Totally confused, he stared at her. "What?"

"I like that you assumed you would be coming with me wherever I go."

Ah, he got it now. "Get used to it, honey. From now on, I go wherever you go."

She wrinkled her nose at him. "I'm pretty sure Eisenhower would frown at your joining the team on our travels."

Evan laughed as he tucked Kiley under his arm to head to the car. Their travels might be in question right now, but he couldn't wait to find out what a lifetime with quirky, wonderfully amazing Kiley Dawson was going to be like.

ACKNOWLEDGMENTS

Thanks to:

New York Times bestselling author Stephen Templin, who learned how to make things go boom in Basic Underwater Demolition/SEAL training. I can't even imagine the talent and skills it took to make it into BUD/S, the Navy SEALS holy grail of military training. Thank you for your generosity in helping me with logistics on how to blow up the dam. Any changes and liberties taken with the information Stephen provided is all my doing. And a special thanks to Sabrina Templin for connecting me with Stephen. You and your brother rock!

The very generous Ron Norris, who continues to give of his time and knowledge in police and military procedures, weaponry details, and information technology. As a retired police officer with the La Verne Police Department and a Certified Information Systems Security Professional, the experience and knowledge you share are priceless. Any errors in or liberties taken with the technical details Ron so patiently explained to me are all my doing.

My wonderful agent, Steve Laube. I appreciate your support, caring, and encouragement more than you can know. You are truly a super-agent

493

able to leap tall buildings in a single bound and make the impossible happen.

My editors, Dave Long and Luke Hinrichs. I'm so honored to work with you. Your notes on this book have truly made it so much stronger. Working with you both and being a Bethany House author is a dream come true!

To the amazing and talented marketing staff at Bethany House—Noelle Chew, Brooke Vikla, and Amy Green. Thank you for your support in introducing the HOMELAND HEROES series to readers.

As always, to my super talented friend and romantic suspense author Elizabeth Goddard. Beth, you make this writing journey so much richer and more meaningful, and you're always there when I need a shoulder to cry on or have reason to celebrate. Even when you are going through your own difficulties, you make time to help me with mine, and I am very touched by our friendship.

And most important, thanks to God. You provide me with the words I need to share stories filled with your unfailing hope. Each day I look forward to seeing what you will do in my writing life, which you have blessed so mightily.

Susan Sleeman is the bestselling author of *Seconds to Live* and more than thirty-five romantic suspense novels with sales exceeding one million copies. She's won several awards, including the ACFW Carol Award for Suspense for *Fatal Mistake*, and the *Romantic Times* Reviewers' Choice Award for *Thread of Suspicion*. In addition to writing, Susan hosts the popular Suspense Zone website, www.thesuspensezone.com. She's lived in nine states but now calls Portland, Oregon, her home. For a complete list of the author's books, visit www.susansleeman.com.

Books are produced in the United States using U.S.-based materials

Books are printed using a revolutionary new process called THINKtech™ that lowers energy usage by 70% and increases overall quality

Books are durable and flexible because of Smyth-sewing

Paper is sourced using environmentally responsible foresting methods and the paper is acid-free

Center Point Large Print
600 Brooks Road / PO Box 1
Thorndike, ME 04986-0001 USA

(207) 568-3717

US & Canada:
1 800 929-9108
www.centerpointlargeprint.com